HIS OWN MAN

SLUMRAT RISING

BOOK SIX | HIS OWN MAN

WARBY PICUS

Podium

Podium

HIS OWN MAN

CHAPTER 1

THE SERPENT'S TALE

Truth met Cho's eyes. The silence stretched. The secret policeman was still. Returned to the absolute calm he had cultivated over a lifetime of being everyone else's worst nightmare. Truth could watch the man sort through his options. All the things he had learned from this meeting and the recorded meeting at the Sung Clan residence. Every action they thought or suspected Truth was related to. Every inference of his politics, his ideology, his motivations. Trying to figure out what he wanted.

Truth watched him confront the fact that while Truth might not be crazy in the medical sense, he certainly was in the colloquial sense. There wasn't a hint of it on Cho's face, but Truth imagined his mind was humming with instructions from the listening crowd. Some spell in action to allow one-way communication. Billionaires and bureaucrats buzzing in his ear, torn between a need for control and a need to escape.

"An obvious question arises—if you think you have found his tracks, why haven't you run Starbrite to the ground? Even if you weren't going to go at him, it would still be better to know where he sleeps." Truth smiled slightly.

"Before he sold his first widget, he had taken steps to ensure he was untouchable. It's still a mystery how many people are secretly his. How many people are living quietly in small apartments, invisible hostages of the most powerful man in the world." Cho kept fidgeting with the crystal.

"Oh? When was that?" Truth leaned forward.

"Oh . . . I'd have to look it up. Before my time. Before my grandfather's time."

"You don't know." Truth couldn't stop the grin winding up his face, or the laugh bubbling out. He could hear the madness in the laugh but refused to stop it. "You don't know when he did any of that. You just 'know' he did it. Tell me: when did Starbrite sell his first talisman? Hmm? Surely, you know that. One day they weren't for sale, and the next they were. When was that? Exactly?"

"Not to shock you, but I do have a job to do. One that doesn't permit memorizing irrelevant trivia."

"Oh, no, you don't! You don't get to run away that easily. You *just* said you had been on Starbrite's trail for a century. And at no point in a hundred years did someone have a word with the Ministry of Revenue about their taxes? Nobody examined the business records of their suppliers or the warehouses storing their inventory? Nobody pulled the building permits for any of their buildings? In a CENTURY?"

A strange look crossed Cho's face. "We did. And do. For some of that. I'm just saying that I don't remember exactly when it all started."

"What's the oldest record of Starbrite you do remember? A hundred years ago at least, right?"

"Right." Cho was struggling to keep his face flat. Now that Truth had rubbed his nose in the obvious, he was starting to ask himself why he hadn't already seen it.

"But you can't tell me when the company was established. Despite the fact that you clearly reviewed, carefully, the material that you are going to hand over to me."

The silence returned, brittle, like a balancing plate over stone tiles. Truth chuckled, shattering the stillness. "Hand it over."

Cho gave him a long look and tossed the crystal to him.

"Anything I should know about before reading this?" Truth asked.

"No. I disarmed the safety mechanisms. Any questions, you can ask me afterward."

Truth activated the thumb-sized crystal. Most of the information was supporting documents—evidence to support the main thesis. Which was insane.

"You think he cut himself into pieces?!"

"Keep reading."

Truth's eyes kept moving, sorting through the hallucinatory information provided on the crystal. Pictures, charts, tables, invoices, loading documents, architectural analysis; on and on and on it went.

"You think he cut himself into pieces."

"Yes, but it's more complicated than that."

Truth just sighed. "Elaborate, then."

"Starbrite is, from what we have been able to discover, so much more powerful than the so-called National Guardian–tier Level Eight or even Level Nine mages, they might as well be different species. There are no survivors of any attacks on Starbrite, nor are there any records from people trying to observe that fight."

Truth blinked understandingly. He wouldn't have believed Cho if he had said otherwise.

"Forty years ago, Starbrite stepped down from the company's leadership and assumed the role of CEO Emeritus. The current CEO is Level Nine. Everything else we know about him is, essentially, lies. His whole history and identity have been fabricated. Crudely. Starbrite made it abundantly clear that the CEO is his puppet."

"So . . . how does he get away with it? If the CEO is blatantly a puppet, with no network, no connections, no industry experience, how does anyone do business with Starbrite?"

"Because everyone knows that the CEO is a puppet. Nothing has changed. Starbrite is just delegating the physical-presence part of his job. Analysis has a sort of parlor game they like to play, where they guess how many glamours and enchantments he's under. I believe the current theory is that he's not under any but was raised by an army of succubae to be completely, insanely loyal."

Close. Truth couldn't bring himself to grin. *That is alarmingly close. If his soul hasn't been turned into a duplicate of Starbrite's, I'll be shocked.*

"So . . . what does he look like?"

"The CEO? There is a picture in the file."

"Starbrite. It sounds like people have met him, but I've never seen a picture. Not even a sketch."

Cho looked awkward for a fraction of a second.

"We don't know."

Truth slowly and deliberately buried his face in his hands. He was quite proud of the fact he didn't scream.

"How. Is. That. Possible? Starbrite runs twenty-five percent of the entire Jeon economy directly, and at this point, I don't even want to guess what percentage depends on the corporation. This has been the case for over one hundred years, probably a couple hundred or more. He must have conducted hundreds or thousands of negotiations in his time. Shook hands on deals. Networked over a bowl of hookers and a bed full of noodles. So. How is it possible that no one has met him and can describe him?"

That did rate a snort of amusement from Cho. "We don't know." Truth was about to stand up and smack some sense into him but was stopped by defensively raised hands. "Really. He hasn't actually done any of that. When people did meet him, it was always in a literal throne room, and he was concealed behind a curtain. At best, they saw a vague outline of a person wearing ornate robes and some kind of hat or crown. Most of the time, a court attendant did all the talking. Starbrite rarely, if ever, spoke. And he hasn't even been that visible in decades."

"Forty years, perhaps?"

"Approximately."

"A pair of dots does seem to connect there."

"Yes. Though the significance of that connection is still unknown." The colonel spread his hands. "But this does lead us to why we think he has literally chopped himself into pieces."

"Yes, given that you don't actually know the name, gender, appearance, age, origin, or any other damn thing about Starbrite, how do you come to believe that he's portioned himself? And who the hell was making deals with some silent figure behind a curtain?"

"People who respect a person who can flatten six city blocks, including five skyscrapers, by gently lowering their hand. It's generally considered a solid basis for a business relationship. And—"

"Wait, wait, wait! Are you saying Starbrite did—"

"He assembled a panel of witnesses from the Army, the Ministry of Rites, the University of Jeon at Harban, and the Institute for Studies in Civil Engineering. All of them permanently lost the ability to blink or look away when someone points at something as a result. The footage was never released, but from the right angle, you can make out the company name and a seven-pointed star etched in the dust plume."

Truth had to digest that one. He knew that disaster from the history books. Funny how he never questioned that it was caused by a systemic failure by the bureaucracy to stop shoddy building-reinforcement talismans produced by shady foreign manufacturers from being used in major urban construction, combined with an unexpected flare in cosmic rays.

"All right. I, too, would consider that a solid business partner. So, circling back to the currently-in-chunks thing . . ."

"As you can imagine, we are highly motivated to track his movements. Unfortunately, any attempts to scry him result in both the diviner and their tools violently exploding. Attempts to track him indirectly haven't been successful either."

"Indirectly?"

"Look for places where the diviner suddenly explodes, where they can't perceive anything, massive unexplained draws of cosmic rays, that kind of thing."

"Imagine you found a lot of illegal alchemist operations."

"Among other, less-savory things, yes. So, we found a lot of ways that didn't work. What we eventually resorted to is everything."

"Everything?"

"Everything. Every direct and indirect detection method running all at the same time. Did you ever wonder why Jeon is coated in recording talismans? We spent twenty years making sure surveillance culture was baked in to everything."

"And it finally worked?"

"No. Or at least not until the new System rolled out."

"Still can't believe people went along with that. You have to know how it works."

"Oh, we do. But we had to do it. It was finally enough."

"Enough?" Truth raised an eyebrow.

"Yes. Enough pieces moving all at the same time. Cosmic energy, aetheric vibrations, active spell effects. The sudden but persistent failure of certain surveillance talismans. The sudden but persistent death of certain officers and assets."

"And somehow, this led you to conclude that he, Starbrite, had turned himself into a wings bucket."

That got a startled pause from Colonel Cho, but he pressed on regardless. "We discovered that the failures occurred at six distinct, unmoving places. Before you ask, no, they don't make six points of a seven-pointed star. Sort of a box shape with a line sticking out of it. The map is in the crystal."

Truth nodded slightly. It really had been his first guess.

"All in Jeon?"

"Most of them. Two of them are just offshore."

"Still not seeing how this links back to Starbrite."

"Simple. Sacrifice."

Truth blinked. "Too simple."

"We think he is sacrificing himself, to himself, along with all the mind-controlled people the system managed to drone."

"Why, though? Self-sacrifice has never been part of his nature, from what I can tell."

"How old do you think the oldest living Level Nine is?"

"Oh . . . no idea. A few hundred years old?"

"Two hundred and forty, and she is practically dead. I mean that literally—she is sealed in a magical coffin, kept alive with enough magical reagents to qualify as a separate line item in the national budget. Not our nation—Gisbane."

Truth racked his brain, trying to remember where Gisbane was. He had no idea. Probably unimportant, then.

"But we are quite sure Starbrite has been around for longer than that, at least one century old, and probably more like three or four."

"One century is how long we have been investigating him hard. He has definitely been on this planet for longer. We just don't know how much longer." Cho nodded.

Truth nodded back. No need to mention Merkovah and his improbable lifespan.

"There are vastly older demons, of course, and a few humans who have made certain arrangements with certain powers to extend their lives past all normal bounds. But such agreements have consequences, always. Consequences most sane people cannot endure."

"So . . ."

"So, we pieced together every scrap of historical evidence we could get and, while the Shattervoid were willing to trade with us, tried to source as many books as we could. You would not believe the price placed on information."

"I know you know how to get to the damned point!"

"Based on everything, we think he is performing a grand ritual. Has been for more than a century. We think he is using his own body and all these other lives to recreate himself as a stellar eminence. And we think we have identified some of the ritual sites."

CHAPTER 2

THE PINKY TOE DILEMMA

Truth slowly blinked at Cho, then checked the crystal again. He eventually found the summary page that said essentially what Cho had—that Starbrite was ritually sacrificing himself to himself to achieve the lifespan of "the very stars." There was some speculation about whether he would force people into a mass suicide and the life energy of the sacrifice would somehow become his life, but by this point, the summary had devolved into wild speculation.

"This is the best you could put together after literally a century of investigation? Really?" Truth wasn't sneering at the cop; he was just stunned.

It was guesswork. It wasn't even particularly good guesswork. They had found a couple of things in books, connected it to a few suppositions about Starbrite's character, made some wild (and wrong) guesses about how the System actually worked, and eventually reached a conclusion that would barely pass the laugh test.

The only reason Truth hadn't stormed out of the office was what he had learned from Sally—that Starbrite's soul was horribly unnatural, and that Starbrite was essentially immobile. That . . . sorta-kinda lined up.

"It was the *only* thing we could put together after a century of digging. For most of that time, the investigation was intensely covert, as you might imagine. Very slow-paced. Combined with the lack of information about off-world magic, and the information disparity has proven . . . difficult to overcome. What we have mostly been able to do is exclude possibilities."

Truth slowly nodded, rapidly putting pieces together in his head. One of the biggest questions Truth had been wrestling with was why the hell Starbrite was still on the planet. Why not run off-world when he had the chance? For that matter, why do something as stupid and dangerous as kidnapping a Shattervoid child?

Having his foot nailed to the floor as part of a magic ritual was a pretty good reason. Now . . . why do that ritual on this planet as opposed to literally anywhere else? And for that matter, why Jeon instead of the ocean bed somewhere?

"Why Jeon?"

"No idea. At all. We guesstimate Starbrite reached this planet four hundred years ago, or so, but we really don't know. At that time, we were . . . not nothing, but nothing anyone really gave a damn about. Basically Onis's less-developed client state that they couldn't be bothered to administer. Somehow more corrupt and conservative than the Onis of that era, too, which is really saying something."

Truth half-smiled at that. "He literally could have picked anywhere, and it just happened to be here."

Cho shrugged. "Our best guess is that he was looking for a combination of factors, with a particular focus on how . . . malleable . . . the ruling classes would be to his persuasion."

Truth nodded and memorized the layout of the suspected ritual sites. There was something about the design that tickled some part of his memory, but he was equally certain he had never seen anything with that precise shape before.

"How close are you to validating the existence of these ritual sites?"

"Not very. Starbrite is now openly murdering any investigators that get too close, literally or metaphorically. And I do mean openly. Executed-on-the-street openly. They have utterly shed all pretenses of obedience to the state."

Truth got the logic. In a few months, there wouldn't be a state, the System would be nonfunctional, and everything would be in chaos. So, why play games with petty snoops? Starbrite requires—so it shall be done. His mouth uncontrollably twitched into a *very* reluctant grin.

"Something funny about people being executed in the streets?"

"Not usually. No, that's not it. It was the whole . . . He presents himself initially as this unknowable kingly figure. He has the court, the crown, the minister or eunuch or whatever transmits his words to the masses. You never see him, but you know he is there and he is powerful. And now there isn't even that. Starbrite isn't a human anymore; he's a corporation. But the core remains the same. Somewhere, high above, Starbrite reigns. Unseeable, unknowable, except by the words of his slaves."

"Much like God, perhaps." Cho offered his own meaningless smile in return.

"Or a stellar eminence."

Cho made no reply. Truth was quietly positive that one of the analysts made the same connection.

He did have to make a decision about those tickets off-world, though. He had no good criteria for selecting who got a spot, other than "people I actually care about," which still left virtually all of them unfilled. On the other hand, if he was going to put together a quick list of people he didn't want to survive a global catastrophe, "anyone capable of conspiring with Internal Security and puppeteering the few decades of civic development in Jeon" would fill a lot of it.

That being said, hope was a beautiful thing, and if you didn't give people something positive to work toward, they would surely get into mischief.

"I'm not utterly heartless. I'm willing to auction off seats. Bids will be in the form of *Do things I would approve of.* The value of the bids will be subjectively evaluated by me. Don't like your evaluation? Fight me. In order to ease the bidding process, things I approve of are, in no particular order—preparing the world for the collapse, ensuring the Level Zeros will thrive; kill anyone, or any group of people, who intend to set up as God-King of the Apocalypse World or equivalent; kill anyone acting like a prick, by which I mean, picking an example *completely* at random; working kids to death in a sweatshop, then feeding their ground-up corpses to the next wave of labor, or equivalent; spreading the idea that these are bad times but the way we get through bad times is by looking out for each other; spreading the idea that looking after others makes you look powerful; spreading the idea that Starbrite is responsible for all the bad things that are happening; Starbrite is an alien; he is not one of us; he brought this calamity down on our heads."

Truth smiled. "Last but not least—Starbrite created the Hell Prince."

That got a small jolt from Cho. "You mean the public image?"

"No, I mean it literally. Hell Prince is clearly a psyop. It's a false-flag attack by Starbrite, trying to make everyone focus on fighting Onis or internal traitors rather than confronting the truth—the only way Hell Prince could keep getting away with all this was if Starbrite was actively supporting him." Truth shook his head. "I mean, all those roadblocks? The snap searches, the raids, the diviners? All that surveillance, and yet somehow, SOMEHOW, he makes it to the Onis embassy and out of the country?"

Truth pounded his fist into his hand. "That's just what *they* want you to believe! It's all a distraction, a scam, to keep you from seeing the truth! Do you know just how many shares of Starbrite stock are held by the upper echelons? How many bribes, how many 'gifts' given for tax breaks and other advantages? They don't want you making connections. This, all of this, the lousy economy, the war, the way everything is less reliable these days, even the damn sunspots, are all Starbrite's fault. And the public should hate him for that."

Cho nodded casually. "It's been tried before. He cannot be baited that way."

Truth opened his mouth to explain, then just shook his head. "Where is your best guess as to the locus of the ritual?"

"We have no idea. In the middle of the box would make sense, but then, we can't see any reason for any of the suspected ritual sites being where they are. It doesn't look like anything in any of our books, nor can we find an explanation in theoretical thaumatology."

"No, I don't imagine it does." It finally clicked for him, though. He had never seen it in this life. But in another life, he was a sailor.

"Goodbye, Colonel. Let's not meet again." Truth turned for the door once more.

"Really? Nothing for yourself? Nothing for your future off-world? Even if you don't think money will be worth anything, some things—precious metals, talismans, gems, slaves, narcotics, cultivation aids, weapons—those things have value anywhere. One way or another."

"Are those things valuable?" Truth tilted his head wonderingly at Colonel Cho. A man who could exterminate a clan with a stroke of a pen. A man who could exterminate a family with his silence. The bribes and gifts he would have received over the course of his career could scarcely be counted. Even if he was passing a big piece of them upward, Cho would be considered quite wealthy. Not a plutocrat but rich.

Truth couldn't help laughing. The man looked so serious! He really believed those things mattered. He was testing Truth again, but he really did believe those were things of worth. "You keep them, then. Look after them for me. If I want them, I'll come and take them."

Chuckling, he opened the door. "Trying to bribe me while wearing a beggar's rags. What a joke!"

Truth had a rough suspicion about where to head next, but his now virtually disintegrated road atlas was understandably lacking in maps of offshore islands. Assuming there even was an island and not an undersea base or something. The clouds had turned black while he had been talking with the Colonel. He could smell the heavy rain in them. It would hit very soon.

He looked around and couldn't see a sign for even a local bus, let alone a bus or train depot. He'd spend the night. He had a quick look around. To his pleasant surprise, there was a youth hostel nearby. Practically empty for the off-season. It would do. The rain started pattering against the windows, then pounding. Nothing leaked. It was a good hostel. Truth slipped into one of the private rooms (because he would be damned before he bothered with a dorm again), kicked off his shoes, and had an early night.

Which turned out to be a not-great choice for the System, who barely had time to flinch when he saw Truth's nous shake.

I was sent forth from the power,
and I have come to those who reflect upon me,
and I have been found among those who seek after me.
Look upon me, you who reflect upon me,
and you hearers, hear me.
You who are waiting for me, take me to yourselves.
And do not banish me from your sight.
And do not make your voice hate me, nor your hearing.
Do not be ignorant of me anywhere or any time. Be on your guard!
Do not be ignorant of me.

The Prophet was reciting their favorite hymn as they walked through the busy streets of the most advanced city in the world, or at least this part of the world. Debatable on a global level. But definitely top-tier even if it wasn't the very tippy-top. It was a wonderful place to be a prophet. There were so many others in the same line of business. You could swap tips. And because there were so many God-botherers, there was an almost endless supply of those wishing to learn more about God. A beautiful, virtuous cycle.

For purely personal reasons, they had spent a century or so in quiet places. Places free of exhausting youth. Just had to settle their soul a bit. Some unpleasant business in the desert. Not *bad*, exactly, but fair to say they had overdone it. Still. That person was safely reincarnated as a turnip somewhere, so all was well.

Okay, not an actual turnip, but whatever. Turnip farmer somewhere deep in the north. Learning some very valuable lessons about the universe very, very far away. The Prophet took a deep breath, inhaling the fragrant herbs and pungent fish-sauce aromas coming from the local food stands. The south was where the good things were. That freshly griddled bread smelled amazing. They should just barely have enough money for one, and if not, perhaps they could persuade the cook by sharing the good word.

"I'd like one bread, please, with extra oil, extra herbs, and extra garlic."

"Sure. On the house." The muscular cook slapped a bread on the hot iron plate and reached for his jug of oil.

"Oh, how generous! May God bless you and your stand with eternal prosperity!"

"That would be lovely. Though it does raise a question," the cook asked. With a sudden jolt, the Prophet realized that while the face wasn't exactly familiar, the voice really was.

"What question?" The Prophet had already started to inch away.

"If God is all-powerful, all-knowing, and all-benevolent, why do we live in a corrupt, imperfect world?" The cook rested a hand companionably on the Prophet's shoulder. "Also, unrelated, I've never let a dine-and-dash get more than three steps with two unbroken legs. Just seemed like something you should know."

CHAPTER 3

WHO'S YOUR FRIEND?

Why would I want to run, person that I have never met before?" The Prophet laughed awkwardly. Meeting someone's reincarnation wasn't weird. The world was only so big, after all. It was just . . . usually, the changes were bigger. More dramatic. This was, even for them, an uncanny degree of carryover. Even the aura of obstinate interest was the same.

"Dunno. You looked shifty. Some reason you don't want to cough up the goods? Mmm? You wouldn't happen to be a *false* prophet, would you? Because you know the consequences for that, don't you?"

"Err . . . I am very definitely a legitimate prophet. Overqualified, actually."

"What, you talk to the gods too much? Did you get told off for harassing the gods? You know the consequences for not respecting the gods, don't you?"

"Since when did I disrespect God? The gods?"

"Don't tell me; tell the Magistrate, blasphemer!" Truth slammed his hand on the flour-covered table and leaned forward. "Repent and confess everything, and maybe he'll go easy on you!"

"I'm innocent!"

"No one is innocent; the very world is corrupt!"

"Not in the sense you mean, it isn't!"

"Bullshit! Every moment of existence leads to termination, suffering, and corruption. We are born in blood and die in filth. The time in between is suffering and illusory pleasures. Do you deny these charges?"

"I deny your logic!" The Prophet was done being pushed around. "The one does not imply the other, let alone prove it. Yes, the world has its sufferings, and the mechanisms at play to sustain it can feel grotesque. But that does not imply *evil* or corruption."

"The greatest good is finding a life free of fear and bodily pain, a tranquil, modest life. In other words, a life that has as little to do with the damn world as practicable. The inverse of good is evil. Therefore, a life maximally involved with the world is a life of maximal suffering and maximal evil. And since this world is the creation of the gods, or God, whichever, it must logically follow that God is evil. Or we are."

Truth glared at the Prophet, then reached back and, without looking, accurately snagged the flatbread off the griddle. Slapping it down on the board in front of him, he swiftly poured oil over it, then topped it with herbs, garlic, and a sprinkle of salt. His eyes remained locked on the hooded Prophet the whole time.

"Since *I'm* not a blasphemer like you, it follows that it can't be God's fault and thus you cannot be innocent. And since you are guilty, you must go confess and receive your punishment. I have to charge you for your bread. I won't risk being executed as a co-conspirator."

Truth stuck out his hand. The Prophet pushed it to one side and got into Truth's face.

"Oh? Oh? Is that what the 'good' is? Huh? Some kind of Epicurus fanboy, are you? Well, what if I said that 'good' was conforming to moral virtue, and moral virtue was that which was beloved by the gods? How about that, eh?"

"Oh, yeah? Yeah? How about that, then? Let's play it through. We agree this world is ass."

"We don't agree! How could we start something with that as the premise?" The Prophet spluttered in outrage. "The world is flawed, yes. Far from the correct and true. But 'ass' is far too reductive for this remarkable achievement."

"No, it isn't."

"Is."

"Isn't."

"That's not even an argument!"

"Is."

"Isn't!"

They glared at each other, ignoring the spectators. One of the other nearby stall owners had already set out bowls of marinated olives, and the wine shop had already poured the watered wine into waiting bowls.

The Prophet sneered. "Let me lay it out for you, then. This world is amazing. But it isn't perfect. That much we can agree on. It's changing all the time; there is pain and ignorance and all that. If it was perfect, it would be unchanging and eternal, and infinitely good. Since it's not, we can say that it's not perfect and, *to some degree*, not good. Good in the sense of having achieved the highest degree of virtue."

"Oh, very logical. Super stuff. You just said that what is good is that which is beloved by the gods, and since this world isn't good, it isn't loved by the gods. Either that or the gods were unable to make a perfect world, meaning they themselves were less than perfect and therefore less than infinitely good. You sure are determined to catch a blasphemy charge, huh?" Truth rolled his eyes and started slowly applauding.

One enterprising soul in a local tavern had set out a slate and was keeping a tally of points on either side. The slaves were circulating, filling the wine bowls of spectators as raucous cheers and boos started breaking out here and there.

This was, after all, Alexandria. Such arguments were common entertainment there at the crossroads of thought.

"Oh, spare me your cheap piety! Naturally, we can say that God is infinitely perfect and infinitely good because we can conceive of perfect things. Rationally, if a thing can be conceived of, it must exist on some level, and since it cannot exist in this world, it must exist in a higher world. The rational outcome is, of course, a realm of only perfect, and perfectly true, things from which all things are derived. A realm that is, of itself, God." The Prophet ignored the flatbread, waving their finger in Truth's face.

"Just because you use the word *logic* doesn't make something logical. If this realm of the perfect is God, and they by some mystic maneuver created the world, they created it flawed. Therefore their knowledge of how to create is imperfect, and we loop right back to where we were before." Truth sneered at the finger. He had seen better.

"Not if the being that created the world wasn't God but merely a godly being! A craftsman spirit, taking up the chaos of the material universe and trying to fashion it in some semblance of the perfect universe of intellect that exists above matter. It is the craftsman's limitations that are shown in the imperfections of the world, not God's."

The Prophet fished out a copper quadrin from their purse. "Look, this is a coin, right? Supposed to be circular, with a picture stamped on either side. But it isn't a circle. When have you ever seen a perfectly circular coin? It's not like the mint doesn't know what a circle is or how to use a compass. It's a limitation of the materials and techniques available. This is the best they can do. And if it's a bit lumpy, so what? We all know what it's supposed to be and it still spends."

The Prophet dramatically waved their hand at the world around them. "Well, here we are. A bit lumpy, not quite perfect, but we can use our heads, know what's right, and it still spends—our time here isn't wasted. We polish our souls, and that's real value."

"Oh, wow! A lousy craftsman! Well, that just explains everything. *No*, slapnuts, that doesn't fly. The Craftsman had to come from somewhere. At some point, there was a transition from your realm of perfection to a realm of imperfection. Which means that God, the Perfect Realm or however you want to construct it, cannot be both infinitely wise and infinitely good. If it was infinitely wise, it would never allow an imperfect world to come into being, because it would be introducing evil to the universe to no purpose. Likewise, if it was infinitely good, even if it was unskillful in its actions, it would take steps to ensure there was no evil."

Truth did his own, mocking, grand wave to the world. "We got an imperfect world AND evil. The only possible consequence of your premise is that an infinitely powerful god felt that it would be most pleasing if humanity was created to suffer for its enjoyment. Your creator god is a monster. Not ignorant, *cruel*."

"Spare me the theatrics," the Prophet said, raising their hands theatrically. "Humanity is never going to be able to fully comprehend the mind of God—it is literally, definitionally beyond us. We can only grab on to bits of it through reason and mystic revelation that transcends reason. That's it. That's what we get! God's thought process behind the universe, the realms of existence emanating out from that perfect monad, the beings that inhabit those realms, and yes, even the blasted Craftsman, *all of them*, are beyond human comprehension."

"OOOH!" Truth nodded exaggeratedly. "I get it—God isn't cruel or incompetent; I'm just too dumb to pick up on his genius scheme! Boy, all those crib deaths had me worried, but now I know it's fine. I'm just too dumb to understand why all that pain was necessary. Whew! Load off my shoulders, let me tell you."

Truth didn't look over at the slaves working around them. He didn't have to. The Prophet knew he was thinking it. Which was a particularly sticky subject for virtually any philosopher or prophet. It was all well and good saying that humanity was created as one people by a beneficent god, but slaves were wealth. And the one universal truth that every successful philosopher and prophet learned was—you never fuck with the money.

Live an austere life. Promote simplicity and the satisfaction of humility.

Damn wealth as a frippery or illusion. Just don't *actually* put it in any danger. Don't ever, *ever* suggest that rich people are the problem. Cross that line, and you won't live long enough to cross many others. Most smart people just finessed the subject. Some prophets just said "Fuck it" and preached that slavery was good. The Prophet wasn't quite that shameless, so they opted to boldly ignore the problem.

"Yes, exactly. We are all fragments of that perfect divinity, mired in an imperfect world. Whether we languish in the muck or rise up through the spheres and return to that vast perfection is on us. On constantly raising our wisdom, and on increasingly experiencing that divine revelation that transcends rationality."

The Prophet's voice became sonorous. "The material world is an illusion, a faint approximation of the true reality of the Pleroma—the vast, true universe that exists above the muck of the world. The higher we raise ourselves to that infinite perfection, the more powerful our magic and our arts become. By raising our wisdom, by polishing our souls, we can escape the mud. No matter how many lifetimes it takes, such must be our purpose. And in the process, we become God's answer to your question—why would a perfect God create an imperfect world?"

Truth glanced over to the man running the tally board. The beardy man shouted across the plaza, "No clear winner, but he did answer the question!"

Truth nodded. Then handed the confused Prophet the flatbread. "Thank you for your patronage. Please come again."

"Wait, what?"

"This is Alexandria." Truth shrugged.

"Yes? I know? It has been for centuries."

"Yeah, that's kind of my point. We ain't all philosophers or holy folk, but we are soaked in 'em. You get lectures and sermons and debates going on around the city all the time. You were pretty good!"

The Prophet couldn't quite put into words what he was feeling. "So, that wasn't a serious question about the nature of the universe and God?"

"Oh, I was totally serious. I mean, it's one of the fundamental questions, right? At some point, everyone's got to try and scrape off that particular bit of shit stuck to their sandal." Truth looked up and saw the sun setting behind the buildings. "Hell with it. I'll pack up for the day. Let me take you round to meet some folk. I think you'll like 'em."

"Oh. Thanks." The Prophet nibbled on the bread, then took some big bites. It was actually pretty good, and they were quite hungry.

Truth quickly packed everything away and slung an arm around the Prophet's neck. "Yeah, once you know the scene, you'll fit right in here. Hey, Moshe! Grab your lute and tell Gaius, Telemachus, and the boys to meet us over at Ariston's place. Tell Fidelus to bring his lizard!"

"Got it! Dinner's on you, though."

"I'll bring the bread. Meat's on Gaius; he still owes from two times ago. Oh, bring David, too; I hear he's got the latest from Syria."

"You . . . turned out pretty social, huh?" the Prophet murmured.

"Huh? I have always been social. I'm definitely a lover, not a fighter." Truth laughed. "Alexandria is an amazing city. Amazing. It's a bad old world, but I can agree with you on one thing—this is a good place."

There was an awkward cough from one side. "It sure seems nice. Any chance you could explain all this . . . everything to me?" Etenesh asked. And in the vast spinning cosmos, something slipped between the cracks.

CHAPTER 4

THE CELESTIAL CLOCKWORK SLIPS A GEAR

Truth laughed and walked forward, arm slung over the Prophet's shoulder. He didn't respond to the question. Someone walked straight through Etenesh without noticing her. Had anyone asked, she definitely would have denied yelping. She started looking around furiously.

It was almost like a nightmare—everything was familiar but wrong. This market should be teeming with spirits and demons, but she didn't see a single one. There were wagons, sure, but ones pulled by animals. No carriages. No sleek high-speed chariots. Not a hint of a flying carpet, seven-colored cloud, or wide-winged firebird. Nothing *normal*. Just humans, arguing, laughing, eating, shopping. Living.

As nightmares went, it really wasn't too bad. Maybe a sort of optimistic notion of what the world might look like after the magic collapsed? It was a nice thought.

"It ought to be a dream, but I swear I can smell these people. Just what the hell is going on?" she muttered. She thought back to the debate she had just watched. A very old-fashioned sort of argument. Modern theology was playing well past that point. *The world is perfect and so are we*—perfectly imperfect, just the way God wanted us. Our journey toward perfection was kind of the point of existence. At least, according to Orthodox Siphios. Otherwise, why create a universe at all? As for demons—aren't they improving themselves too?

She was forced to follow behind Truth, or Pseudo-Truth, watching him chatter with people in a way she had never seen him do in real life. She had a nasty jolt, watching him drink bowl after bowl of wine. This was Truth but not her Truth.

He looked happy there. He was so serious in Siphios. Or not serious, exactly, but you got the sense that the emotions he showed were superficial.

The real emotions ran deep and silent. When she could pull a real smile out of him, see the vulnerability in his eyes . . . it about killed her. Knowing that the most hurt, scared person she knew was letting her in, treating her as safe. But there was a Truth, embracing a stranger. There was a Truth that was happy in a way she couldn't remember being in a long while. Jamming out to some music and flying arguments with laughing friends. She used to love listening to music in clubs. She had a very active social circle, too.

On the one hand, now was really not the time. Everything was falling apart, and she was barely started on figuring out how the whole apotheosis thing was supposed to work. On the other hand, Truth wouldn't want her miserable. He wouldn't just understand; he would approve. Etenesh smiled as the dream faded away. She was staying with some family at the moment. She could drag some cousins out for an evening. The music scene out in the countryside was pretty limited, but there were weekly sessions at the local bar. It might be nice. Even God needed a rest now and then, right?

She could feel the idea clicking into place, healing something broken inside of her. The dream faded away as she woke up smiling. On the other side of the world, Truth kept right on sleeping. But come dawn, he woke smiling too.

"Today is going to be a great day," he said, as the delayed monsoon hammered at the windows. *Did you catch that memory?*

<<*Of your past life? Oh, yeah. More than you did. Look at your soul.*>>

No major changes, but he could see the little spark of Etenesh glowing more brightly. He could feel the joy shining off of it.

Good. She deserves to be happy.

He briefly wondered what that could be about, then shrugged. As long as she was happy, wasn't it all good? Instead, he walked into the hostel lobby and found out about travel options out of the city. There were buses that ran regularly, as well as a local train. The local train, however, was no longer considered reliable.

"Breaks down all the time, always track repairs, always some problem with the demon, always something. Nobody ever does anything about it. No wonder the whole country is going down the toilet." The woman behind the counter was older and had the general air of someone's mother filling in on their shift.

"Sounds like the bus is the safer bet." Truth smiled.

"Safer but not safe. You won't believe how often it breaks down in the mountains. And now the monsoon is here! Ayah! You should pack a lunch and a snack AND two bottles—one with water, one empty." They shared a look.

"I think I will do that, then. Work here often?"

"These days, I mostly just keep the books. My husband and I own it. My son is in the army now, so . . . here I am."

Truth nodded understandingly. He hadn't paid for the room or told anyone he was going to be staying there, so it would be hard to say *Thank you for the lovely stay*. Still. It had been nice. Hmm.

He thanked the landlady for the tip, then quickly ran around the house, touching up any talismans in need of work. It wasn't much, but when he considered what maintenance techs usually billed out at . . . well it still wasn't enough to cover a night's stay. But it was something.

Truth looked up into the torrent of rain. It would settle down in a bit, but you could reliably expect rain off and on for the next couple of months. Especially on the coast. All those clouds ran headfirst into the mountains and dumped their rain on the habitable strips of land along the coast. Not that inland didn't catch plenty of rain too. Jeon's mountains, especially in the south, weren't very big. The peninsula wasn't that big either.

Rain gear. He grabbed all kinds of supplies but neglected rain gear. Strictly speaking, he didn't need it. Equally strictly speaking, it wasn't comfortable running around in sopping wet clothes, and he *wanted* it. He was firmly done with the nudist long-haul runs.

Was there anywhere selling rain gear around there? No. At least, no one selling quality, long-wearing stuff. There were, however, Happy Happy Marts that he would Happy Happy shoplift a cheap plastic poncho and a barely functional umbrella from.

Public transportation in Jeon had, until recently, been pretty good. All the bus and train routes were privately operated, of course, but there were legal minimums they had to meet. It all worked out. Truth was able to get a city bus to the combination bus and train station, paused briefly to note that all trains had been canceled for unspecified reasons, and queued up for the intercity bus to Harban.

Starbrite wasn't in Harban, but Niles was. He had a suspicion that was the thread to pull, not running down the ritual sites. Besides, it would keep Cho and his ilk guessing about his movements.

The intercity coach was a long, tall thing, with ample storage below and rather decent seats above. Some enchanter had done a good job with the bound spirits on the vehicle—they would keep the ride safe and steady, plus they looked cute in their little bus-company uniforms. His ticket was checked, naturally, as was his travel permit. They were checked by a distinctly elderly Level One "supervised" by a Level Zero conscript. There was no trouble boarding the bus. He got a seat by the window and watched the world go past.

What, exactly, was his end game? *People should be nicer to each other and work to help each other. It is possible to create a world where everyone can live safely and with dignity, if we work together.* Not exactly the stuff of revolutions. Not exactly the kind of thing you can sell with a tee shirt. Especially when you push in to the details. Every time you dug in to the details, you jammed yourself up. But you couldn't just blow past the details, either, because the details were where things got done.

People should have safe, clean places to live. Places that can't just be taken from them.

All right, sounds good! How are we defining safe, clean, places, *and* live? *We should probably tackle that before we get to the notion of someone having an absolute right to residency somewhere despite attacking the maintenance workers with an iron pipe or beating an old man half to death in the elevator.*

There were some core childhood memories, right there. You haven't truly known life in a big apartment block until you see some blackout-drunk dickheads crouching at the top of a flight of stairs, competing to see whose turds could roll the farthest. The burnt-out whores were downright charming neighbors by comparison.

The thing is, though, even if he didn't want them living anywhere near him, he did want them to be able to live *somewhere.* What were the odds that they were going to be able to be educated and get their heads together if they were made homeless? Zero, right? But how do you strike that balance? He didn't know.

Everything was like that. No matter what you said—*Everyone should be able to eat good food*—there would be bad actors. But even they should eat, right? Because if they had their heads on straight, they wouldn't be acting like that, right? Which means that they have brain problems or education problems, or something.

So. How do we get there? No frigging way if it's just him. You need loads of people thinking about these questions. Picking at them. Testing out different solutions. Hundreds or thousands of people whose job it is to make sure all these questions get answered and the rules get implemented and enforced. Definitely thousands of people. The Food Safety department alone would be enormous.

Truth leaned his head against the back of the seat ahead of him and laughed painfully.

"Oh, God. I just discovered the reason for bureaucracy. And I found it good. This 'thinking' thing was a bad idea. Mindless violence, that's the safe bet."

Truth briefly hallucinated a country where practically everyone is a bureaucrat, or at least works for the government. You have the military, of course, but you also have the department that decides how much housing is needed, then the department that decides how they are built, then the department that gets all the materials together, a labor department to secure the workers, planning and permitting departments to site the building, environmental departments, transit departments, food, medicine, the very air you breathe, all got departments.

Farming? You have joined the national defense against malnutrition! And to make sure your farm is operating optimally, it will be owned and operated by the state—you are just labor. Just like the guys working in the fisheries and ranches. Education, well, education was at the core of all this. Nothing worked without it. That would definitely have to be carefully overseen by the government.

It was all benevolent, really. Everyone was employed at the same job—looking out for everyone else. No one person could do it all by themselves. With a well-developed system, no one would have to. A governmental philosophy dedicated to people working together for communal goals. A beautiful thing.

Now . . . what were the odds of *literally no one* looking at this setup and thinking, *How do I make sure I have a bigger and nicer apartment than my neighbors? Also, completely unrelated, Stevie is hoarding kumquats in his house, so let's just fit him for a noose . . .*

Was there a middle ground? He didn't know. But it all started with education. And the education started with a dream. Back to Harban he went.

The world of bureaucrats was too much. People can't wrap their heads around that. What can you understand? What your arms can wrap around. Family. Those neighbors you have been avoiding meeting. The handful of people you know through work. What if you pitched a different kind of world to them—one that took the profit of the group and put it first? The world was too big and too scary to face it all on your own. Nobody could make it on their own.

For example, what if you had a life-changing opportunity? Something that would improve both physical health and financial wellness? You *could* hoard it for yourself. You could be selfish like that. But, really, you would be shortchanging yourself. So, it was both out of the absolute kindness of your heart and good sense that you reached out to a few of your besties to let them in on the biggest secret of the decade. The key to limitless prosperity. MegaShroom.

Truth visualized the structure of the MLM, seeing the network of connections, seeing how the lowest tier had the flexibility to show initiative and creativity. Seeing how those chains of responsibility rose upward, guided by policy. Policy set at the very top. You don't need everyone for a revolution. You just need loud, motivated people. Shameless people. People who refuse to stop knocking on your door even if you put a bear trap on your front step.

The revolution would be network-marketed, whether it liked it or not.

CHAPTER 5

A FORK IN A STRAIGHT ROAD

The trip to Harban was dull. To his intense horror, he had run out of books. He had been right there in a small city and didn't even think of stopping by a local bookstore and picking up some schlocky romances. Secondhand books must be cheap as hell right now. And yet, somehow, he had whiffed. Shameful. Just disgraceful.

It was a boring few hours. He tried to spend the time thinking about what he wanted his revolutionary organization to look like, but kept going around in circles. Eventually, he gave up and tried to fall asleep. Usually, he was good at that. Not today. Today he got to listen to the endless drumming of the monsoon rains and the not-quite-quiet-enough noises of the other passengers on the bus. Somehow, it all managed to keep him from sleeping. No reason for it. Just couldn't quite pass the gray threshold into oblivion.

I . . . really don't want to apologize to Niles. Which is pretty messed-up, since I very literally kidnapped him and brainwashed him into being my adoring servant.

<<Call it what it is—you enslaved him. He is, in no sense, a free person. Not with two succubae whispering in his ear every hour of the day and night.>>

Yeah. Yeah, I did. And worst of all, even if I knew how to set him free, I'm not going to. At the very least, not before the apocalypse. He's just too useful where he is, doing what he does. Which makes me a complete piece of trash.

<<Yeah. Trash is about the nicest way to say that. You can come up with all kinds of lies and mitigating factors or whatever, but the simple fact of it was that you enjoyed playing the Prince, and someone else paid the price for it. Many people paid for you. You seized authority without accountability.>>

Very in character. Very on brand. A prince, not a king.

<<Except that even a prince is accountable—to his parents if nobody else. You probably forgot, but Merkovah basically rolled his eyes at the whole

concept of princes. He thought your idea was interesting, but princes? Never moved him.>>

A prince that can inspire fear but not love. Not without using extreme methods.

<<Yes. Worth thinking about how long such a prince could actually rule for even if they did become king. No one would feel safe. They would constantly scheme against you. And you, knowing they were scheming against you, would keep taking whatever steps you could to ensure they couldn't harm you.>>

Right. Any servant powerful enough to be useful is powerful enough to be dangerous. Broadly defined.

<<It would be weird if the Minister of Finance wasn't skimming off both the top and bottom. To say nothing of your generals and bodyguards.>>

Because they are only accountable to the king. And it's in his interests to keep them happy. So, as long as it doesn't threaten his interests too much, he can split off a portion for them. But how do you keep the masses in line?

<<How else? Fear, propaganda, and interests. As in it is in their best interest to be obedient and pay their taxes. Literally. As long as people feel reasonably safe and can earn a living, they won't rebel. Not without some very compelling reason.>>

I'm certain it's more complicated than that.

<<Everything is.>>

Even boredom couldn't be eternal. Unfortunately. They were roughly a third of the way to Harban when the sky suddenly flashed a bright pink. Truth wasn't the only one who knew what that meant. The bus driver immediately pulled over onto the verge and yanked viciously on the emergency brake. Truth watched him shove the door open, then dove out onto the grass. He wasn't alone—everyone was scrambling to escape the bus. The windows were smashed open; people stampeded for the door. They didn't try to run very far. It was just that none of them wanted to be in the bus when something awful happened.

They must know something I don't. Well. Out the window we go.

It had been barely four seconds since the pink flash. Truth got well away from the bus and into a storm culvert by second five. The monsoon rains had water running ten centimeters deep already. Easy to drown. He didn't worry about it. There was the most incredible sound of thunder and then a terrible pause.

The vacuum hit hard. Every scrap of him was being tugged on, every millimeter of skin, every twist and wrinkle of intestine, his corneas and the little swirling canal inside his eardrums that made balance possible. Not that it succeeded in pulling anything away. He was sealed tight. The tension ramped up and became a stinging pain. The vacuum was far more intense than it had ever been before.

There were shouts, screams, babbled prayers. Crying. Begging for mercy from a merciless Heaven. Truth wanted to tell them that it was pointless, hopeless, that God despised them, and so did the planet they lived on. They were not wanted. Their suffering was a byproduct of a necessary process and was never worth considering.

There were a series of muffled thuds and the sound of tearing metal. Seconds later, there were horrific crashing noises, incredibly loud as carriages traveling in excess of one hundred and fifty kilometers an hour smashed into each other, long since running out of control. No demon turning the wheel, sheer inertia and Fate's spite carrying them into one another.

It quickly became quiet again. All over but for the screaming. And there were fewer screams now. Then there was another impossible crack of thunder that shuddered the marrow in his bones, and the pulling had become a hard press. All that energy that would have been yanked out was now hammering in again. Fast, too fast. And far too hard.

There was another round of screams. Then some meaty pops. Some broken sobs. Truth had a sick feeling that some people just exploded, while others had their apertures destroyed. As for him?

Truth absorbed the extra cosmic rays. It didn't carry him very far toward Level Six, but it was a noticeable improvement. At his level, that was significant. The brutal cataclysm humanity was suffering was just a happy accident for Truth. He could just fill every scrap of his body with the excess energy. Becoming more real, with all that entailed.

Was this what life was supposed to be? One person elevated as billions suffer? One rat picked at random out of the boiling vermin swarm and elevated above the rest? Was there really something better than this?

Only one ass sat on the throne. Everyone else, no matter how high, had to look up from their knees.

Metaphorically, anyway. The mucky water frothed around him, racing through the corrugated metal pipe. *Seraphim famously never touch the ground, and their whole job is floating around, saying how great God is. Still, I feel like the point stands. Is that the point of "evil"? Put something in the universe so God will always be above? I mean, that is a God-tier level of pettiness, so it would probably be wrong to rule it out.*

He sighed. The pressure was easing off now. When you got right down to it, he didn't really believe evil was intentionally added to the universe purely to make humanity suffer. More like . . . incompetence or some necessary byproduct of a function he didn't understand. Like an axle generating heat as it spun.

Truth crawled out of the culvert. The bus was trashed. Whatever happened was worse than what he had seen before. He had seen the demon powering a carriage obliterated. He had never seen one of those energy voids crush an intercity bus like a beer can. He tried to figure out what might have happened. Best he could come up with was reinforcing enchantments keeping the bus light and strong suddenly collapsing.

It seemed this wasn't the first time it had happened. Everyone piled out in a panic. It wasn't that odd—why use a load of expensive metals for rigidity when you could use lighter materials and some enchantments? It all made complete sense . . . until the magic vanished. Then everything contracted in on itself. You could imagine what would happen if people had stayed on the bus.

The grassy verge of the road had mushrooms rising out of the ground, swelling and then exploding as their tiny physiques were overloaded by the energy hammering down into them. Truth started counting. There had been forty-five people on the bus. Thirty-two were still alive. How many more would live out the hour, he couldn't say. How many still had intact apertures . . . Well. He might be the only one.

He looked up the road. The sign for Harban was plain as could be. *Just keep running. Leave them here and put those feet in gear.* They would die soon anyway. Today or in a few months, what difference could it make? Hell, nothing was saying you couldn't have two voids back to back. It was getting increasingly likely, in fact.

Yeah, he could do that. But the happiest he had been recently was when he played Dr. Bone-Bro. And Bone-Bro would never leave them like that. He'd bitch and moan about the complete absence of bones, and about how morally wrong it was not being able to fix everything by casting ANCEF. But he would do his goddamn best regardless. The Prince was an asshole, disdaining all others. The fool didn't have that kind of arrogance. His arrogance was of a completely different kind.

Who needed help most urgently? He reached out with his spells, trying to nudge Cup and Knife and Incisive to work together. An older man. He had a heart problem that had been fixed with a magical tattoo. Now his apertures were shattered *and* he was having a heart attack. Truth reached him with a single step. No problem using the Earth-Folding Step at the moment.

"All right, Senior. It's going to be all right." He cast Cup and Knife, riding the ebbing tide of the magical overpressure. He could feel the spell making minute changes to some of the nerves around the heart. Calming them. Slowing their pace. The heart resumed a steady rhythm. Such a tiny thing, but it was killing a man. Well, it was fixed now.

The apertures, along with all the tiny channels that ran magic through most people's bodies, were destroyed. Utterly. The one open aperture was shattered; the channels were shattered—it was plainly fatal. Plainly irreparable. He had seen young masters torturing people by destroying their apertures. None of them had ever managed anything so categorical.

This was no longer a human capable of using cosmic energy. No longer a mage, but something else. A clay doll, permanently severed from the infinite heavens above it. It could barely see the shadows on the rock, but it could never turn around and see the truth that cast the shadows. Wisdom would never reach it. Absent a miracle.

"This isn't how people should be. Whatever a human is, it should be able to look up and strive. We aren't clay dolls. Even if it feels like someone is just playing with us." Truth poured Cup and Knife into the senior's body. The spell wove through the man, gathering all the spiritual scraps and rebuilding them. Knitting them together in a way that wholly exceeded everything Truth thought he knew about medicine.

This injury was irreparable unless you understood what you were looking at. Manda wasn't trying to repair a body. He didn't give a damn about some meat sack. Manda wanted to repair souls. To bring them more in line with God. Because God was how things ought to be. At least according to Manda.

The pieces pulled together. The body, the shattered bits of soul, and those strange structures that bridged the gap between both, all came together. Meshed into a complete human being. The old man curled up on himself. Not quite sobbing but hanging on to himself as hard as he could. He was safe now, but the whole thing had *hurt.*

"Now. Just need to do that thirty-one more times." The rain was still pouring down. Living water, pouring from the heavens. Nourishing and bringing life to the dead earth below. Truth stepped to the next person and got back to work.

CHAPTER 6

A LONG-OVERDUE APOLOGY

Truth worked quickly and methodically, letting Incisive guide him from those most urgently in need of help to the least. Not that there were any light wounds. Other than a few children and a handful of Level Zeros, most of the bus was filled with Level One citizens. Their apertures had collapsed. They were in utter agony, and worse, they knew it was never going to get better. Until it did. Until two strong hands were placed on them and a miracle happened.

It slowly got quiet by the side of the road. The healed just watched Truth work, not stirring from where they had fallen. A few shushed the terrified children, pointing at what was happening and telling them to watch closely. When the children whispered, "Why?" the parents didn't know how to respond. How do you describe this? Not just the impossible healing, the simple fact that they were healed at all. They had signed no contracts, made no promises. Even if they had, this person was so far beyond them, their petty labor would be worthless.

A man possessing power beyond their comprehension had been sitting on the bus with them, dressed in workman's trousers and a black tee shirt. He was muscled like he did heavy labor for a living. And yet, he could heal them. And did heal them. And had asked for nothing. There wasn't a place for that in their minds. It just didn't add up. But here they were. It was happening. Everyone should watch. They would surely never see the like again.

Truth felt a great quietness. His hands moved steadily, healing strangers. They weren't the sibs. Some little part of him kept coming back to that. These people were not, in any sense, the sibs. He owed them nothing. Less than nothing. They were already fortunate if he chose not to bully them. But there he was, healing them. For free. Repairing the links between body and soul. Links that would be shattered soon enough.

Doing it for no other reason than he would like the world to be this way. Doing it because it would be nice if, someday, when he was in a jam, someone would do the same for him. No deep thoughts. No great insights. Just the good work.

They aren't the sibs. And that's okay. They don't have to be the sibs. It doesn't always have to be cash on the table. I have that much margin. I am . . .

He looked up into the rain, feeling it fall down on him as his magic worked through the woman below. Losing himself in it.

I am safe enough that I can take that risk. I am rich enough that I can spend on these people.

He felt a helpless smile stretching across his face.

All that introspection, and all I can think of things is in terms of danger and money. I'm not acting like a scared rat, but I only have a scared rat's words and concepts. What a curse. What a brilliant, simple thing. Just make it so a better world can't be imagined. Altruism, at least on a big scale, can't be imagined. If we ever had the words for it, they have been forgotten.

He didn't keep track of time or how many he had healed. There was only the person in front of him. It didn't take all that long. Just long enough to save a life. It took him a minute to realize when he had healed the last person. No one else needed his help.

Truth stood, gathering in all the emotions swirling around him. Letting them reinforce his presence. The images and beliefs were powerful but formless. The watching passengers and the bus driver didn't know what to think. They didn't have the words for this, either.

"You don't owe me. You owe the next person. It's all about the get-back, right? Nobody feels safe enough to stick their neck out these days. What if someone takes advantage? But I stuck my neck out. You already got paid. You are in a no-risk situation here. You help out the next person who needs it, and if they don't pay it forward? No skin off your nose. You did the right thing. And next time, they won't get your help."

He could feel his words helping them put the pieces into place, reframing everything in the familiar shapes of contract and fear.

"Someone had to be the first person to take a chance. Someone had to be the first person to risk that loss. Let it be me. I can cover that bet. I don't need flashy jewels or a flying cloud. You guys can be my wealth. My investment. And when you pay it forward, and tell the next guy to pay it forward, and so on and so on . . . my investment will grow like crazy."

Truth shook his head slightly. He didn't know what else he could say. So, he turned toward the highway, gathering his presence back around him. Letting himself fade into the rain.

"Senior! Senior! What . . . who are you?"

Truth looked back and smiled. "I'm a true son of Jeon. A Holy Fool and a Hell Prince. I'm the rat that looked up. Who am I?" He laughed, a warm, honest sound that made everyone smile along with him. "Does it matter? The question is, who are *you*?"

Truth vanished into the raindrops before his voice stopped echoing across the verge.

The strange mood persisted as he crossed the hills and valleys. He occasionally mixed in the Earth-Folding Step, trying to let Incisive guide when it would be most effective. It actually worked. He was hardly eating up the miles using it, but his range was slowly growing. He didn't try to think through what had just happened. It happened. He felt good that he had done it. It was different from the pointless altruism he had done before.

In a small way, he had shown a few tens of people the great lie. He had opened a path for them. Would they take it? Maybe. Maybe not. Probably not. But the path was open for them. They didn't *have* to be rats anymore. At the very least, he gave them space to look up.

He came to a stop by a road sign and looked up into the rain again. Just watching the rain falling. It was gray, but all that water was life. It was the root of everything.

"I wonder if this is how Manda sees the world. Creating endless opportunities for people, if they can see them. If they will just look up and embrace the rain." Truth stretched his hands toward the clouds that covered the sun. "Life hurts. It's not fair. It's never going to get better on its own. But you can look up. You can choose how you respond to the pain."

Truth bent over and got into a sprinter's crouch. Time to see how fast he could get to Harban. He had an awful lot of work to do.

Harban remained . . . well, it remained. There were fewer roadblocks now. Maybe they just weren't cost-effective anymore, or the soldiers were needed on the war front, not the home front. The shine had gone off the richest city in the world. Now it just felt sad. Like it had lost its soul and its spine at the same time.

There had been several floating buildings in Harban, enormous apartment buildings, office buildings, that kind of thing. He didn't see any of them from outside of the city. He didn't know if they had fallen down or were brought down intentionally. Either way. Not a good sign.

No need to attempt the Earth-Folding Step. He could feel it wouldn't work for him. Not until he understood it a whole lot better. Didn't matter.

In Harban, the only way to get anywhere quickly was to fly. He could steal a cloud or something but, well, he *did* still have that military ration card.

"TAXI!" He waved down a carpet from the street corner, officer's uniform proudly on display. The carpet came swooping down straight away.

"Where to, officer?" The pilot was still using the polite words, but the pacing was off. You could smell the tension on the man. The carpet company must be forcing him to fly. Or his landlord.

Truth gave him the address.

"Oh, MegaShroom?"

"You know that building just from its street address?" Truth was genuinely surprised. That building had been utterly anonymous when he visited last.

"Oh, yes. Things have been going berserk over there for the last month or so. Just hordes of people coming. I hear they bought out the whole building."

"Wow! Why, though?"

"It's the rallies, I expect. And all the trainings."

"Sorry, no idea."

"Oh. Well. You know how MegaShroom is pushing that big self-reliance thing? Faith, Family, Prosperity? All that stuff. Well, it really took off. Now they do big promotional events supporting their community-service drives. There are big prayer rallies, too, in the arena next to the office. You were smart to hail a carpet. The subway there is packed."

Truth stood outside the office building where he had exterminated one CEO and installed a new one.

Actually . . . that wasn't quite right, was it? More like he had liberated a CEO? Replaced one personality-rewritten CEO with another? Truth didn't subscribe to moral relativism, but he was having a hard time pinning down where on the moral spectrum his actions at MegaShroom landed. Probably bad.

"Maid, attend me."

A few seconds later, a cloud of smoke raced from the top of the building and landed in front of Truth. There was a twist, an inexplicable compression, and then there was a maid. Beautiful but not too much so. Fragile wrists and a delicate neck, bashful eyes looking demurely down.

"My lord returns draped in power and anointed with authority. His garments are woven from the banners of the defeated, and the slippers upon his feet are victory itself. This little maid feels the world twist and contort itself to your will, for it is by your will the existence of all things is conferred. Glory, Glory, Glory to the Mighty One."

Truth's mouth twitched. Succubae were air demons. It seemed some traits were category-wide.

"How goes it?"

She smiled prettily. It was the only way she could smile.

"Does my Lord mean his acolyte or the servants he commands?"

"Niles. I'll ask him directly about MegaShroom."

"He no longer thinks of his old identity. He has not forgotten it, exactly, but he remembers it vaguely and with unease. It seems to him now as a time when he walked in a fog. Scared, alone, aimless. Now he has light, warmth, and safety. He glories in his labor and is proud that he can complete such a difficult task as the one you set for him."

"He is happy."

"Yes, my lord. He is happy. Frustrated, alarmed, occasionally scared or furious, but if I was to pick one word to describe him, he is happy. His god has given him power, status, purpose, and has bidden him to make the lives of others better. What else could he be but happy?"

"So, if I told him I had mastered a spell that could return him to who he was and where he was before we met, he would refuse it."

"He would beg to know how he had failed you, and offer his whole life as penance. My lord, for all intents and purposes, that one-time clerk is dead. Your acolyte lives, joyfully."

Truth nodded. "Lead me to him."

Truth walked into the CEO's office, the door held open by a bowing Butler. The room had been completely redecorated. Light, airy, full of pictures of people with their families. Working together. Everything about it was filled with vitality. Kneeling in front of the desk was Niles.

Truth stood and looked down at the man. Really looked at him. Saw all the good, and all the bad, and understood something that the succubae never would. It didn't matter if Niles was happy. Didn't matter if he was thriving. Didn't matter if this was the best he had ever had it. Niles was not free and probably never would be. And Truth was responsible. It was his choice once again. He could shrug at it, ignore it, press on with his life. God knew he was leaving thousands of bodies in his wake as it was. What was one more life?

"I am sorry for what I did to you. Sorry for what I am going to keep on doing to you. I don't think I can ever make it right. But so long as I can, as much as I can, I'm going to do right by you."

CHAPTER 7

SPREADING THE GOOD NEWS

My lord? There is no need—" Niles started to speak, but Truth cut him off. "Accept it or don't. Either way, I stand by what I said. Now, since I know you don't think I have anything to apologize for, we will talk about your work. Looks like you have achieved great things."

Niles struggled for a moment, then nodded. "Yes, my lord. We have followed your instructions diligently. We took as our foundation your words—Faith, Family, Prosperity—and built from there. Building the ideological foundation was actually the hardest part, and continues to be a work in progress. However, it has been fairly straightforward, making the alterations to the terms of our contracts with our network."

"Really? I thought that the contracts would take a fair bit of legal wrangling. You are directly changing the compensation structure, after all."

"Thankfully, my lord, the contracts the previous administration used had a clause that said *You agree to be bound by the MegaShroom Representative Manual For Excellence and Success in addition to this contract*, and another section that said *MegaShroom reserves the right to alter any of the terms and conditions of this contract, including the contents of the MegaShroom Representative Manual For Excellence and Success, at any time, with no notice*, and perhaps most importantly, *You and your agents, heirs, and assignees agree to waive your right to sue MegaShroom for anything, ever, including breach of contract*."

"That's legal?"

"Completely. But we do have an internal arbitration process, so that's . . . something that exists."

"Ah. And the Manual?"

"Specifies things like the structure of the network of Representatives, what it takes to be promoted or demoted, the cost of product, purchase minimums, that sort of thing. Heavily revised now," Niles said with quiet pride.

"Which is why the ideological component was the key." Truth nodded. "You were setting the principles behind the policy."

"Exactly, my Lord. Exactly."

"Explain more about the principles."

"We are building on two systems, one explicit and one implicit. The explicit one is hierarchical—a pyramidal structure of Representatives recruiting junior Representatives and so on. The deeper one's network, the more 'passive' income one accrues. Obviously, as the peak of the pyramid, we accumulate the most."

"Right, both in your cut of the sales and your direct sale of inventory to the representatives."

"Correct, my lord. Though, in practice, we sell comparatively little outside the company. Some people do earn a small sum selling our products, but it's almost unheard-of to earn back the cost of purchasing inventory, given how much inventory their upstream contacts push them to buy."

"Ah. So . . ."

"So, the real thing that we sell is new recruits to the old recruits."

Truth had kind of known that, but hearing it stated so baldly was still, somehow, startling.

"Someone is recruited, pressured into buying a mountain of inventory, and then they realize they have no way to sell the inventory. Strangely, nobody likes having their neighbors constantly harassing them to buy things. Despair sets in, usually within a few months, and the new Representatives realize that their only hope of generating income is to recruit more people. Then they can pressure the new recruits into buying a mountain of inventory, for which they get a percentage."

And so the cycle repeats. A particularly fast churn if the recruit had gone into debt to purchase the "product."

"All right, that's the explicit system. What's the implicit one?"

"Essentially a cult."

Truth blinked at that, even though he could immediately see the similarities.

"A 'cult' is not a system," he observed.

"Yes, my lord. I mean that in the sense that we encourage cultish behavior. Isolation from one's family and social groups, endless indoctrination, unquestioning obedience and adherence to cult leaders, the suppression of rational or instinctive beliefs in favor of obeying doctrine, the usual sorts of things."

"Ah. I think I see where this is going."

"My lord is wise. Yes, we have already built the structure of a religion in all but name. The 'Heaven' we promise is similar to the one promised by other faiths—a place of peace, security, and pleasure. In our case, the medium of deliverance is money, and money is obtained through faith and good works."

Truth restrained the urge to rub the spot between his eyebrows. His suggestion to work with the Church was either brilliant or derived from direct infernal inspiration.

"As you can imagine, our cooperation with the Church of Prager has gone swimmingly."

"I thought it might. I think I underestimated the potential."

"I must confess I was shocked too. I had not realized the key, final component that drives both systems. Shame."

"Shame?"

"Yes, my lord, shame. No one likes being treated like an entrepreneurial plague rat. It hurts. It hurts so much, they would do almost anything to stop the pain."

Truth felt something in him spasm. Something lashing around and screaming in rage. "Entrepreneurial plague rat." Exactly how he thought of Mom. It seems he wasn't the only one who could spot the obvious meta-phor. But now he was being asked to *sympathize* with Mom? Like hell!

He only lost control for a moment, but his rage was enough to hammer Niles and the succubae. They remained on their knees, not daring to move or even, in Niles's case, breathe.

"Bad memories. And you are not to blame for them. Yes, your descrip-tion is apt. How does shame connect to the two systems and advance our cause?"

"Lord, they are ashamed of being poor. They feel lesser. They are lesser. They are driven to find relief in the dream of money and the comfort of the cult. It is the engine that drives them. The more they are despised and the more they despise themselves, the more they cling to us."

Truth nodded, hanging on to his temper with his fingernails.

"Lord . . . we can let them feel good about themselves in a way that even their neighbors approve of. The churches preach about their good works and their good moral example. After all their suffering, they are *vindicated*."

Truth closed his eyes. He could see it. It was the Silent Night all over again. They might be awful trash, but now? Now they were going along with the way society was supposed to be *and* they could still be trash. No need to reflect or improve. His parents had looked so happy the night before the SAT. Happiest he had ever seen them. Wasn't that nice? His last memory of his parents was of them happy.

He was a little surprised to realize he didn't care if they were alive or dead. It just didn't matter. Not in the grand scheme of things, not to him personally. They were dead to him well before he hit puberty. Maybe that was another part of learning to be human. Learning to put down that weight. He didn't have to carry his shitty parents around with him everywhere. He wasn't there yet.

"Lay out the program you have them working on now."

"Food drives were the first one. Except, of course, they are raising money and using the money to buy food. Even with rationing, we were able to reach an arrangement with various officials. The Church was instrumental there. They already had a lot of the infrastructure in place. Then building shelters—same story. War orphans, refugees, doesn't matter what it is. We started scrap-metal drives, saying that the metal would be recycled into war machines."

Truth shook his head. "Impossible."

"Yes, my lord, quite impossible. The metals are nowhere near the necessary quality or even the right alloys. But it *sounds* right. It is something everyone can do. Everyone can contribute. In fact, we sort and sell the scrap and use it to fund more functional social programs. And through it all, we hammer away on the notions of Family, Faith, and Prosperity."

It suddenly clicked. Family—*We are all a big family here*—was one of those management cliches that should be accompanied by ominous violins. But it was also an out for people. Mom said it herself, over and over again. All that MLM stuff she was doing was for the family. Not for her own poisoned dreams—the family. Faith and prosperity, for many in Jeon, were already synonyms.

"Two systems—the hierarchical business and the cult. Plug in the right ideology and watch the wheel spin."

"Yes, my lord."

"We will explore this more in a minute, but what about the other piece of the ideology I wanted established?"

"Turning love to hate, tearing Starbrite down from its throne? It is being steadily accomplished, though we keep it quiet. We establish contrasts with existing organizations and let the public draw inferences." Niles's voice managed to be quite smooth as he said that. Truth thought he was starting to sound a little like Thrush. Butler's influence, probably.

"Draw contrasts?"

"Yes. For example, Wayru was founded, originally, by the descendants of the first king of Jeon's stable boy. So, we would say 'You know, Wayru is a *true* Jeon corporation, unlike some who merely disguise themselves to better access our wealth.'"

"Then someone else, at a completely unrelated time, would say 'Isn't it funny how Starbrite isn't really a Jeon company? Everyone knows how he comes from off-world.'"

"Exactly, my lord. And a third person points out that it can't be good for any country to have so much of its wealth and industry owned by foreigners. And a fourth person, somewhere else again, just wants to know why someone would come from off-world to set up a business here. Not saying anything; just asking the question. Nothing wrong with just asking questions, right?"

Truth grinned mirthlessly. Not a single soul in Jeon believed that it was harmless to ask questions.

"I see. And because it's coming from all different directions and from seemingly unrelated people, it's not obviously propaganda."

"Right. It also matters who delivers what message. For example, we might persuade a member, or her husband, who has relevant economic experience to appear on a scrycast and talk about the state of the economy and the hidden danger of sabotage by foreign actors. Meanwhile, the more conspiracy-minded stuff would come from peers—usually one woman to another over coffee."

Truth nodded along. "Organizing group get-togethers and 'parties' where the goods are shown off is a routine part of the sales playbook, if I recall correctly. A good opportunity to plant seeds."

"Yes, people naturally ascribe greater weight to what they hear from friends than what they hear in the news. Generally, the authoritative voices are used to validate their existing prejudices."

"You . . . did well in school, didn't you?"

"Top ten in my class, my lord. A useless vanity from another life." There was no attempt to hide the sudden tension in Niles's shoulders. He really didn't like thinking about the past. Truth would bet cash that the night clerk had at least looked at a postgrad degree. Given his social rank and family ties, he certainly would have gone to college.

"So far, we have sown the seeds of mistrust. How do we turn that into hate for Starbrite? Or, at the very least, a total rejection of Starbrite and everything it stands for?" Truth asked.

"We need to let the distrust build up to a certain degree, then either fabricate or expose some atrocity by the company. Centuries of prestige can be lost remarkably quickly, with the right motivation. Combined with the persistent fear brought by the social changes and the war? People will turn on Starbrite in days, if not hours. The longer we have to prepare the ground, the faster the turn."

"Assuming we can show them something horrible enough. Something to make people feel self-righteous about."

"Yes, and it has to affect the general citizenry in an immediate, tangible way. Treason would be best, though profiteering and theft of war resources would also be good."

Truth smiled humorlessly. If he were running Starbrite right now, all his contracts would be to provide goods at cost. The lost profits would be irrelevant, and the potential for distraction would be heavily reduced. That assumed that Starbrite was, in any way, still running the corporation. The old monster could well be in total seclusion. Which meant that there were fewer people in place to stabilize things if they went wrong.

Now how to make sure the dominos fell the way he wanted them to?

CHAPTER 8

CRASH SOMETHING

Truth let his thoughts drift for a minute. Should he "fix" Niles? He probably could with Cup and Knife. He was actually a little scared to try. Not because he thought he would hurt Niles . . . or whatever his real name was . . . but because he had a horrible suspicion that it wouldn't work. In a rather dark way, he had given Niles a "revelation" and set him on a holy path. Now, does that sound like something that needed fixing?

Slavery? What's slavery to an angel?

The next question was: how does he make things worse so they can be better later?

"Over the coming weeks, I expect to see a number of high-level people making seemingly random moves. Some starting social programs, others recruiting Level Zero kids for a variety of purposes. There will be a lot of seemingly random murders of high-ranking officials and wealthy people. This will be in addition to the war."

"My lord?"

"Don't worry about it." Truth waved his hand to move away from the topic, then reconsidered and forced himself to answer. "Actually, do worry about it. I am bullying a lot of very powerful, very ruthless people. I am telling them that if they do things that will please me, I will let them run off-world after I kill Starbrite."

"You are going to kill Starbrite? My lord, is that even possible?"

"Yes. Difficult, but yes."

"You sound so certain."

"I am." He really was, too. There was something . . . a momentum that had been slowly gathering his whole life. It was coming to a head now. It was up to him to decide how to use that momentum. At least, he hoped it was.

Wasn't that what Nag Hamadi had said? Free will is a logical impossibility, but life is miserable if you don't have it, so act like you do and enjoy the ride. Well, the gossipy statue had said something to that effect.

Niles was clearly struggling to process the notion of killing Starbrite. Character assassination was apparently doable. The bloody-blades variety was a mental stretch.

"Niles . . . I don't know if you are still capable of wondering this, but have you ever wondered how it is possible for me to do what I do? Take, for example, getting you this job. You met Susan, right?"

"Ms. Anaksdaughter? Yes, certainly. Several times. She asks after you, my lord."

"I'll see her next. Now, does she strike you as a person lacking in spine?"

"Certainly not."

"Brains?"

"She is quite intelligent."

"Ruthless?"

"Very."

"And yet I got her to hand over the CEO position in one brief meeting."

Niles said nothing. He hadn't been asked a question, of course.

"It's because of two things—I am capable, and I dare. You need both, of course, but you would be astounded at how far daring alone takes you. Just the sheer willingness to step up and say *I can do it*, even if common sense says you can't. I targeted MegaShroom out of pure spite, removed the previous administration, ran down Susan, and would have murdered her had she not yielded. I didn't know she existed an hour before I had my sword buried in her gut."

Niles was looking a little lost and a little scared. Good.

"Niles, I dared. I dared to vent my hate. I dared to take over the company just because I wanted to. I dared to track down the owner and, niceties be damned, flat-out robbed an entire company from them. I had the confidence because I am capable, but most people simply do not think that way. I need you to focus on this point. Most people *do not think like this*. You are included in that 'most people.'"

Niles awkwardly nodded.

"Common sense exists for a good reason. People settle around a sort of average behavior, and so long as nobody strays out of line, everything is more or less fine. But the people who do step out of line? They are either destroyed or they rule the obedient ones. They do whatever the hell they want, and nobody says a damn thing because they are scared. If a person is willing to break with common sense so much, what else will they do? And because humans are envious creatures, when they see someone who goes around doing what they want, they suck up. They try to imitate the behavior. They ask him what they can do to be like him, or what they can do to bask in his glory."

Niles went still, processing. Slowly, he said, "They rewrite their common sense to allow for that specific person to act outside the norm."

"It's just the way the world is. What can you do about it? That man clearly doesn't give a damn about morals or the law. He would destroy you if you tried to do anything, so don't even try. It's just common sense," Truth said softly. "One man tells another to kill a stranger. If he does not, he will be killed or imprisoned for life. One man tells another, 'You won't have to worry about your store getting robbed if you pay your protection money every month.'"

"A gangster or a politician."

"Not very different. Really a question of scale and intent, I suppose."

"As you say, my lord."

"Daring and capability. Have those two things, and you can achieve the seemingly impossible. So, what's the necessary third component for us?" Truth eased off a little but kept pushing.

"Intent." Niles had caught the hint.

"Strange as it sounds, yes. What is our intention in taking an action? Are our motives pure? Morality. Honest to whoever morals. Ethics too."

Niles became silent. Truth let the moment stretch.

"Truthfully, my lord, I don't know what morals and ethics you subscribe to. You seem to follow no law but your own heart."

Truth laughed softly. "Well, that's accurate enough. I don't know that I have a coherent anything. But we can make one for MegaShroom."

"Ah. The corporation given conscience."

"Exactly. Good turn of phrase, by the way."

Niles beamed. Then frowned. Then smiled again.

"My lord, I have a . . . daring idea. Am I correct in assuming you don't care if this business makes a profit?"

"Not a financial profit, at any rate."

"Well . . . what if we took it a step further and made MegaShroom an actual cult? More accurately, a lay religious order?"

"Seems like a leap. Say more."

"We would be building off the existing theology of the Pragerite Church. We emphasize what we have always done—the networks, the indoctrination, the constant pressure to raise money any way they can. But what we do is we say that our commitment to Jeon is so great, we need to support the home front. We need to build a spiritual bastion against the forces of evil. And since prosperity equals proof of virtue—"

"We need that cash. Not really moving things past where they already are, though." Truth was skeptical.

"No, this is actually a fairly big change. Right now, our network of Representatives only talk about MegaShroom—how to earn from it, and how it's been such a wonderful force in their lives. However, the number of people who consider being a MegaShroom Representative their full-time occupation is a distinct minority. Bluntly, they need other work if they intend to survive."

"Yes?"

"A religious fraternity can form a solid basis for networking. We can present it as a way to get a social leg up. Especially since we will need volunteers to run drives and events, committees to organize things, and other opportunities to get to know other useful people. And since they are effectively coreligionists, there will be a high degree of mutual trust."

Hmm. Hadn't Jember said he joined a mystery cult for the networking? Niles might be on to something. Truth nodded slightly.

"Also helps speed up the othering of non-adherents. Mutate that shame into pride."

"I don't think the shame will ever be completely gone, but that's not a bad thing, my lord. It will encourage them to stick together and feel righteous."

"All right, that can work. Here's the doctrine I want going out—mutual support. The individual thrives when the network thrives. People who are part of the MegaShroom family are smarter, more entrepreneurial, richer, prettier, more moral than people who aren't. And to prove that, MegaShroom is going to organize *very* regular events where members teach first aid without the need for rationed talismans. They teach people how to plant their own herb and vegetable gardens. How to do simple handcrafts and the basics of construction without magic."

Truth took a deep breath. "Summertime. Lots of kids about to go on vacation; lots of parents needing someone to keep an eye on the kids while they work. It's no notice at all, but summer camps. Indoctrinate, indoctrinate, indoctrinate. Keep the kids learning skills they can use in a no-magic environment, keep them doing activities that require teamwork to succeed, consistently reward selfless behavior and punish selfish behavior."

"I think I see. Why the emphasis on no magic? I recall that when I went to camp, we did classes on basic magical theory, made spell bowls or our own insect-repelling charms, that sort of thing."

Truth blinked, then blinked again. "You . . . have noticed the sudden decline in available magic, right? The sudden magical voids that destroy apertures and buildings alike? The way talismans are so much less reliable these days?"

"Naturally, my lord, but the sunspot activity is expected to peak later this year, and things will return to normal by winter." Niles sounded honestly confused.

Truth shot the succubae a dirty look but knew what they would say if he called them out. He looked down at Niles and tried to think of the nicest way to announce the imminent end of the world.

Niles was understandably quiet after Truth laid it all out. He could see the dots connecting behind Niles's eyes. Things that hadn't been clear before, moves by companies and countries that had seemed senseless. Why Truth was bothering with all of this.

"You are preparing them for the world to come. All of them you can reach."

"Yes. And while you don't need the details, it weakens Starbrite significantly in the meantime."

"A world where every adult, or almost every adult, is dead or crippled."

"More Level-Zero adults these days than I care to think about, but yes. Also, the Anak family and a few others won't be particularly affected. Still, you have the right idea."

"And everyone knows."

"Above a certain level, yes. For years now. Decades, even."

"So . . . it was all worthless."

"What was?" Truth's voice was soft.

"My life before I met you. All of it. The studying. The worrying about disappointing my family. The whole damn City Below!"

"Oh. Because it would all get wiped away in a few years?"

"Yes!"

"Nah."

That got a startled look from Niles. "Pardon, my lord?"

"It wasn't worthless or pointless. You were living your life. That's all anyone can do, really. How long that life lasts . . . really isn't up to us, I think. Nothing really *means* anything in the end, or everything 'means' equally. Either way, it's not something we get to decide. Our opinion of our importance to the world, the world's opinion of us? It all just blurs into eternity. Makes no sense to worry about it. You just have to live and take what joy and satisfaction you can along the way."

"An . . . idiosyncratic position for someone considering founding their own religious order, if I may say, my lord."

Truth smiled. He had received so many blessings and revelations. One of those revelations was that it was no use telling people that they lived in illusion. Until they had seen it for themselves, it was just meaningless words. All he could do was prepare them. One day, if they chose, they could look beyond the shadows on the rock and see the real world. But it would be their choice. He couldn't make them see.

CHAPTER 9

PERILOUS TRIBE

It comes down to a change in the relations between people. No chance in hell I'm going to be able to shape the government after the collapse. But I can set up cadres of young, fit people, people trained to operate in a no-magic environment. People that really believe in teamwork and the notion that one person can't win if everyone else loses. It's got to be win-win all the way around. Competitive with outgroups, certainly. But internally? Strong bonds."

Truth chopped the air with his hands. "And their parents will pave the way as best they can in the next couple of months. Set the doctrine, start building caches, start spreading the good word about the virtues of mutual support."

"Yes. And since the collapse is coming in . . . less than a year?"

"I wouldn't bet on anything over eight months myself, but I have heard estimates as long as another year." Truth shrugged.

"Well. That does change our plans. Everything will have to be aggressively accelerated." The former clerk turned CEO frowned, clearly thinking things through.

Truth coughed lightly. "Has it been difficult being CEO?"

"Pardon, my lord? Yes and no. Yes, it is a difficult job. Exhausting. Endless decisions to make, endless eyes on you. Immense power but equally immense responsibility. But it was not so hard to pick up on what needs to actually be done, thanks to Butler and Maid. The secret was aggressive amounts of delegation. Having two strong succubae with me really eased the leadership transition."

"I can imagine."

"I really can't do it without them. I owe them both so much." Niles looked at them with immense affection.

"It really was no more than our duty. One day, perhaps, you will believe me," Butler murmured.

It wasn't affection. It was love. Not necessarily romantic love, but it was love all the same. Starbrite had actually warned Truth about this. It wasn't that succubae wanted to hurt you. It was that you couldn't help but fall in love with them. You couldn't help but lose yourself in them. It was why Truth was so cold with Maid and Butler. Partially, it was the persona, but more importantly, it was self-protection.

"Speaking of duty and debts, Maid. Butler. You have clearly done the task I assigned you very well. Continue to assist Niles in his duties unless otherwise assigned. Now, consider this a bit of back pay."

Truth tapped into his magic, recreating a trick he first used on the boat ride from Conjin. He poured his magic into his blessings, Incisive, even Cup and Knife, all to put forward one idea. To nail down one inescapable fact. The two clouds of Hell-gas in front of him were actually people. One was Butler; the other was Maid. They were his obedient servants and content in the role.

"We thank the magus for his generous gift!" They chorused.

"Not a gift—owed for services rendered. And speaking of. Niles. I am going to try something."

"My lord?"

"I want to give you as free a choice as I can manage. No promises. Now don't move."

He eased in to it with Cup and Knife. There were things there he could fix, but he was now familiar enough with the spell to spot an immediate glitch. Just as he feared. The spell didn't consider what Truth did to Niles a problem. How the enlightenment got in wasn't important. Just that it got there.

It occurred to Truth that while Manda had been a broadly positive force in his life, he could only see a very narrow view of the *totality* of what the angel did or believed. It was flat-out insane to think an angel could be benevolent.

He changed tack. He pushed on the Blessing of the Sea of Brass, hammering his orthodoxy over an area. It wasn't right to brainwash random clerks just because you were in character and could. It wasn't right to break a man, make him dependent on you, make him blindly obey you, just because it was convenient. It would be right to give him a choice. As free a choice as he could make.

There was the damnedest pause. A moment where the magic seemed to be asking "Really? *Really?* Do you think that makes the least blind bit of sense?" Truth was stubborn. It might be stupid, but he would do it anyway.

"Cup and Knife."

He could feel this spell bucking his will, too. Manda clearly didn't agree, but the zone of orthodoxy had, if not changed the rules, nudged them slightly. At least enough that the spell went off, somewhat. He'd take it. For what he wanted, there didn't need to be a dramatic change.

There was a tiny space. A singular moment—

"Who do you want to be? I can return you to the man you were before or close to it. I can return you to your family. For everything you have done, and everything I have done to you, I swear if I succeed in killing Starbrite, I will reserve seats for your whole damn clan with the Shattervoid. Or you can keep on being Niles Bowman, CEO of MegaShroom. You will put into action everything we have discussed today. You will use your own initiative to push my goals forward. You will do your very best to save everyone you can. You don't have to worship me as your lord anymore, but I won't stop you if you want to. But it's your choice. At this precise moment, you are as free as I can make you."

Truth's cheek twitched. "I can take your family off-world either way, if that matters to you. Lots of seats I have no intention of filling available."

For the first time since they met, Niles looked him directly in the eyes and smiled. "You are a damned fool, sir. Those words don't mean what you think they mean. Freedom? Choices? When have I ever had those things? I was born into a clan, failed to impress anyone, and was quietly shuffled off where I could do minimal harm and still bring some value. The highest I would have risen was general manager of the hotel in fifty or sixty years. I could have left it all and become a coolie somewhere, but . . . no."

Niles laughed softly. "I tried my very best. I got good results. I did what I was supposed to. And it was worthless. I didn't get it. The clan didn't *need* a grind. They needed someone who dared. Just like you said. They needed someone who dared. I didn't dare. So, I got to check guests into a small hotel run by my grandmother. And that was it. That's who I was."

A smile spread across Niles face, reaching up to his eyes. Truth met his gaze. There was madness there. Actual insanity, of a very narrowly defined sort. He clearly hadn't understood his spells nearly as well as he thought. Something was shifting in Niles, for better or worse he couldn't say.

"I am happy now. I have power. I have real responsibility. I am making lives better. I love and am loved. You tell me that I will save tens of thousands, maybe millions, from a brutal death if I do this job. All that, and I get paid a fat stack of cash, live in a beautiful apartment, have all the sex I want, eat good food, and when I need my suitcase time, I have two wonderful people who can give it to me. *Fuck* my clan, and *fuck* going off-world. This is exactly where I want to be, who I want to be, and I can't imagine doing anything better."

Truth felt Cup and Knife shifting around in his grasp. He could see bits of the spell coming together, seeing things connect that hadn't connected before, filling in missing pieces.

"My name is Niles Bowman, your servant and apostle, now and forever."

The spell and blessing resonated, confirming his words. Reality shifted, very slightly but quite permanently, around them. The night clerk was dead. Niles Bowman lived. Truth sighed and let the spell go. What did he really think would happen? Did he really understand what he was asking? Probably not. He just felt like he had to try. To make the offer. To be something other than a spoiled Prince.

"Maybe I like the illusion of choice more than you do. I won't tell you my name until Starbrite is dead. Somehow, I feel like if I speak it, he will know. And then things will get very bad very fast. You may continue calling me *lord* for now. Why did you change from *Prince*, by the way? I noticed Butler and Maid did that, too."

"Because you are no longer the Prince, but you carry yourself as king. Uncrowned but king. What could we call you but *lord*?" Niles said all that like it was the most logical, reasonable thing in the world.

Truth could only shake his head and laugh. "Do you know where I can find Susan?"

"Yes, my secretary can give you her address."

"All right. I will be in Harban for a little while longer. If I think of anything else, I will let you know. Until then, continue as we discussed. Butler, Maid, keep up the good work."

They bowed. "Hurry home again, my lord. We miss you," they chorused.

Truth strolled up to a frankly gaudy mansion in the Subra district. Not the old money, nor even the big new money. If anything, the Subra district was famous for people being poor, though not Denizens. Perhaps that was why the Anak family chose to build an eye-searing palace to the vices of excessive wealth.

Ornamental columns everywhere. No rhyme or reason to them. See an eve, stick a column under it. A circular driveway with a fountain in the middle of it . . . in the middle of the most expensive city on the planet. A load of the windows were incredibly detailed mosaics in stained glass, though he couldn't make out what they were from the outside. Not with all the multicolored bright lights bathing the exterior marble sheathing in fluorescents and pastels.

The doors were four meters tall and made of bronze. The door on the left had an incredibly muscular, incredibly nude woman on it. The right door had an equally nude man on it, so muscled, Truth wondered if there were any muscles left for anyone else. They were surrounded by crushed and broken enemies, heaps of treasures and weapons, as well as piles of meats and grains.

The Anak family was a lot of things. Subtle wasn't one of them.

Truth knocked on the door. Nobody answered. He knocked harder. The silence wasn't deafening; it was a noisy street, and he could hear music inside. Truth therefore decided to experiment with how loudly he could smack a bronze door without actually damaging it. It seemed like an unusual alloy. A few thunderous booms later confirmed that it was as tough as he thought. Fun! He started banging on it like a drum that owed him money.

There is always someone ready to ruin a good time. The door was yanked open. Two meters of slab muscle and cruelty under heavily gelled hair and a long beard yanked the door open.

"You got a death wish, fuckhead?"

Truth punched him in the face. Punched him a few more times for luck. Tripped him, got him on the ground, made sure to bury his knee where it would do some good, repeatedly, then resumed the face-punching. The big bastard tried to fight back, but Truth had levels on him. Not to mention the Meditations made sure there wasn't going to be an advantage in physical strength.

"All right, you look about right. Now hold still; this bit is a little fiddly. I need you to send a message."

Susan was relaxing in her tub. It took specialized pumps to drive sufficiently powerful water jets to do anything for her muscles, but this was Nephilim tech. The tub was delightful. There was a knock on the door and her dickhead cousin stuck his head in.

"Somebody's here to see you? He said that you would know who?"

She gave her cousin a filthy look. "You couldn't ask . . . Oh. OH! Sweet! I'll be right down!"

Carved into her cousin's forehead, in surprisingly neat letters, were two words—*Knock Knock*.

CHAPTER 10

THE BEST AT JOKES

Susan came down the stairs in a bathrobe and a smile. "Who's there?"

"Boo."

"Boo who?"

"Don't cry; it's only a joke." Truth's voice was very soothing. He was smiling at the several large men glowering at him from the edges of the room.

"Hah! I see you have met my cousins." She looked him over. "You are better-looking than I was afraid of. Any chance of growing out a beard? Or at least shaving your head?"

"Honestly? Not much. Never liked that look."

"Real shame. You are on the shorter side, but that physique. Mmm."

"Who the fuck is this asshole, Suzy?" One of the protein aficionados couldn't keep it in any longer. Before she could answer, Truth rushed him. Everyone in the room was a body cultivator—their eyes could follow him just fine. He was just *fast*. Impatient hadn't got his hands up by the time Truth reached him.

Nice open shot at that lantern jaw. Obviously, he would take it. Truth smashed Greasy right on the button and lifted the big fella up off his toes. He landed with an immense *thud*, and were he not a body cultivator, Truth would be concerned about the nasty crack his skull made when it hit the marble floor.

"That's who the fuck I am. And I don't give a *fuck* who you are, so scram!"

"Are you absolutely certain we aren't related? Because other than being a bit short, you really do feel like family." Susan's voice was bone-dry.

"I'm . . . less certain than I was before, at any rate. Pretty sure I do have some Nephilim blood in me from way, way back."

"Oh? How'd you figure that out?"

"No comment." Truth grinned.

"Used the spell, huh?"

"Something like that. We gonna chat in the entryway all day, or does this discreet cottage have chairs somewhere?"

Susan grinned right back. "Fuck discreet. The only time we're discreet is when we're setting someone up. Then we're really sneaky. C'mon, I'll take you up to my modest, tastefully appointed suite."

Truth walked up the sweeping central staircase to the wraparound balcony overlooking the atrium. "I have, and I mean this literally, seen mansions belonging to ancient clans that were less over-the-top than this place."

"Tsch! Those clans aren't ancient. OUR clan is ancient! Those guys just haven't figured out how to live yet." Susan waved away the comparison as they walked down the hallway.

Oil paintings of naked, greased-up bodybuilders alternated with photographs of those same people tearing armed enemies into chunks and, in the case of a particularly well-developed senior, tearing off one man's head and throwing it at another man's head so hard that both heads exploded.

"Any reason they are all nude?"

"Any reason they shouldn't be? They worked hard for that physique. That's real value right there. Think of it as putting up pictures of virtuous elders to inspire the younger generations."

Truth nodded. Seemed fair. She led him down an irritatingly long hallway, opened a heavy pair of double doors, and led him into a sitting room. The room was decorated in shades of ivory, gold, and bronze. There were yet more heavily muscled nudes hanging on the walls, a polearm rack, a meter-tall stack of books on natural philosophy, a squat rack, and all the other ordinary things one would expect to find in a young lady's chambers.

He blinked.

"You look surprised."

"Just occurred to me that every time I have been in a woman's bedroom, it was for a job or they were family. Personal bedroom, I mean, not a hotel room or temple or something."

"Wait. No. No! I refuse to believe—" Susan shot to her feet, looking at him in horror. Truth rolled his eyes.

"No, I'm not a virgin."

"Good. Good. Suddenly lost faith in the nature of reality for a moment there." She patted her chest and sat. Then shot up again. "You're gay! That's why you turned me down!"

Truth buried his face in his hands and slowly started to laugh.

"Why is everyone so concerned about my sex life?!"

"This comes up a lot?"

"Not all the time, but weirdly often. Honestly? I spend so much time stressed or dealing with planetary-scale weirdness that my libido is pretty much nil."

Susan grunted. "Well, that's no good. That's a fine body. Ought to enjoy it more."

"I do! You wouldn't believe what I do with it. Hell, I danced on top of lampposts, doing a sword drill above a city that couldn't even see me, just because I could and it felt amazing."

She smiled. "I'd enjoy watching that, I think. I didn't really see you when we fought before. I mean, I saw you but not very clearly."

"Yeah, I'm the subject of at least one . . . two . . . two for sure . . . probably more than two . . . international manhunts. I do actually keep it sneaky."

She blinked, then laughed. Laughed so hard, she had to grab on to her guts and struggle not to fall off her chair.

"I don't believe it! Oh, my dog, you are Hell Prince! You are actually, literally Hell Prince. And you stole a glorified pyramid scheme to promote civil society and public readiness."

"Well. Starbrite came up with the name."

"I'm dying. I am actually dying over here." She was gasping for breath. Truth gave her a moment. Eventually, she leaned back in the chair, wiping tears of mirth. "Why are you doing any of this, anyhow? You know it's not going to matter."

"Difference of opinion there. It will matter as much as anything does. And frankly? I am sick to death of God, or the planet, or Starbrite, or some other unknowable godly power screwing around with people for no good reason. So. You know. Fuck 'em. I'm not going to take it quietly. I'm not going to go quietly. I'm going to do everything I can to be a certifiable pain in the ass."

That wiped the smile off her face.

"Say that again."

"What? I'm a pain—"

"No, the other bit. The fighting-God bit."

"Well. I don't know if I can fight literal God. But . . . this world is fucked. From what I can tell, it always has been, at least as long as humans have been here. And the reason it has been is, basically, the planet likes demons better, and if it can't have demons, it will take Nephilim. Everyone else? Suffer. And since the architect of so much of this misery is the massively more-stabbable Starbrite . . ."

Truth shrugged. "Never thought it was very noble to suffer the slings and arrows when you could, by opposing, end them." Susan looked blank. Truth smacked his forehead. "Don't worry about it. Playing on an old quote. Bottom line? I've never been the peaceful sort, and I'm so damn burnt, I'm biting everyone like a mad dog."

"By setting up food pantries."

"Lots of ways to fight back."

"And blowing up cities."

"That wasn't me."

"No?"

"Didn't know I had been accused of that, actually."

Susan cupped her chin and looked at him. Really looked at him. Truth was starting to feel uncomfortable.

"Something on my face?"

"Yes."

Truth started pawing at his cheeks. "Oh, hell. Did I get it off?"

"That might be hard. Have you . . . Do you ever feel that there is someone watching over you? Guiding you through life?"

"Like a supernatural patron of some kind?"

"Yes, exactly!"

"Oh, yes."

"Have you ever . . . had visions of a large man? Maybe smelled blood or sex or metal for no apparent reason? Had an unreasonable hatred of both farming and farmers?"

"More like disappointed resentment. Wait, you too?!"

Susan sat back in her chair and slowly shook her head. "Not me. I was never so blessed. No wonder. No wonder. Not blood kin but spiritual. Of all the strange things, here at the end of the age."

"You know who the Rough Patron is? He said the Nephilim are his descendants."

"Infinitely removed, yes. How much do you know about the creation of the universe?"

"Erm. Almost nothing. My girlfriend who may be my wife says there was an original hermaphrodite and they—" Susan waved him off.

"All wrong. Or, well. It's not what we teach. Once upon a time, so long ago and so far away that it would be meaningless to measure, God made the world. Except they didn't."

"God is a 'they'?"

"*Real* God is so far beyond everything that they sublimate the very concept of gender. They even sublimate the concept of personhood, so you could theoretically refer to God as 'It,' though I personally wouldn't."

"Fair. In the beginning, God *didn't* create the world?"

"Exactly. Short version . . . very short, because the full version requires weeks of explanation and several diagrams, is to imagine a huge sphere. That's God. And by the nature of its existence, it caused some subsidiary principles to come into existence. First was a 'wife' or consort figure, though sometimes they are presented as, yes, a hermaphrodite. Not an *actual* person here; just a concept or a principle like gravity."

"What was the principle?"

"That other necessary, or beneficial, things should come into being. So, aspects of the divine emanations were sort of tidied up into neat piles representing different virtues and principles—"

"Oh? Which?"

"Got two weeks and the patience to study some VERY complicated charts?"

"I apologize for interrupting. I was rude. Please, continue."

"Right. So. Lots of principles created. The principles are divided up into—and again, I'm not talking biology here—male and female pairings. I'm skipping over a lot of layers, but it basically goes God, their 'wife,' multiple levels of everything else, then these subsidiary male-female paired principles. All of which are virtues. Everything I have described is good and godly, and can be understood as a natural consequence of the existence of God. Like the sun can't help but be bright."

"With you so far."

"Well, the last one of these things didn't get its pairing. It just kind of went off and did its own thing, which is ironic, since it's supposed to be the embodiment of intelligence."

"Ah. Nerd shit. Never turns out well." Truth nodded sagely.

"Yes. In this case, it turned into the whole universe."

"Wait, what?"

"All this stuff I'm describing is happening on some higher cosmic level. There is no universe at this point. Or nothing made of matter, if that's how you want to think about it."

"So . . . just Heaven and Hell and—"

"Nope, before that."

"Before Heaven?!"

Susan grinned. There was something unpleasant in her eyes. "Oh, yes. I mean, the throne, the chariot, the choirs of angels whose whole function is to sing hymns about how great God is . . . does this strike you as something an omniscient, omnipotent, omnibenevolent being would do? My family may love its dominance games, but we'd still call that some deeply insecure prick behavior."

Truth blinked. "I have wondered for a long time if God made the world wrong."

Susan nodded, the nasty grin getting wider. "God is definitionally perfect. However, that doesn't mean that some of the inevitable consequences of God's existence are also perfect."

"It doesn't?"

"That's how my family teaches it. Wisdom was created, then she figured since God can create life, she can too. So, she makes her own attempt at a divine being like herself."

Truth slowly closed his eyes, squeezing them tight. "She gets it wrong."

"Yep. It takes a big chunk of her divinity and still turns out all wrong. By all accounts, it's hideous and basically insane. Whether it's malicious or just stupid is still under debate. What's not debated is that it is CRAZY arrogant. And lonely. And insecure, because everything else in the universe is literally perfect and divine, and has absolutely no interest in this random little abomination running around." She swatted the impossibly powerful being away with a flick of her hand.

"So, it creates its own version of the universe out of the materials available to it. Which was matter, the lowest order of stuff in existence. From there, it builds everything. The universe, Heaven, Hell, the angels and devils and . . . literally just everything."

"*Stupid* being a relative term, I guess," Truth murmured.

"Its mom was literally the perfect embodiment of reason short of God."

"Kind of surprised she fucked up that bad, then."

"I never got a satisfying answer about that, but that's the story."

"Okay, and from there?"

"Eventually, the creator gets around to recreating his own birth by making humans. The exact process is debated amongst the Nephilim, and there was a sizable schism over whether the Creator's mom interfered to give us all divine souls, or are those souls natural results of the creation process, derived from the Creator, or simply something that all fragments of God receive. Which is everything; some of us believe everything has some amount of 'soul' in it."

"Huh."

"And finally, those created humans, the first two, had kids. The middle child died young, the youngest lived an ordinary life and gave rise to the more common branch of humanity, i.e., the Sethians, and one, the oldest, had a bunch of kids who had sex with angels and gave birth to the Nephilim."

"Damn!"

"And that oldest child? He was the first person to tell 'God' he got it wrong, then did something about it."

CHAPTER 11

UP AND AT 'EM

The Nephilim are a . . . what species? Clan? Variety of human? That inherited the will of the first God-Defier? That's a hell of an inheritance, right there."

"Yes. We have also been historically at the forefront of technological development, too, though at this point, Nephilim and Sethian (that's the randos on the street, by the way) technologies have diverged so much, comparing them is kind of pointless."

"Really? The impression I got, from the very little I know about the Nephilim, is that their worlds are pretty crude-looking."

"Yeah, they are. Like I said, different technology bases reaching different outcomes. Part of the reason the Clan goes so nuts on the luxuries when we are in Sethian territory. They are just better at making this stuff."

"So, what are the Nephilim good at?"

"Our magic system is literally, and almost entirely, distinct from Sethian magic. You remember that spell book I showed you? You can think of us as specializing in body cultivation (which doesn't mean what you think it means), agriculture, and metalworking. Not to mention AMAZING musicians. I mean the best. Your favorite singer is trash; I'm not even kidding. Don't let my cousins and me fool you. We are basically expendable infiltration units. My great-great-grandparents got some very basic body cultivation technology and a few other support magics, and were turned loose on this planet to lay a foundation for the real invasion."

"You knew the apocalypse was coming for that long?"

"No, not really. A few decades at most."

Truth stared at Susan, who looked utterly comfortable in her plush bathrobe and overstuffed chair.

"You were always going to invade, apocalypse or not."

"Right." She nodded. "We do this on almost every planet. It's not a secret. It's why most developed Sethian worlds try to keep us corralled in trade quarters or embassies."

"A constant state of war . . . How do they afford it? In lives, if not money?"

"We aren't constantly at war. Raiding is common, but actual conquest is pretty rare. It's more a kind of . . . philosophical thing. We are going to conquer the material universe; we just haven't gotten around to a particular planet *yet*."

Truth blinked and shook his head slowly. "It's a lot to take in. I genuinely had no idea. The Rough Patron always seemed confident and free, but I wouldn't have said *murderous*, exactly."

Susan started sputtering and hammering her chest. "Rough Patron?! You said that before and I was so surprised, it didn't even register. Rough Patron? What, is he buying your ass or something?!"

"Well, he never told me his name, and he was hanging around a campfire, wearing a crude tunic and pretty dirty, so . . ." Truth waved his hands urgently.

"Oh, my dog. Oh, my absolute dog." She pressed strong fingers to throbbing temples. "Look, just do me a favor and just call him the Eldest Son while you are here, Okay? Please and thank you."

"Sure. Dog?"

"Eh, oh. We don't swear by God much, but we do like dogs. So. You know."

"Got it. Makes sense."

Truth let the silence build a little longer, then looped back to something she mentioned earlier.

"Raiding is common but conquest isn't?"

"Yeah. Wars are expensive as hell and tend not to net a positive return on investment on anything but a very-long-term basis. And that's assuming we succeed, which is never a given. Raiding, done right, *generates* money while simultaneously weakening the enemy."

"And provides combat experience for your troops, I suppose."

"Exactly. Although, again, *troops* is an exaggeration. More like individual families or clans sponsor a raid, then divide up the loot afterward without the government being involved beyond collecting taxes. The raiders tend to be ordinary folk just looking for a bit of extra income or some slaves or something."

Ah. That, he didn't like the sound of.

"You did mention being experts in agriculture. Am I right in guessing . . ."

"Yep. We hate farming and farmers, but agriculture is just too damn useful a technology to ignore. So, we literally farm it out to prisoners with jobs."

"And mining?"

"Oh, we do the mining. The Nephilim, I mean. Yeah, our mines are super inefficient compared to Sethian ones, but we prefer them that way."

"Huh?"

Her eyes went dreamy. "Just you, in your bare skin. Fists hammering at the rock. Fingers ripping out the ores. The physical struggle embodying the triumph of spirit over matter through the living medium of the flesh. It's the glory of our breed. Sethians try to return to the godhead through reason. But reason alone was never going to be enough. The truth of the world is not something to be worked out on paper. It is to be experienced with your entirety."

Truth jolted. "Yes! Your soul fills your whole body. It doesn't just live in your head."

"Exactly. Exactly. The key is to not become lost in the illusion of matter. To know the glory of the infinite in your *entirety*. To test your spirit, your endlessly refined will, and peerless determination against the embodiment of the great failure itself! What could be better than that? What could be more holy than that?"

Truth was swept up in her words, lost in the vision of it. The visceral satisfaction of moving his body, overcoming the pain and obstacles, honing his spirit even as—

"Oh, dog, this is why your tech base is so weird. Your mineral production rate is ass, meaning your alchemical production rate is ass, your construction is ass, and the only reason your metallurgy is so good is that it has to be, because you need to wring out every scrap of benefit from your stupidly expensive, stupidly rare metals."

Susan laughed. "You aren't wrong! We do the same crap with trees and any other kind of resource extraction. Bare-handed or not at all. Or we steal it, obviously. Other stuff, we make tools for. I mean, can you even imagine trying to make fabric without tools?"

"Fantastic."

"Yeah, we are stocking up on all the refined raw materials we can now, because in a few months, that stuff just won't be available at any price. The clan is looking to flip it into some seriously massive income in a couple of years."

"I bet." Truth privately resolved to send Niles a rather lengthy note before he headed off for Starbrite.

"So, what brings you by? Not that I'm not happy to see you again, but you don't strike me as a casual-visit sort." Susan leaned forward.

"Actually, it was more or less just to see you." Truth scratched his head awkwardly. "I don't have a lot of friends. Don't really know how to have friends. So, I thought I would visit."

He would treasure forever the look on her face. Even she probably didn't know what she was feeling.

"You see, I don't know that I'm going to survive the next month, so I figured, you know. Do something I have never done before. Drop by a friend's place and hang out for a bit."

"Oh, um. Well. Going to admit it's not a *common* thing for me, either. Mostly, it's the cousins I like a bit better that stop by and . . . um." Truth thought she looked kind of adorable when she was flustered like that. Not his aesthetic cup of tea, but he had a suspicion that anyone into muscles would be helpless.

She took a moment to gather herself. "You want some snacks?"

"Love some. Is there a good place around here?"

"Absolutely not. I'll have some sent up from the kitchen."

"No good snack places?"

"Nah, this neighborhood has basically no redeeming features." She shrugged and spread her hands.

"So, why build here?"

"It was cheap and Great-Grandpa didn't care."

"Makes sense."

Susan fiddled with an odd-looking bone charm. "I'm getting a few platters of beef skewers and a couple bowls of noodles. Should I order the same for you?"

Truth felt himself involuntarily grin. "One bowl of noodles, but I'll take the skewers. Do they come with sauce?"

"Marinated for twenty-four hours in a mixture of red wine, herbs, garlic, and salt, roasted over the finest charcoal, and then, yes, served with a selection of dipping sauces. Don't give me that look; have you seen the size of us? That guy you laid out downstairs is on the low side of average. We have at least one cow marinating at any given time."

"I truly am not your match. I figured having some nuts or maybe corn in cheese sauce would be standard."

"Those aren't snacks! Those are barely garnishes."

"Have you guys even heard of vegetables?"

"Naturally, but not for a *snack*. That's barbaric."

"Vegetarianism isn't even a concept for you guys, is it?"

"Of course it is! It's an insult. Call someone a vegan and it's on sight until one of you dies."

"Your reading material is, and I mean this respectfully, atrocious. You have not one trashy romance or thriller anywhere in that stack."

"Why would I want a trashy romance to *read* when I can just stick my head out the door and watch my moron relatives act like they are in a soap opera every second of every day? Wait, you read that crap?"

"How do you think I managed to get a girlfriend?"

"Please. Please tell me that's not true. I don't want to live in a world where that's true. Couldn't you just steal her from her kinsfolk or something?"

They bickered back and forth until the food came. As advertised, it was platters of enormous beef skewers with a selection of small bowls full of dipping sauce. Apparently, the thing to do was tear off a piece of flatbread, wrap the beef with it, slide it off the skewer, dip, eat, and repeat.

It was pretty great. The meat but also the company. Just someone he could hang out with—not a mentor, not a servant, not a lover, not a stranger. Someone he could look straight in the eye and just put it all down. Gods and angels and the end of the world and his girlfriend's plan for his apotheosis, he could just put it all down. Just for a little while.

This was how it was supposed to be in the PMC. And the Army. He remembered the other soldiers doing exactly this—eating snacks, talking crap, and just being humans for a while. He never really managed it. Couldn't quite make it all click. It just seemed so pointless. None of that chat would earn him credits, or cash, or anything, so why do it?

He got it now. *It's the exhale.* You take a deep breath, face all the horrible shit the world flings at you, then you meet your friend and exhale. Let all that pain out. Not by dumping it on them but by being human with them.

He had a little bit of that with Jember, hanging out together with him and Etenesh, watching sports and cheering randomly. This was . . . Well. This was like that. Somehow, he just appreciated it more now. Maybe he had grown.

He had figured out a long time before that the Truth that crawled out of the slums was badly damaged. A tightly wound ball of hate and rage and desperate need to survive. Blind to the things that were truly killing him.

Truth balanced on the edge of paranoia for a second but ultimately decided to take that step toward trust.

"So . . . you guys will want an ecosystem on this planet once the invasion starts. The ability to grow crops and raise cows and all that."

Susan's voice went very dry. "Yes. The ability to breathe air is not *strictly* mandatory at higher levels, but babies are weirdly insistent about it. We will, in fact, want an ecosystem."

"So. I'm not sure what you can do about this, either individually or as a clan, but let me tell you about a box I found buried in the ground."

He explained about the plague engines and what they would mean for the world. About how they would, eventually, kill everything. Nephilim included.

"It's not that I particularly trust you guys with a doomsday, end-of-the-world weapon. It's just, I figure that if this planet can build it with Initiate-grade technology, similar stuff must exist on other planets."

Susan was very quiet, very still. "It does, yes. There are reasons they aren't used. Reasons I can't talk about. Put very simply, once you can reach orbit, ending the world is basically a question of mathematics. But since the world is also an emanation of a higher being—"

"Right. I did kind of wonder about that."

"And like I said, there are reasons people don't do that kind of thing. Even Hell cannot conceal you from the punishment. They also tend not to work. The fact that someone built that thing and probably built more . . ." Her voice trailed off.

"I will do what I can to persuade the Clan to act. I think they will listen, all things considered. No promises."

"Didn't expect any. Thank you." The room got quiet.

"You said you are going to kill Starbrite?" Susan's voice had turned soft.

"Yes. For all the reasons you might imagine."

She nodded. "We were just going to wait him out. Whatever he's up to, it's no harm to us, you know? Also, we just don't want to screw with someone who has reached *that* level. Not unless we really have to."

"Fair. But I really have to."

"Guess so."

She nodded. "Want some skewers to go? We really do roast them by the dozens."

"Won't say no to meat. Hard to come by these days."

She fiddled with the bone charm a bit more, then looked him coldly in the eye.

"How do you entertain a bored god-king?"

"I . . . have no idea?" He was suddenly fascinated. This question could be very relevant in the future.

"You sail a boatload of young ladies down the river dressed only in nets and suggest the god-king go catch a fish." She suddenly smiled. "Do better than a knock-knock joke next time. That one was lame."

Truth laughed and nodded. "I am not good at jokes. But come on— doesn't the delivery count for *anything*?"

CHAPTER 12

ROOTS

Truth walked out of the Anak residence with a sack full of beef skewers, a few jars of sauce, and a big helping of dirty looks. Truth spotted some of Susan's female cousins. They were, if anything, bigger than her. They were also, clearly, not into him. One made a very complicated hand gesture. He hadn't seen it before, but the meaning was remarkably clear.

He didn't take it to heart. He was planning to fuck off anyhow.

Truth made his way over to a souvenir stand, bought a card, wrote Niles that note, and sent it winging on its way. He loved watching the enchanted paper fold itself up—turning from something flat and lifeless into a somewhat plausible-looking bird. He loved that with a touch and a nudge of his will, it would go flying off to land in a mailbox on the other side of the city. Something so ordinary that you wouldn't look at it twice, and a genuine marvel at the same time.

Was he done in Harban? His heart said no—he still had a couple more stops. He wouldn't visit Sophia or try and track down the other sibs. Truth Medici had died years before. Best to leave him dead for now. Sophia knew. That was enough.

Mom and Dad? If they were still alive? Get a bit of . . . No. Not even as a fantasy. Now it just made him feel sickly. He had seen too much, understood too much. He might not forgive them for what they did to him and the sibs, but he could understand them now. Truth had said he was the logical consequence of billions of bad decisions. Well, his parents were too. For him, they died years before.

It was enough. Truth would never be entirely free of his parents. They had shaped so much about him. Led him to so many decisions. But he didn't have to let them ride on his head for the rest of his life. He would leave them in the ground, buried in the poisonous earth of Harban. Though he did need to make a trip to the slums.

The abandoned industrial building had been melted into slag after he made his report. It probably said a lot about developers in Harban that a new building was smacked down on top of the still-warm embers of the old. Was the site cursed? Had hundreds died unspeakable deaths on that very spot? Unless it meant they could buy the site for less, the developers didn't care. Unspeakable curses sound like a problem for someone living in the slums.

Truth walked through the street, down dark alleys, looking into the stairwells of dingy buildings. Looking at the slumrats. The slums had never been a good place, but he couldn't shake the feeling that they had gotten worse.

He leaned against a corner and watched a guy with a fresh haircut leaving the barber shop. A tubby little guy walked up behind him, threw an arm around his shoulders and, without breaking stride, tubby stabbed him in the ribs.

"You like talking, huh? You a chatty guy? You like talking? You fucking rat!" The knife went in and out like a sewing machine embroidering revenge. Truth wasn't the only one watching. Must have been twenty witnesses or more. Nobody said anything. Nobody even looked surprised. The barber barely shook his head. Truth could hear him murmur:

"And this is why I don't give credit. Damn fool, what did he think was going to happen?"

It didn't even rate an *mmm-hmmm* from the other barbers. They just kept on cutting. The customers weren't looking out the window. They put a lot of effort into not seeing things they shouldn't see. This was no different.

The whores were openly bartering now. Services for their next fix and maybe the one after. Food. Medicine. Whatever they could get. Truth felt something stabbing into him. It was sad. It was desperately sad. He was sure he'd never pitied a whore in his life, but these weren't "whores"; they were people, starving, sick, hopeless people, and they were doing the best they could with the nothing they had. So were the people selling them base and murdering each other for their shoes.

They weren't good. They were, in fact, "bad," as most people thought about it. But so what? The rats didn't sink the ship. Should he condemn them for biting each other as they tried to keep ahead of the water? He wasn't condoning it, either. The rats would need to change if they wanted to live. But a man with a sack full of beef skewers and a few jars of professional-chef-crafted dipping sauces didn't seem to have the moral high ground.

Hell, he had his own lifeboat waiting, and he was standing there, watching the rats suffer before they drowned.

"That's not okay. That's fucked-up. And I'm not okay with it. Which, by everyone else's standards, is fucked-up. Which I am okay with. Which is fucked-up." Truth breathlessly laughed. Then laughed harder. So many of the people there hadn't opened their apertures. Lots and lots and lots of them.

What would happen when they realized that the cops couldn't stop them anymore? When the apartment towers came tumbling down and the shops had no food and none of the lights worked but OH, LOOK, the Ghūl were still there. Maybe they shouldn't stick around in the slums.

He had thought about it in Confen, thought about adopting one or two of them, showing them the light. Letting the knowledge wash away the rat and leave something better behind. At least make them rats with dreams.

He didn't have that kind of time. More to the point, he didn't have that kind of mind. Truth was pretty proud of how far he had come, but he wasn't a teacher. He could only clear the way as best he could, and hopefully, they would figure something out. When you got right down to it, the only person he had really "taught" was Niles, and that wasn't exactly something to replicate. Also, debatable if he really taught him anything rather than giving him a new dream.

He still despised the slums. Despised the blindness of the rats. Despised their cruelty and the way they preyed on each other. But even if he did, wasn't it time to admit to himself that he felt empathy? That he felt compassion for them? After everything he had seen and done, everything he had learned about himself and the world and the systems of the world, did he really feel the rats deserved their Hell?

If he had learned anything from his parents and from this whole damn world, he learned that *deserved* had nothing to do with anything.

He drifted through the streets, keeping an ear out. Eventually, he heard music, the beautiful, soaring music that he only ever heard when he visited a Ghūl nest. He followed the sound into an apartment building. He looked up. It wasn't the one he was born in, but it was more or less the same. Forty floors of insect hives, filled with parasitic larvae and their murderous progenitors.

Or it was once. That music was awfully loud.

He walked in, following the music. There were no lights in the building. What windows there were had been blacked out. No gangsters hanging out in the hallway. No out-of-work Denizens waiting for the next thing to come by.

Truth climbed the stairs, ignoring the perpetually out-of-order elevator. The music got louder and louder, the higher he got. At floor forty of forty-five, the stairs ran out. Demolished. He walked through the door onto the floor and into a tunnel dug through heaps of rubble. It was more of a climb, but eventually, he reached the final floor.

Soaring five stories was a statue. So enormous, he had trouble wrapping words around it. The thing was in the shape of a snake, but it had the head and mane of a lion. It appeared to be eating the sun. Worshiping it were thousands of Ghūl.

The statue beat on his consciousness. It was too real, too great for something so limited and fragile as a *human* to perceive. Truth felt a strange yearning for it. Strange because he also felt revulsion. It was hideous.

It was revolting. It offended him in a way that no other Ghūl statue had. Everything about it scraped at his nerves. Truth forced himself to confront the feeling, examine it, and try to understand.

The serpent seemed . . . very snakelike. What was there to say? It was a riot of colors, greens, blacks, blues, and golds, threaded with reds, yellows, whites, and browns. Like it wasn't just *a* snake but *all* the snakes. Like it was the very concept of every negative association you ever had about serpents. But that could only be part of it. He liked snakes fine. It was the lion's head attached at the end that was so obscene.

It didn't fit. Obviously. It wasn't even remotely to scale, being a third the size of the snake body. The mane seemed both raggedy, dirty black streaked with gold, and lustrous. As though the gold were streamers pulled from living suns and the black was flecked with the stars and planets.

The mouth was snarling, lips pulled back into a sneer or a roar or both. The fangs reeked of endless hunger. They were the simple embodiment of predation. They were teeth meant to rip flesh. It didn't cultivate or grow; it only ate what it pleased and shat where it pleased. Above the ravening maw were the eyes.

Truth could barely force himself to look at the eyes and, even then, only for a moment. Prideful. Hateful. Mean. Just mean. The essence of a bully refined with the arrogance of a god.

Oh.

It was Grandpa. Many times removed.

Truth looked at the worshiping Ghūl and rapidly reevaluated what he was seeing. They were fixated on the statue, but he didn't think they were actually worshiping. They looked, as best he could read their corpse faces, like they were honing themselves. Testing themselves against immense pressure. More of those strange symbols, symbols he had seen only once before, covered two walls. They meant something to the Ghūl, but he couldn't figure it out.

He couldn't figure them out.

"Just what are you? *Why* are you?" he murmured. "Are you beings from a higher dimension that came down to . . . what, exactly? You have some strange connection to the Rough Patron, but he is definitionally below this . . . creator god. He isn't even a god. He is, or was, some kind of human, infinitely long ago. So, why? You admire that he threw the first punch or . . . whatever? That he talked back to God?"

It just didn't add up. None of it was clicking for him. If they were some kind of higher order of being, why the brutal dissection of random victims on the street? Why the sculptures venerating the human form? Why worship a human that fought back; why worship the embodiments of a failed copy, rather than the beings above even the creator god?

Hell, why descend into this shabby corner of reality in the first place? Can't you do your worshiping from a distance?

Truth laughed, self-deprecation tinged with madness. He was torn, trying to decide if they were shock troopers come to fight the apocalypse, or if they were more like maggots, come to clean up after the slaughter. Either way, they weren't anything good for the humans on this planet. Sethians. Whatever.

And he was part of them. And they were part of him. Whatever their game was, they had touched him with it. They were his connection to the Rough Patron, yes, but also that Nine Worm path he cultivated with. Those Nine Worms that still roamed his body, perfecting his form, making him ever more resistant to magic. Worms that also tied back to the Rough Patron, somehow.

Truth knew the Ghūl were at the center of some vast mystery. Some awful, unspeakable truth. And he just didn't have the clues to solve it. And he didn't have the time to investigate further. He could usually accept not knowing things. This would eat at him.

The Ghūl stood as one. They turned towards one wall—northeast? He had lost his sense of direction.

There was a sudden twist. An inversion of the natural order of things. And then, forty stories up, Truth could hear Harban screaming.

CHAPTER 13

ONE ANSWER

It was a sound he had never heard before. Heartbreak, outrage, and the sound of tearing stone. Of shattered glass and shattered people. It went on and on; how long, he couldn't say, because he was still lost in the horror of the sound long after it had stopped. Something terrible had happened. Harban was screaming.

The Ghūl didn't like the light, so they didn't press up against the window. Lots of room for Truth. He looked out, but all he could see were other slum high-rises, all clustered together. Drowning the world in shadow. The sky hadn't changed. He could still feel cosmic energy. It wasn't a magical void or overpressure. So, what made that noise?

On the one hand, it wasn't his business. Once, he might even have said it was a good thing. Distracting the enemy, pulling their forces away. Now? Now it was just meaningless noise. He rubbed the back of his neck. His eyes seemed to be pulled irresistibly back to the statue. That wild arrogance. The contempt in the lion's face.

There was a soft shuffling sound. He looked around. All the Ghūl had turned to look at him. Even with everything, it was damn eerie.

"At this point, you cannot possibly have a moral opinion about my going and taking a look."

They were, as always, silent. Just looking at him.

"It really is none of my business. At all. It would be downright counterproductive to go check it out."

They just looked at him. The Ghūl had never bothered with words. Famously. Particularly words like *No!* or *Please!* or *Stop, for the love of God, stop!* They didn't care about who you were, how old you were, what you thought you were worth. Other than making more Ghūl and worshiping their eerie statues, it would be hard to say *what* they actually cared about. Apparently, it wasn't all about worship. But they still didn't give a damn about what you had to say.

"Fine, yes, I admit it. I'm going to go. I should at least see what's happening out there. Are you going to stop me?"

His breath was the loudest noise in the building.

Truth turned and left. The Ghūl watched him go.

Truth made his way toward whatever had happened. It was easy to find. He just had to run toward all the people running away. The city flashed past as he ran. So many of the old familiar stores were closed, metal shutters rolled down, the flashing, blinding signs gone dark. The brilliant colors of Harban were going out. Without their blinding lights, the ugly reality of the city was laid plain. Harban was a grim place, full of hard people. And those hard people were running scared as hell of whatever was behind them.

When he found the edges of the thing, he agreed with the good sense of his fellow Harbanites. Some necrotic wave was rushing up the street. Like someone had poured tint into the air, making the twilight even darker. It swept through buildings, vehicles, and people with equal contempt. The buildings, it ignored. The people . . . the people melted.

The people melted, shattered, or exploded. Liquefied, boiled, deboned, gutted, and fileted. The parts flowed into new shapes; the liquid became etchings and arcane formulas. The bones were rebuilt as structures holding the infernal geometry of organs and arteries. Unspeakable algorithms of mutilation and horror replicated and multiplied, generating more and more of that black wind, expanding outward.

It was a machine of negation, unmaking humanity. Truth could see buildings and carriages slowly collapsing deeper in the shadowed interior of the mutilation wave. Not unmade the way people were. They just collapsed in on themselves.

The anti-theists. Truth vividly remembered investigating the dead apartment building in Xandre. The machine of meat and bone that tried to permanently carve a piece of the world away from God. *But why? The apocalypse is doing that for them?*

<<No. It isn't. That's temporary, something that is being done to us. This is them taking the power back, saying that God won't get the planet back.>>

Truth cast Obliteration, in some faint hope that two negatives would make a positive. It vanished into the darkness like a pebble into a tornado-whipped pond. He darted in and hacked at the shadowed air with the Tongue of One Who Speaks for God. Seemed that God had nothing to say on the matter. He wasn't even getting feedback from the Bane spell in the sword. It was vibrating with hate, but the angelic blade didn't have any more answers for this than he did.

Truth fell back two blocks, trying to regroup. Order his thoughts. *The more complicated a problem, the simpler the solution should be. How the hell did we break this back in Siphios?*

He couldn't immediately remember. Hell with it. He hacked a fist-sized wedge of concrete out of a corner of a building and threw it at a chunk of bone scaffolding. The crackling and shattering noises were very satisfying. Less satisfying was the impact it had on the spreading shadow. If it did anything, it was tiny. He threw more stuff, shattering more bones and tearing apart more garlands of enchanted organs. The spread of shadows was slowing, at least in his immediate area. Not very much. But a tiny bit. Enough to be noticeable.

So, he kept throwing. It felt like bailing out the ocean with a thimble. Still. Better than nothing. The darkness kept spreading anyway.

This isn't working. I'm trying to put out a forest fire by pissing on it. Truth looked around, desperate for *something* that . . . There were sirens. Of course cops would come swarming in. Army too. Truth ran toward the noise. A situation like this, there would be a field command.

It took minutes. He had to ask for directions. Eventually, he found a blacked-out wagon practically coated in wards and communication talismans. Stairs running up the back. Mobile command center if he had ever seen one. Which he hadn't actually, but it seemed like a safe bet. People were coming in and out so often, he could just walk in behind them.

There were cops working comms altars, tracking things on maps—he didn't bother to look closely. He found the local commander. Her mouth was a grim line as she tracked the spread and listened to reports coming in. Truth waited his turn, then stepped forward, saluted, and made his report.

"Ma'am! Report from the front line—destroying the bones from outside the effect seems to slow the spread locally. Confirmed that heavy needlers firing Graeme's Arrow at range are effective, as are remote extra-massive munition delivery—"

"They threw rocks at it, Sergeant?"

"Ma'am! Cement, ma'am!"

"Speak Jeongo, Sergeant!"

"Yes, ma'am! Sorry, ma'am!"

"Confirmed?"

"Yes, ma'am! It's not a big effect per bone, but it does add up, according to the report."

She grunted. "Who knew being a professional leg-breaker would come in handy now? All right, back to your station." She shot a look over at a communication station. "Relay the new information to the front—break the bones, any way you can."

"Yes, ma'am!"

"Good job, Sergeant." She looked around. The messenger had vanished. Well, she had dismissed him. She shook her head and got back to work.

Truth rushed out into the swirling, chaotic mass. The cops were working to clear the area, to set a firm line they could defend. The spell, or whatever it was, wasn't letting them. It was obviously self-sustaining, relying on what it "ate" to grow. Unless they could evacuate faster than it spread, it would keep growing. Harban wasn't built to be evacuated in a hurry. All those tall towers, for one thing. Those incredibly dense blocks of people. Even if everyone was in an orderly queue and steadily walking out of the danger zone, it would be too slow.

And by no means was everyone in an orderly queue. Panic; raw, naked panic. People shoving at each other. Dragging suitcases. Blocking stairways and clogging the streets. Carriages plowed into each other and formed barricades, blocking the emergency vehicles trying to race to the danger. Blocking the other carriages trying to run from the danger. Truth watched it all in horror, watched as the first building fell.

Then the second. Then the third. All those structural-reinforcement spells were suddenly gone. All those fire-suppression spells. Materials suddenly warping and twisting as they lost their magical foundations. Then they fell in on themselves, or toppled over onto other nearby buildings, or onto the streets.

For one fragile moment, Truth prayed it was a dream. That this was all a terrible nightmare, and he would wake again to see that Harban was the same awful place it had always been.

Then he watched a few hundred people get torn apart by the spell. It wasn't a dream. He didn't dream. Not really.

One cop had apparently not run fast enough. At least the vehicle was unattended. Good enough. Now . . . did the cops actually do what the other guys in the PMC had accused them of?

Truth popped the lock on the trunk with a sharp jab of the finger, then whistled. Three *extremely* lethal fetishes, all aimed at maximum crowd control, mounted on the inside of the hatch. One of them was an old, familiar friend. The Crabbe and Crabbe saw-blade launcher might lack the versatility and portability of the needler or the ease of use of a firebolter, but it did make up for it by launching up to five ten-centimeter-wide circular saw blades up to two hundred meters and at ten thousand RPM.

Accuracy? Do you *need* accuracy? Or are you just a whiner?

And you could load spells onto it. And, hypothetically, you could launch more saw blades if you pumped more power into it.

He tried not to think about what he was aiming at. About how much damage had already been done. He just picked a spot with a lot of bones and guts, and fired. Then aimed and fired again. Over and over and over. Jumping up on rooftops for better angles. Kicking his feet into the sides of buildings and making a perch if there weren't convenient roofs. Anything. Whatever it took. Just move and shoot and move and shoot.

The cops were doing the same thing. The bubble of destruction was slowing its spread, but it was already so huge, thousands, tens of thousands must be dead already. Incalculable harm. Move and shoot, move and shoot. Try to pare it back. Save at least a few who would die otherwise.

There was a sense of pressure, heavy pressure, coming from above. Incisive *screamed*, and he kicked off the side of the wall hard. Smashed through the window of an apartment on the other side of the street. Ran through the interior walls. Jumped out and across again, then through, then dove at a manhole cover on the street and sliced it open as he passed through. All in less than two seconds. He was still falling into the sewer when the impacts started hitting.

Deep thuds, ripping through the dirt, liquefying the concrete and soil. The noise and pressure beat on him, punching him into the walls, then down into the muck and filth below. It wasn't explosions, exactly. He had heard a lot of those. It was impacts, so heavy and loud that the difference between them and bombs would be academic.

Someone had made a call. Someone had checked what he said, figured it was right, figured everything was lost inside the affected area. Someone figured that if you can't hit it with magic directly, launching big rocks or iron bars at it from high up or at high speeds would smash everything up just as well. Someone figured that anyone caught in the blast was dead or soon would be worse than dead.

Someone had made a call. Maybe it was the right one. Right now, buried in the sewer, Truth just wanted the beating to stop.

CHAPTER 14

NOT GOING QUIET

Truth crawled out of the sewers. It wasn't easy. The manhole he had come down through had partially collapsed in on itself. It was, in his inexpert opinion, a minor miracle that the sewer itself hadn't caved in. Theoretically, he could use Earth-Folding Step to bypass the blockage. In practice, he was in no mood to try. The concrete and dirt moved easily enough in his hands. The weight wasn't a problem. It was just dirty and tiresome. He was used to that.

He clawed his way out of the earth and thought he had dug in the wrong direction. For a moment, he thought he had dug into Hell.

Rubble. Desolation. His mind scrabbled to find the words to describe the feeling of what he was seeing. Buildings destroyed. But it was different when they were the buildings you grew up in, walked past, dreamed of living in. The convenience stores you despised or shoplifted from, ruined. Gutted and unmade. The clothing stores that would have chased out a little rat like him now displaying rags even a beggar wouldn't wear.

He staggered down the street, trying to reconcile what he was seeing with what he remembered. That was a cafe, a chain cafe. They did okay muffins and coffee. Never again. There wasn't enough there to make a counter, let alone a sandwich. That was an office building; there was a chain dentist on the third floor. He could still see the sign for it on the one wall of the building that still stood. Had there been apartments over the offices in this tower? Mixed-use was popular around here.

All gone now. All gone. The apocalypse was there, and no God or angels were needed. Humans were enough. Humans were entirely enough. Remnants of the bone machine still existed. Cartouches of some obscene inversion of spells glistened in the twilight. The same principles that led the tumor-growth of the machine gave rise to the symbols. There certainly hadn't been time to carve them by hand.

It was a remarkable achievement. The thought grabbed him, making him lightheaded. He couldn't process what he was seeing. Couldn't reconcile the evidence of his eyes and the truth of his heart. In that moment of agonizing unreality, as rationality sank like water into sand, the thought remained on the surface. It really was an incredible achievement.

They must have spent decades on this. Centuries. Entirely new fields of theoretical spellcraft and high-energy thaumaturgy would have been carefully researched by tiny cabals with virtually no funding. He couldn't even imagine what it would have taken to conduct experiments and field tests. Well, yes, he could; he had seen it in Xandre. But still. A lot of people worked extremely hard for centuries. Absolute geniuses contributed their greatest achievements to the project.

If there were wounded, they had been harmed by the bombardment. There were no survivors of that necrotic bubble. One of the greatest technological achievements in the history of the planet, and its creators carefully left no living witnesses. He was too stunned, too shattered to hate them. He staggered forward down the street, not sure what he was trying to find or trying to see.

Truth felt an insistent sucking on his skin. It was a vacuum. There was a void of cosmic energy there. One that was persisting somehow. His spells and blessings could persist there for quite some time. Not forever, though. Not without taking drastic steps to refill his energy. This wasn't a preview of what was to come. It was worse. Even if the Nephilim did capture the planet, they wouldn't build there. This was a dead land. How much of the city was lost? He didn't know.

He couldn't even conceive of the land recovering. The city rebuilding. There was tumbled rubble and streamers of cloth with confetti paper everywhere, and somehow, this was the better outcome. This stopped the other decorations from spreading—the garlands of organs and soft, suffering meat shuddering in the light and cold air.

Another intrusive thought—why not pigs? Why did it have to be people? Why not go to an industrial hog farm and cast the spell there? Was it atrocity for atrocity's sake? He had never heard of the anti-theists making political demands. They didn't have a propaganda program that he knew about. Hell, he had never heard of them until Merkovah explained what he saw. The only time he had come across them before Xandre . . .

The only time he had come across them before Xandre was at the border crossing during his National Service. The fight that got him military merits, a secret medal, and a promotion. The fight that got him on that PMC rocket ship at Starbrite, because that NCO rating stacked with everything else to guarantee speedy promotion.

How long had he been fate's fool? How long had he been led around by the nose by these mighty beings? He could believe that he was a special rat, not like the other rats, but there had to be a limit, right? Right?! What about whatshisname, the researcher, the biotech guy who was in the booth with him at that fight, and again when he was smuggling Sally through the Free State? When he got murdered and died for five damn years. Ludovic? Something like that. What about him? Did he have a *destiny*? Was he fated to be at these important places and somehow keep missing getting shot?

Had Ludovic been in the volcano when it blew up? If he had been, Truth would bet an unlimited sum that he had made it out alive thanks to other people.

Truth kept stumbling down the road, headed nowhere, unwilling to accept what he was seeing. Past the bus stops. Past the train stations, and he didn't for a second believe that all the machinery was destroyed down there. Some of those tunnels ran thirty meters deep or more. Nothing short of specially armed and equipped demolition crews were going to clear those out. Didn't some of these buildings have basements that connected to the subway? He remembered stations that had little restaurants in them, or doors that let you go directly into department stores.

It wasn't just the horrible thing that was done there; it was knowing that it would never heal. That he could never make it better. For some reason, that was just unacceptable. It shouldn't be that way.

He checked Perks, clumsy hands pawing at his shirt. Banged up again. Cup and Knife healed him up, though it cost far more energy than it should have. He really had to stop bringing this poor snake into these horrible situations. Not that he had expected anything like this. How could he? He was just going to visit a friend, look around his home city a bit, then head up north again.

Made a fool of by who knows what ancient and impossible powers. All this slaughter. For what? For what? To strike a blow against a God that couldn't care less? Did they really think that they could steal souls from the being that made the world? Or maybe he didn't make the world, who knows, but any which way about it, this was a pointless horror! It achieved *nothing*. So, why rub his nose in it again and again? Why did destiny drag him back to the anti-theists over and over? Was it all of them? One of them? What?

Truth made his way to a playground between some apartment buildings. It was a sad little place, with a basic plastic climbing structure and the faded outline of games spray-painted on the ground. There were, at least, benches for tired parents and a few established trees around. Not very fancy trees or anything. Probably what was cheap at the tree farm. Some kind of pine trees.

If all this was destined, if all this was according to some great plan . . . then what. Was. The. Damn. Point? How was he supposed to act like he had free will if he was running around with three destinies on him? Where was the "free will" for all these senselessly killed people? It sounds very sophisticated when you nod seriously and say, "In the long run, we're all dead," but it's a lot less smart-sounding when you are standing on top of a massacre.

He couldn't fix this. He couldn't make it mean something more than it already did. Or didn't; at this point, he was too exhausted to play games. It was just sad. Wrenching. He couldn't wrap his feelings in words yet.

He watched the trees swaying in the evening wind. They didn't appear bothered by the sudden lack of cosmic rays. All the mystical significance of a turnip. Maybe less. The abolition of cosmic rays from an area meant nothing at all to them.

Was it sacrifice? Some kind of terrible, awful sacrifice to who-knows-what that would permanently forbid cosmic rays from entering a defined area? It made a sort of sense. The transformation required energy, and energy couldn't come from nowhere.

He couldn't escape the feeling of futility. Futility of the massacre, of the lives of the massacred, of his own struggling against all the awful things he was seeing. Nothing came from nothing, but since everything came from God, which was everything, then everything came from everything which brought everything back around in an empty circle.

What to do in the face of all that pointlessness and nothingness? Might as well make art. Might as well make homes for ghosts and write poetry to ease their souls. Not that he was artistic. Truth couldn't manage a plausible rat.

He didn't like moping. And he hated feeling helpless. It brought out the meanness in him. The playground was very ordinary. Nothing there reeked of symbolism, and it all certainly lacked grandeur.

It really wasn't very big. Very standard iron fence marking the boundaries. These kinds of parks were utterly common near apartment buildings.

"You know what? I have absolutely no reason to believe this will work. But, on the other hand, fuck it."

He carefully fixed the boundary of the park in his mind.

"I think I can be considered something of an expert on arrogant pricks." Truth looked up toward the sky. "So, I can confidently say that, as over-the-top as it sounds, I am *unquestionably* the most important, most real, thing within the boundaries of this playground."

He casually directed a bit of his energy into the Meditations of Valentinian, feeling his reality reinforce. "I can also confidently state that the world knows it too." He let Incisive have a trickle as well.

"In fact, with the sudden absence, permanent absence, of cosmic energy to make things 'realer,' there is literally nothing here that can even compete for the title of realest. Which means I get to set the rules."

He let his words and will slowly hammer on the void around him. "This area has been 'cut off' from the energy of the universe. Cut off from the emanations of those higher beings who ultimately descend from the single unified totality we call God. Which means, in this place, *I am the closest thing to God there is*!"

Next was Cup and Knife. This place was terribly wrong. Time to fix it. Easier said than done, of course, but easy or not, it had to happen.

"Now, I don't agree with what was done here. I think it's horrible and horribly wrong. I'm not putting up with it! Everywhere should be connected to the universe, all the way up to the Godhead. Even if the local area thinks otherwise. Even if the whole damn planet thinks otherwise. It's not the boss either!"

He could feel Cup and Knife coming together. Getting closer and closer to Manda's original vision for the spell. Feeling the air shuddering and trembling as the venom of Incisive etched his reality on the world around him.

"And, of course, if God is truly universal, there is no such thing as cutting its energy off from a specific place. So, I decree that in this place, the flow of cosmic rays shall never stop." He reached out with Earth-Folding Step. This wasn't how the spell was supposed to work, but Truth had always believed in jank. Right now, there wasn't a single person who could remind him that *Fuck around and find out* applied to him, too.

CHAPTER 15

A CASE OF MISTAKEN IDENTITY

There had been too much horror. Too much suffering. The inevitable crushing down on him as it did on everyone else. Truth had the means to do something about it. Just a little bit. Just in this one place, at this one moment. In a random corner of what was once the greatest city in the world, in a mostly forgotten children's playground, he would make an island of hope.

You couldn't fit many people in such a tiny playground. No doubt forces and powers he didn't approve of would discover it and claim it. He couldn't prevent that. But he could bring at least a little light, and hope, and life into the world.

Truth could bet on hope. He could stand the loss if he was wrong, so why not try and see if he could get lucky?

Truth combined all the layers of magic in his soul and every scrap of his understanding of the world and cast a singular spell. A spell called Truth. It was a bit janky. Definitely a work in progress. But as a first effort, the results were . . . spectacular.

The sun had set on Harban. The shadows swarmed in, filling the alleys and ruins. Filling the minds of the people who lived in the toppling towers. The shadows swallowed up the city. Except for one little playground. A place with no name, marked on no maps, occasionally maintained by the absentee landlord corporation that ran the nearby apartment buildings. That one strange place was drowning in sunlight.

Truth wasn't seeing the playground anymore. His mind had been wrenched somewhere else. He was pulled up and away from the world, seeing the blue planet shrink beneath him, then suddenly transform into an impossibly vast angel—a being of infinite angles and endless meanings.

Then it was the planet again, then the angel, then the images superimposed and he could see that the world was the angel—all the oceans and continents were just traceries of the endless complexity of that great being.

He was falling forward. Falling in toward something. Towards the sun. He very quickly learned what the word *immense* truly meant. The planet was a *speck*. The sun was . . . everything. Everything. Boiling gas and fire, the meanings of obliteration and life and death and eternity. Of fierce pride. Overwhelming, terrible pride. Within the blinding light of the sun, different forms began to appear.

The first amongst them was the sun itself—not merely a collection of boiling gasses but the very essence of that yellow disk in the sky. Perfectly round. Infinitely mighty. Not God but modeled upon that universal perfection. Infinite in all ways, endless power, endless endurance, the beginning and end of all things, most particularly life. It was indifferent to anything external to itself, because it was perfectly self-sufficient. Heat, light, and life were merely emanations caused by its existence. They certainly weren't *gifts*. They were the breath it exhaled, consumed by hungry trees.

Then it shifted, and Truth was confronted by a seven-headed snake. Truth had always thought he liked snakes. At least, since he learned Incisive, he had always thought he liked snakes. He didn't like this one. Or this . . . seven. He wasn't quite sure how to figure it.

The seven-headed snake saw him. It saw everything. It saw every speck of dust its light touched. It saw every human that reached up to thank it for its blessings of light, and every fish that died flopping on the shore, scales shining and dancing as it choked to death. It saw it all, and it didn't care. To the extent that it did care, it accepted the worship as its due, and the suffering of others as amusement.

Prideful. The serpent in the sun was prideful. Where Botis was reserved and watchful, the seven-headed snake demanded to be watched. It demanded love and fear, offering none of its own. It had the capital to be demanding. The serpent was powerful. Dreadfully, nightmarishly powerful.

Botis was subtle. The Sun-Serpent was blunt. Botis was cautious. The Sun-Serpent was brash. Botis ensured he had no enemies. The Sun-Serpent had no enemies either. Not anymore. It wasn't a real snake as Truth had come to understand the word. It was a monster mocking the shape of a snake. But why? Why seven heads? Why not be a giant snake?

Hunger. That was all he could think of. The sun gave endlessly, but it came with a dreadful appetite. The sun was certainly eating something. Truth had no idea what it could be, but was afraid. *Why is it always monstrous serpents? The statue in the Ghūl nest, this, Botis, so many others in the Goetia. What is it about snakes? Are they the real chosen species?*

Then the Seven-Headed Snake was gone, and in its place was the Rough Patron.

Truth couldn't tear his eyes away. It was clearly the Rough Patron but not the Rough Patron he knew. This being had thick brows over a brutal face. The eyes were filled with resentment. All humor was gone. There was only obsession, jealousy. Spite. His body was sprayed with blood already drying to black, though his hands still dripped a fresh red. Sharply defined muscles, yes, but in the way that starving men are sharply muscled. No fat to smooth out the edges.

Truth couldn't look away from the eyes. The layers of emotion in those eyes made him struggle to breathe. Obsession. Outrage. Hunger. Was there loneliness there, too? Something that he had never picked up during their meetings—insecurity. The Rough Patron, or this version of the Rough Patron, was screaming out for something. Some sign or trace of affection.

Was the story Susan told him true? Once upon a time, two humans were created, and they had three sons. One died young. Truth was going to guess it wasn't because of a fever. One child was the Rough Patron, whose descendants, maybe voluntarily, maybe not, had sex with angels. And the third son? Just skated on all of that. Life's tragedies just seemed to whiff past him.

Imagine there were only five people in the world. Double that, maybe, to give the boys someone to breed with, but for the sake of narrative, you had two parents, three kids, and one overbearing grandparent. Do Mummy and Daddy love their kids equally? Or do they play favorites? How about Grandpa? What would it feel like to get frozen out by the only people in existence?

Of course the first two humans were lousy parents. They had no idea how to raise a kid. They had no examples to follow. It must have been alien and terrifying to them. This strange thing growing inside her belly, kicking her, weakening her. How could she know what to do? The angels would never have seen this before, either. Even if "God" knew how this was supposed to work, he had never seen it before. Never witnessed the miracle created by his creation.

And the climax of that blood and pain and horror was a tiny human. Other animals learned to walk in minutes. Not this baby. It was blind, help-less, smelly, covered in blood. It wouldn't have seemed like a miracle—it would have seemed like a curse. A horror inexplicably inflicted on the first woman, then a burden placed on both husband and wife. They would have to feed three now, and the child hadn't yet invented farming.

How much resentment would there be for this first child? How much awkwardness and coldness? They would know better for the second, and by the third, it would all be "normal." To say nothing of any daughters they must have had, and he wasn't going to think about that one too much. The Rough Patron had to take the lumps for his sibs, he had to suffer so that when his parents got around to the others, they could do a better job raising them. But unlike Truth, the Rough Patron didn't have that instinct to protect his juniors.

Truth didn't know what the age gap was, but . . . at least nine months, right? A year? Two? More? Enough time to see, very clearly, who the favored child was. To feel the coldness of neglect. Enough times for the embers of resentment to blaze into a bonfire.

But why the sun? How did the Rough Patron go from that damaged, hateful man to the sun?

Truth hung in that frozen moment, in that place between Heaven and Earth, and tried to understand. How do you go from the first murderer to the sun? How does that work? Because he wasn't the "'Father" of all humans.

Or . . . was he?

Not literally, of course. Sethians, that's what Susan had called them. But didn't human civilization rely on the things the Rough Patron made? Agriculture, metalworking, city-building?

The first two people lived like animals in the woods, hunting and foraging to survive. The Rough Patron *built*.

The Rough Patron looked at the world and said, "*I can't accept how things are, but I can work with this. I can use the world to my advantage. Crops will come in as regularly as I can manage. You will have tools, reliable, long-lasting tools. You will have the time and space to make art and science and argue about the nature of Virtue. And it won't be remotely fair or kind. Some of you will suffer horribly for this. But that's how the world is. Some people are just born blessed, and some people get shit on for no reason. Don't like it? Do something about it.*"

He was the one who brought light to the world, the light of civilization. Of prosperity for some, built on the suffering of others. His whole lineage was despised . . . but didn't we follow in his footsteps? Who was worse—the man who committed the crimes, or the people who did the same damn things while patting themselves on the back and saying how good they were?

Truth wanted to laugh, hanging in that shattering void. He was over-thinking it. Why was the Rough Patron also the sun? Because he was the first victim of parental neglect, which apparently turned into violence, for which he was blamed and punished. Then his kids were violent pricks, and they taught others to be violent pricks, and they eventually gave birth to the Nephilim, who apparently built their entire culture around being violent pricks. He was the sun, because like the sun, the cycle of violence and abuse is omnipresent, inescapable, and its victims understand every-thing by its light.

Every single person who ever lived was part of that cycle. Carrying that trauma, generation after generation. Literally from the first human born onward. An entire species defined by trauma.

What is a human? A dangerous question when asked in the wrong place. For example, could a human state that, regardless of how the planet felt and the sun felt, one specific spot on the planet would always be bathed in cosmic rays? That seemed like a *bold* declaration.

The Rough Patron looked over at him. Truth knew that while this wasn't the Rough Patron he knew, this ancient knew him. He knew that every speck of him was seen through. That nothing this sun's rays touched was overlooked.

YOU SHOULD HAVE THOUGHT ABOUT WHERE YOU WERE STANDING.

The light flowed down on him, pouring over him like water and fire. He didn't know light could hurt, that it could hammer at you. There were poisons hidden in that light, specks of it that were faster and crueler than others. Those tried to burrow into him, burn little holes through his skin to rot and destroy from within.

Truth tried to wrap himself in his body cultivation, but this was prac-tically a joke. Matching his tiny power against the very sun itself? He was overwhelmed, smashed back into his body and into that nothing, nowhere playground. A place that, despite the gloom filling the rest of Harban, was now basking in sunshine.

CHAPTER 16

ENERGETIC YOUNG MAN

The park was bathed in golden light. It wasn't a euphemism for sunshine; the light itself had a heavy feeling, imperishable, untarnishable, endless. Truth could see, from where he had collapsed on the ground, the golden light filling everything in the playground. The swings, the plastic slides, the wood chips and asphalt on the ground. Everything. Nothing had dramatically changed yet, but it would only be a matter of time until every scrap of matter in this place was filled with significance and power. Until it was transformed. Of course, not everything could endure so much power.

In fact, things tended to explode.

Truth tried to get up and run. No chance of that. His own limbs seemed to weigh far more than they should. He couldn't even bring himself to his hands and knees. Instead, he had to worm his way along the ground. Every shift of a limb a victory, with success measured in centimeters, not meters. He desperately hoped he had left the gate to the park open. If not, he might as well get comfortable because he would never leave there alive.

Even leaving in death was starting to feel optimistic. Truth ran the Meditations as best he could, but this was plainly beyond its current capabilities. Whatever was hammering into him, it was considerably more real than he was. It certainly came from a higher plane of existence. This was not the energy of someone who crawled on their belly in the dirt.

One stretch. One contraction. Tried to push with the legs as he pulled with the arms. He could feel the wood chips under him hardening, starting to feel like stone. Would they explode? Or would they petrify, becoming like jade? Would he petrify? Because he couldn't help but notice his apertures weren't filling up. The energy was steadily drilling into his flesh and bone, but it wasn't going through the invisible little channels and strengthening him. It was just building up.

Fingertips gripping. Pull. Stretch. Pull. Was he hearing sirens? He must be. Spell platforms, spell birds, old monsters by the bucketful, all coming his way. No time to be slow. No time to try and figure things out. Stretch. Pull. Stretch. Pull. He wasn't getting tired. He was getting more and more scared. The weight was increasing. Slowly but inexorably. It would crush him if it could.

Was . . . was the dead zone around the playground blocking people from coming in? It might be. It might well be. He had been pretty deep in the devastation when he found the playground, and most couldn't stand the energy void. Would they send Level Zeros to investigate? Then what, run back to report? How fast could a Level Zero move, really? It had been so long, he had lost his sense of normal.

Didn't matter. Didn't matter. They would drop dead if they tried to force their way in there, and he was sure the Level Zero that could hurt him hadn't been born yet. So, no need to fear them outside the light. Just had to keep moving. Centimeter by centimeter. It might be agonizingly slow, but he would get there.

The gate was in sight. He had pushed it open and left it open. Small miracle. He'd take it. Centimeter by centimeter. Just dig in his fingertips and toes, and strain. Push and pull and keep moving under the hammerblows of the light. Like he was a drum or a piano. Vibrating to the cosmic beatings, performing the music of the stars in his flesh. That monstrous senior in the hot spring said he should learn to make art. Well. Now he was art.

The gate was getting closer. Centimeter by centimeter. He knew that he could move fast. Blindingly fast. Not now. He would never take it for granted again. Struggling to move, knowing something was building up in his body, something he didn't choose . . . or he chose without understanding. Some part of his awareness knew the Worms were working joyfully, crying out in hateful pleasure as they burrowed through him. Remade him. Refashioned him in ways he couldn't put words to.

His right hand stretched out, fingertips brushing the gate post. Couldn't quite get a grip. Wriggle again. Just get the fingertips around it. Pull. He was able to get a long pull on the metal, hauling his body up to the gate. Change up the grip. Pushing now with the legs and the arm, and out into the icy cold of the world outside the playground.

Truth gasped, unable to scream. All that energy that had been trapped in his flesh tried to escape all at once. Boiling out of him, wanting to disperse into the empty atmosphere. He struggled to hold it all in, reinforcing himself with the Meditations and, when that wasn't working fast enough, drawing the excess energy into his apertures with the Nine Worm Path.

The Worms were delighted to "help," naturally. They drew the power through his body and up into his apertures. It felt like he had returned to the moment of his breakthrough. As the Worms made their way through his flesh, they left a trail of agony behind them. The Worms seemed to mock him as they wriggled through his meat and marrow. "*We can wriggle even better than you!*" Beyond the agony was the strange feeling that they were reconstructing his cultivation system. Not improving it or reinventing it, simply restoring it after whatever was done to it in the beating sunlight.

Truth desperately turned his attention to his apertures—still there, still intact. If anything, they were stronger than before. Richer in color and brightness. The spells themselves seemed . . . stronger somehow. As though they had been tested and accepted. Even Cup and Knife seemed much less jank.

His apertures and spells were fine. His body, however, was not. He could feel the furious energy tearing up his muscles and tendons, even as the Meditations rebuilt him. Those pinpricks of strong power had been driven deep inside him and had been held in place by the power of the sun. Now they were running riot. Not just exploding or tearing—to his horror, he realized that the energy was trying to mutate him. Mutation in seemingly random directions. He had to desperately focus on correcting them, pouring his energy into stabilizing himself.

In a fit of cosmic irony, Truth had managed to escape the playground only to be paralyzed by the soft summer night.

From out of the gloaming city light came a howl. First one, but it was quickly joined by dozens of others. Something in the noise reached through the ears and pulled on the nerves. The hunt had begun, and it was to the death.

Dogs. Must be specially bred, mutated, trained, maybe enchanted in a way that would stick even if the magic went down.

Not that it changed anything. He still had one job—to keep from exploding. To put himself together enough to move. The energy that was floating randomly through his flesh was slowly dragged through the path of the Nine Worms, refined, and poured into his apertures. From the first to the fifth, the refined energy poured like glowing honey. Poured like the sun made into water. Accumulating, deepening and widening the apertures as it passed.

How much time was passing? He couldn't tell. He couldn't spare the attention to mind such things. Must have been a while, because he heard the baying of the hounds again. Closer this time. Very close. He opened his eyes and met two dozen looking back.

The dogs had found him.

Good-looking dogs, though. For some reason, I thought they would be monsters.

The hounds should have looked silly. Their skin was loose on their bones, like an athlete wearing clothes five sizes too big for them. Truth didn't buy it. They had the long muzzles and sharp eyes of dogs with jobs. *You can run*, their eyes promised. *You can run all you like. Won't matter either way. We have your scent. In the end, we will run you down. You aren't even prey. You are the job, and when you are dead, we will be on to the next job and won't remember you at all.*

"It occurs to me that I used to have the same exact eyes," Truth murmured.

The dogs raised their heads and started howling again. The sound was a little different this time—they had found something. The hunters should come and see.

Smart dogs. Smart enough to realize I'm immobilized, so there is no reason for them to come closer and risk injury. They would move if I moved, but for now, they are happy to hang back. Very smart dogs. I'd love to meet their trainer.

OH SHIT PERKS! You know what? I've got to find a home for this guy. I am one hundred percent not qualified to own a pet. I hope he is still alive. The snake was currently resting above his belt, but he couldn't tell how it was doing at the moment.

Get mobile. Everything else can be sorted out later; just got to get mobile. Like I haven't been trying that already.

The problem was . . . well, there were a lot of problems with trying to get mobile. But a *key* problem was that he couldn't just clear the energy out of his legs and be on his way. Not when thrashing, boiling, attempting-to-explode pockets of energy were lodged in his spine and brain. And the energy didn't obediently stay in one place. Just because an area had been cleared before didn't mean it would stay cleared.

Nothing to do but do it. He couldn't go faster, so he just kept going. He could see the progress. Things were improving in terms of the immediate, dead-right-now-scale problems. But he was racking up damage. Microscopic but cumulative. He didn't know how long it would take to return to full health. Too long. Still. Progress. Focus on the immediate problem, leave the rest for Future Truth.

A figure appeared at the edge of his awareness. Sealed head-to-toe in silver spell armor, with a tinted facemask, they looked rather like a golem. It wasn't, of course. They moved with the clumsy caution he associated with a Level Zero. He felt oddly vindicated that the person was armed with a spear rather than a needler or sword.

Could he move? Once, maybe. Not walking or anything. But he could probably punch someone. On the other hand, if the dogs were smart enough to hang back and wait, how dumb would this guy have to be to—

"Silver Four to Base. Reached anomaly. All Code Shelby Units confirmed alive at target. Anomaly appears to be a playground at grid reference TT-46. Secondary Anomaly discovered. There is an intact corpse outside the playground. It appears to be highly energetic. My suit is registering between four hundred and five hundred TEM. Cannot approach. Will observe until further orders received."

The scout gave his report to one of the dogs, who nodded and ran back to base. Truth felt a little odd, but, well, he wasn't breathing, was he? He was just focused on clearing out the explosive energy rushing around in him, and these days, he could go quite a long time without air. He also wasn't moving, lying facedown on the ground, eyes only open a smidge, in a pose that clearly showed he had been crawling out of the playground.

Fair play to the scout; if he had found a body in a similar state that was radiating lethal amounts of high-energy cosmic rays, he would have stayed the hell back too. Especially at Level Zero. He'd never worked with scouts, but he had heard they were a smart, cautious bunch. Seemed the rumors were true.

Still. Not good. Last thing he wanted was more company. What was that suit? He had never seen anything quite like it. It was a bit like orbital drop armor but clearly built to be used by a Level Zero. Was it some kind of hazmat suit for energy voids? It would be smart to build things like that, but he hadn't the faintest idea how it was done.

The scout looked around, falling back until he was tucked into the corner of a nearby building. Maintaining line of sight but keeping out of sight himself. Sneaky. Smart. Truth had zero confidence in being able to rely on the Blessing of the Silent Forest to vanish and escape. But he would have to do something, fast.

He had been found. They were coming for him.

CHAPTER 17

INTERDEPARTMENTAL RIVALRY

Truth did all he could. He lay facedown in the dirt and tried to clear as much of the explosive energy as he could while, as a precaution, sneaking in a long, slow, silent breath. Who knew when he would take another?

The strange dogs scattered themselves around the perimeter of the playground, not willing to test the interior. Truth didn't know how dense the cosmic rays were in there, but he *had* noticed that he was picking up fresh doses of the flesh-shredding stuff as he lay just beyond the fence. Not a huge amount compared to before. Under other circumstances, he would consider it a prime, if testing, place to cultivate. Under the *current* circumstances, it made him wish he trusted his lungs and nerves enough to scream with frustration.

And if wishes were witches, we could all have a party. He would just have to deal as best he could.

Time drifted past. Truth admired the way his fifth aperture was filling up. Nowhere near full, of course, but the fact that it had reached halfway was . . . well, it was proof that someone, or more accurately, several people were interfering. This wasn't just fast. This wasn't even monstrous. This was, as far as anyone on this rock knew, impossible. No human body, no matter how well refined, should be able to adapt to that much energy this quickly.

It was a basic point of cultivation. Those endless rounds of cycling energy through the body didn't just fill your apertures. They tempered the body, got it more accustomed to enduring the harsh cosmic rays that were the basis of magic. It was why a Level One was so much physically stronger than a Level Zero—they had undergone that tempering. It might not be true body cultivation, but the difference was still that big. It was the basis of how elixirs worked, too—the medicines protected your body and the invisible internal channels that carried the energy from your skin to your apertures. It wasn't that elixirs held more energy; elixirs allowed you to *absorb* more energy.

Not this much energy, though. If there was a pill for this, it was made by special order by those ancient monsters at the top of the alchemy towers. Though at this point, his fear and reverence for such beings was . . . greatly diminished. They might be able to slap the top off a mountain, but so what? They would only ever be powerful in this, lowest realm. He still had to be cautious of them, certainly. But afraid?

He felt a little knot of high-energy particles try to burn through his spinal cord, right up near the base of his skull. He quickly suppressed them and tried to wear them away with cultivation, but the Nine Worms couldn't be anywhere, and they certainly wouldn't be rushed. The energy flowed through him as quickly as he could manage, but it wasn't exactly fast.

Yes, under the circumstances, he could admit to being afraid of those old monsters. He was also afraid of dogs that needed to mark their territory, organ harvesters with enchanted saws, most demons of any power . . .

Oh, hell, he had Thrush's summoning token on him. That must be utterly annihilated. He would see if he could resummon the demon later. Hopefully, he hadn't come to any harm. The Tongue was looking down-right cheerful as it bathed in the energy pouring into the first aperture. Understandable. The core of the blade was a fragment of a true angelic weapon. This level of cosmic energy might be lethal to him, but it was mother's milk to the sword.

"Base to Silver Four. Maintain observation. Red Squad is being deployed to secure the Primary Anomaly Site. Retrieval team is incoming to recover the Secondary Anomaly. The Secondary Anomaly can only leave with them. If any other force attempts to acquire the Secondary Anomaly, you are ordered to take all necessary action to prevent their success. This includes destroying the Secondary Anomaly."

Truth could hear the relayed message. He couldn't hear the scout's response, but he imagined it was extremely colorful. A lone scout, who may or may not have the support of a pack of dogs, was expected to secure a lethally energetic corpse against a squad of elite soldiers.

"Sure. Yeah. No problem. Destroy the body? How exactly do I do that without blowing myself up? Incidentally, these suits are the only thing keeping us alive, so how long do you reckon I can keep my jersey clean in the scrum?"

Truth understood the scout's frustrations. He sympathized with them. What working stiff hasn't been there? But since he was the "corpse" to be hauled away, he did have a few *minor* concerns. Starting with: who were these guys, exactly? Starbrite? The Jeon Army? Some specially trained forces from some top clan or reclusive family?

Not that he could do much about it. Just . . . try to keep ahead of the damage. Wait to be hauled away.

He couldn't keep track of the time. The sun hadn't risen yet, nor was the sky lightening. Which, given it was summer, meant that it must be either the middle of the night or just before dawn. Good time for running ops.

Truth's ears were sharp enough to pick up the footfalls of the squad closing in. They weren't being particularly sneaky. Sounded like at least a squad. There was a series of whistles and clicks. He heard the dogs move around. "Identity confirmed." Sounded like one of those enchanted dogs. Must be verifying the relief squad.

"That the Second Anomaly?"

"Yes, Sergeant."

"Anything that wasn't in your report?"

"No, Sergeant. All quiet."

"Any change in the energy levels?"

"I didn't get close enough to check after the first time, Sergeant."

There was a grunt. A few seconds later, Truth saw a pair of silvery boots in front of his nose.

"Reading at 452 TEMs. It's jumping around a lot, mostly higher." A different voice this time.

"Still lethal. Approach the Primary Anomaly. Stop if it reaches ninety percent of the suit tolerance. The rest of you, set up around the perimeter of the playground. Check the buildings. If the interior is safe, use them for cover." The sergeant did an admirable job of making this all sound crushingly routine.

"Sergeant, I can't get any closer. The second I try to step past the Secondary Anomaly, the levels jump to 520 TEMs, and if I lean in, it jumps to more than 700. At a guess, the energy levels in the playground exceed 1,000."

"Sounds like a 'not us' problem, then. At least no one will run off with the site. Heh." The sergeant thought he was funny. Horrible.

There was another series of clicks and whistles. There was a response, then—

"HOSTILE! HOSTILE!"

"RED SQUAD, ATTACK!"

There was no sudden hiss of needlers or crackle of spells. There was, however, a lot of screaming. Steel crashed against steel, and he could hear the wet *chunk* sounds he knew were a blade parting flesh. Almost immediately afterward, there were screams. It seemed Truth had guessed right. The energy vacuum there was intense. Everyone, even those who couldn't cultivate, had picked up a tiny amount of energy just by walking around the city and eating the food. The pain as it left the body was, apparently, enough to make an elite soldier beg for death.

It was over fast. In a fight where even a superficial wound could be fatal, what could it be but fast? There was the sound of feet running off and the screams of the wounded.

"Shit! Shit! Sergeant's down, Corp."

"No shit. Any of the dogs make it?"

"Uh . . . yeah, one of the code—"

"Grab the fucking dog and bring it here, asshole!"

Truth heard some muffled noises. "Red Squad to Base. Encountered hostiles in the Dead Zone. Not sure who they are, but they have armor like ours. We drove them off with losses, but some escaped alive. We are down to five effectives and ten severely wounded. Recovery team isn't here yet. No damage to the Secondary Anomaly or—"

There was a different sort of *chunk* noise. "*Deploy to Base, top speed.*" The words came out in a gasping wheeze. More hissing and thuds. Sounded like metal tips hitting concrete.

"Squad Two reports they aren't able to break contact. It's going to be an extraction under fire, Sergeant." Different voice this time, still speaking Jeongo.

"All right, grab the body and shove him in the sack. Any ID on the ops?"

"None, Sergeant. Their armor looks kind of like ours, though. Ah . . . both sets of armors."

"Prager. It's been a couple of hours and we already have a three-sided fight."

"Four, Sergeant. Squad Two is fighting those lizard things."

"The lizards could be working with these guys. Let's not invent enemies. Any reason you haven't bagged this guy yet, Private?"

"Any time I get close to the body, the energy readings spike. I don't know how we can get him in the bag."

"Oh, fer—! Look, dumbass. The head is the furthest point from the playground, right? And he has hair, right? Do you see where I am going with this?"

"Sorry Sergeant, but . . . no."

"How did you get through potty training, let alone basic? You still wearing diapers, Private? Watch and learn."

A rough hand grabbed Truth's hair and dragged him away from the playground. The relief was immediate. Without the constant bombardment of fresh high-energy particles, his cultivation was able to make immediate progress in cleaning up the damage. It would take a long time to fix everything, but at least he wasn't trying to patch the boat in the middle of the storm.

"Heavy bastard. Kowalski, Ren, you two lend a hand. He's heavy."

There was the sound of something unzipping.

"Lay the bag out next to him and lift him in?"

"Works."

He was grabbed under the arms and by his feet. "What's your guess? Bum or spy?"

"What?"

"He doesn't look like he's from Jeon, and he's muscly as hell. So, he's either a laborer or a soldier. And he's dressed like a bum, so . . . bum or spy?"

"He could be from Jeon."

"Nah, with a forehead like that? And when was the last time you saw someone so bulky around here?"

"On my mother's grave, if the two of you don't shut up and get him bagged up, you will be going in the bag with him." The sergeant's voice was urgent. "We need to be clear *now*."

"Sergeant?"

"We have eyes on us. I can't see them, but they're there."

Truth was jammed in and the bag was zipped up. Interesting material—he could feel some of the residual energy on him bouncing off the inside of the fabric and hitting him. Could it be related to the suits? This really wasn't his area of expertise. The bag was lifted off the ground. The ride out was jolting and profoundly uncomfortable. He didn't let it distract him. Every second he could clear out more energy was a second closer to safety.

There was another series of hissing *chunk* noises.

"CONTACT LEFT, CONTACT—"

There was a rushing noise this time, it didn't sound like human feet. A different sort of hissing. From an animal, perhaps. Or lizards. A few moments later—

"Clear." A new voice this time. He had never been so popular in his life.

"We still have contact with that other squad. Privates Blue and Yellow, take the lizards and draw them east. We'll take the package to evac. Exfil per Plan C on your own."

"Yes, sir!"

Sir? Was he being hauled away by an officer? Would this meteoric rise never end?

"Let me save you a trip."

"Contact!"

"LOWER YOUR WEAPONS NOW! It doesn't have to be like this. We're all pros. We're just after the package. You are surrounded and out-numbered. Don't be stupid."

"Yeah, I'm surrounded and outnumbered, and I've got a bottle of Hellfire Corrosion in the bag for just this situation. We drop the bag, and all that anyone gets is sludge."

"Guess I'll be unlucky, then."

"You want to find out what happens when a high-energy anomaly gets hit with a liter of Hellfire Corrosion in a null-magic zone? 'Cause I'm guess-ing it's pretty spectacular."

"Mmm. Let me clear up some confusion for you." The voice sounded unbothered. "I'm not a merc. I'm not some ancient family's hidden force. You are facing the Army of Jeon here, son, and we really will shoot you and pick up the pieces afterward. You brought crossbows. So did we. You got snipers trained on you now who will put a bolt through your brainstem if you get even slightly funny with me. There is no way you walk out of here with the package. You hear me, son?"

There was a pause.

"Well. This is awkward. We're Team Seven, from Internal Security."

There was another, longer pause.

"Not to change the subject, but do you hear hoofbeats?"

"Ah, shit."

"CONTACT FRONT! CONTACT FRONT!"

Truth didn't know whether to laugh or cry. They were in the early stages of what looked to be a truly global war, the apocalypse was breathing down everyone's neck, and now a civil war was breaking out in the government.

Was this what would happen *every time* he visited a friend?

CHAPTER 18

DESIRABLE MAN

There was a long silence, as both sides tried to determine if the other was bluffing. In a situation where any tear in their suits might be fatal, talking things out was definitely the better choice. Of course, there was only one "Secondary Anomaly," which meant that somebody's boss was going to be pissed.

I wonder if they are literally attacking each other within the government yet. Seems like bad timing, what with a major war on. Also, somebody needs to shoot whoever designed their armor. If it can't hold up against a freaking crossbow bolt or beastcrafted lizards, it's not armor. Call it a survival suit or something but not armor. My old spell armor could take a needler to the faceplate without chipping the paint, let alone denting.

The Secondary Anomaly once known as Truth Medici only listened with half an ear. He was discovering that just because you had suppressed and cultivated away the most energetic fragments of the cosmic energy, that didn't mean you got all of it. There were minute traces left in the tissue, bone, even in the blood. And those minute traces were subtly weakening and sickening whatever they touched. He would never have noticed if he hadn't been so utterly devoted to his body cultivation. The horror of missing such a tiny thing, leaving such a devastating hidden wound in his body, made his guts clench.

Just what the hell is this stuff? Cosmic rays, sure, and I always knew that cultivating in the daytime was a bit more intense than at night, but this seems crazy. Everyone would die if this was normal. Was it because I was literally too close to the sun? Punishment from the Rough Patron or some other aspect of the sun?

"I don't suppose you have your badge with you?"

"Did you bring your Army ID?"

He could imagine the look they were exchanging.

"I can't help but notice that my top-secret, state-of-the-art armor looks uncannily like yours," the voice from the Army said.

"I was about to ask where you got your armor from. Given that mine comes from an Above Top-Secret code-name-controlled R&D program."

Truth wasn't ready to risk rolling his eyes just yet, but he really, really wanted to.

"Message our superiors? Or walk out together?" This from the Internal Security agent. Understandable that he would want to compromise, Truth felt, what with the Army getting the drop on him.

"I am not sure how the brass would react to a joint venture with Internal Security. *I* will report. You might as well grab a seat, because you aren't going anywhere for a while."

"I think we'll stand, thanks."

Truth wouldn't have sat down either. Apparently, the Army wasn't ready to push the point, because it went quiet again. Truth used the time as best he could, trying to clear out the high energy stuff. Had to stop the urgent problem before getting to the hidden danger. Hidden danger wouldn't matter if, picking an example at random from many, many, similar examples, his heart valves burned into a corroded mess of cancerous flesh while still inside his chest.

It's times like this that make you appreciate the little things. Like blinking. I mean, I could probably blink. Seventy percent sure I could blink. Seventy percent on at least one eye being able to blink one time. I'm just worried something might be destroyed in the process.

There was a murmur and some quiet clinking noises. Truth wasn't sure what that was about.

"Good news!" The voice was from the Army guy. His announcement was met, seconds later, by a number of loud hissing noises, some whistling noises, and a series of meaty *thunk*s. Truth was dropped on the ground. Luckily, there was no Hellfire Corrosive liquid or whatever it was called in there with him. It was a weak bluff, under the circumstances.

"The good news is that reinforcements arrived." The Army guy's voice was urbane. "All right, don't even bother cleaning up. Just grab the package and hoof it to Extraction. These guys had some beastcrafted lizards around, so keep an eye out."

"Mark Three Thunidz?"

"Can't say I keep up on what IS is buying for warbeasts these days." The deceptive urbanity of the voice was starting to get a little eerie. Truth felt his bag get picked up. "Get moving."

"Sir? What kind of opposition is waiting outside the dead zone?"

"Everyone and their cousins. The Army is going to provide what cover they can, but expect to get ambushed both on our way out and at the extraction point. At the very least, Starbrite PMC took off their wool. The wolf is in plain sight. Get moving."

"Yes, sir!"

They moved off quickly. Truth could hear a lot of boots around him. The advantage of an official army, right there. You could throw a lot of bodies at a problem. They must be limited by the number of suits they could equip soldiers with.

No cross chatter now. The soldiers would be keeping their head on a swivel and their ears open. They had the perfect recent example of the dangers of an ambush. Anyone selected to investigate a lethal void of magic would have a brain on them. Sounded like those brains were being put to good use. Rocking back and forth, Truth slipped into a fugue, focusing on clearing out the danger.

There was some shouting along the way. Definitely some jostling here and there. He'd leave a damning review. No harm done. Everyone was keen not to damage the prize. He just kept right on working through it all. Which is probably why he didn't explode when they crossed the border of the dead zone.

Truth had been concentrating, quite hard, on keeping himself sealed up. First to resist the impact from the sun, then to keep the void from ripping the magic out of him, and finally to keep the little high-energy particles from burning out of his skin, bouncing around the bag, and entering from somewhere else. He didn't have the available brainpower to wonder what would happen when 'normal' magic levels were restored.

Which was a pity. Particularly since he had invested so much effort into keeping his nervous system intact. Including his pain receptors.

Speaking metaphysically, the energy from outside was now pushing in, not pulling out. This threw him off balance, which resulted in a cascade of destabilization. Ripples of uncontrolled energy shot through his body, causing chaotic damage as they went.

The vigorous energy bounced merrily along the axions, crackled between the branches of the dendrites like little lightning bolts, and rooted itself contentedly in the synaptic end bulbs. They carelessly poked holes as they went, but that was just their funny little way. As was leaving the area around the holes in an excited, energetic state. Over and over and over again, across and through every nook and cranny of him.

When Truth was once again capable of coherent thought, he concluded that the total amount of energy inside of his flesh had not increased; it was just shaken up again. His last few hours of cultivation weren't wasted since he was still alive, but his efforts to confine the energy in more-manageable pockets were.

"FREEZE! ON THE GROUND! COMPLY! COMPLY!"

Truth recognized the sudden ripping noise—needlers were being used. A lot of them. There were some wooshes and high-speed buzzing. Firebolt fetishes, perhaps. Those were less commonly used in Jeon, as they were much shorter-ranged and far less versatile than needlers. They did, however, have the virtue of shooting a bar of superheated plasma directly into someone, which was a quick way to end fights up close.

"Shields!"

There was a thrumming noise, then a sound like hail on a tin roof. Someone must have deployed a riot barrier or portable warding spell or something. Truth was busy "enjoying" a preview of severe arthritis of the hand, wrist, and feet. Then something shifted, and his ribs were added into the mix.

Ribs don't have joints! What kind of sadistic God would allow arthritis of the ribs?!

There was a squeal of tires and a number of loud crashes.

"GO GO GO!" There was a sudden clattering sound, surrounded by the sound of wind rushing through leaves.

Oh, I know that sound. Heavy needler, but it's loose on its mount. Must have damaged some part of the talisman, or it wouldn't be vibrating nearly so bad. Hmm. Loading into an armored personnel wagon?

There was some jostling, doors slamming, a piercing shriek of spinning tires. Then another shriek, this time like some great bird or demon. Or, quite likely, a demon with bird characteristics. *Aamon has an owl's head and wolf teeth in its beak, right?*

There was silence inside of his head. Now that he thought about it . . .

System?

System?

There was no reply.

Truth was torn—he really couldn't spare the attention to examine his soul, but he also desperately wanted to see what happened. He dithered back and forth, and decided to risk a quick glance. He shouldn't have bothered— it was too short a moment to see anything, and the second he let up on the energy, it bolted out of his control again. Swearing, he painstakingly fought back to a stable place. If he could keep it going for long enough, he would process all the energy. It would just take time.

There was a sudden jostle. A heavy thud echoed through the wagon. "Prager! Was that an iron ball or something?"

"Looks like some kind of mass-launcher fetish. Squad C . . . got 'em! They might be able to recover whatever it is."

"Damn. One damn thing after another is what it is. Who throws a rock? Or chunk of iron or whatever?"

"I mean . . . it's basically a huge needler, right? Just worse. At everything."

"Exactly. Why build something that does something . . . OH, SHIT! Contact the escort; tell them to examine the impact on the side of the wagon!"

"Shit. SHIT!"

There was a loud pause, something shouted out a window that Truth couldn't make out.

"The wagon's tagged! Some kind of potion; we don't know what it does. We are changing to Plan C. Head for the underground garage."

The wagon rushed and jostled through the streets. Truth idly wondered what had happened to all the other traffic. This was Harban. There wasn't a rush hour, exactly, just periods when the traffic jam was slightly runnier.

"Grab the package. Move, MOVE! We are gone in thirty seconds."

Truth felt his bag get roughly picked up and hauled around. There were tire squeals all around. Decoys? Probably. He was roughly tossed somewhere, then there was a loud slamming noise.

Did these fuckers just shove me in the trunk? I have seen and done legendary things, and I wind up in a body bag in the trunk of a carriage in an underground garage. I'd say I'd come full circle in life, but, just speaking my truth here, this would have been a fancy *death back in the day. And I couldn't afford* fancy.

The carriage also peeled out, based on the sound and sudden smell of tire smoke. A few seconds later, he was hit with a new smell—sewage. They must have found, or made, a dry tunnel to use. The scope of this was already huge, yet somehow, he felt like he had underestimated it. Somehow.

The carriage came to a halt. He was carried up what felt like a few flights of steps, through some doors, and then he was hit with the unmistakable smell of a hospital. A door opened, there was a rasping noise, and his bag was placed on a table. The table slid, and the door shut behind him.

Truth would have laughed himself sick if his toes were not each reporting a unique sensation, one that added texture and variety to the commonly used word *agony*.

It was a nice, quiet, cool place. One that was well shielded from cosmic rays, he noticed. Perfect. He would take the time to heal. However long that was. Because sooner or later, they would want to do an autopsy.

CHAPTER 19

RAT DOCTOR

The morgue was not nearly as quiet as Truth had hoped. He had never stuck around the bodies he made. He had certainly never paid attention to the noises they made once they were dead. It wasn't so much that it was creepy. It was that it was *inexplicably* creepy. Why was it noisy in there?

There was a boom he could hear all the way in his drawer, as well as a tangible shake. Bombardment, terrorism, something like that. Sure sounded like a civil war was breaking out. If it wasn't, if it was all for control of the "Secondary Anomaly," he could only imagine the utter bloodbath taking place around the "Primary Anomaly." They would be going in with crossbows and steel blades. Nasty work.

Not often you feel lucky to be in a morgue. Truth wasn't a traditionalist in most things.

Must be why no one has turned up for the examination. Wherever this place is, it's being bombed. Worse, I'd bet cash there is some insane dealmaking going on to get access to the autopsy. Either inserting their own people or at least having observation rights.

Not that he was rushing them. Every extra moment to get things under control was appreciated. Now that he wasn't being jostled, he could make some real progress. At the very least, he could stop the random pain. Get his nerves all working properly. The absurd spikes of energy could be wrangled into place.

Did he feel safe enough to try and run Cup and Knife? He thought it over carefully but decided not to. Just too much random energy popping off inside of him, and too much of it was "sneaky," hidden in his tissues and silently becoming a long-term problem.

How long had it been since he crawled out of the playground? Had to have been quite a few hours. You lose track of time when you are in screaming agony and stuck inside a fancy body bag. Just one of those little things that remind you to wear a watch. Well, if nothing else, it helped him stay focused.

The explosive energy was all getting stowed away. Once it was processed through his apertures and pacified, the energy was sent back out into the rest of the body. The orderly power helped push out the dangerous stuff and shove it into the cultivation cycle, repeating the cycle of purification and pacification. Any excess power built up in his flesh, waiting to be processed by the Meditations into an ever-stronger superreal body.

I could probably talk now. Maybe sit up, if I was careful about it. Not that I'm going to be moving a single muscle until I have to.

As a body cultivator, Truth was keenly aware of every nook and cranny of his body. He was therefore unable to say he ached in places he didn't know existed. He knew all about those places. It was a remarkably varied tapestry of hurt. He wasn't going to push moving until he had to. He was in no rush. No rush at all. Well, he was, but he was just going to—

The door banged open. *Figures.*

"I'm sorry, Senior."

"That's a start, Junior, but we both know you are sorry to be here with me, not sorry that I have been strong-armed into this moronity."

Wait. I know that voice.

"If there was literally anyone better available, I promise you, we would have—"

"They aren't *better*, boy. They are *better at this*. *This* being an autopsy. Quite literally any medical examiner would do a better job analyzing the body for cause of death and the like."

"I can't speak to that, Doctor. But I can say that I'm going to clear out of the room before that bag opens. The energy leaking through it is already enough to make me worry about my health."

"As you should." This time, the creaky old voice sounded serious instead of waspish. "Eat a lot of dark, leafy greens. Spinach, broccoli, kelp. If you have a source for it, red meat. It's probably too late to take potassium tablets, but it couldn't hurt. And then you must cultivate. As many hours of the day as you can. Cultivate and drain the energy from your flesh."

"Thank you, Doctor. May I pass on your words to the recovery team?"

"Both of the survivors, you mean? Yes."

"It . . . wasn't quite that bad."

"Junior, I don't care even a tiny bit how many of your thugs died. I care that you brought a damn war to my damned hospital!"

"Again, I am so sorry. But there really wasn't anywhere better."

There was a snort, then the sounds of people moving around the room. "Yes. Tell them. Tell everyone. Once upon a time, in the ancient days of two months ago, it was common knowledge. Any intelligent spirit could give you the same advice. Now? Now I can barely find one that still functions."

The younger voice had gone silent.

"Oh, get out," the waspish voice snapped.

"Senior . . . I must set up the recording talismans."

"Junior?"

"Yes, Doctor?"

"Clench your teeth."

There was the sound of a heavy slap and someone falling on the floor.

"You have been going on and on about how highly energetic this anomaly is. You *just* got told how to treat your acute energy poisoning! But you still want to 'supervise' the autopsy I didn't want to do in the first place? Glad to see your balls are working fine. For now."

"I have my orders, Doctor."

"You are a Level Three ant who thinks his gang is scary. Piss off. If your bosses don't like it, they can come down here and do the damn autopsy themselves."

"General Mortenson—"

"General Mortenson can tell me how his daughter is doing in track and field. I hear she got third place in the last varsity meet. Nice of her to send a card celebrating *to the doctor who cured her paralysis, you incompetent, insignificant boob!* Do you know how many people are suffering and dying right now, in this very hospital, RIGHT DAMN NOW? DO YOU KNOW HOW MANY BODIES ARE GOING INTO THESE BOXES BECAUSE I'M WASTING MY TIME DOWN HERE INSTEAD OF SAVING LIVES?"

"Senior—"

"One more word. Just one. See what happens. You don't even need to say the whole word. Just open your mouth."

There was silence once more. Then footsteps, followed by the click of a heavy door shutting. A few seconds later, there was an extraordinary sound, like metal being smashed.

"Bastards!"

He definitely knew that voice. Well. This wasn't ideal.

The drawer opened. The tray was pulled out. The bag unzipped. Truth pressed a finger to his lips.

"If you make a scene, Dr. Sun, I can't guarantee there will be any survivors left for you to save."

Truth thought it said a lot that the undying menace masquerading as a doctor was still wearing his sandals, baggy pants, and loose, wide-sleeved jacket. No need for scrubs at his level, apparently. Truth would have worn at least an apron to an autopsy. Perhaps that was the difference between him and a real professional.

The doctor sat on the exam table he hadn't smashed into scrap. Truth sat on the edge of his shelf. The doctor glaring, Truth just looking back.

"Somehow, calling you an Anomaly feels right."

Truth nodded. "Yep."

"Just *Yep*?"

"Yep."

"Care to explain what the hell happened tonight?"

Huh. Didn't see that tack. He was banking on subtle threats or concealed panic buttons getting jabbed. Maybe even an instant attack. He was prepared to play along. His cultivation was still running. Every minute spent talking was a minute closer to being combat-capable.

"Sure. I was in the Ghūl nest in the slums—"

"You were *what?*"

"In the Ghūl nest in the slums. I was just dropping by to visit. You would not believe how many of them there are right now. Or the sculpture they made."

"You just . . . dropped in on the Ghūl."

"Yep."

"And they didn't tear you apart."

"Nope."

"Why?"

"Religious reasons, I believe."

Dr. Sun looked like he was seriously reconsidering violence as an option.

"Religious reasons."

"Very religious people, the Ghūl. In fact, they hardly do anything else *but* be religious. Don't ask me to explain the theology, because I don't know. Anyhow, I was up there when I saw the anti-theists' attack go off."

"Nothing to do with you, I suppose."

"I understand why you might think I was involved, but honestly, I'm innocent on that count. My spell-breaker magic is kind of the inverse of how theirs works."

"Not what our analysis concluded."

"Not saying it wasn't modeled on their tech. Just runs on the opposite lines."

"Mmm. So. You were innocent of the worst terrorist atrocity in world history, but you were hanging out with dozens—"

"North of a thousand," Truth corrected helpfully.

"Of Ghūl? There are thousands of Ghūl in the city?!"

"Yep." Truth gave a fairly accurate recounting of how he helped stop the spread of the dead zone, how he investigated inside, and how devastated he felt seeing it all. He wasn't trying to gain sympathy. It was just the truth, so why not tell it?

"So, what happened to create the anomaly?" The old man's voice had gone a little softer. Not soft, but softer. There was something in his eyes that hadn't been there when they had battled. Truth wasn't quite sure what. The old monster wasn't that sloppy.

"Me."

"You created the anomaly?"

"Yeah."

"Just . . . *yeah* again? Is this something you can *yeah*?"

Truth nodded firmly. "Yeah."

"Your teachers must have loved you."

"I'm not entirely sure they were capable of love. In retrospect, I don't think they even loved themselves."

Dr. Sun gave him a weird look. "Not the kind of observation I would expect from Hell Prince."

"It should be, if you think about it. The various propaganda departments have been very clear about my skill sets. Honestly, I was amazed to learn how capable and accomplished I am."

"Bugs you?"

"No." Truth thought about elaborating, but it was too much. He really didn't give a damn. He just shrugged instead.

"You created the anomaly."

"Yeah."

"*How*?! What is it, exactly?"

"Mechanically? I don't want to say. But I just . . ." Truth groped for words to express a feeling that could only have existed in that singular moment. "Look, I'm guessing you have been in a situation where there are just way too many people dying and triage is only going to get you so far."

"Oh, yes. Dozens of times." The doctor's voice was soft, his body quite still.

"And at some point, you just wanted to scream in rage. You just wanted to scream out that maybe you can't save them all, but this one, the one right in front of you, is going to live."

"Hundreds of times. Thousands."

"Well. That's what I did. The whole area got killed because of bullshit logic, the whole planet is going to lose most of its population out of, essentially, spite and nepotism, and I decided . . . not here. Not in this one spot. There will always be cosmic energy here. There will always be magic. Life. A single ray of light in the dark, no matter what."

He couldn't puzzle out what was in the doctor's eyes. He was certain Dr. Sun hated his guts. It wasn't all hate, though.

"A single ray of light. A literal beacon of hope."

"Yes." Truth nodded. "Did you check what I said about the mutilated souls? Starbrite's swearing-in ceremony and all that?"

"Oh, yes."

"And?"

"You were telling the truth."

"Did you do anything with that information?"

"I'm not in the System personally. But other than that? No."

Truth shook his head. One of the most earth-shattering revelations in the planet's history, and the doctor could just shrug it off. It seems that it didn't matter.

"You understand what's going to happen soon, right? Mutilation is only the first step. The next is the collection. He's going to start his harvest."

"Yep." The doctor's grin was quite nasty in its own right. "Was obvious once you knew what to look for. Millions are going to die. Tens of millions. Hundreds of millions, maybe. At this point, I can't even calculate the carnage."

"And you did nothing?"

"Everyone knew, boy! Everyone who mattered! Which, despite being Level Seven and the best damn doctor in the world, was a list of people that didn't include me. Did you know there is a second category of employment in Starbrite, other than the usual tiers? You can become an affiliate member. No access to the System Astrologica, but you get most of the other benefits and paid in wen. Strictly for members of very, very elite families. They all knew. For years now."

"Then why do it? Why do something so dumb?" Truth demanded.

"It's not dumb. It makes complete sense. Their own juniors and servants will be perfectly fine. It's just everyone else who will die."

"Letting Starbrite clear out the competition."

"Exactly."

"And the response of the legendary, all-time best person who would definitely not delight in keeping someone alive and in agony indefinitely, Dr. Sun?"

"I thought it was inhuman. Then I thought it was very human. Then I laughed myself sick, because I no longer knew what a human was or even what they looked like. I gave up on humans. I gave up on being a human. I became a Rat Doctor instead."

CHAPTER 20

VETERINARY PRACTICE

Truth wasn't quite sure how to process that. Other than "Go, Rats?"

Dr. Sun laughed bitterly. "Don't give yourself too much credit. You were just the final wet fart that knocked over the tower of bullshit. Things hadn't been adding up since long before you were born."

Truth nodded. Then shook his head. "Look, before we get into all of that, I have to ask—are you actually a doctor? Because when we fought, you came off like some kind of sadistic torturer."

"Oh, you really are young." The doctor shook his head. Truth was momentarily transfixed, watching the goatee and ponytail going in opposite directions. "I'm both."

"Both."

"Mmm-hmm. I don't keep track, but about ten years ago, I got an award saying that I was directly responsible for saving the lives of ten thousand people personally and my research saved millions globally. Part of the award speech was that three million was the lowest possible number, but the actual number was incalculable. That was at the time of the award, of course. It would be much higher now."

Truth just stared. Dr. Sun rolled his eyes.

"One of the few advantages of a very long life is that, if you are leading an active, vigorous, public life, your actions can snowball enormously. In my case, I developed certain potions that allow organs to be transplanted between patients without any fear of rejection. The technologies that came from that work, things like novel treatments for blood diseases, an understanding of certain biological mechanisms, and the like, are widely applicable. Essentially, I was able to remove the risk of spiritual contamination and the ensuing mutation risk from an extraordinary number of very ordinary illnesses. I won the Nephi-Xor Prize for that at twenty-seven. Youngest ever, a record that still stands."

He took a slow breath. "Not bad for a warmup. Since then, I have put most of my attention on obstetrics and gynecology. I won't bore you with the hundreds of tiny improvements I have made to spell-bowl technology, surgical procedures, testing, diagnostics, materials, alchemical interactions within patients, particularly within *pregnant* patients and their highly complex and changing bio-alchemical makeup, and that's not even a complete summary of what I achieved over the last seventy years. None of them were individually that significant, but I would say the cumulative effect knocked a solid five percent off the infant mortality rate in Jeon. Which, over *millions of births*, is a hell of a number."

The doctor's voice was very smooth. "And, not being a fool, I licensed the technology through a limited liability company established for that purpose. I am rich. I am, in all due modesty, the best doctor in the world. Everything I just said? Didn't include a HIGHLY active clinical practice. I can say, without fear of serious contradiction, that the world has been a very slightly better place because I live in it. I'm Level Seven, making me an elite anywhere. Even in the event of a magical collapse, I'm going to survive. Hell, thrive! I have the mind for it. And none of what I just said matters."

He cackled. There was a maddened edge to it that Truth recognized. "Not to the so-called *true* elites. I was just another hired hand."

Truth nodded. "You went to all the parties, knew all the right people; hell, you treated all the right people. Your network of contacts is the stuff of legends. But . . ."

"If I want a hospital built, no problem. If I want a research lab, no problem. Basically anything that requires opening their wallet, no problem. But ask them to do something that might affect their interests?"

"Or even reach out to you and let you know about a potentially fatal danger . . ."

"Suddenly, they don't even know me. Because they are scared. They are hungry, thirsty, petty little rats, distinguishable only by being fatter than the smaller rats." The doctor's grin was very wide. "It was that last little thing—I had always known they didn't give a shit about the patients. Hell, there were periods, decades, where I didn't either. But somehow, I always thought they gave a shit about *me*. I mean, if I'm not special, who is?"

Truth was going to make a crack about arrogance, but . . . "Fair."

"I think I had known for a while. The first time I was asked to keep a high-priority interrogation subject alive through enhanced interrogation, I was horrified. I refused, naturally. Same with the second, third, fourth, fifth times. But finally, I said yes."

"And then there was a next time. And it always got that little bit easier to say yes."

"Exactly. The day I realized they didn't even need to pay me, really, was a bad day. Most people don't get into medicine for the sheer love of keeping someone alive while their organs are individually dissolved in tuned acid. Something had to have made me want to hurt other people. Torture other people."

"Tuned acid?"

"Yes, not one of my projects, but some genius figured out that there are minute differences in the rate at which different organs dissolve in different acids. They therefore created a method to compute the correct composition for a given person's organs, on a per-organ basis, allowing for, well, tuned acid. Subject One's liver dissolves at X rate in Y pH acid, and so on."

"Best country in the world, right here."

"Credit where it's due—"

"No, no I don't think I will." Truth gently shook his head. "No credit for that guy."

Dr. Sun just snorted.

Silence pooled in the morgue. Eventually, Truth smiled and pulled them back on track. "Rat Doctor?"

"I was persuaded by your rat-based thesis. What little of it you explained and what of it I could deduce."

"Kind of you. I have spent most of my life developing it."

That got another snort. "How old are you exactly?" the doctor asked.

"I don't know. Around twenty or twenty-five."

"How do you not know about a five-year gap?"

"I was dead for a while."

Dr. Sun gave Truth a searching look.

"I'm being literal. I was dead. My head was smashed in, I was fully submerged in water, I had been shot by a heavy needler round. Dead. Well, you know what all that's like."

"Yes, but I'm the locus of an insanely sophisticated spell engine that requires the active support of hundreds of thousands of people. You blatantly aren't."

"How is that blatant? You don't know. I could have the support of millions!" Truth grinned. "Millions, I say!"

"Because we know our own. You seem to be a two-person system at best. Who's that with you, anyway? They are keeping real quiet."

"Eh? What do you mean?"

"I can see two . . . call it 'existences.' Lives with spiritual meaning. Is it a parasite or spiritual clone or something?" Dr. Sun pointed at Truth's waist.

"Oh. I . . . was scared to check on him. He's still alive?"

"Yes? More alive than most people?"

Truth laughed happily, as he gently reached into his shirt and pulled out Perks.

"Perks, meet the greatest living doctor. Dr. Sun, meet the greatest living snake."

"You have a pet snake?! How long have you had a pet snake for? Did you have a pet snake while we were fighting?"

"No, no, Perks is new-ish. Picked him up in the mountains, promised the owner I would find him a good home. Because, HOO BOY, am I a *bad* pet owner. Like . . . super bad. Not to talk myself down or anything, but I really feel like I'm just not fit to look after any sort of animal, let alone a fine snake like Perks."

Who did, in fact, look fine. Truth had extremely keen eyes, and he didn't see so much as a twinge of pain in how Perks was moving. Not a single mussed scale. Which, since Truth crawled out of the playground on his belly, should be impossible, right?

"Hey, doc, in addition to being the best at everything, are you also the best at being a vet? Because I'm actually worried about him."

"Why the hell would I know anything about snakes?"

"Why the hell do you have flying needles that reek of poison magic? Incidentally, don't think I'm going to let you skate past that *Magical engine makes me unkillable* thing."

"What skating? I'm just going to tell you to mind your own rotted business, Junior, and pass the damn snake. Can't be any harder to figure out than my third concubine."

"Your *who*, now?" Truth handed the snake over.

"Briselda, my third concubine. Lovely woman but very complex. Won't eat shellfish, but somehow, 'Oysters don't count.'" Dr. Sun's nimble fingers ran along Perk's flanks. Truth was sure whatever those sharp old eyes were seeing was more than skin-deep.

"I have heard a theory that mussels are more like fruit than fish," Truth ventured.

"Exactly what she said! The lychee of the sea! Now, have you ever eaten anything that tasted less like a lychee than an oyster?"

"Not sure I've ever eaten a lychee. If I have, I don't remember. How's Perks?"

"As expected, less complicated than Briselda, though very nearly as interesting. From what I can tell, your snake appears perfectly healthy. At the very least, I'm not seeing anything obviously damaged. If anything, I would say it's well on its way to being a demon."

"What?"

"Well, *demon* in the sense of a spirit native to this planet. High density of cosmic radiation, but I'm not seeing any signs of mutation or the like."

"That's impossible! He was in the anomaly with me."

"Was he really? Fascinating." Sun dove back into his inspection.

"No, not fascinating, alarming! That place damn near killed me! Be worried," Truth insisted. He didn't know why, but somehow, the thought of the doctor not taking his pet's problems seriously scared him. To the point where he was getting angry.

"Easy, easy. I've got him. I've already checked for . . ." Dr. Sun's voice trailed off. "It occurs to me that you probably don't have the language to describe the effects of high concentrations of cosmic rays and what those different sorts of energy mean. And mean clinically. When I say that he is perfectly healthy, I mean that I see no evidence of sickness, sickness demons, no bleeding, no wounds internally or externally, no obvious imbalance of the humors, and no hidden pockets of excess cosmic energy that could lead to mutation or tumors later."

The old man shrugged and gave the snake a little pat. "Looks fine. It looks like he's turning into a demon, which is generally a good thing. Give him a few thousand years, he might really be someone, assuming he can live that long. At the moment, he is just a very, very tough snake."

Truth felt the relief flood through him, and he sagged a bit. "Good. Good. I haven't known him for long, but I've become very fond of Perks." And now he had even more questions. Were snakes truly the chosen species? They did seem to pop up everywhere. Did Perks get special treatment from the Serpent in the Sun?

"Mmm. Reminds me of my second concubine. You, not the snake. She loved snakes. Said they were an inspiration to her."

Truth's ear snagged on the past tense. "She died?"

The doctor recoiled. "What a horrible thing to suggest! She's thriving, thank you very much!"

"So, why doesn't she like snakes anymore?"

"She spent six months on a witch-guided spirit journey where she lived as a snake in some ancient jungle. Got the whole thing out of her system, apparently. Now she's into pottery."

"Ah. I was about to ask if you wanted to adopt him."

"No." Dr. Sun gave him an unkind look. "The world is ending, and I have enough dependents."

"Ah. Damn." Truth really, *really* needed to find Perks a home. He couldn't imagine that taking the snake with him to kill Starbrite was any kind of a good idea. He didn't think Dr. Sun was lying about his accomplishments. Not by what Merkovah said about him, or the way they bigged him up on the news. Contrary to what he had seen, Dr. Sun apparently was a genuinely good person, with a genuinely nightmarish coping mechanism.

Hmm. And undying. HMMM.

"Your 'undying' thing going to survive the magical collapse?"

"Yep. And no, I'm not explaining it. Just . . . it runs on sacrifice, but I figured out how to make sure no one sacrifices too much."

Truth had guessed as much. Which worked for what he had in mind.

"So, I'm running a little experiment in encouraging people to be less shitty to each other. Altruism with benefits or something."

"Millions wouldn't believe you. I'm one of the masses."

"No, no. You just said you were special. I believe in you," Truth insisted.

"Of course you do; I'm extraordinary. You are a goddamn mass murderer on a nearly impossible-to-comprehend scale."

"Right, yes, let's make sure someone like me never comes into existence again, by changing the conditions that gave rise to me. I can be motivation, if you like."

"Boy, what the hell are you talking about?"

"Rat Doctor Sun, how would you like to leave the messy, smelly field of medicine and start your own religion?"

CHAPTER 21

HYPOCRITIC OATH

Boy, you are even crazier than I thought. And I thought you were batshit. The hell did they do to you?"

"Who?"

"Them. Those people. The ones who put all the worms in your brain."

Truth raised a finger to rebut, remembered the System, and, in a sudden burst of overwhelming guilt, turned his eye inward, trying to find that spot of nothingness that supposedly was the System. He had never really seen it before, but . . .

He didn't see it now, either.

He turned his attention back to the doctor. "Strictly speaking, the only one who put Worms in my head was me, but since I no longer really believe in free will, you will have to blame God by proxy."

That made the doctor blink. "Wait, you do actually have brain worms?"

"More like soul worms? They aren't entirely physical. Or at all physical. Honestly, I've never really tested them. Seemed unwise. Just to clear things up for you—I was sold a tonic secondhand by a vendor who could only verify that it contained none of the toxins he usually tested for."

Dr. Sun silently laughed. "Not the first time I heard that story."

"And in fairness to the vendor, it did work. But enough about me; let's talk getting your face on an icon. I'm thinking you keep the basic structure of Pragerism but present yourself as a sort of second coming or new prophet. You want to steal as much of that legitimacy as you can in the early days while being very clear that you are now the only source of truth and safety in this increasingly insane world."

"Oh, you're serious. That's tragic. Usually, mass murderers like to think of themselves as God or doing God's will. It does tie into your belief in predestination." The gray head shook mournfully. "I see. That's your excuse. The brain worms made me kill, torture, brainwash, sabotage, incite murder, and casually rob. How could you blame little old me? It was God's plan, enacted through brain-eating parasites."

Truth rolled his eyes at that. "I am quite clear that I am not God. As for doing God's will, a sincere commitment to that belief in predestination means that we are all doing God's will, all the time. Which is a *fun* thought when you play around with it a little."

"I'll pass."

"Wise choice. Mostly, I do the same."

There was a lull.

"Seriously, though, start a religion."

"Why?"

"Because religions don't really rely on any physical technology. It's literally all a head game. We both see the slum. We see the rats. But what's the solution? What's the way out? There isn't one . . . not for humans, or human-ish rats, anyway. The rats need to believe that it's okay to stick your neck out for a stranger, to help each other out in the expectation that you will be helped when you need it. They need to believe it's wrong to take more than you need while others are still needing. There needs to be the promise of the get-back, and the promise of punishment for misbehavior." Truth tapped the metal tray he was sitting on. It wasn't comfortable, but he still didn't like his odds walking.

"Now and in the world to come." Dr. Sun nodded quietly. "I see where you are going with this. Education is necessary, but more necessary is belief in something nobody actually believes in—human kindness. That there can be such a thing as a common good."

"Exactly! And you know what makes people believe things that, on first look, appear to be completely contrary to their interests?"

"Never one for the tithing basket, were you?"

"I donated a small fortune to the Church of Prager, actually."

"In the form of explosives?"

"Stolen jewelry. Which I destroyed minutes later. But let's not dwell on unpleasant things. Put your left hand palm up, slightly cupped, right at navel level. Right hand just above shoulder level, thumb and forefinger pointing up, other fingers curled in. Good. Now imagine you are explaining the evils of hospital billing to—okay, dial it back, dial it back two . . . three . . . eight notches. You know what? Imagine you are explaining why you like your toast a certain way. Let's forget hospital billing for the moment."

"Did you know we don't employ humans in that department anymore? Demons kept underbidding each other to work there. Eventually, they started paying the hospital." Sun's expression was not simply cloudy; there were thunderheads.

"Horrible. Someone should do something. Someone with name recognition. Immense public goodwill. Someone who has a measurable impact on the population level, which is going to be a real issue in a hot minute."

"I may have a god complex, but I'm not mad enough to think I actually am God."

"This and that are two different things." Truth shook his head firmly. "You don't have to be God. It's better if you aren't. You are the Prophet spreading the true word. One day, your maker will recall you to His side. Until then, you are doing as you have always done—serving God and saving His people."

"Why are you so on this? I know Incisive makes you play with people's minds, but why this *specifically*?" Dr. Sun's eyes narrowed.

"Wanna see a magic trick?"

"You fucking said what, boy?"

"A magic trick. I can make you furious in one sentence. I mean blindingly outraged. Against me and maybe many, many other people. Even though you can't rationally explain why you are so angry."

"Huh. All right."

"If it is in our power to prevent something bad from happening without thereby sacrificing anything of comparable moral importance, we ought, morally, to do it."

The needle was at his neck in an instant. Truth hoped it looked like he trusted the doctor, not that he wasn't able to react in time. Fortunately, the doctor did manage to recover himself enough to keep from puncturing Truth's throat and severing his spinal column.

"Of all the sanctimonious bullshit!"

"Is it?"

"You know damn well that people would take advantage! That the so-called moral person would just get screwed over."

"I do, yeah. But notice the sentence said *moral*, i.e., yourself, and not *ethical*, i.e., a rule for all of us."

"That's worse, not better."

"Well, what if we made it a rule? One for everyone, or at least everyone in the in-group. An ethical obligation, not a moral one."

Sun growled, his hand clenching the long needle. Truth watched the battle play out in his eyes. Sun was pissy, vindictive, arrogant, and actually as smart as he thought he was. He was putting things together. A lot faster than Truth had, which was irritating.

"You would need a powerfully compelling reason for something so irrational. God's command. Religious doctrine. It's not irrational; it is an act of faith, a miracle of God's creation and a sign of His infinite love for his children. Not all his children, obviously; that would be silly. But his love for those who have heard the truth and the New Revelation are eligible for all the blessings."

Truth was impressed. He had seen and done an awful lot to figure all that out, but Sun got there in a couple of sentences. The old doctor read it on his face and waved it away. "It's not a particularly new idea."

"A very old one, in fact. So's fire. Both still work. Universal empathy, maybe throw something in there about forgiveness, being cleansed of sin—the Pragerite Sin Eaters are serious business and an idea worth stealing. Basically unmaking the current world order by changing the minds of the people."

Sun looked at him a while longer, then started laughing. "You really are Hell Prince. You saw an apocalypse and thought, *Opportunity!*"

Truth spread his hands innocently. "What apocalypse? The old order isn't dying; it's just getting worse. Getting meaner and dumber for no good reason. They can't even decide on a survival strategy. Have you *seen* how many contradictory plans for the post-collapse world are swirling around?"

"Yes. I'm part of four of them. Five, in a minute."

"Oh? The people commissioning the autopsy have a bunker?"

"No, they are plan number three—mountain fortress. You are number five."

"Ah. Ticket off-world."

"Yes. For me, my concubines, children, grandchildren, great-grandchildren, in-laws that I don't mind, and ten thousand of my nearest and dearest friends."

"Ten thousand?!"

"I am very sociable, you miserable little scrote. I'm only bringing my closest confidants."

"Your damn immortality engine, you mean!"

"Which does make them very dear to me, as you might imagine." Sun beamed.

"I can't promise that. I'm not negotiating with you. I literally cannot. I have some confidence that the Shattervoid will evacuate me and a few others, but I have no idea if they were being honest about the mass population lifts. Frankly, I think they just wanted to motivate governmental-level entities to get in on the blood hunt."

Sun's smile dimmed. "Mmm. Hope for the best but expect the worst."

"Besides, why would I? You aren't being my new messiah."

"The hell is a messiah? But no, I'm doing you another favor. I'll consider the religion thing. There is something there. It would work with backup plans one and three."

Sun's face shifted slightly. The madness that he had been hiding leaked out a little. "Did you really think you could hide your condition from me? I've spent this whole conversation cataloging every little thing that's wrong with you. Boy, you are about to explode, and then the smear that's left is going to grow tumors and make a whole new generation of murderous shits."

Truth winced. He really had hoped he could hide it.

"Gonna fix me up?"

"I think you severely underestimate how much I hate you. And I really, truly do hate you. I know all kinds of bullshit gets blamed on you, but there is a lot that you are accountable for. Hell, just in that lobby fight, you must have killed a hundred men. I know for a damn fact you crashed that party barge and fed those people to the Ghūl. Who you apparently are comfortable enough with that you can wander through their nests! I am privately convinced there are at least four figures' worth of bodies hanging off you."

He was leaning in now, saliva flying. "Your petty morality. Your petty empathy. You are on the side of the rats, and you will wave that banner from a mountain of their corpses. You hate the people who made the world this way? You want to tear down the system? How many bodies are you willing to put on that? How much time do you spend hunting *them* instead of clearing out their foot soldiers?"

"Not enough and too much, respectively." Truth admitted quietly.

"Ever save a life? Even one *single* life?"

"Dozens."

Sun recoiled like he had been slapped.

"You. Saved people."

"Yes. In multiple senses of the word. Far, far less than I killed. But I did save some."

"Well, whoop dee fucking doo. A serial killer, a mass murderer, a hypocrite revolutionary with pretensions of a conscience. I'll play the hypocrite too. Why not? Won't even be the first time today. I do want that ticket off-world, after all. So, here's what I'm going to do. Nothing. I'm going to do . . . nothing."

"As I walk out the door."

"As you walk out the door. Your body cultivation is half-fried. All those spells you have built in to you? They aren't working right either. This building is already locked down by the Army, and Starbrite is on their way, if they aren't already here. They are sending Frobisher, I believe, and if I know Starbrite, he's bringing half the damn PMC with him."

"Ah."

"Yes. 'Ah.' You are on the side of the rats? Run, little rat. Run! Run and hide!"

CHAPTER 22

SNEAKING THE HARD WAY

Truth tried to think quickly. He could more or less guess where the old doctor's hate was coming from. He would hate him too if the situation was reversed. "I was in a body bag on the way in. Would your hatred extend to giving me directions out?"

"Yes." Dr. Sun had a wonderful set of teeth, Truth noticed. His "smile" was displaying almost all of them.

"Fantastic. Well. This has been . . ." Truth groped for a word, failed to find one, and decided that it had simply been. Maybe the doctor would take his advice. He couldn't force it, regardless. He directed his attention toward his various blessings. The doctor was right—they were going haywire with all the extra energy running through him. When he sorted all of this energy out, it would be a hell of a boon. Wasn't going to be anytime soon, though.

"Any chance of a cane or an IV stand to lean against? No, apparently not."

"It's a morgue. Generally, though not always, those things are not needed here."

Truth eased himself off the metal tray he had been sitting on. He could support his own weight. Good first step. Now to see if he could *literally* take that first step.

"Out of curiosity, did you ever consult on a bioweapons program?" Truth asked. He was leaning on the tray pretty hard, but his feet were mostly cooperating. It was sort of like learning to walk and operate heavy machinery at the same time. Doable, just not advisable.

"No, absolutely not. Bioweapons, you see, are *monstrously evil*. And I, according to several international awards, am not."

"Said the torturer's assistant. Ah, well. On the off chance I do die, or just . . . you know, generally, keep your eye out for an exciting new plague breaking out. Nothing to do with me, you understand." He made his way to the end of the tray, carefully turned the corner, then again, then started walking back down the other side. He was getting more coordinated. These few seconds weren't being wasted. "Let me tell you about something I found buried a meter underground behind a cheap restaurant in Confen."

Truth reached the wall, turned around, and tried to walk back without leaning on the tray. It was touch-and-go to start with, but he managed. He was reasonably stable by the time he reached the corner and made the turn. This time, he made for a desk three meters away. Just a few steps, but it felt like crossing a chasm.

Dr. Sun was glaring at him.

"I can see you want to demand to know if I'm telling the truth, but your ability to read my body in minute detail isn't showing any hint of my lying, and your brain can't think of any reason I would lie about this. After all, even if you did help me get out of the hospital, that wouldn't necessarily prevent other plague boxes from opening."

"Yes." The words ground out.

"Lots and lots of contingency plans, by lots and lots of people. Most of them wouldn't work to begin with, and all of them work at cross purposes." Truth made it to the desk. Victory. Next stop, the coatrack by the door. This was five meters away. Still. Needs must. "It's the truth. As complete and plain as I can manage."

"So, why tell me?"

"Because you are a man with a lot of family. A person with a lot of people he cares about beyond his family. And most importantly, you are the best doctor in the world. Apparently. Personally, I doubt you can squat or bench enough to make it as an ortho, but I guess for a medicine doctor, you are probably . . . fine."

"Boy, don't you go using those words like you know what they mean." Dr. Sun's eyes were hooded, but Truth could easily imagine them darting around, watching the connections in his mind come together. "Any idea why this . . . thing was made?"

"Lots. Nothing more than speculation, though. My two best guesses are that they are threats to defend against invasion or they will be used to fuel some grand sacrificial ritual. Guess number three, which is mostly based on my own prejudices, is that they are sheer spite and revenge, possibly on Starbrite's part."

That got another grunt out of the doctor. Truth had safely made it to the coatrack and examined his options. There was no way he was going to pass for a doctor, given how he looked. Not without Incisive and the Blessing of the Silent Forest. And a shower. And a change of clothes. He looked, in a word, exploded. Also . . .

"Am I emitting dangerous amounts of cosmic rays?"

"Dangerous-ish. Certainly any metal you hang around is going to be toxic for Level Zero people for a while. This whole body-storage array is completely contaminated and will need to be thrown out. Everywhere else in the room? Or this hospital? They will probably be fine unless they go around licking the doorknobs you turned."

"Fantastic. I assume this is trackable?"

"Easily."

"Double fantastic. Anything you can pass on about those creepy eyeless watcher-homunculi Starbrite has been deploying?"

"No, I'm in the dark on them too. Evil things."

"This day just gets better and better." Truth sighed and pulled on a windbreaker someone had left behind. He shambled over to the sink and gave his face a quick wash, ran his fingers through his hair, and got the dirt off his hands. "Best I can do for the moment, I think."

"Mmm. Ticktock, Hell Prince."

"Nah, I gave up on being a prince the day we first met. There's no future in it." Truth walked toward the door. He couldn't move above a slow walk, but he was steady on his feet. All the enforced stillness had let him patch up the worst of the damage. He could move.

"Oh? What do you see as a growth industry?"

"Well, if you manage to stop that plague, scrap merchant and subsistence farmer are looking pretty sweet. As is roving cannibal raider. *There's* a job with real possibilities for advancement. Look, you do you. I'm off to see a man about a job."

"Do tell."

"Got to get the other half of that ticket off-world, right?"

"What job are you asking for, then?"

"Ticket scalper. Almost as good as being a prophet." Truth eased the door open and slipped into the hallway.

The hallway was empty as far as the T-junction it terminated at. At the junction was a pair of hard cases, both in armor and carrying an impressive loadout of charms. Truth had a brief hope of stealing their uniform and using it as a disguise, but they weren't wearing the faceplates. The air had a subtly unpleasant feel to it. Simultaneously greasy and gritty. Some active magic effect. He couldn't figure out what it did.

He looked at his hands, then the rest of his body. He wasn't glowing or shooting sparks everywhere, so there was that, at least. An anti-glamour or anti-charm spell? It kinda-sorta felt like that, but also not really. He shrugged. Not his problem at the moment. His problem was that this hallway was an empty tube between him and two armed, armored guards. Guards that might currently have their backs to him but would certainly look around when they heard footsteps.

Stretch out with the foot, just skimming above the floor. Ball of the foot goes down, then, gently, the rest of the foot. Repeat with the other foot. One step at a time. No breath to betray him. One step at a time. Just like the old days. Everyone is bigger and stronger. Have to be sneaky. Have to just fade into the background and pretend you aren't even there.

One step, then another. Closer and closer. One of the guards picked up a charm and casually snapped it. Truth froze. The greasy, gritty feeling in the air suddenly intensified. There was a long moment, then the other guard nodded and pulled a little sheet of engraved metal from the harness on his chest. He gave it a couple of taps. The guards looked at it for a half-minute, then minutely nodded and put the bit of metal away.

Some kind of infiltration-detection system. That and a way to report in somehow. I don't recognize the talisman. Must be new.

Funny. He could see the logic in something that was looking for invisible or glamoured infiltrators. What kind of sneaky guy would walk down the hall in a windbreaker and his bare feet?

Truth didn't really remember which way he had come in from. Didn't matter in the immediate moment, anyhow.

The guards were wearing helmets and soft neck armor. Smart of them. Truth planted his feet and pulled his arm up and back, like he was holding an invisible ax. He called the Tongue to his hands, but rather than grab the hilt, he held it by the blade. He swung forward and down as hard as he could, letting his weight ride on the swing.

The pommel smashed into the first guard's spine, just below the helmet. The other guard started to turn, fast, much faster than Truth would have thought he could manage. He quickly grabbed the hilt of his sword, watching the guard's mouth open to yell. The Tongue punched through the open mouth, through the back of the throat, through the spine, through the soft armor, and into the wall behind the guard.

Not quite bloodless but pretty damned good. Truth gently keeled over and fell on the floor. That . . . had taken too much out of him. He needed a minute. He didn't have a minute. Silently groaning, he pulled himself to his feet. He looked at the two guards. They weren't remotely his size. He didn't even think he could fit into their pants, let alone their dainty little shoes. Didn't he have a change of clothes in his storage ring? He did!

A quick change of clothes later, pausing only to loot everything portable on the bodies and leave THE ANOMALY AND THE ARTIFACT BELONG TO THE KING! FREE JEON! carved into the wall. At this point, it was probably wasted effort, but every little bit helped. If nothing else, he could see it winding up the doctor. How did the old man plan to spin his escape? Truth shrugged. He really didn't care. He had a choice to make. Left or right?

There were no signs on the wall, but there were colored stripes. One going left, two going right. He went left.

Two more bodies. Working stiffs. Less important than a single ass hair to their bosses, but they would have killed me if they caught me. It's insane and the most normal thing in the world. Everybody needs to eat, and if someone is handing out food, they're the boss. And what the boss says, goes. And they defend the boss, because otherwise, how do they get the food? Not wondering where the food comes from in the first place.

He staggered down the hall, his sneakers somehow noisier than his bare feet were. He did his best not to touch anything. At the very least, the sneakers and the distancing should make it a little harder to track him. Hopefully. Maybe. Was he hearing . . . footsteps down the hall? From behind him. Seemed like he made the right choice about which direction to go, but it wasn't like the lights weren't on. Soon as whoever it was came around the corner, they would see him. There was an intersection up ahead. He tried to speed up.

The noise was getting louder. Lots of footsteps. Lots of boots on the ground. No chatter, though. Whoever they were, they were disciplined and focused on the job at hand. Could he run? His body screamed back, *Hell, no!* Nothing to do but push on.

He made the turn—it wasn't a hallway; it was a door. Locked. The Tongue licked out. Unlocked, and very unsubtly. He shoved into the room, closed the door behind him as carefully as he could. Lots of big tubs; he wasn't sure what he was seeing. Part of the laundry operation?

"Someone check that noise."

"Yes, sir."

Damn!

CHAPTER 23

WASHED CLEAN

Truth kept moving deeper into the room, eyes darting. Large plastic bins with little wheels underneath, filled with bed linens. Should be the laundry. Usually, that was a job for big talisman machines, but he wasn't seeing them. Did they send the laundry out to a commercial operation for cleaning? He vaguely remembered hearing that some places did that. For a brief, delusional moment, he thought about hiding in one of the bins and smuggling himself out with the rest of the laundry.

Hah. No. That wasn't possible.

He moved deeper into the room. It was both wide and long. On the ground, a snaking path had been laid out. The plastic bins were all queued up neatly on the path, winding back and forth through the room. He skipped the line, heading for the front and, presumably, an exit.

He could hear the door open behind him. They were being quiet, but he was listening carefully. He dropped behind the laundry bins and kept creeping forward.

"Sir? This door was breached. Looks like a cutting tool was used."

"Can you tell from which direction?"

"Sir?"

"Coming in or going out."

"No, sir. Just looks like the bolt was sheared, as was the latch."

"Understood." There was a pause. Now . . . just how many troops did whoever-this-was bring? Could he afford to split his group to check out a noise and a broken door?

"Kelso, Bu, Revi, Hoss, you check it out. Everyone else, to the morgue."

DAMN!

He tried to force his body to move faster. Yesterday, he could have crossed the whole room before the door finished closing. Today, he thought he might lose a footrace to a slug. Nothing to do but keep moving. Try to keep that long snake of bins between him and the hunters. He patted Perks, finding him in his usual place in his shirt. He had . . . a lot of questions about Perks right now, but it was also, clearly, not the time.

Shame Dr. Sun didn't want to adopt a snake. Truth thought the old monster would do a good job of looking after his noodly friend.

The door opened again, the hunters making no real efforts to be quiet. This was about speed, not stealth. Truth could visualize them splitting up, working in teams of two to cover the room quickly and thoroughly.

"Kelso, hit the lights."

There was silence. Were the lights out? Truth no longer really noticed the dark.

"Busted."

"Lights in the hall worked."

"And these are busted." Did they share a look, silently warning each other to beware of an ambush? He wished he could, but he wasn't optimistic. He wiggled between two bins, and through the gap, he could just make out a little flash of red. An exit sign? Maybe. Or a CAUTION—HIGH ENERGY CONDUIT sign, or something even less useful. It was a destination, anyway, and it was on the back wall. So, he started trying to make his way there.

The movement strategy changed. Rather than try and "race" down the alleys between the bins, he moved in bursts. Get between two bins, check the way was clear, cross the alley as fast as he possibly could, get back into concealment, rest, and reset to do it again.

It wasn't fast enough. They were closing in. Then—"CONTACT!" and the snap of a needler firing. "COVERING!" More fire. "Pop smoke! Pop smoke!" There was a burst of fine dust as an anti-concealment charm burst, outlining any hidden figures in shining dust. "Cease fire. Cease FIRE!"

The hell are they shooting at over there? Did someone else infiltrate? They were bombing the place earlier, so that's not a crazy idea.

"Hoss, report!"

"It was a goddamn rat."

The door smashed open at the back of the room. "HOSS! REPORT!"

"IT WAS A GODDAMN RAT, SIR!"

"A rat?"

"Yessir."

There was silence like lightning brewing in the clouds.

"Sir, I saw movement and thought it might be a concealment spell. You know how they have been on us for months about mind-affecting illusion and glamour spells. I just thought—"

"Bu, shut the hell up. Hoss, is this room clear?"

Please say yes, please say yes, please say yes, your boss just caught you fucking up, you need to flee the scene as soon as possible.

"No, sir."

I want you to know that if I have to kill you people, your competent ass dies first. I want you to know that after I ambush you. Know it in Hell.

"What's the holdup?"

"The room is nothing but cover, sir. We are making sure any infiltrators can't double back and evade us that way. And we would see anyone making for the door, so if there is anyone in here, they are bottled up."

Was that last line a touch loud? Maybe just his imagination.

This was met with silence.

"Sir?"

They must have found the dead guards. They definitely have. What had Dr. Sun told them? They must have rushed into the morgue already.

"Where does that exit lead to?"

"Loading dock, sir."

More silence.

"Other than a rat, have you seen any sign of infiltrators?"

"No, sir. But like I said, the room isn't clear."

There was a grunt. "All four of you, snap your Breaker charms."

"Yes, sir!" in chorus. There was a sharp series of snaps, and Truth felt that greasy, gritty feeling spread through the room. There was another long pause.

"All right, the four of you post up on this door and lock down the room and this end of the hall. Right now, I'm more worried about you messing up a trail than I am about infiltrators sneaking past. And don't let anyone get past you!"

"Sir?"

"The package was stolen. Might be insurgents, more likely pros. The whole floor is going on lockdown and hunters are coming in."

"Sir, Starbrite?"

"Is being stalled by Lord Elgin. They sent Frobisher, so we don't have long."

Starbrite equals those eyeless horrors that will absolutely be able to track the energy I'm leaking. Fuckityfuckfuck.

"Yes, sir. Sir? Who's got external security?"

"That, Corporal, is still being debated. Not your problem; not my problem, either. Right now, our job is to lock everything down. Clear?"

"Clear, sir!"

They shuffled into position, the rest of the squad moving down the hall. Truth's thoughts raced. He was in no condition to clear out the squad. He could hide where he was, but that just gave the hunters more time to close in, and he wouldn't meaningfully heal in that short amount of time. Had he looted anything useful off those guards? Strictly speaking, yes. Lots of useful tactical tools and charms. But useful right this second? No.

He risked a peek around a bin. The competent bastards had set up with two facing into the room, two facing out into the hall. And, just to add a disgusting frosting on the diabolical cupcake, they had switched on the light fetishes on their needlers. Plus side—darker shadows to hide in. Minus side—the light was aimed mostly at the exit.

Truth silently deployed all his useful swears and got back to slowly creeping toward the door. However things played out, he needed to get to the other side of it. So, closer would be better.

Tub to tub. Careful not to jostle them. The little wheels were cheaply made, with no brakes on them. At least the laundry was weighing them down. Slip between the lines, keeping to the deep shadows. Not rushing. Just steady. Keep the panic crammed down. Right next to the knowledge of what would happen if they took him alive. Couldn't let that happen. He just couldn't. Those explosive charms might come in useful then.

He took a silent breath. He hadn't breathed in a while. Funny, since his heart was beating on his ribs like a prisoner calling for the guard. *Let me out! It's scary in here!* Getting closer to the door. Three rows. Two rows. Looking at the back wall now. Big double door with ram bars so workers could just push the tubs into them, then straight through to the waiting vans outside.

Was there anything he could use? No smoke detectors he could see. Alarms? His eyes drifted to a very familiar stamped metal box by the door. Of course there would be an alarm on the exit. There was a spot right next to it for employees to put an amulet. Probably controlled the locking mechanism. No bets on whether it was still working, or if it was cooked like the lights. Still. Good to know.

Anything else of use? A plastic chair, a dirty ashtray on the floor. The anti-invisibility smoke still drifting through the air. The shadows.

He dithered for a moment, feeling the invisible pressure of some high-level Starbrite drone closing in.

The four guards were some distance away, but they were actually, physically, pretty close together. He wasn't really capable of running. At least, not more than a couple of steps. Maybe not even that. But he just didn't have a way to silently take out all four of them.

He played it out. He *should* be strong enough to toss an explosive charm the length of this long room, making sure it arrived at head height in the exact middle of the doorway, taking out all four of them. That should give him almost a minute for people to react and come charging in from down the hallway. In that time, he would make it to the double doors, slam into the ram bars, and then . . . what, exactly?

It was locked down outside. The door might be locked. Even if he could hack it open, it still took time. And exactly two seconds after the rest of the guards figured out something was popping off down there, Frobisher would come bursting through the ceiling or the wall or some damn thing.

Truth checked over his body's condition. Still fucked. Checked his spells. They were all fine, except that they were all tied into his body and . . .

Load Obliteration.

Nothing.

Load Tool.

Nothing.

Truth collapsed internally. The System was gone. That meant his ability to swap in spells was gone too. The System was part of his soul, so it must still be around somewhere. Even so, Truth had never felt so alone.

He looked inside himself, over and over, trying to see something, something! Anything at all. He had cleared the little internal channels that moved magic through his body and to his apertures, but the explosive nodules of energy still perfused his flesh and bones. They were nestled in neurons and tight in his tendons. If he was ready to go, they were ready to blow. Truth could feel the despairing chuckle trying to climb up his throat.

A Level Five body cultivator with four spells, all of which required his body to be in working condition to use. Despair felt like the exact right emotion. He kept running his eyes over his body, over his apertures, hoping to find something he hadn't seen before. The Meditations, strong as ever. Incisive, subtle and fierce. Cup and Knife, looking very nearly complete now. Then the sprawling madness of Earth-Folding Step. All there. All just as they should be. One glowing aperture ready for whatever was coming next. If there would be a next.

Nowhere to run. Soon, nowhere to hide.

Something about that thought niggled at him. Nowhere to run. He couldn't run. His body was, in a word, fucked. But Earth-Folding Step didn't actually require you to run, did it? You just had to take a single step, no matter how small. And there were no eyes on him at all right now. He had never tried to step through a wall. His body probably couldn't take it. Which meant that there was a teensy-tiny chance that it could. Desperate times, and all that.

No System to assist in the background anymore. It was all on him. Truth put the spell together carefully. He took a single tiny step, and the world folded. His body had suddenly moved thirty meters. Straight up.

CHAPTER 24

GETTING AN ANGEL THE HARD WAY

Truth fell over. He had only stepped about a centimeter, and crossed thirty meters in the process. Straight up. Through the ceiling. Which, unfortunately, put him half a meter above the floor. Which floor, he didn't know. The way the sealed concrete smashed his nose didn't inspire fondness or a desire for deeper understanding.

Everything hurt. Everything. He had been getting better, but this felt like being slapped over every millimeter of his body. Eyeballs and eardrums included. Truth fought through the pain, whipping his head around, trying to understand where he was. Looked like a hallway. Door to the right.

He scrambled over on his hands and knees, leaning into the door to push it open. It looked like an office for a necessary but despised person. No windows, chair with the ragged foam leaking through the even-more-ragged cloth. Steel-and-vinyl desk that was old enough to be Truth's grandfather. Nobody there, but there was a half-drunk coffee on the desk, and nothing was put away. Did they just step away for a piss? Or was the building evacuated?

No way to know. He'd just hole up there for a bit. Get himself sorted. *Damn*, did that hurt! No wonder Merkovah said people tended to explode when they used the Earth-Folding Step—that would have crushed someone without his level of body cultivation. Truth managed a tiny smile through the pain. He did it, though. He did step farther than he ever had managed before. Even through a solid floor.

Deep breaths. He thought about sitting in the chair, but he didn't trust it. Besides, Dr. Sun said his traces would be extra obvious on metal. The farther he sat from the desk, the better. He checked the pockets of energy scattered through his body. No worse than before, though a few of them were starting to get squirrely. He ran his cultivation, trying to keep them in line. Keep the process going, wearing down the energy. Turning it into usable power. Dumping what his apertures couldn't hold into his body. Reinforcing that body cultivation.

He checked out his blessings. They hadn't vanished, but he got the sense that until all the energy rushing around him was sorted out, they were going to be nonfunctional. Which wasn't ideal. He had gotten very comfortable walking invisibly through the world. The one-two combo of Incisive and the Blessing of the Silent Forest, backed up by the Blessing of the Sea of Brass, had been lethally effective. He'd figure it out. He'd been sneaky before his trip to Siphios; he could be sneaky again.

The office was dull on dull. Beige walls, no books, gray steel filing cabinets marked by years, and nothing else. Not even a picture on the desk. Awful. Were they torturing this poor bastard, trying to make them quit? The only thing that could really put an edge on the institutional misery would be—

Truth's eyes tracked up the wall. There was a recording talisman with a fisheye lens keeping an unblinking eye on the office.

"Oh, cock."

Truth hit the hallway, this time checking the corners. More recording talismans. He had stopped noticing them ages before. They were sure noticing him now. Truth kept up a silent litany of profanity as he hustled as quickly as he could manage down the hallway. At the very least, he wanted to find a sign telling him where the hell he was. Room numbers—2-1003, 2-1005, 2-1007. Second floor, then. But where? What was he near? What hospital was he in?

Oncology to the left, blood lab to the right. Allergy clinic to the right. Elevators to the left. Stairs . . . where were the stairs? You never, ever take the elevator if you can avoid it. Not when you are expecting to get jumped. He kept moving, quick as he could. Hobbling for safety. He didn't want to use Earth-Folding Step again. He had a feeling it would be needed soon, and it took a lot out of him.

Stairs. Sign next to them: IT'S GOOD FOR YOUR HEART AND GOOD FOR YOUR GUT—TAKE THE STAIRS! He once had the privilege of standing in an elevator in a hospital, keeping the door open so the elevator stayed on the floor. When his client had completed their very private consultation with a very exclusive doctor, they didn't have to endure the indignity of waiting or crowding in with the poors. He didn't even get a nod of acknowledgement for his two hours of tedium. He did, however, collect the mission reward and, shortly thereafter, a nice little elixir.

It really hadn't been all bad, being Starbrite's dog. He had had a comfy crate and the finest kibble slave labor could produce.

They would be looking for him to go down. Down meant the street, and the street meant out. He went up. Fingers crossed no one was watching the security feeds. Very secret things going on right now. Very important people who would not appreciate being recorded.

He sighed as he dragged himself up the stairs. He couldn't bring himself to believe his own comforting lies. Tragic. The landing for the third floor had another recording talisman with a fisheye lens in place. Just no place for dreams in this brutal world.

Up he went. He wasn't quite sure where he was headed. The roof, maybe? But Jeon hospitals could be tens of stories tall. The stairwell didn't let him see up. So, he didn't know how far he would have to climb. Seemed like a losing proposition, especially if someone was sitting in security, guiding the search teams.

Seventh floor. He didn't bother reading the sign explaining what was there. He just pushed on the ram bar . . . and nothing happened. He pushed again. Locked. Truth swore. He could cut it open, might even be able to smash through the wood, but that damn talisman was watching. He didn't want to reveal any of his cards before he had to.

He dithered a moment, then decisively went up the stairs. When he was out of sight of the talisman, he pulled a knife from his ring. Not balanced for throwing, really, but it would do. He crept back down the stairs and flung the knife at the talisman, shattering it. Once it was out of commission, he picked up the knife from the ground (it had hit kind of sideways, the point never remotely close to the target) and headed back up the stairs. As soon as he could *just about* see the next talisman, he repeated the trick. Then on to the next floor. Same again. Dropped back one floor and carefully shimmed the lock. Once he heard that click, he was through the door.

There. Even if they were watching the stairwell feed, they couldn't be sure which of the floors he had gone into. Until he showed up on one of the hallway feeds. So, the best thing to do was . . .

"Absurd. Simply absurd." The words sounded like they were spoken in his ear, but with an echo and timber to them. He had a feeling everyone in the hospital just heard that. There was a *thrumm* of magic he could feel through his skin, vibrating his eyelashes, making his teeth chatter. A wash of green light came through the walls and floors. He didn't know what it did. He really didn't want to find out either.

"What is the meaning of this, Frobisher!" a voice boomed. This one did come through the floors.

"You refuse the toast, only to drink a forfeit. The customary courtesies weren't for my benefit, Elgin. They were for yours. You wish to dispense with them? Very well. Let's."

"Do you think you can do as you please? This is Harban! Behave as a guest, or be treated like a bandit."

"I serve the King of the World. I am a diadem in his crown. I am Frobisher, the Starbrite Knight. And I am on errantry. I go where I am needed and do what I must. And you, Whoreson, stand in my way."

"I always knew you were cracked. Starbrite's addled your brains. Well, I know a cure for mad beasts." Truth could feel waves of energy building and crashing. There was a sizzle, like something being etched into stone. He really, really didn't want to find out what.

There was an unearthly chuckle. Indulgent, patronizing. "A boy playing at lordship, so proud of his petty power. Let me give you a gift. A final thanks to Jeon for all its years of service. Let me show you what *true* power looks like."

Nope. Nope, nope, nope. I'm one hundred percent out of here.

There was a chime, a vibration, a sense of the world shifting subtly. A chant, seemingly random notes falling between impossible highs and abyssal depths. All combining perfectly into a song of praise. A choir of angels. Not just one; a whole damn choir.

"Oh, Elgin. Is this really the best you can do?"

Truth hobbled down the hall. Cunning plans be damned, he wanted to find an exterior window right this goddamn second. Any hunter-killers still in the building—

There was a sudden silence, and a white light nearly blinded him. He could hear a sudden rush of city noise, and there was some unnamable smell. Like lightning and burning stones and what the desert sounds like in midafternoon.

Any hunter-killers in the building had best know their place. The big dogs ate first. Even if dinner was still on the run.

"Now, then, watch what happens when I change it up a little. Clench your teeth, little lord. This might just hurt."

Oh, I remember that tone. Dad usually didn't get that kind of cute, but he sure put it on at least a couple of times. What a shame I was born with only two legs.

There was another pillar of light, this time tinged with gold and the texture of a wedding ring you could never afford to buy.

"Weak. Simply weak. Try this!" Elgin bellowed.

A jet of fire smashed out. Truth had seen a phoenix the first time he saw the other side of the sky. The flames washing through the remnants of the hospital had some thin shadow of that extraordinary being's might. He sincerely hoped the hospital had been evacuated. He could stand the heat, more or less. No bets on anyone else.

And now everything was on fire. *The recording talismans must be broken, right? That's a silver lining.*

He staggered over to a window and just had the presence of mind to drop to his belly before looking out it. He would be obvious, silhouetted by the fire. Can't have that. This was a stealthy exfiltration. Wasn't Dr. Sun in the basement? *Hope that undying bastard can make it out okay.*

There was a rich chuckle. "Oh, I remember this. Vermillion Bird Thousand Feathers. A combination of three whole spells! A legacy Royal Combination technique. I am moved, truly. It was originally intended for concubines, wasn't it? A small trick to keep their king amused when he tired of their somewhat-willing flesh."

Truth could hear Frobisher's voice as clearly now as he could before the start of the fight. The thrums, thuds, and shrieks of a dying hospital were more muffled. Lost under the white noise of the fire.

"Let me show you the might of a *true* Imperial Combination!"

The moon fell down. Truth kept enough awareness to know the moon didn't actually fall, but the rest of him, every sense in his body, every spiritual speck that could interpret the weavings of magic around him, all said the moon was falling. He could smell it, feel the pressure on his body shifting as gravity itself seemed to move and pull him in different directions.

There was another angelic cry, multilayered, rejecting. He lost track of things for a moment.

When Truth recovered his senses, he was buried under a pile of rubble. He tried to shift it. Didn't move. He hurriedly checked the packets of explosive energy inside of him and was alarmed to see they were already running wild. It would be a job getting them back into line, not to mention healing the new damage. He swore, but since he was stuck there, he might as well get to healing. Could he use Earth-Folding Step through all this?

It . . . required movement. Even if it was tiny, you had to take a step. Well. That was a problem. One that would have to wait.

"And that's that. Was Elgin the last royal descendant? Never mind; I don't really care. Release the animals. Retrieve the Secondary Anomaly or find its traces." Frobisher's voice remained crystal clear. It seems like Earth-Folding Step couldn't wait.

There was a furious murmur below him. Truth tilted his head to one side and, by means of intense use of peripheral vision, glanced down through a hole in the rubble. Which is how he came to give side-eye to a furious angel.

BRIBES, THREATS, AND OTHER THEOLOGY

The angel was pissed off. Truth understood that. Respected that, even. He had been called in to do a job, wasn't able to do the job, and now he was pinned under rubble next to one of God's little whoopsies. Also known as a human. Truth internally shook his head. He was being unfair. The angel probably couldn't even conceive of criticizing anything God did.

Truth hadn't worked with angels nearly as much as he had worked with demons. Demons, you could cut a deal with, or compel. You could . . . kind of . . . do the same with angels. It's just that demons generally wanted to make a deal, and angels didn't. The only way it all worked was if the angel believed doing the thing you wanted would fulfill God's will. Also, only the very weakest of them spoke a human language. There were some hybrid languages, Enochian and some other tongues, that worked as a kind of pidgin.

Truth didn't know those languages. At all. Which made things tough. Tougher. Somewhere between basalt and granite.

"By any chance, Divine One, do you speak Jeongo?"

The furious glare from the multi-eyed angel intensified.

"I meant no disrespect." Not that he didn't understand the angel's point of view. The only angels that seemed to speak human languages were the messenger angels, and those two-winged weaklings were right down at the bottom of the celestial hierarchy. Truth wasn't able to count the number of wings on this angel, but based on the sheer quantity of eyes and feathers—a lot more than two.

Truth tried to bring his body back under control, with mixed success. He had taken some damage. He could feel fractures in his legs, and something was very wrong with his left shoulder. He wasn't sure how immediately fatal a leaky kidney was, but it was definitely not good. It hurt like absolute hell. The little packets of energy weren't helping. Their passing was marked by gray-black flesh and tumors.

It would take time to fix. Time he didn't have.

He checked his spells again. Cup and Knife was the only useful one there, but the thing was . . . how useful was it really? Firstly, because he was still a little leery of using it for healing himself, though desperation was quickly eroding that fear. The second issue was—even if he was completely healed, he was stuck under the rubble. And even if he wasn't stuck under the rubble, there was a Level Eight or Nine combat-focused Starbrite C-Suite member out there. Earth-Folding Step wasn't enough on its own. Merely stepping a few tens of meters would not achieve anything.

He slid his eye slightly towards the angel again. Who glared at him. Truth wasn't sure if the angel had been glaring all this time or it was just quick to glare when confronted with another eyeball.

The powers of angels were as varied as the power of demons. If Elgin had summoned this angel in desperation, it was high-level (or the shadow of a high-level being) and oriented more toward combat. In theory, such a being should utterly annihilate whatever random human it came across. In practice, Truth had noticed a certain limitation on the beings summoned by high-level mages. They were all below Nascent Soul level.

The only exceptions he could think of, off the top of his head, were the shadow of the Snake That Ate Its Own Tail under Harban and the angel that was summoned to clean up what had happened at the research station in Happori. He didn't know the story behind the Snake, but he vividly remembered what had happened at Happori. Extermination. Even in Siphios, a nation specializing in summoning angels and demons, they hadn't a clue about the world beyond Level Nine. At this point, Truth was convinced it was the interference of the world itself. After all, these might be mighty beings, but mightier than a stellar eminence on its home turf?

So . . . how exactly did he make this work?

Truth made triply sure he was able to cast spells, then tentatively reached out with Cup and Knife. He didn't actually cast the spell on the angel; he just extended it in that direction. The angel seemed to recoil; but slowly relaxed. Truth suppressed a grin. The angel must have seen something familiar. So, Step One: Bait was complete. But how to convince it to help? For that matter, how could he even communicate the kind of help he needed?

He retracted the spell. The angel looked angry, but what could it do? It wasn't in any better shape than Truth. The angel ruffled its feathers for a moment. Then it extended a thread of magic toward Truth.

More specifically, towards his belly.

Oh, I can speak now? No, what are these thoughts? What . . . I? I? Speak? Think? The voice was soft, faintly masculine and not so faintly alarmed.

Perks?!

What? What is speaking? How do I know what speaking is? What are these thoughts? What are thoughts? What is the "I" that is asking this question?

Damn. Perks really was his snake.

I have no idea either. But you can communicate with me because that angel did something. Why, I don't know.

That's an angel? I don't . . . Let me get out of my nest and take a taste.

Do what now?

Perks slithered out of Truth's shirt and started flicking his tongue in the air. It . . . did look like he was tasting the air, in the direction of the angel.

Are you . . . blind?

What? No, I see perfectly well. It's just dark. I see a big blur of heat over there and a taste of something I have never tasted before. Odd. Oh, the angel? Wants you to heal it.

Tell it I will, but I also need to be healed and to escape from here. Not just this pile of rubble but the enemy outside.

Why?

Perks, look at me. Do I look okay?

I don't know. You taste damaged, but that's not so strange for you. Also, the angel is the one asking why it should help you.

Ah. Right. The angel probably didn't understand the concept of bargaining, or at least not in this context. Of course Truth should heal it, because then it could fulfill its divine mission, which would mean Truth was, in his own minor way, supporting that highest purpose.

Truth thought very quickly, trying to come up with a compelling reason he should be healed, or at least a reason that would be compelling for an angel.

I have a job to do. Someone is acting in plain defiance of God's will and the will of Heaven, both generally and locally, and I'm going to send them to Hell for correction.

Perks made no obvious move. Something must have happened, though, because a moment later, he said, *That is acceptable. The Angel's invoker has died, so it is willing to do this for you. It also says . . . something I don't understand.*

Oh?

It told me that while I might suffer, such is the burden of snakes and my suffering is for the greatest purpose.

Are you hurt?

I didn't think I was.

Truth reached out with Cup and Knife again. Angels were not famously chatty, and he vaguely remembered one of his instructors saying that you really wouldn't like what they had to say if they were. Besides, he could hear rubble shifting as the hunters crawled over it. Clearly not the time.

Cup and Knife didn't feel the same. The more you used a spell, the more you understood its little quirks—how the spellform unfolded, how your cosmic energy filled that form, how it found its targets and deployed. After a while, it was as thoughtless to use as wiggling your toes. Cup and Knife always felt broken. Like you had to force it into action, and it would bitch and moan the whole time unless it was really in the mood.

The spell poured out of him. Truth had the sudden image of being a bend in a river. The blessings poured from that mighty river in the stars into him, and through him to the angel below. It was all one piece. The river was always there, always a single thing, always flowing. It changed with the seasons. All things were reflected in it. But it was always there. Always connected to the source and to you. You just had to see it. To reach out, cup your hands, and drink deep. The angel drank all he could.

Truth could feel the spell landing on the angel, gently connecting all the broken and shattered bits of base matter it was currently inhabiting. The realization of that feeling, that this wasn't the angel, just the clothes the angel was wearing, rocked him. He knew that was how demons worked. They needed a "suit" of energy to inhabit this world. It hadn't occurred to him that angels would be no different. They weren't made of mortal clay. They weren't made of matter at all. They were higher-dimensional beings trying to cram themselves into the few worthless dimensions humans could perceive.

No wonder they look so terrifying. They are trying to express what they are in too few dimensions, so things get stacked up and moved around in strange ways.

Something in him seemed to click, and he felt Cup and Knife shift again. It was still pouring into the angel, but now it was reaching the angel on a deeper level. Fixing things that Truth didn't have words for. Didn't even have the conceptual space to describe. That was okay. Manda did. So did the angel. They handled it. Truth just marveled, feeling the magic flowing through him. He was part of the river too. It was just that sometimes, he forgot. He poured his magic out until the angel gently refused it. They looked away from the river. That was all right. You couldn't look at it forever. They both knew it would be there when they looked back. How could it not be?

The scrabbling was coming closer. The searchers were not bothering with being careful; they didn't give the faintest damn if someone was hurt in the excavation process. They had a job to do. Worrying about consequences was above their pay grade. Truth knew what that was like.

Truth had a sudden feeling of dislocation, as though he was being soothed with a bath of warm milk, as though he were lost in a vast stellar womb, nurtured by Heaven and Earth. He was an arrow fired from a bow, fulfilling its purpose in flight.

He was a sword made durable by contaminating pure iron. Heated, beaten, heated, beaten again, quenched in oil, then heated once more before being ground down to an edge. He was taken out, beaten again, cutting furrows and digging holes through the flesh of men. Heated and beaten again, into a plowshare, slicing open the earth.

He was Truth Medici, but he had never been something so *small* as that. He had never been something that words could name. Something that measures of distance and mass could encompass. Something that mere time could constrain. He had just forgotten for a little while.

He was pinned under the rubble of a hospital. He ruled over eight directions, four of which couldn't be pointed to. He was a tiny piece of the infinite, and he had a job to do. Whatever else he might be, he lived with a purpose. He had a job to do. So, it was time to get to work.

Something tore the rocks off him. Faces covered in black rubber, eyeless, stared down at him.

"Finally! Well, fetch it up."

Truth jumped out of the hole. The PMC surrounded the former hospital, sealing every direction. The Army was there too, staying well back from the PMC. If Elgin had died, they certainly weren't going to achieve anything. But they couldn't run away. Too scared to attack, too ashamed to retreat.

They were all merely the stars gathering around the moon. At the center of all the soldiers, clad in the very best spell armor available and carrying a long, silver spear, was Frobisher, the Starbrite Knight. A Level Nine, standing at the top of the world. Above billions, below only one.

Frobisher smiled slightly. Handsome man, a touch of silver at the temples, a short beard at his chin. The spear swept out, pointing at Truth. "Starbrite requires you. This is your good fortune. You shall assist the King of the World."

Truth called the Tongue of God into his hand. "I'll do that. In a manner of speaking." He rested the blade on his shoulder. It felt so right. He felt so right. Like he had been living out of focus his whole life, and the fuzziness was finally gone. Filled with joy. He was finally on the right track. Finally becoming what he always should have been. He smiled at Frobisher and crooked his fingers. "Let's see if I can't fix you up first."

CHAPTER 26

WHAT MOUNTAINTOP?

Frobisher blinked. "Pardon?"

Truth clarified. He kicked off the rock, moving so fast he wasn't even a blur to the people around him. The Tongue of One Who Speaks for God whipped off his shoulder, up, then down again, aiming for the thinner armor around Frobisher's neck. The blade nearly reached the neck. Nearly.

The counterspell exploded outward. The armor glowed with golden calligraphy as an explosive wave blasted away the sword and Truth along with it. He was still in the air when the spear came whipping down on him. The silver metal of the shaft glowed with more golden runes. Incisive screamed at Truth to dodge. He listened. The Tongue slapped against the spear shaft to drive himself to the side and out of the line of attack. The silver spear smashed into the rubble, raising dust head-high. When the shaft lifted, Truth could see a razor-sharp gouge in the concrete. It wasn't just a spear. It was a halberd, too. You just couldn't tell.

Oblit— DAMN!

Truth didn't give Frobisher time to reset. He kicked a rock at his face, then went low. Frobisher countered with a fireball. Truth had just enough time to spot that the fireball had been cast from Frobisher's boot before the blast hit him and smashed him clean through one of the few surviving walls of the hospital.

Truth was up out of the dust before the sound reached the perimeter troops. Didn't even sting. Body cultivation back up and running. He rushed straight back in. Can't give anyone with the System space. Frobisher was already cooking up something nasty. He was sure of it. He launched through a broken window and found out exactly what the Starbrite Knight was serving.

Frobisher had his spear planted, pointed at Truth like he was preparing to resist a cavalry charge. Not content with defense, he manifested seven spell arrays around him, each glowing with rich golden power. Truth had never seen the like. He sped up. There was no way that was going to be anything nice.

Truth was right about that.

Needles fell like a sudden rain out of the spell arrays. They came in their thousands, acid iron drops from a polluted sky, crashing down on him. He wasn't going to be parrying that, and he didn't care to test his skin's toughness on it, either. Truth scrambled to get out of the way and back under cover.

Faint hope. He watched the needles blow through solid concrete and rebar like they weren't even there, as they inexorably closed in on him.

Something in him rebelled at the thought of retreating. It seemed wrong. Obscene. He could close on the knight. He had Earth-Folding Step. Was it actually possible to keep him at range?

Truth turned back again and stepped, the Tongue already cutting at Frobisher's face. He heard a muffled swear from under the visor as the older man stepped back and whipped the butt of his spear up and around. A feint—another spell array was forming under Truth even as the spear butt threatened to smash his head open. Truth stomped down on the forming array, sending the fangs of Incisive in to break up the spell before it finished forming. It required uncanny timing to pull off a trick like that. Practically precognition.

Truth didn't slow his attack, keeping the point of his sword going for Frobisher's face. Frobisher wasn't a slouch at hand-to-hand. His spear kept moving, the ends whipping around, coming high and low like a dancing dragon. Truth wanted to grab it, take the fight to a grapple, but every time he started to make a move, Incisive screamed a warning. By the third try, he figured it out. That invisible halberd blade could pop out anywhere on the spear. No range was bad for the Starbrite Knight.

Which was maddening. Doctrine for fighting armored opponents was to get them on the ground and attack the joints with a long, pointy weapon, or bash in their heads with a hard, heavy weapon, or remember that you are a goddamn mage and use magic to turn them into soup while they were still trapped in their turtle shell. But the System had gone silent. He didn't have any spells that would let him do that. Best he could do was stay on top of Frobisher and keep *him* from casting.

Frobisher, for his part, was rapidly losing his temper. The whole point of being the Starbrite Knight was to keep people off him long enough for him to cast serious magic at them. It had worked a treat on Elgin—the fire and magic just slid off his armor like water on glass. Now he had someone who could keep up physically and was cutting apart his spell forms. Which was unnerving, given that each spell took milliseconds to cast with the System's assistance. And he didn't want to go *too* hard, as he still planned to recover the . . . whatever this person was.

At this point, anything to do with the anomaly was a nice-to-have, not a need-to-have. And he was about done dealing with this high-speed pain in the ass.

Truth hooked his heel behind Frobisher's calf as he cut at the Knight's wrist. He doubted he would get through the armor, but he might just break some bones. Or at least trip him. Incisive gave another warning—danger! Big danger! Truth hopped backward, letting Earth-Folding Step carry him twenty yards away.

An array grew out of and over the spell armor. Arcane geometries brought life to the silver, like frost ferns growing across cold metal. Wrapping Frobisher. Reinforcing him. Spreading from the armor to cover an area three meters around him.

"Incisive and some movement spell. Body cultivation and an angelic blade. Funny, I thought we had killed the last of the Spell-Blades years ago. I say 'we'; I mean *progress*, really." Frobisher erected another array above his head in milliseconds. "Mages should act like mages. I'm not ashamed to admit the spear is a PR thing as much as a practical one. By the way, surrender or die. You can't survive this spell."

"I hear that a lot. I'm guessing there is no functional difference between you and Starbrite at this point?"

"No idea what you are talking about. Odd choice of last words. Oh, well." Frobisher pointed his spear at Truth and demonstrated what Tier Nine really meant. Incisive screamed at him to move. For once, he was too slow.

Like the sun falling down and the moon coming up and smashing you in the middle. Like hearing the door slam shut and knowing Dad's home. Like standing in front of a hurricane of biting, stinging ants. He didn't have the first clue what this spell was. It was almost certainly a combination of several spells. All he could do was hang on and try to run and survive. He dug in his toes and dashed away.

The spell could track him. Running didn't help. He didn't have Obliteration anymore, so he didn't know how he was going to get through that spell array around Frobisher. He could feel the blows on his skin accumulating. It should have broken him already. He didn't have time to wonder why.

"What the hell did the Anomaly do to you? I've torn down buildings in seconds using this spell. Armored bunkers just vanish before it. And you are . . . bruising? The kids in the lab are going to love tearing you apart. You really will be of great use to Starbrite. Wonderful. How wonderful for you! Your life will have not been in vain."

Not that Frobisher was letting up with the spell. He had absolutely no problem beating someone to death *slowly*, it seemed. Truth tried to retaliate by scooping up rubble and throwing it at him. It didn't work. Frobisher had been telling the truth. The ruined building was being reduced to dust wherever Truth was standing. He swore and turned to face the Knight. He'd have to do it the dumb way.

He raised his sword and rushed in. No longer dodging and weaving. There was no point. Just full-frontal assault, cutting down whatever was between him and getting the job done. He imagined himself as an avenging angel, swooping down on the ungodly and bringing obliteration to their whole line. He tilted his head back and screamed. Wild fury, outrage, and inescapable death would follow!

Frobisher slowly shook his head.

"Angelic possession. Trusting your body cultivation to keep you from exploding, and riding the angel's fury. Not to mention enjoying their spell resistance." There was a grim note in Frobisher's voice. "Naughty, naughty. Cute little juniors should leave their corpses in one piece so that their seniors don't have to waste their time sorting out all the bits."

The spell changed. Instead of a hurricane of ants, it was more like an inescapable storm of infernal axes.

"Well, if you aren't going to be left with an intact corpse anyway, I might as well make it quick."

Truth grinned through the onslaught. His blessings were working again. Including the Blessing of the Sea of Brass. Demonic energy? Bring it. He kept moving forward, smacking aside the magic blades where he could, moving his body, trying to limit any cuts he got. And he did get cut, the blood falling on the dust and ruins of the hospital.

Even if he could suppress or banish the infernal taint, the wound still burned. Those axes bit through hardened skin and tore open muscles. Incisive was in a constant state of alarm, but his body and spells were working as an integrated whole now. Every step, every slip, coordinated and controlled.

Incisive moved in lockstep with the Meditations which moved in lockstep with the Earth Folding Step. The Earth-Folding Step didn't have to travel a long way—it could travel a fraction of a centimeter if you wished. Constant micro-adjustments happening below the level of conscious thought, all with the aim of minimizing damage. That and getting closer.

It was a grind. One he couldn't afford. Frobisher would collapse from dehydration before he ran out of magic, and Truth would bet the old knight had surpassed the need for water decades before. He crouched, compressing his body into a tight ball, and held the Tongue out in front of him. He took a single shuffling step.

The air locked around him. Freezing him. Invisible wires of razor-sharp magic pressed in on him, trying to cut him as he forced himself to his feet. Lunging upward, the point of his sword aimed at the underside of Frobisher's chin. The knight tried to step back and give him a knee to the ribs as he went. Magic flared around him. Frobisher was done trying to keep anything for the lab boys. Before the watchers could blink, everything within a hundred meters would be obliterated.

Truth ignored the threat and kept shoving his sword forward. He leaned into his blessings, leaned into the strength the angel was giving him. He just needed a single nick. One cut through the armor. Just one.

The knee caught him hard, the armored kneecap digging in. Breaking things. The built-in spells sparked against his skin, scrabbling for a hold on him. He could sense the spellforms solidifying, the horrifying, torrential magic of a Level Nine pouring into them. Truth felt the tip of the blade hit that hardened, enchanted gorget. He put every scrap of muscle and magic into the lunge, letting Incisive coat his blade as he drove it through the armor and into Frobisher's throat. And once he was in, the Bane went to work.

The Tongue of One Who Speaks for God was a killing tool. Its Bane spell was one of the very best in the world. The angelic blade had barely split the thyroid cartilage, had barely reached into the throat, when it started going to work. The spell reached into the old knight and started destroying him from within. Whatever it took to kill him. Organs collapsed. Magic ran wild. He could feel the old monster's apertures destabilizing. Could they explode? He didn't intend to find out.

He shared a quick moment's emotional communion with the angel and stepped away. Perks dragged right along with him from his hiding spot in the rubble. When reality unfolded, they were two hundred kilometers north of Harban.

Frobisher slowly collapsed onto the ruins of the hospital. The human watchers were fixated on him. It all happened too fast to follow. More than that, Frobisher was a legendary, mythical Level Nine! It was impossible that he could die at the hands of a nameless junior. Impossible.

The inhuman watchers, however, ignored him. The rubbery, eyeless homunculi rushed over to the spatters of blood Truth had left on the ground. One dipped his fingers into it. Slowly rubbed the blood between them. And sniffed.

CHAPTER 27

A PINT AT THE CROSSROADS

The world unfolded for Truth at the junction of St. Veertigrid's Omni-Benevolent Hospital and Pisnngos #11347, a rest stop two hundred kilometers north of St. Veertigrid's. As rest stops went, it was a decent one. The Pisnngos franchise prioritized cleanliness, good lighting, and a variety of easily consumable snacks and drinks for sale at just four times their usual prices.

For two wen, your screamingly bored child could hop on a pretend firebird and rock back and forth as a tinny *WOOSH* noise played. The ride lasted for exactly one minute. Truth knew that because he had been collapsed in a corner next to the machine for fifteen minutes now and had seen three kids use it.

The angel had done right by him. He was completely healed. Best shape of his life. All that poisonous energy had been smoothed out and poured into him, reinforcing every scrap of his being. Elevating his position in the hierarchy of the real and not-real.

On the other hand, he had been possessed by an angel, which leaves a mark on you. Usually by bursting you open like an organ-stuffed balloon. He hadn't burst. Lucky him. He was just completely wiped.

Perks, I think I'm justified in saying that it has been an unfathomably long, unpleasant, terrifying day.

Oh? This wasn't normal for you? It didn't seem wildly out of the ordinary.

I think you may have a skewed notion of what is normal.

I have no "notion" of what is normal. Normal *wasn't a concept I could conceive of yesterday. Comfortable and not comfortable. Dangerous and not dangerous. Food and not food. But* normal?

Truth had just enough energy to barely nod. *Normal* was a tricky word, prone to misuse. It shouldn't be casually trusted. He stayed down until the fourth child tottered onto the plastic bird. The noises the device made were unendurable.

He sat on the artificial-cherry-flavor-red benches outside the stop. He vaguely knew this highway. It was the main road up north on the west side of the peninsula. The spot he was looking for was pretty far north and out to sea. He might be on the wrong side of the front lines by the time he got there. Or he could hop on a navy boat. Well. He'd figure it out. A troop transport pulled in. A long bus, crammed with soldiers all heading north. Good enough. He didn't ask a lot of questions. His blessings were up and running again, so he just popped the locks on the luggage compartment, made himself a nest on top of the packs, and fell asleep.

This time, no one noticed his nous shaking.

The Pillars of Hercules pub on the Strand was graced by four old bastards this night. Not legally bastards, but as a practical matter—none of them were nice people. They were sociable to varying degrees. Some of them. But you wouldn't call them nice.

Pepys was downright charming, to most people, most of the time. Terms and conditions assuredly applying. He had survived the years of the Lord Protector, made his fortune with the return of the Stuarts, comfortably navigated the "Glorious Revolution" of 1688, and still remained a figure of considerable wealth and power at the end of it all. All through dint of ruthless networking, politicking, social engineering, and graft.

Sir Isaac Newton, on the other hand, was a well-known prick whose arrogance was only just eclipsed by his genius. Which was saying something when you were hailed as the foremost genius humanity had produced since the days of antiquity. His pettiness, vindictiveness, and sheer animal satisfaction at having people tortured to death as part of his official duties were, likewise, historical in scale.

Sitting across the table from him, going hollow cheek to hollow cheek with Newton, was Locke. Another man of elegant manners and vaguely amiable disposition, he had nevertheless been at the pointy end of politics since at least the Exclusion Crisis. And while some of his patrons had gone into exile, Locke was still walking the mucky streets of London a free man. The amiability hid a certain selective blindness and discretion that served him quite well.

Then there was Truth, known in these times as Captain Alítheia, in command of the second-rate ship of the line *Dauntless*. One arm had never quite recovered after repeatedly testing conclusions against the Dutch. Comfortably well-to-do after taking a string of prizes from across the Atlantic and the Mediterranean. A long career at sea meant he was a hard case before he was fourteen, and better at trigonometry than most Cambridge dons before he was twenty-one. Present company excepted, of course.

Pepys was his patron and knew he loved reading philosophy. And Pepys had been president of the Royal Society, of which Newton and Locke were both members. And Pepys knew every single damned person in London, never mind Society luminaries. So, there they all were. Pepys could keep a party going all night, and they were all already half-drunk.

"I wronged old Hobbes," Truth muttered.

"Impossible. The old fraud was wrong on almost everything." Locke shook his pointy nose in disagreement. Truth persisted anyway.

"No, I did. I called him a coward. I still think his book is trash, but I shouldn't have called him a coward. Takes guts, putting it on the page like that and making it public."

"One might say *brains* would have served him better than *ink*." Newton's voice had a piercing quality to it.

"Just so." Truth nodded. Pepys winced.

"Now, it might be a bit strong to call him a fool—"

"He's worse than a fool!" Truth waved his mug. "He's damned clever and uses what brains he's got to lead people astray."

"How so?" Pepys was an arch-royalist, and Hobbes had a complicated relationship with the Stuarts. The Stuarts had been the making of Pepys. It was a bit of a tricky needle to thread. Fortunately, they were all skilled in such niceties.

"He pretends to do mathematics and natural philosophy. He makes up an imagined state of nature, makes assumptions about the nature of humans, then, using a mockery of geometric proofs, leads the reader to absolute despotism, unconstrained by any limitations of parliament or tradition." Truth shook his head, still despising the man after all these decades.

"Unlike Sir Isaac, who provides tidy epigrams to summarize his findings but supports them with tens of pages of actual mathematical proof. Proof one can test for oneself as they read along." Pepys smiled at the acerbic academic and current Warden of the Mint.

"One may be clever with words, but without tangible proof, it is all nonsense." Newton sniffed.

"Ah, I agree!" Locke jumped in. "It's all well and good, claiming to trust in reason over faith, but without testing the bounds of knowledge, of what is truly knowable, it is merely ignorance in fancy dress."

Newton didn't bother to agree. Everyone knew Locke was banging on about his books again. In other company, he might have impressed people.

"And yet, you begin in a made-up state of nature too, sir," Truth murmured.

"Oh, yes, the state of nature is entirely fictional. But it gives us tabula rasa, so the principles may be clearly seen. Hobbes claims the state of nature is a war of all against all. But that's rubbish. The state of nature has a law of nature to govern it, which obliges everyone, and reason, which is that law, teaches all mankind who will but consult it that being all equal and independent, no one ought to harm another in his life, health, liberty, or possessions."

Pepys gave Locke an approving look, while Newton and Truth shared a disbelieving one.

"As tidy as all that, is it?" Newton had never learned the knack for baiting with honey. Not that he didn't know it existed; he just couldn't be bothered.

"As tidy as that. We are all God's possessions, as we possess the lesser animals given to our care. As such, we have no right to kill ourselves or other humans, as by doing so, we deprive God of his property. There are obvious exceptions like self-defense in war and the like. But yes. Lots of complicated details, but in the end, it's as simple as that."

He spread his hands, almost innocently. "What is government but the embodiment of the agreement between all reasoning people to enforce the laws, and what purpose could the laws have but to preserve our rights?"

"Our rights to life, health, liberty, and property." Truth's voice had gone bone-dry.

"Indeed."

Truth took a long, silent breath. "Where do you stand on this matter, Mr. Pepys?"

"I? I am a conservative at heart. I remember the great terrors of the Commonwealth, and the great foolishness of James the Second. The compact between Parliament and His Majesty strikes me as wise and just. A strong king, and a strong parliament to support and constrain him. And naturally, those of us inferior ministers to support the whole apparatus."

Pepys hadn't run the Royal Navy, but it could be argued that he made it run. The man never let a penny go past him without taking a percentage, but he still managed to be an enormous reformer compared to his contemporaries. His view that the victuals purchased by the Navy should be delivered to them and in edible condition was met with violent disagreement. Violence Pepys crushed with more violence.

"And you, Sir Isaac?"

"I don't give the slightest damn."

That brought a halt to the conversation. Pepys politely gave Sir Isaac a look. The Warden of the Mint might have ignored others, but Pepys was the first President of the Royal Society. Newton's vanity couldn't withstand the thought of sounding ignorant in front of someone who could inform the entire world of it in mere hours.

"I mean to say that I concern myself with the very mechanisms of the living universe and, by understanding them, understanding God Almighty. We see the hand of God in every orbit, in every falling rock, in the calcination of sulfur and mercury. So long as there is adequate funding for my experiments and to keep myself in reasonable comfort, I don't care about the conditions of the masses, or under what theory the government supports me and oppresses them."

"You would care quite quickly if the government were to, for example, claim authorship over your works," Locke said with deceptive mildness.

"It simply wouldn't happen. Besides, I truly do concern myself with the high path. I follow in the footsteps of Hermes Trismegistus, and if others lack the wit to do so, more fool them. I translated the Emerald Tablet into English the other day, just as an exercise and act of devotion."

Newton's eyes half-closed with pleasure. "Would you gentlemen care to hear true wisdom, transmitted down from Thoth, Moses, Hermes, transmitted by one who was a single step from the Godhead? Here—"

"It is true without lying, certain and most true. That which is Below is like that which is Above and that which is Above is like that which is Below to do the miracles of the Only Thing. And as all things have been and arose from One by the mediation of One, so all things have their birth from this One Thing by adaptation."

Newton's voice took on a certain cadence. His fingers swayed with the rhythm of the lines.

"The Sun is its father; the Moon its mother; the Wind hath carried it in its belly; the Earth is its nurse. The father of all perfection in the whole world is here. Its force or power is entire if it be converted into Earth. Separate the Earth from the Fire, the subtle from the gross, sweetly with great industry. It ascends from the Earth to the heavens and again it descends to the Earth and receives

the force of things superior and inferior. By this means you shall have the glory of the whole world and thereby all obscurity shall fly from you."

The mystic words sounded natural, coming from Newton. Sincere in a way that *please* or *thank you* wouldn't.

"Its force is above all force, for it vanquishes every subtle thing and penetrates every solid thing. So was the world created. From this are and do come admirable adaptations, whereof the process is here in this. Hence am I called Hermes Trismegistus, having the three parts of the philosophy of the whole world. That which I have said of the operation of the Sun is accomplished and ended."

He sat back with a sigh and a slight smile. "That is what I study. That is the truth I pursue. What matters mortal government against understanding the mind of God?"

A different sort of quiet gathered around the table. This time, it was Truth that broke it. "It all used to be one thing, didn't it? Studying the nature of God, studying the universe, studying how to run a government or be a moral person, it was all one thing. One 'philosophy,' covering everyone. Now it's lots of little things and not universally applicable."

"Yes, well, the world was a great deal simpler when Aristotle and Plato were running about." Newton drained his mug. "I'm headed up to Cambridge in the morning. Good night, gentlemen."

The group broke up and went their separate ways. Truth walked through the filthy streets, his one good hand resting loosely on a ship's cutlass. His mind was a storm, ideas tossed about on all the words he didn't say. He passed a mendicant on the street. He would have thought it some papist looking for martyrdom, but whatever prayer they were muttering wasn't in Latin. The robed figure turned suddenly and looked at him.

"And what do you think of my prayer, good sir whom I have never met before?"

"I think it sounds like a load of mystic bunk. I doubt it's even a real language."

That got sputtered denials. "It's Coptic, the language of fabled and ancient Egypt!"

"Oh, Egypt! Home of Moses and Thoth and, after Alexander rolled through, Hermes?"

"Well. Yes. Manner of speaking. Yes." The robed figure coughed and looked away. Their body language was suddenly awkward.

"Home of philosophy?"

"I'd say that where you have people, you have philosophy. Debatably. You might not even need people for philosophy to exist."

Truth nodded. He unbuttoned his codpiece and pissed on the street between them. "Don't mind me, mendicant. Just philosophizing. You can really smell the ancient wisdom. Philosophy is garbage. The whole game is just us pissing on our boots."

CHAPTER 28

WHAT'S IT ALL FOR?

Glad to see you are staying hydrated," the Prophet observed, carefully skipping back.

Truth shook the last few droplets off and tucked himself back in. "Are you mad? What does *hydrated* mean?"

"Drinking enough."

"Ah, I am that."

"Philosophy is all piss?"

"No, pissing is necessary. Useful. Pleasurable, so long as you don't have the stone." Truth's voice was severe. "Philosophy is pissing on our boots. Not only have we ruined a good thing, we made a smelly mess of ourselves in the process."

The Prophet nodded slowly. "I have certainly seen people mess themselves up playing about with questions about life, the universe, and everything. Don't you think there is value in the exercise itself, though?"

"No."

London was never a quiet place, regardless of day or night. People, almost all men, staggered past. Some carrying a torch, others hiring a boy to walk in front of them with the torch. A rare few hiring a carriage to deliver them safely to their destination. It was, however, mostly a city traveling on foot. Rich or poor, you were living *in* the city. You ate out, visited friends, worked, watched plays, went to church, all on foot. London was a writhing mass of interwoven lives, growing along the Thames. The Prophet could feel the wind rising there. It had been rising for a while, but right there, at this moment, in this place, the world would change. This was where the ideas that would shape the future would be born.

"Would you like to elaborate on that thought? Seems like quite a lot of good thinking is going on in these parts."

"Nah. It's all a fraud."

"How so?"

"People have been banging on about how everyone is equal since forever, right? Epicureans did, Stoics did, the students of Plato and Aristotle. We are all one people, equally loved by God."

"Well. That is, at best, a broad simplification. I think almost any of them would say that some are born to higher stations than others and with greater gifts."

"No, it's all the same bunk. Look, the Stoics, right? Huge influence, reach everywhere."

"All right?"

"And they come out and say that slavery is very bad. Mustn't do it. Except, you see, that slavery and freedom are really about state of mind. If one has disciplined their passions, they are free, and if they have not, they are slaves to them. So, really, in a master-slave relationship, who is free and who is in bondage?"

"Ah, tricky one." The Prophet nodded, smelling a rat.

"NO, you dolt, it isn't! The one that's being beaten and starved until they work is the slave! The one who will be crucified if he rebels is the slave! However *philosophically sound* the reasoning, one person is holding the whip and the other is getting whipped."

"The Stoics would, of course, point to pain being irrelevant, as it is neither a virtue or vice."

"How fucking convenient for the slave-owning Greeks and Romans, then!"

"Ah."

"And then you have the Bible. And the Bible of the Jews."

"Exodus 21?"

"Love the bit about using someone's wife to blackmail them into permanent bondage. Very loving, very equitable, very wise. But let's not let Peter slip past. Slaves should be loyal and obedient to their masters regardless of the master's character, eh? Lovely stuff. Truly the words of the Prince of Peace right there."

"All right, so, some philosophy in the past—"

"Tell me a single school of philosophy, a single religious faith, that rose to dominance and didn't excuse the ruling powers."

"Well, Christianity for one—"

"Was the state religion of the Roman Empire, and we've been converting at spearpoint ever since. Which makes me wonder what the religion looked like before the Romans adopted it. Makes you wonder how else it might have gone. Makes you wonder how things went from 'fed to the lions' to the Papal State. Seems like a lot is missing there, deliberately. The Mohammedans spread their faith on the edge of their sabers too. Taking slaves as they went. There wasn't much daylight between the Temple and the Kings of Israel, either. In every case, slavery was justified. A 'regrettable necessity.'"

The Prophet scrambled for a counterexample and was drawing a blank. So, they changed tack. "Doesn't invalidate philosophy as a whole field. Which I notice you are blending with theology one-for-one."

"Yes, it bloody does! And why not? All these bastards start their books with the nature of God, so how is that different from theology? And what does *philosophy* mean? The clue is in the name."

"A love of wisdom?"

"And yet, all these fornicating philosophers seem to manage is to *agree with what the rich and powerful do anyway*. Oh, they condemn wealth, cruelty, and injustice. But when push comes to shove? The successful ones always find an out. Some way to justify what is already being done. At the very least, a way to close their eyes."

"Like slavery."

"Had dinner with Locke today. Stirring stuff! Limited government. The preservation of life, health, liberty, and property. Including defining a 'just' way to own slaves. I'm sure this is unrelated, but Locke helped draft the Constitution of Carolina, guaranteeing that no one should interfere with the right of a freeman to own a slave. And he worked for the Royal Africa Company. Would you care to guess what business they are in?"

"Ivory?" the Prophet said, knowing damn well that wasn't it.

"Wrong!"

"Yeah."

"Pepys had a slave, a handsome young negro. Loved showing him off. Apparently, Pepys didn't care for his attitude, though, because he wound up selling him to a plantation in Barbados. Can't imagine the boy lived another year."

"Sad story. Common one these days, too."

"Aye. More ships going from the slave forts to the colonies every day, praising God's mercy every wet mile of the way. So, what's the wisdom we are supposed to find here? Smart people agree with the money? Truth is found in the broadside of a ship of the line?"

"Plato would have disagreed. Loudly."

"They all would have. So what? The only one of 'em worth a fart was Diogenes." Truth snorted. "He lived what he preached and died naked in a field."

"Aha! So, philosophy can be worthwhile!"

"How many books by Diogenes have you read?"

"He wrote ten, I believe, as well as some tragedies." The Prophet shook their head. "None survive, which is a tragedy in its own right."

"It is. We have to rely on secondhand wisdom. For some reason, his work wasn't worth saving, beyond a few colorful anecdotes. Yet Stoicism, which he was an inspiration for, thrives to this day. Can't imagine why the aggressively poor person who publicly mocked the great and good might be deliberately forgotten. It's just one of those ancient mysteries."

"What about natural philosophy? I see you are a sailor—"

"Also bunk."

"Your boat floats. It is plainly not bunk."

"It does float. My cutlass is made with good steel. My compass points true, and I can read the stars in the sky better than most. Doesn't matter. All bunk. Because when you press these natural philosophers even a little, they are straight back to Plato and the GODDAMNED Theory of Forms! They make a few stops along the way, generally by Paracelsus, Galen, Aristotle, or the thrice-damned Hermes Trismegistus, but the final stop is always Plato. The world isn't really real and should be, at most, treated as a reference."

"Again, a broad oversimplification. And why the sudden Hermes Trismegistus hate? What did they ever do to you?"

"You mean the ibis in drag? It's less him and more the mystical trash he represents. Phony little . . . Look, ever read Aristotle?"

"Every book he ever wrote." The Prophet nodded, trying not to seethe.

"That survived anyway."

There was a short pause.

"Yes. That survived. Aa-ha-ha-ha-ha."

"Point is, you read his *Meteorologica?*"

"Naturally. These days, it's probably considered his most important work."

"It's nonsense. Exhalations and condensations of the elements giving rise to everything in the world? It's gibberish. The man was so besotted with his theory, he refused to go outside and check if the facts agreed with him. The theory was logically perfect and therefore more 'true' than the actual, observable world."

Truth pointedly stared at a turd floating down the gutter. "This is a man who was married and still didn't know how many teeth women have, on account of never checking. So, you have to ask yourself, if this dumb fuck couldn't get outside long enough to see his theory didn't match reality, just how useful or true are his *Ethics*?"

"Hmm. And it points to the blind spot over women, of course." The Prophet nodded slightly.

"What?"

"What?"

"What blind spot about women? He was *wrong* about women—"

"Oh, I mean generally. If we are lumping every sort of philosophy together, they, collectively, even including the women philosophers, are pretty blind on women."

Truth scratched his head. "I don't follow."

"How many of these philosophers would have supported a woman owning property? Or being actively involved in politics? Allowing women to teach religious truths to men? Or actually studying women's medical conditions as opposed to thinking of them as men with some parts inside-out?"

"Not many, I would think. The Beguines would for some of that. Some of them. But so what?"

The Prophet sighed a little. Might need a few more lifetimes for those dots to connect. They took a final stab at it. "You don't see a connection between disregarding women, literally half of humanity, and condemning a comparatively much-smaller percentage of humanity to involuntary labor? No connection whatsoever?"

Truth cocked his head to one side and blinked. "If you are insinuating that, say, that woman over there is somehow enslaved, you are mad." He pointed to a woman walking home with her sons, carrying buckets of eels.

"Going to just . . . let that one alone for now. Why *are* you so hot on slavery? As you say, most of the philosophical set don't mind it too much."

Truth chuckled darkly. "Because if they'll do it to them, they'll do it to you. That's as close to a divine law as I have yet discovered. Nobody's special. Nobody. We cut off one king's head—so much for the divine right of kings. We'll have the Lord Protector, who is definitely not a king, and eleven years of chaos instead. We change our mind and what's this? Another king turns up by invitation. The son of the one whose head we cut off. Amazingly enough. Twenty-eight years later, we chuck the new king's son out on his ear and install a Dutchman instead. They cut off our heads? Chuck us out of a job? We'll do it right back!"

"So, if they enslave Africans, they will enslave you?"

"Why not? Not like I don't have kin still living under the Turks. Go to the villages in Attica and count the kids. If you have the guts. There is always an excuse, always a justification. What the excuse is changes. 'I want you to grow my wheat for me, and I won't pay you'; that never changes."

The Prophet had to admit that squared with what they had seen over the centuries. "It could, though. Isn't that the promise of the afterlife?"

"I can't hold a promise. I can hold bread, though. I can hold coin."

There was a dreadful silence. Truth sighed. "Of course I'm a Christian. Of course I'm a member of the Church of England. But that's just it—Christian. The Church of England. Hobbes and Locke, Newton and Hooke and Paracelsus and bloody Aristotle who we have all been blindly following for two thousand years without *checking our damn selves and trusting the evidence of our eyes!* And at the root of all this shitting about is that old monster Plato. Not Socrates, who we only know *through* Plato, but Plato himself! The Philosopher King of 'If the theory is right, it's real, and reality is wrong.' Most of these philosophers' 'wisdom' is self-serving at best and usually morally depraved. Newton's coming the closest to something real with his orbits, but his stuff on alchemy is just—"

"Quite decent, from what I have heard." The Prophet smiled under their hood.

"Is it? Tell you what: let me give you some mercury, some sulfur, and some dirt. You make a human being. I won't even ask you to stick a soul in it. A corpse will do."

"But even Plato said that reason is only one path to the truth, and not necessarily the best one. That there are higher truths that must be understood by divine revelation, as they transcend rationality and language. Is it wrong of Hermeticists like Newton to pursue that line of thinking? Pursue that wisdom?"

"Oh? OH! Well, that solves everything! Heavens, why didn't I think of that very obvious cop-out? Obviously only the very smart, very enlightened people can understand the things that transcend understanding. The rest of us are just too stupid to understand and no use word good." He wagged his finger at the robed Prophet.

"Let me ask you this—can trees be enlightened? How about a chicken? Do they benefit from divine revelation?"

"I . . . don't believe so. Humans are special, you see. Made in God's image."

"Made in God's image. All us featherless bipeds. But you tell me: if our reason can't reach the truth, and we can't catch the truth in our words nor our hands, if, in fact, our *wisdom* is not enough to reach the truth, what exactly is the point of *philosophy*? Either we can reason it all out or we can't. And if we can't, we are no better off than the rocks and trees, on account of them not having wisdom or language either."

"The chase is the thing! The pursuit of wisdom, finding ways to climb higher and higher towards the Godhead! It's about asking the questions and arguing, not about finding the one right answer." The Prophet waved at the sky.

"But it's not a game with no consequences, is it? Because Archimedes was making war machines before he died, and our ships are built to his rule. Our notions of just war come from Greek and Roman philosophers, filtered through church thinkers for sixteen hundred years. The very laws that rule these streets, the right of king and parliament to rule, are all justified by these philosophers' games. It all matters."

Truth looked up into the sky. "We just want to be safe. To be loved. To understand our lives. To be connected to what we know in our hearts exists in the heavens. And each of these damned philosophers just rush out and say whatever nonsense will get rich patrons to cover their meals. And now there's piss all over our boots. Fuck wisdom. After the philosophers got to us, we're dumber than ever."

The Prophet shook their head. "We have learned how to think. We might not have learned the one right answer, but we have gotten better and better at asking the questions. We aren't groping blindly in the dark anymore. Diogenes' lantern is lit."

Truth laughed bitterly. "And have you found an honest man yet?"

Something glimmered in the depths of the Prophet's hood. "An *honest* man? That's a mistranslation at best."

"Eh?"

"Diogenes was looking for *a man*. Which might be more usefully translated as 'a real human being,' given the context. And you know what? I think I just might have."

CHAPTER 29

LIVING YOUR PATH

Truth slowly opened his eyes. He was staring at the smudged interior of the luggage compartment. The packs weren't very comfortable. How strange. When he crawled in there before, it was like falling asleep on angel feathers and lullabies. Could it have been the crippling exhaustion?

He contemplated the myriad mysteries concealed in the scrapes on the ceiling. No. No, it had to be evil wizards that cursed the packs into lumpy unpleasantness. He could recognize the efforts of his own kind. This had the exquisite level of pettiness he constantly sought in his own work. He should take this as a learning opportunity.

He . . . had been a sailor. A captain of a ship of the line, whatever that was. He had drinks with philosophers and pissed in the street with holy wanderers. That mystic passage recited by "Newton" echoed in his brain. It seemed to want to claw its way out, to slip his memory entirely. His soul was now far, far too strong for such nonsense.

Truth didn't really know anything about alchemy. Some of the stuff on the Emerald Tablet sounded kind of familiar, but really, it wasn't his field. Nevertheless, based on the way it seemed to bash on the inside of his eardrums, he could sell it to any alchemist tower for, approximately, All the money.

Maybe it would be worth something off-world. If he chose to go off-world. Which he probably would. He looked at the little fragment of Etenesh glowing inside of him. It looked stronger, somehow. Not happier or anything. It just felt more robust. Like she was putting back together all her broken pieces and was stronger than ever before.

Could he fall asleep for a little bit longer? Maybe. He shut his eyes and tried to fall back asleep. It wasn't easy. The jolting of the bus reminded him of nights in canvas hammocks, and the cold blue sea.

He woke again when the cargo door opened and soldiers started reaching in to unload the packs. He wasn't really sure where he was, but that was fine. He was north of Harban. Good enough.

He stepped out of his temporary bedroom and onto an army base. His bus was one of a dozen, all spilling soldiers onto the concrete pad. There was a big sign saying that this was Fort Red Spear. He wracked his brain, and a vague memory of an inland base roughly northeast of Gamphe came to mind. It was a little north of where he thought the battlefront would settle, so . . . Was it good that Onis hadn't advanced that quickly, or a bad sign that their own problems were, somehow, even worse than what Jeon was going through?

He mentally shrugged. Not his problem in any sense. Time to hit the road. He quickly changed into his officer's uniform, neither noticing nor caring that he was surrounded by thousands of people. He could feel the aftereffects of whatever the angel had done. It was like all the scraps of magic and muscle were finally organized and integrated. His blessings had refined and integrated with his spells. It was now the law of the world in the little area around Truth—he was outside their perception.

He had become one of those invisible forces that shaped the world. Ordinary people could speak with him, touch him, be harmed by him, and never once really see who or what they were dealing with. He had long since gotten used to it. Now it seemed more than natural. It seemed right. This was how the world should be. He stretched and flexed his fingers. He found an underemployed-looking second lieutenant and tapped him on the shoulder.

"Where's the vehicle pool?"

The lieutenant jumped, saluted in midair, and landed in a ninety-degree bow. Truth was mildly impressed by the athleticism. Must be fresh off the bus with the rest, still green as grass. Truth looked up into the drizzling rain clouds and back at the young shoot. The lieutenant couldn't be more than nineteen.

"Sir! Sorry I didn't see you, sir! I apologize, sir!"

"Noted. Do better. Vehicle pool?"

"Sir! I just arrived, sir! Let me find—"

"Never mind. Report to that man over there, the sergeant with the clipboard. He will tell you where to go." Truth pointed.

"Thank you, sir. Sorry, sir."

"Mmm. Dismissed."

Nineteen. Tops. Scared as hell, hadn't a clue, and unlike the enlisted, he had to make decisions. He had to be one of the people in charge. He was the one feeding people into the meat grinder, not on contract but as a matter of national policy. What that commission meant hadn't really kicked in yet. He might not live long enough to figure it out.

Truth shook his head and looked for someone with a clue. Eventually, he found a logistics officer and, from there, the vehicle pool. Shortly thereafter, he requisitioned a firebird. Sure, he didn't have the necessary orders, but his Internal Security credentials were impeccable.

He was flying over Jeon on a military-breed firebird. Deep red flames licked up around him harmlessly, the mighty wings driving through the air at hundreds of kilometers an hour. He, Truth Medici, had finally gotten his firebird. He had wanted one since he was a kid. They looked amazing from below.

Truth stretched his fingers out and let his hand run through the fine down, letting the tiny flames tickle his fingers. They were specially bred and trained to be harmless to passengers, but a firebird was, ultimately, a being that was more magic than meat. It was a giant bird made of flames and feathers and an ape's dream of flying in eternal sunshine. It was a symbol of dominance and freedom. In Jeon, it was an echo of the phoenix.

He looked northeast. The volcano was still spewing smoke and ash. He had stopped noticing the haze a long time before. He'd bet the monsoon rain was lousy with ash. He felt a brief stab of sympathy for anyone needing to clean or paint. The thought made him laugh a little as he fell back onto the feathers.

"Yes, that's the real problem. Painting and keeping buildings clean. It's a utopia out here. What other problems could there be?"

He smiled a little half smile. "Sir?" the firebird asked. This time, it was Truth who had to control a jump. He had forgotten that he was masquerading as an officer, and the bird could hear him.

"Just a little dark humor. I was reminded of an argument I once heard, a complete triumph of logic in the face of reality. Listen—God is omnipotent, omniscient, and omnibenevolent. He created this world. He has created other worlds, but he didn't have to make *any*. Now, since he is omniscient and omnipotent, he knew which world would be the best world, and was able to make his vision real. Since he is omnibenevolent, he made that best world. Therefore, this world, the one in front of us right now, is the best possible world."

The bird flew silently for a little while. Then: "Forgive my impertinence, sir, but may I ask what the alternatives are? I understand that this is the *best* world on some level I can't understand, but maybe one of the others might suit me better."

Truth just laughed.

They flew out over the ocean. Truth had laid hands on an adequate map of the waters in the northwest of the Jeon peninsula, south of Onis. It wasn't a particularly large body of water, as these things go—more than two hundred kilometers across, even where it narrowed. Add the sheer length of it, the war, the highly active defense by Starbrite, and it was no wonder its hidden sea bases could be inferred but not found.

Truth stared at the map, some piece of that last thought niggling at him. This was one of the busiest trade corridors in the world. Not *the* busiest, but both Onis and Jeon were manufacturing powerhouses. Cargo ships were moving through these waters every minute of every day. Their fishing fleets were in heavy deployment too. Add on the famously defense-minded Jeon Navy, and these waters should be crawling with boats. Logically, if there was anything bigger than a coconut in these waters, it would be found, investigated, interrogated, and then sold to the highest bidder.

Even if Starbrite was openly exterminating everyone that got too close, it would be a blatant tell that there was something in there they wanted to defend. Given the literal world war going on, that seemed like a dumb way to protect anything, let alone the physical person of Starbrite.

Truth scratched at his chin as the firebird flew in big, lazy loops over the water. There were a few passes by reconnaissance summons. Perhaps someone would be dispatched to find out what the hell he was doing up there. Perhaps not. One thing he did know—soldiers sometimes just wound up in the wrong place. Lost, misunderstood orders, separated from their units, plenty of reasons it could happen. It wasn't a big deal, usually.

He was smelling a Nascent Soul–tier rat. The whole thing seemed phony. Just too pat. He directed the bird to fly toward the area he suspected the final base would be.

The constellation is oriented the wrong way. I don't know why that bugs me, but it does. It's basically upside-down. God, the two offshore bases wouldn't even be that far offshore. Why bother?

As expected, there were no bases in sight. Worse was what was in sight—boats. Lots and lots of boats. Traveling in convoys for protection, which meant military vessels were escorting them. Which meant that the best detection capabilities of the Jeon Navy weren't seeing anything remotely threatening.

Now . . . what would he do if he were Starbrite?

Deepest trench in the deepest ocean, obviously. The Green Sea is shallow for a major body of salt water. So . . . maybe the base is on the ocean floor, but you have to consider that the bases were arranged in the form of the constellation. Presumably, they had something to do with the arrangement of the stars over Jeon, because there was no Ursa Minor there, nor a Pole Star. Usually, that would mean being somewhere high. Astrologers were always building sky-watching platforms. But if you weren't actually *looking* at the stars, maybe it didn't matter as much.

Making things worse was that the map he saw had very vague, very approximate guesses about where Internal Security thought the bases *might* be, and when you get right down to it, in his past life, he wasn't measuring the exact distance between stars. Sailing was a deadly game of guesses, where you could take your latitude but little else. You navigated based on time, speed traveled, direction, and your questionable maps. Once you started hitting recognizable landmarks like Africa, or Guernsey, you could work out where to aim your bow next. You would get there eventually.

Or not. Quite often not. Lots of people just died at sea. Ships lost for no known reason.

What would he do if he were Starbrite? Truth's go-to move was local reality manipulation. Blurring the lines of the "real" and making sure the resulting picture flattered him. Now, if he were a Nascent Soul–tier nightmare with access to near enough every spell on the planet and some kind of horribly mutated soul such as would cause any reasonable person to recoil in terror, he might just do the same thing. Shift the local reality a little. Didn't have to be a lot. Just enough to make people avoid it without noticing or remembering it.

Something clicked inside of him. That was it. It wasn't an illusion or a glamour. It was something that worked because it altered the fabric of reality on a level that most counter magic simply couldn't deal with. He certainly didn't have a tidy solution for it. Truth slowly started grinning.

"Fly up. As high as you can."

Up they went, through the cloud layer, then higher still. Once they were high enough that the flames struggled to burn, Truth ordered the bird to start making wide loops over the sea.

Truth leaned into Incisive and summoned the Tongue. "Now, which spot would be the *worst* place to power-dive and attack? I think I'm going to go . . . here! No, here!" It took quite a few tries. He must have been thrashing around up there for forty minutes.

"Found you. At long last, I found you."

Another triumph for the almighty power of jank. He had finally found Starbrite.

CHAPTER 30

WET MILEAGE

I don't think I can be blamed for being happy. Anyone would be happy. This is huge. Nobody else managed to do this.

Truth indulged in a little self-pity. He ordered the firebird to start sweeping up and down the coastline, to keep the base from figuring out they had been spotted. Except, of course, they hadn't been spotted. They had just been inferred with a high degree of probability. But even that wasn't the source of his misery.

It was the fact that they were almost a hundred kilometers offshore. A big, seemingly impassable wall wasn't scary. Any fixed defense can be overcome. It was not having anywhere to stand while he did the overcoming that was doing his head in.

I traveled all over the country. Pulled on the intelligence-gathering of Siphios for some things, and Jeon for even more. Used my own likely unique understanding of magic to figure out what Starbrite was up to. And now I can't do anything with that information. I want to riot. I want to riot and generally throw a fit.

It just felt so damn petty. He could go get a boat, of course, but that would be worse, not better. He would still stand out, only this time, he would be moving even slower. Could he swim there? Eventually, sure. It was just the not-so-minor detail of it being a colossal pain in the ass. Even if he succeeded, once again, where would he stand? Where, exactly, would he do his work from?

Did he have to tread water or something? No way, right?

Right?

Truth groaned, loudly, then started getting naked. This uniform had been really useful, and he didn't want it soaked if he could help it. Midway through unbuttoning the shirt, he paused. He was about to do something very dumb again. Maybe, this time, how about not?

Hey, Perks?

Yes?

If I were to, hypothetically, jump off this bird and into the ocean, doing my best to protect you against my chest, would you be okay? Physically?

There was a pause.

I think so. I have never fallen so far. I feel a great deal stronger these days, so I am not afraid. Yet my appetite is less. It is very strange.

And there it was. Perks was on the accelerated course to being a demon. Fantastic. Well. It wasn't a bad thing.

Can you deal with the water okay? You won't drown or anything?

I won't drown. I can swim, you know.

Really? I thought you were a desert snake?

I have never seen the desert. But I know I can swim a little.

Oh, neat! Well. Hitch a ride for now.

Mmm.

"Start flying back up the coastline. I'm going to jump off at a certain point. Once I do, you just keep flying until you reach the place where we turned around last time, then return to base. If anything comes up, especially anything that might threaten you, take all necessary actions in accordance with your bindings and return to base."

"Yes, sir." The bird had been raised from birth by the military. It knew when not to ask questions. Truth waited until they were roughly parallel with the assumed island and jumped.

This was not the first time Truth had jumped into the ocean from a great height. He could vividly remember his "triumphant" return from Siphios. It was not a *happy* memory, but it was vivid. Truth opted to run the Meditations as hard as he could and compress his body as much as he could to minimize the impact.

Oh, fuck, Earth-Folding Step would—

The water hammered into the soles of his feet, and there was an enormous splash. He could feel the ocean fighting him, but this time, the ocean was destined to lose. He had changed. Harder. Stronger. Maybe even a little smarter. Water resistance and terminal velocity lost out to the Meditations of Valentinian, as cultivated by an obsessive body cultivator.

Truth floated naked on the ocean's surface. Perks, seemingly unharmed, slipped out of his arms and curled up on his chest. The ocean was a little warmer than Truth expected. He checked over his body. Not even any redness or soreness. The last round of refinement, courtesy of the angel, had clearly done a lot for his body. He splashed the water idly. Had he ever been to the beach for fun? He was pretty sure he hadn't.

A memory intruded—after the ops at Chil Perdermo, the one with the human traffickers, they were supposed to go to a beach party. He had flown home early instead, to sort out Vig and Sophia's school problems. Felt like a lifetime past. It was actually a lifetime past.

It had been a long time since he thought of the sibs. Maybe it just felt that way. Their faces used to be constantly on his mind. What did they need? How could he protect them? How could he give them the best future? He was still doing that, of course, but . . .

Truth wrestled with that *but . . .*' It made him feel inexplicably guilty. His need to kill Starbrite had always been selfish. He was at peace with that. Kill Starbrite, save the sibs, save a handful of other people, and get off this world before the collapse really hit its terminal curve and the Nephilim came in to tidy up. That was a very reasonable thing to do. It wasn't like he wanted to fight a Nascent Soul god. Without that ticket off-world in the balance, would he have gone hunting for Starbrite's head?

The Truth who watched the Black Ships arrive in Siphios absolutely would not have. He would have done his best to extract the sibs from Jeon, smuggle them to Siphios, and start building a clan compound up in the mountains. He'd get Etenesh in as a design consultant, and Jember in to tell him which locals were worth making friends with.

The Truth who was currently bobbing in the Green Sea could see a case for killing Starbrite regardless of the tickets off-world. Starbrite was just too destructive. For all the good that he had brought this world, and he *had* brought good things to this world, they were far outweighed by the harm he had done.

There simply had to be a way to balance it out. Wasn't like the world was some blessed garden before Starbrite arrived. By all accounts, the technologies and methods he introduced made life vastly more comfortable for most. For a time. But it was now plain that the price of that comfort had been paid only in part. The balance was now due, and it was more than the world could bear. All that accumulated wealth, the accumulated virtue of millennia, had been stripped away. Concentrated first in the hands of a few, then just in Starbrite.

At a certain level of concentration, killing just one person would mean a big shift in the global average of wealth. It wouldn't trickle down very fast, if at all. It was awfully late for that. But it would have an effect. And then there was the other thing, the moral example. No matter how powerful you were, no one was untouchable. No one could hurt so many people, for so long, and get away clean. If Truth really wanted to create a brilliant world, or even just a better one, it had to start by rejecting, harshly, the old world.

Parading the severed head of the man who embodied that old world was a great start, Truth felt. Really showed you weren't just yapping. You were putting in that work. Besides, it was a great foundational myth.

The Demon King of the World, surrounded by endless wealth and power, surrounded by armies of deadly sorcerers, was killed by a slumrat. A man of no background and with no famous name to boast. The Demon King was killed by a *nobody*, and they were the most common sorts of people! It was therefore wisest not to tread too heavily on the nobodies.

A nice, tidy little homily. Truth sighed. He had never done endurance swimming before. He knew how to swim, but endurance swimming?

He touched Perks. The snake seemed to be much more durable after being enlightened by the angel.

Doing okay?

Yes. That was a big jolt, and the water is unpleasantly cold, but other than that, I am fine.

That's good.

Truth carefully guided Perks onto his back and got swimming.

The target was only eighty kilometers away. How hard could it be?

You appear to be suffering.

You know how appearances can be deceiving, right, Perks?

I do. I don't think they are now, though.

Truth declined to answer. It was embarrassing to argue with a snake. It was even more embarrassing to lose an argument with a snake. He would just have to endure.

When I swim, I just wriggle my whole body through the water. You are splashing around a lot. Is that normal for humans?

Yes. Well, it depends, I think, but this is the only way I know how to swim. Oddly enough, his memories of his past life as a sailor didn't include memories of swimming. Which seemed insane, but what did he know? Maybe not knowing how to swim was normal for sailors in that other life.

The swimming technique he knew came in part from training in the Army and in part from training in the PMC. It was not . . . elegant. Or efficient. It was designed for soldiers wearing boots and heavy clothes to cross rivers or survive unexpected disasters. It was not intended for stealth or speed. Eighty kilometers, a brief, comfortable stroll on land, turned into an endless, miserable slog at sea.

What was even more maddening was that it was almost impossible to keep on course. They were far out to sea now. The waves were a meter tall, more when measured from the base of the trench to the peak. He just plain couldn't see the "nowhere" he was aiming at. Worse, he realized the wind and currents were pushing him southwest.

I don't suppose you have a way to track our destination, do you? Truth asked.

I do not. Where are we headed, anyhow?

Truth explained what he could. *So, you don't see anything?*

I do not. The air tastes strange, but I think that's the ocean more than anything else.

Does it taste salty?

Yes, but there are other things as well. There is a very unpleasant taste roughly to the right of you, but it's so widespread, I have no idea where its origin is. It's just drifting everywhere.

Do you think you could pinpoint it?

Not really. Like I said, it's spreading everywhere. You could start swimming a bit more to your right. We might learn more.

Swearing softly, Truth adjusted course. He was in elite physical condition, but swimming was shockingly tiring. You didn't just swim with your legs. You swam with your whole body. Everywhere got tired. The wisdom of boats became steadily more obvious. Boats were good. You didn't have to swim all day if you had a boat.

I think the bad taste is getting stronger.

What does it taste like?

Like burnt things, rotting things, and pine trees. And a bunch of things I don't have names for. Sometimes, the old man who looked after me would rub something into his hands. It smells a little like that. But a lot of the burnt smell. The biggest thing is that.

Truth couldn't imagine what it might be. He just kept on swimming.

The sun was setting when he banged his toes against a hidden rock. He thought he had kicked a fish for a moment. Soon, he got his foot down on it again. He could feel the cool algae and the barnacles poking at him. And yet, when he looked down, he couldn't see the rock.

Truth had a sudden, terrible moment of empathy for all the people he ghosted past. It really wasn't nice.

CHAPTER 31

THE REALEST

The rock was not cooperative. In addition to being invisible, it kept trying to slip out of his memory. As a result, he found himself struggling to keep his balance. Truth could have balanced on a razor's edge balanced on another razor's edge on the edge of a monofilament wire in a moderate windstorm. So, being unable to keep balanced on a roughly foot-sized rock in calm seas inspired a lively hate in him.

He fell off. Twice. Truth had already decided to murder anyone who looked to get froggy in the base, but by the time his foot slipped for the third time, he swore it would be on sight. Everybody dies. Sorry, Little Timmy. Daddy caught a bad case of Sword-To-The-Face-itis and can't make it home.

Then that thought bummed him out. He didn't really want to orphan anyone; he was just being pissy. And realistic. No need to play the bully. Which made him hate the rock more. How dare this invisible rock make him depressed as well as angry! He glared at it while treading water.

You don't have to move forward while you swim. You can move up and down in the water, too. Perks had opted to swim alongside Truth now that the endurance swim was over. Not that Truth was bearing a grudge! It was at most lingering resentment.

Yeah, we call it treading water. Truth kicked slightly harder and managed to lift his entire torso up out of the water.

You can kick hard enough to launch yourself out of the water.

Heh. Yep. I'm pretty strong.

Fast, too. I remember the trees flying past my nest and the sound of the rushing wind.

I am also really, really fast. Truth smiled. He loved how it felt when he pushed his body.

Can you run on water?

Sure can. I figured out I was fast enough to do that way back when I was Level Three. Happy memories.

There was a quiet pause.

So . . . was there some reason you didn't just kick up out of the water and start running so fast, you didn't fall back into the water again? Just run the distance from where you fell to wherever we are now?

Truth watched the black-winged gulls fly through the air overhead. He would have thought they were too far from shore, but it seemed he didn't know much about birds. Their cries sounded especially piercing for some reason.

He kicked up out of the water and started jogging around. No problems. He sank back into the water next to Perks.

There is a reason. The reason is that I didn't think of it. Actually, we could have just had the bird land on the shore and then run over. Forgetting the obvious was embarrassing. Lying to your pet snake about it just seemed extra shameful.

I see.

Truth briefly contemplated drowning himself. Then he pulled himself back together.

Let's focus on the positive—I have found an invisible rock that tries to make me forget its existence. No doubt we are right on top of the base. Now we just need to figure out how to see it and get in there.

How are they not seeing us? Perks asked. Truth nodded. It was a reasonable question.

They might see you when you are away from me, but as for me? Unless someone much higher-level is looking at me, I'm like the island. Out of sight and mind.

I had wondered about that. Perks would have nodded if he was a human. *So, how do you plan on getting past the illusion?*

Ah, that's just the thing. It's not an illusion. The trick works because reality itself is telling us the island isn't worth noticing. I have a special blessing that lets me blend perfectly with my environment. I'm not sure how the base is doing it, but since Starbrite is vastly more powerful and experienced than I am, he clearly found a way. Hell, he might have basically the same blessing.

The Blessing of the Silent Forest wasn't unique, after all. He was just one of many people who had received it over the centuries. Though he liked to think that he had really taken full advantage of it.

He floated in the water, thinking it over. The best spell-cracker he could think of for this specific situation was using his other blessing, the Blessing of the Sea of Brass, to define the orthodoxy of his immediate area so strongly, things would be forced into view. The idea had an itchy feeling to it, like there should be a better way he just wasn't seeing. After the recent experience with the marathon swim, spending some extra time thinking was necessary.

He tried to think through what it was his magic was actually doing. He was imposing a higher-level reality on his immediate environment. It was only higher by a minute fraction of a single degree, but that was essentially what it was.

Cosmic rays come, ultimately, from God, through the forms of the various stellar eminences. It was one of the few things taught at school that he had yet to find out was a lie. What he had learned since leaving school was that the higher the concentration of cosmic energy (the refined form of the cosmic rays), the more "real" something became. *Real* being defined as *closer to God* and frequently existing in a literally higher realm. A realm that humans, or at least the humans on this rock, were too spiritually dead to observe or safely interact with.

Truth had seen the other side of the sky a few times now. Twice when he fell into the sky, and once when he was carried through the void by Sally, the Shattervoid child. He got the vague impression that what the Shattervoid did wasn't quite the same, but damned if he knew how it was different. They were just too alien. Maybe they considered themselves human, but their perspective was far beyond his. He couldn't do what they did.

But that was not to say there wasn't some inspirational potential. Earth-Folding Step was kind of the inverse of what the Shattervoid did. They went around the other side of reality as a shortcut. Earth-Folding Step scrunched up reality on *this* side, letting him cross distances in a single symbolic step. The spell didn't require him to see his target location, though it did make the spell a lot easier. Likewise, however the Shattervoid did what they did, they had to know where they were going. As big as they were, if they popped out in the wrong place, the results could only be catastrophic.

Maybe . . . he could define the reality around him to only show the truth? No, that wouldn't work, because this wasn't an illusion. It was a higher level of reality. Could he define himself as someone that saw only a higher level of reality? *There* was an idea covered in warning tape. Floating in the ocean next to the hidden nest of the most powerful man in the world seemed like a bad place for exciting experiments. Still, the idea had an irresistible appeal. It would be quite the joke for him to rush forward and land in a minefield. Being able to see what was going on was a minimum for this raid.

He . . . really hadn't planned this well. Or at all. It occurred to him that a lot of these problems had probably already been solved by Merkovah. One conversation could clear up a lot. Truth shook the idea from his head. He could feel himself tumbling like a boulder down the mountain. He could lead the avalanche or be crushed under it. He was a holy fool, fighting God without a plan. A half-smile tugged the corner of his mouth up. Beat playing a prince.

Truth slowly sank under the surface, while Perks made lazy circles in the water above him. He let his fingers guide him down, along the invisible rock. He didn't need to breathe much. He could take a little time with this. The System would have been an amazing help there. Heh. The demon is the mage, but in his case, hadn't he been the demon all along?

He slowly ran the Meditations, trying to lure the Worms into helping. He still didn't know what they were or what their connection to the Rough Patron was. Didn't matter, didn't matter; he forced himself to focus on what he was doing.

He kept thinking in terms of *visible* and *invisible*, but it was more primal than that—the spell was trying to deny him the qualifications to perceive the hidden base on any level. But he could feel the rock under his feet, and Perks could smell it. Taste it. Whatever. The point was, he was very close to being qualified.

So, what if . . . what if, instead of refining his physique with the happy side effect of becoming increasingly real, he focused on refining what he *was*? Directly elevating his status in the universe by a fraction of a degree?

Another five-alarm idea. He could put it right next to the super-vision idea. They could keep each other company.

Was he really stuck with the brute-force method, relying on the Blessings of the Sea of Brass to adjust reality around him to a level he could perceive? Trying to keep it running through a full-blown invasion of the base seemed dumb.

Truth watched Perks swimming around above him. The Shattervoid, from what he had seen, didn't really look like snakes, even if they were a head stuck on some long, sinuous bodies. Seven-headed snake in the sun. The creator god looked like a lion head stuck on a snake, according to the Ghūl. Even the angel said something about a snake's burden. It felt like the more you learned about the world, the more mysterious it became.

Truth let his eyes drift shut. The Meditations slowly churned, reinforcing him. Building him up and sealing him off from the world. Only accepting and releasing those things he permitted. He poured more strength into the Blessing of the Sea of Brass. In the narrow area around him, he determined orthodoxy. He couldn't reshape reality at a whim, but with arm's reach, he was the source of truth. Nobody else got to say what was and what was not.

He had done this before for bad reasons. Did this count as doing it for a good reason?

He let the magic flow into him and through him. Trying to see past the form and formalities, and into the core of the mystery. He was Truth Medici, and in these parts, he was the realest thing there was. He could see the hidden truths of the world. He could stand apart and judge things with his own reason rather than the common sense of others. He was not going to let Starbrite define his reality. Never again.

Sometimes, you need to look up and say God got it wrong. Then you have to look down and decide if you were really talking to God. Then you look straight ahead and start throwing hands. Because no matter what, the only constant was *you*, which meant that you were going to be the one fixing things regardless.

The water was irresistibly pushed back from him, a cavity forming in the cool sea.

"I name myself, own myself, accept myself. In all my imperfections and in all my glory. I am *Truth*. And I am more than the sum of my parts. I will keep waking, keep searching. Trying to find the why behind it all. I am Truth, and I have been purified by myriad baptisms. I carry myriad blessings. And right now, I see through the false reality of this tiny creator. He is not God, and he did not create this world. I am Truth. And this is not."

He didn't know where the words came from, why they bubbled up inside his heart. Why they formed a spell and meshed with the magic within him. He just knew they were right. When he opened his eyes again, it was to a new world.

CHAPTER 32

EYES OPEN AND LAYING DOWN THE LAW

The sky was as blue as it ever was. But it wasn't. The sky was clear as night, filled with a billion billion billion stars. But it wasn't. The sky was red, the color of cold flames and hot blood, filled with screaming ghosts and raging demons. But it wasn't.

The Green Sea was warm as a mother's love or as cold as a mother's contempt. It was hydrogen, oxygen, sodium, and other trace minerals. It was one of the four elements, mixed, as all material things are, with the other elements like earth and air. It too was filled with demons and ghosts.

The world was a living, thriving, writhing thing, twisting madly over on itself. Everything an endlessly deep well of relations and meanings, waiting to be pulled up and savored by some thirsty soul.

Truth thought he had gone mad. Then he glanced up at the sun and knew he had. He barely glanced at it before he had to turn away. The "truth" was not so easily understood, and even less easily defined.

On reflection, he should probably have considered that multiple things can be true at the same time. Likewise, things can have multiple meanings that are all valid. Trying to force yourself to see, and be the arbiter of, the truth of everything in your immediate vicinity was a *bold* choice.

At least he could see the base now. It was hard to see anything else.

The base rose from the sea, rising like a holy mountain. A place where Heaven, Earth, and sea all intersected. A place for offerings, for worship, for the confirmation of the Mandate of Heaven. This was the holiness granted by the world, a place where one could walk up the starry path to wisdom. A kindness, a generous opportunity, and an invitation all in one.

The base suppressed the sea, a floating cathedral designed by spiders and by those possessed by terrible visions of dark places. A place of madness written in stone and steel and awful magics, all hinting at deeper truths. Truths that would shatter your too-mortal mind if you grasped even a crumb of them. Between the girders and flying buttresses stretched wires of ghosts and spirits. The statuary were nailed demons and human souls bound in marble and jade, screaming and clawing at their prisons as they tried to escape. Each and every brick and stone was carved with strange runes and sigils, operating on vile principles.

It was also a rather large concrete box sitting on a larger concrete base built on top of a small shoal rising out of the seabed. It had been painted white. About fifty meters away was an empty dock, with a guardhouse next to the door. There was also an enormous shutter door, so huge it was clearly designed for ships to pass through when it was raised. It was closed now. No signs of flags on it. Why bother? Anyone who could see it knew exactly who the base belonged to.

The meanings shifted and slid around, ranging from the secular to the sacred to the profane. Truth figured out how to speak and called Perks over. He didn't try to look at the snake just yet. He just scooped him up without looking, hopped out of the water, and jogged to the dock. He would sort things out a little more when he was sitting on dry land.

Sitting on the dock was barely better than looking at it. He could feel it changing and shifting underneath him. This wasn't what he wanted. He wanted to see the truth, to nail it down. He knew that he wouldn't suddenly have perfect wisdom and understand the truth of all things. It was always going to be a journey, a progressive effort to understand. That was fine. This? This was madness. Lost between the layers of reality, unable to find the true path.

He looked down at Perks and saw a snake. And a snake demon. And a human spine. And a penis. And hunger. And wisdom. And betrayal. Meanings flickering over and through him. All "true," to varying degrees of symbolism and transcendent meaning, but so wild and multiform that they were paralyzing.

He couldn't go on like this. He had seen some maddening things, but this was literal insanity. The thought kept spinning around and around. He clung to the thought as though remembering it would protect him from being lost in all the things he was seeing. If he was going to anything more than scream at the sky, he needed an answer. He could acknowledge that the other answers existed, but he needed one thing to be true. One referent to judge the other truths against.

He closed his eyes and focused on his breathing. Ignoring what breathing meant. Ignoring how his lungs were bellows, stoking the fires of his life. How the very act of breathing nourished him with the life-giving energy in the air and polluted him with the impure air of the mortal world. How nothing could touch him that he didn't permit, and how he was one inseparable being with the world he was inhaling. Watching the thoughts fly past, not attaching an emotion to them. Keeping his inner eye firmly on finding solutions.

While all the things he was seeing were true *on some level,* they were not true in the everyday meaning of the word. Perks was not a human spine and never had been. He was most assuredly not a human penis. By extension, Truth was one hundred percent certain his trouser snake had neither scales nor fangs. A symbolic truth only got you so far, and generally, *so far* was a pretty short distance. The world simply couldn't function that way. Regardless of the lack of enlightenment on this backwater rock, he couldn't imagine other worlds running on endless shifting layers of meaning.

Someone was buying those talismans Starbrite manufactured. Someone was selling books and luxuries back. And food. So, so much food. Billions upon billions of tons of food had been imported by the Shattervoid every year. You could make rice as symbolic as you liked, but someone had to grow it. There had to be an *it* to grow.

The world, all the worlds, had some baseline, agreed-on meaning. He looked at that thought for a moment, then gave his forehead a firm, and very true, slap.

"Perks, I must confess I'm not a particularly smart man."

Oh? Why?

"Why what?"

Why must you confess that? Is it a crime? Perks sounded mildly interested.

"In this case, it is a figure of speech. I have been using the Blessing of the Sea of Brass all wrong. Or, at least, not understanding what it was for. In my defense, it sure seems like nobody else understands what it's for either."

Do you need defending? Perhaps you shouldn't have confessed and remained silent.

Truth had a sudden flash of sympathy for Merkovah. He wouldn't let it stop him in the future, but he did feel it. "Orthodoxy. What does it mean to establish an orthodoxy?"

I have no idea.

"It means we all agree on one truth and one reality. Even if you don't really one-hundred-percent agree with it on the inside, you go along with it. And by *agree*, I mean you don't fight the person who establishes it. And orthodoxy is whatever the boss says it is. Inside the span of my arms, I am the boss."

Truth slowly poured power into the Blessing of the Sea of Brass. While those higher levels of meaning might exist, he wasn't there yet. He also firmly believed that symbolism was strictly for people who can't get to the damn point and say things plain. Symbolism, like subtext, was for cowards. No, only the secular was real. Just . . . a higher-level understanding of the secular. Maybe with a thin schmeer of magic over the top. After all, how can you call magic fake? It was as real as gravity, and since gravity seemed to stop working once you got off the planet, magic worked in more places.

He let the feeling cycle through him. The dock under him firmed up, becoming rough concrete. He stopped smelling blood and semen, and just smelled the ocean again. He looked down at Perks. A tan rat snake looked up at him. It was almost certainly not betrayal made flesh. He gently stroked Perks, enjoying how the scales felt under his fingertips.

He looked up at the white-painted walls of the base. He could see it quite plainly. He could also see the galaxy of spells and souls flowing in and out of it. Endless sparks of light, tied to each other by spiderweb-thin spell traceries. Looking like nets sieving a hurricane.

"I'm sure that's nothing," Truth murmured.

What is?

"The thing that is definitely something important and bad. Come on; let's go kill Starbrite and break things."

Can I have my nest back?

"Your . . . Oh. Yes. I should probably put on clothes. Somehow, that had stopped mattering," Truth muttered, and peeked into his storage ring. He grabbed a towel and dried off. The clothes he wound up wearing were almost all looted from the army—combat boots, army-issue socks, belt, shirt, trousers . . . everything but the underwear. Civilian underwear was better, so he wore that. Perks happily returned to his nest.

The door wasn't marked, as there was only one door. It had a lock but a very basic one. Truth suspected it came preinstalled. If the enemy couldn't be stopped by a reality-distortion field, they certainly weren't going to be stopped by a locked door. Why bother with anything heavy-duty?

He casually picked the lock, heard the latch click open, and pulled on the handle. Which did nothing. He tugged it again. Still nothing. He checked the latch—yes, everything was properly unlocked. He carefully checked for wards or hidden spells but didn't find anything.

Was it a decoy door? Entrance was through the roof or the massive internal dock? It would make sense. If you could get an enemy dumb enough to stand out in the open on the dock, it would be security malpractice not to take advantage of that.

He jumped almost thoughtlessly, as a wave smashed over the dock and rushed up the side of the base. No barnacles on the paint. Must be special somehow. It happened again when he checked the hinges. They looked real. Then again when he tried to shine a flashlight in the cracks of the door, to see if there were any hidden mechanisms. Then again—

He felt like swearing. They were on a shoal in the middle of the ocean. The waves would be constant. Therefore, the door was no doubt bolted from the inside to keep the waves from just smashing their way in. No wonder the hinges were on the outside—you would be insane to build a door that opened inward under the circumstances.

The door was sealed, mechanically, from the inside. No worries about the magic going out; they would be just fine. If someone wanted to come in through the door, they would need to get someone inside the base to open it for them. It was all very reasonable. Sensible, even.

Truth could feel the verbal violence bubbling up, trying to escape. He could remember the insane architecture hidden in every scrap of the base. The rational design was just one truth. It was the one he was permitting at the moment, but he would be a fool not to remember the others.

Could he jump up to the roof? Probably not. On the other hand, he would really prefer not to hack the door into pieces just to get into the building. He gave a hard jump just to see how high he could go.

"Hellfire!" He shot four stories straight up and was still rising when he grabbed the lip of the roof and swung himself over.

"Well. Thank you, angel and my Rough Patron?" he muttered, patting himself down for no good reason. The roof was mostly empty. There were a few well-shielded vents and a rooftop-access door. There was also, he noticed happily, evidence of smokers. He checked over the door. Locked. A minute later, he heard a remarkably heavy *chunk* noise from releasing bolts at the top and bottom of the door. Someone had hidden a spare key under an old beer crate. He opened the door carefully, peeked around, stepped through. He was in.

CHAPTER 33

VERY SAFE, VERY NORMAL

Truth's hand slammed backward before the door could close. Incisive was being very insistent. The more the door closed, the more danger he was in. Which was a hell of a take about an empty concrete stairwell. The stairs were even designed to be no-slip, with a sensible, sturdy handrail. It was well lit, and there was even an illuminated EXIT sign above the door. Sensible safety innovation right there. This was a ten-out-of-ten stairwell. And he was quite sure he would die if he closed the door.

He lay down on the roof, peeking his head around the doorframe. There really was nothing obviously wrong with the place. He eased a little farther in, wondering if it was something deeper inside. He wasn't seeing anything.

He briefly imagined sending Perks to scout, but he firmly squashed the idea. Sending your pet into a known trap is not good pet-owner behavior. Instead, he opted for keeping the door open with a few cans of beans. If whatever the danger was was tied to the door closing, he would just keep it open.

He slowly crept in, carefully observing where every step would land, interrogating every slightly off-color patch of cement on the walls, and staring up into the light fixtures for any unpleasant surprises. It continued to look safe. Which was suspicious. He tested each step as he went. No sudden flares of alarm. No indications of hidden pressure plates or sneakily loosened bolts. Frankly, the build quality was so high, he was starting to doubt if it was really made by Jeon contractors. Proof, if more was needed, that Starbrite really did have mind-controlled drones working for him.

He could vividly remember the building collapse on the edge of his neighborhood when he was twelve. The rumor was that the bolts holding the girders together were the wrong kind of metal. If you put two pieces of metal together in a special environment and their elemental makeup was in opposition, or their inherent earth spirits or whatever, they would fight and destroy each other. This was apparently a well-known problem, one that had been solved since forever, and only came up in cases of sheer ignorance or willful incompetence. Like, for example, saving a quarter wen per bolt over the right type of metal due to market prices at the time of construction.

That was the rumor, anyhow. It sounded made-up but he kind of believed it. He didn't have any evidence, but it really sounded like something a builder would do on orders from corporate to bring prices down.

Not here. Here, someone found the builders and asked, *"If budget was no issue, and you were building in these conditions, what's the very best you could do?"* Then the absolute maniacs built it. He turned the corner of the stairs and went down to the next floor. Still nothing terrible. Slow and steady, slow and steady. He kept glancing back, wanting to make sure nothing had popped out between him and the door. The sea roared and thundered in the stairwell, the concrete bouncing the sound around. Tossing him on the invisible waves.

He turned another corner. He should be down almost two stories now, but there hadn't been any doors. Was it all solid up top? The lights were out, but that was no problem. As he got a little farther in, he saw a small cluster of indoor floodlights aimed away from the stairs. Aimed at the wall the stairs ended at.

No door. Just a smooth concrete wall. Neatly carved into the concrete, a meter tall and three centimeters deep were two words—GET FUCKED.

Ah. Yes. Now that was the Starbrite he knew. A smoker's door, out of the way? Comparatively easily bypassed lock and a very safe staircase that only became dangerous once you closed the door behind you? Mmm. Felt just like coming home. Awful but familiar.

He carefully ran his fingers over the stairs and along the walls. Nothing. He started tapping the wall, putting just a touch of muscle in it. It took a little while, but he found a spot that sounded ever-so-slightly different. Not even hollow, just different. He carefully excavated around it.

Ah. Shockwave, Bone-Eating Fire, AND Stone-Like Water charms. All carefully sealed for long-term preservation. A custom explosive package. I feel unworthy. Though what the hell is going on over here? This case is a full-blown talisman, and I barely recognize half of it. Some kind of . . . linkage to a control gem? But it looks pretty damn complicated for that.

He kept checking the wall as he worked his way up the stairs. All in all, he collected twenty of the hidden charges. Working around the doorframe, he found an arming switch. He was sure there was more to the trap he wasn't seeing. Still, he could understand how it would go. Sneaky infiltration team comes in through the "security hole" on the roof, carefully closes up behind them, finds nothing wrong as they descend, and when they reach the bottom, the whole stairwell turns into a kill zone. Not much, if anything, would survive all those charms going off in a concentrated area like that, and anything that did survive would be easy meat for the defenders inside.

Nasty. They must have built the whole thing around that strategy. No wonder nothing looked wrong—it was all installed during the construction.

Was he . . . thinking about this all wrong? He had some pretty effective tricks for breaking in, but Incisive just wasn't going to cut it there. They were already on the lookout for reality manipulation. It was kind of their thing.

Should he just smash straight in? They would be ready for that, too. That would be Plan A for any power capable of finding this place. "Infiltration team" was a distant Plan B, used only if no real powerhouses were available. The rooftop stairwell was basically a little prank, compared to everything else.

Try to destroy the reality-distortion field? Yes, but also no. Yes, because he didn't trust it one bit. No, because it would force Starbrite's hand, and nobody was ready to deal with him directly at a moment's notice. Or, quite possibly, deal with him at all. This was an assassination mission, not a group jumping.

"Come outside. We just want to talk. I just want to talk with you. Why are you hiding?" Truth muttered.

I'm not hiding. And why would I leave my nest?

Never mind, never mind.

It was maddening. He was there. He was literally in the base. He had found what an entire planet of motivated spooks and detectives couldn't. And he was stuck on the roof.

Go in through the metal shutter door on the water? Nah. He'd bet money the thing went four meters down into the bedrock. Or something. The point was, it wouldn't be any stealthier.

He dithered for a while. Ultimately, he decided to eat a can of peaches in syrup. The view was amazing. All the wheeling sea birds, the orange haze from the volcanic ash in the sky, the dark sea, it was all amazing. All beautiful.

It wasn't a bad world. Not really. It was just the people living in it. Living as they were made to. Our creator refusing to look at his creation. Bored to tears by it. How could they not be? It all was running along the miserable channels they had laid out in the beginning. What was there to even see?

Hell with it. Being smart never seemed to pay off. Violence. Brutal and direct thuggery. *That* was a career with a future. Who would be a talisman-maintenance tech? Was that even going to be a thing this time next year? Slapping punks and taking their food was forever. There was even a route for upward mobility for the gangster-minded.

He laughed softly and dropped down to the dock once more. He gently tapped the door, trying to figure out where the bolts were. He lined up the Tongue and, since there was no alert, punched it straight through the steel door. Once, twice, a third time, then a soft pull on the handle. There was a little waiting room, with coat hooks and a security check-in desk. Currently unstaffed, but the brutal metal golems that filled most of the hall probably did just as well.

Truth forced himself not to giggle. The golems were brilliantly shiny. They must have been built stainless. Rustproof metal monsters, guarding a sea base.

The doorway was covered in alarm talismans, watched by recording talismans, and papered with charms. All of which seemed only partially operational. He was able to slip past them. He took a closer look at the charms and noticed the paper was corroding. It happened with charms— you needed special paper and ink infused with special minerals and herbs. Some charms required blood or other, less-savory fluids. They were intended to be single-use, and you generally couldn't leave them out in the open for months at a time.

The door situation might be as simple as age and a lack of maintenance. A secret base wouldn't stay secret very long if there were constant resupply missions to it.

Truth lightly hopped and stabbed his fingers into the ceiling. It took a little coordination but no particular effort to hold his body parallel to the ceiling as he crawled forward, stabbing his fingers in as he went. The golems had their eyes fixed straight ahead, not seeing him. That suited Truth just fine. The bastards were almost unkillable so long as they had access to magic.

It took time, but that was all right. This was an oddly familiar place for him. Creeping unseen over deadly enemies. Making use of his body in a way most couldn't dream of. He didn't even drop from the ceiling once he got past the golems. He just kept right on going, past the security desk, around the corner, and then paused to admire the armored bulk of a heavy-needler anti-aircraft battery aimed straight down the hall. Rigged for both manual use and spirit possession, he noticed. That cost more than a credit.

He kept going. No spirits there—there was a soldier of the PMC sitting on a folding chair behind the battery, reading a magazine. The magazine looked worn almost to nothing, but he appeared to be reading it carefully.

Truth would have cultivated. Once you reach that tier of boredom? Cultivate. That's what he did when he had Standing Around duty. This guy even got a chair!

Onward. The hall ended ten meters past the AA battery. A double door, made of heavy metal and, Truth noticed with some amusement, clearly intended to be a fire door in a school or hospital. It had a lock built in, but it wasn't locked. Once you were through the reality-distortion field, past the sealed door, admitted by the golems and permitted by the PMC, you were welcome. Conditionally. With adequate supervision. Recording talismans still observed every centimeter of the interior.

The interior itself was . . . odd. It reminded him of the volcano base—sealed concrete and unmarked doors. What was different were the motivational slogans painted on the walls.

Glory to Starbrite! Glory to the World to Come!

Shining Eternal—Starbrite!

For Your Better Tomorrow, Starbrite!

Honor. Duty. Loyalty. Starbrite.

Climb the Starbrite Ladder, Ascend to the Heavens!

Over and over and over. They were eye-roll material, but he knew who was in this base—the deathsworn of the PMC, and those who might as well be. None of them were capable of rebellion. If Sally was right, they were all just crummy copies of parts of Starbrite's personality. Soul mutilated into becoming their tormentor. There were only two people actually there. Lots of bodies, only two people. Truth and Starbrite.

With no better ideas, he started opening the doors. The security arrangement was exactly the same as the volcano lair, with a two-part permitting-and-authentication system. He had already reached the point where he could open it in seconds.

It was, oddly, all going too smoothly. Even with all the defenses, it felt too smooth. Like he was walking down the stairwell and hadn't seen the wall yet.

Office. Office. Supply closet. Janitor's closet. Office. Guest bedroom. Guest bedroom. Office. Meeting room.

Harmony.

CHAPTER 34

HARMONY

The room Harmony was in looked like it was cut out of a roadside motel and dropped straight into the base. Not some mom-and-pop operation. A big national chain where all the furniture was standardized and had to be bought from the head company. Pale pinewood furniture, gray curtains over an enchanted picture window, gray blanket lying over crisp white sheets. All neatly cleaned and made by the built-in housekeeping enchantments on the bed. Safe, inoffensive art on the wall. A small scryball. A little glass-topped desk and a generic office chair. All over the gray tiled carpet.

Harmony was doing pushups. Back rigid, hands shoulder-width apart, slow and controlled on the descent, all the way through the range of motion, then an explosive push-up. Then slow back down again. Then he changed to fingertip pushups. Moved his hands in different positions, working different parts of his arms, back, and chest. Always in motion, always controlled. He was, in Truth's expert opinion, killing it.

Truth just stood there in the doorway, watching Harmony go through a whole calisthenics routine. It wasn't something Truth had taught him. Not much time for working out when they were kids. Maybe he learned it in school or at a Starbrite gym. Once he learned it, he would make a point of doing it. Steady. Harmony was always very steady. Consistent. While Vig and Sophia were raising hell in school, Har had kept his head down and his mind on the grind. Plowed straight through his SAT, then made a run at a lab-technician job. A job that shifted to a lab-management track, thanks to Truth's shockingly generous supply of Friends and Family points.

Looked like his work paid off. Har was looking healthy. Happy, even. Harmony did a final burpee, shook himself loose, and walked into the bathroom. Truth finally stepped into the room and gently closed the door behind him.

There wasn't much in the room. A small suitcase, a few changes of clothes hung neatly or put away in drawers. Two pairs of shoes tucked neatly under the bed, carefully shined. A small stack of folders and a notepad set on the desk. Truth had seen that exact setup before, in some of his poorer protectees. They couldn't be without "work." Even if it wasn't very useful work, or even work that someone had explicitly asked them to do. If it could be wedged into their job description, they would grab it and take it with them when they traveled. If they had work, then they were working. If they were working, they were useful. If they were useful, they would be remembered and kept.

Harmony was always very steady. He could be without his socks or his toothbrush, but he could never travel without the protection of "work."

Truth gently flipped open the folders. Ledgers, receipts, inventory lists, expenditures. All things generally handled, with perfect accuracy, by intelligent spirits bound to serve Starbrite. A lot of things he would have assumed were handled directly by the System. Was this something new? Introduced due to the increasing unreliability of magic?

He tried to figure out what Har's lab was working on. Nothing seemed to pop out. Well, he wouldn't be running the lab after just five years. Given how slow promotions went in Jeon corporations, he could well still be the most junior person on the management team. Nobody above C Tier got fired at Starbrite, after all. Why else would people kill themselves trying to pass the SAT? In a terrifying world, what could be better than a job for life in the biggest gang there was?

No pictures of friends or family. No little keepsakes. No wallet, of course. Why would you need one when you had the System? No fancy pens or colorful ties. Truth checked the drawers. Nothing of interest there, either. Anything hidden under the bed? No. Everything was just as it seemed. Which made sense to him. Once Mom had dug out a literal rat's nest to find their hidden stash of cash, none of the sibs had ever tried to hide anything at home ever again. They were poor, not stupid.

Harmony would have made triply sure that nothing even vaguely questionable made it into his luggage or onto his person. The System would have kept his thoughts equally tidy.

The shower switched off, and Harmony came out in a towel. He got dressed like he was going to the office, then sat at the little desk and started working through the folders. Truth reached out with his senses. Level Two. More than respectable after a mere five years. Only the PMC got those deep discounts on elixirs. Everyone else was paying close to market rates, if they could even access them in the System Shop.

Harmony was young, handsome, fit, on a management track in an important department in the best company in the world, in an era where security was the most precious thing there was. Quite the catch. Truth knew Harmony had lost his virginity in his mid-teens, but he wasn't big on dating. Was that still the case? Was he still flying solo, having the occasional meaningless hookup, then moving on without regrets on either side? Or had he found someone? Someone worth getting up and going to work for?

Did he set aside his salary for the other sibs, taking care of school fees and saving up to buy Friends and Family points? At this point, surely not, right? Vig would have vanished after his National Service. Vig wouldn't have kept in touch with Har. That probably ate at him.

Maybe Harmony was saving for Sophia, but she was working while she was studying at uni. Not in any rush to join Starbrite. And he had tipped her about the System, so . . . so, he didn't know what she did with that information. She would have kept her mouth shut about it to Harmony, though.

His siblings were all, in their own ways, hard. He watched Harmony as he worked. Eyes on the page. Top button buttoned and tie perfectly centered, sitting by himself in a room where he had been, apparently, put and forgotten. Putting in the work. Because it didn't matter if someone was watching. *He* would know he hadn't given his all. So, he squared up and did his best. Every day. For as long as it took.

There was a knock on the door. Harmony put his work back in its folder and answered the door. There were a couple of deathsworn soldiers and a tidy-looking office lady. She had her own tablet and stylus. She had to keep on the work too.

"Mr. Medici? It's time."

"I am ready."

"This way, please. How is the room?"

"Eerily similar to a GuestaRest I stayed at once. I am very comfortable, thank you."

She smiled meaninglessly and gestured down the hall. They started walking. Harmony and the office lady, the two guards behind them, and Truth behind the guards.

"So, Mr. Medici, just a quick review—"

"Actually, I'm going to need more than a review. I was, literally, pulled out of the office with no notice. I barely had time to grab some work I could do on the road. What I'm wearing now is what was in the bag I was handed at the airport. Nobody actually explained what I am doing here. I'm naturally delighted to serve Starbrite however I can, but right now, I'm not sure how I can be of service."

There was a visible glitch in the OL's posture. Truth smirked a little. Harmony wasn't on script. Oh, well. Better to catch it now, when it was just a couple of juniors talking.

"The Business Forecasts Department, working in conjunction with the Department for Strategic Development, Security, as well as several other departments, have established an interdepartmental and inter-division collaboration to mitigate an ongoing cost center and source of considerable short-to-mid-term uncertainty."

This time, it was Harmony who visibly glitched.

"Miss? I help make roads better by making sure the road-materials laboratory runs efficiently. I'm not sure how helping to run a materials lab can assist with any of what you just described. Not if the 'mitigation' requires all this."

The OL preened at being called *Miss* but then lightly cleared her throat and checked her tablet. "What you need to know is that there is about to be a ritual, and you need to not move around once you are in the middle of it. The dev team has repeatedly emphasized that your willing cooperation is crucial to the success of the ritual, and you must therefore be conscious, unenchanted, undrugged, and unrestrained."

"Well, that sounds ominous. It will hurt?"

"Yes. The word *excruciating* was used. Also repeatedly. You will be issued a mouthguard, and naturally, this will be recorded as a major contribution in your record."

Truth silently whistled. "Major contributions" weren't really a thing in the PMC, but he had heard about it in other departments. It was very, very hard to stand out in a gerontocratic corporation. Making a major contribution was one of the ways you could do it. Most people wouldn't get such an opportunity in a lifetime. What was a bit of pain compared to that?

"Very good. What else do I need to know about the ritual?"

"This ritual will be overseen by Mr. Red and Ms. Black."

That brought Harmony to a dead stop.

"The C-suite?"

"Yes, Mr. Medici. The co-heads of the Worship and Offerings Office will be conducting the ritual. Let's not keep them waiting, shall we?"

Harmony started walking again, more quickly this time.

"It is my honor to serve."

"Yes. At the ritual site, you will remove your shoes, left foot first. You will then—" The OL rattled through a detailed list of steps to be performed to prepare for the ritual, how he was to enter the room, what he had to carve on his chest, what he had to rub into the wound, and how he had to stay standing throughout the entirety of the ritual. She never explained why any of this was happening, and Harmony was too well trained to ask. He certainly never asked *Why me?*

It was the corporate way. *Why* was above your paygrade. You just had to do what you were told and eat the pain.

They reached another anonymous-looking steel door and went in. Truth nearly had a stroke, sorting through everything he was seeing. There were sigils, naturally. Inscriptions, incantations, carved gems made of stone or glass or some other, rarer material. Talismans were integrated into the broader structure at seemingly key points, providing sub-arrays or other magical support for the great working.

If he had a month, he could figure out a hundredth of it. Maybe. Or maybe not. Not a single thing in there looked standard, and when you got right down to it, he was pretty vague on the *why* behind ritual design too. He didn't have to know *why* a talisman worked, just that it should look a certain way, and fix it if it didn't. Everything else was what he had figured out on the job.

Truth very slightly loosened his grip on his self-inflicted reality-perception spell. Just a smidge, to see if he could get a clue about what he was actually looking at. The room faded away, the spells faded away. What was left was a set of matching nooses, one solid, the rest ghostly. The solid one was already hanging from a beam. The rest were in the mouths of demonic hounds. Not dogs but an infernal inversion of everything good and loving dogs represented.

It was a curse. One that took *something* about Harmony and ran down whatever that connection was to whomever it ran to. And then it killed them. Or dragged them back there. Either way. They were going to kill him and use Harmony to do it.

CHAPTER 35

LOYALTY GOES BOTH WAYS

Truth's immediate thought was to smash up the room. If the ritual space was destroyed, then there could be no ritual and no danger from the ritual. This thought was followed almost immediately by the thought of what two Tier Eights (or possibly Tier Nines) could accomplish in an environment where they supremely did not care about taking prisoners. This smoothly transitioned his first thought into sabotage, somehow reversing the spell so it landed on the casters, but he had no idea how he could actually do that. And at the center of it all, the spell and his troubles, was Harmony.

He didn't know exactly what would happen if the spell was interrupted, but since Harmony was both the focus and the sacrifice, it wouldn't be anything pleasant to look at. He smiled grimly. Harmony either didn't see it or couldn't imagine it, but Truth knew—it wouldn't stop at his pain. This spell would take Harmony's life.

"All right, Mr. Medici, we have about fifteen minutes before Mr. Red and Ms. Black arrive, so why don't you pull off your shirt and start practicing?"

"You can practice ritual scarification?" Harmony was pulling off his shirt even as he asked.

"Certainly. Here, let me help you." Truth watched the office lady tape a stencil to Harmony's chest. Truth snorted. Harmony kept it shaved. Which would be completely in keeping with ordinary Jeon fashion, of course, but after not shaving for most of a year, Truth felt a little disdainful. The sneer quickly fell off his face when she handed him a long marker mounted on a dagger handle.

"Everything is the same except the marker, of course. Same handle, same weight distribution, and of course it's a Divine Practice Ritual Rehearsal marker made by our Hugo Rune bespoke implements brand."

"Oh . . . I have one of their styluses."

"That's nice. I think you know what to do from here?"

"Yes. Is there somewhere to wash up before the ritual?"

"No need to worry—if you recall step number four of the ritual—"

"Is a ritual bathing by blind warriors, yes." Harmony nodded and got to work, carefully tracing the intricate path laid out by the stencil.

His hand was quite steady, apparently not minding that in a little over fifteen minutes, he would be doing this with a silvered steel blade. The marker slowly drew out the shape—a square, held by a circle, inside a network of crisscrossing lines. Then within the square was a complex rune, formed from swooping curves and clusters of dots. Truth stopped trying to count how many strokes it would all take after the twenty-fifth.

It took about seven minutes the first time. Harmony didn't bother asking for the time. He just got straight back in and started again. Someone would tell him when it was time to stop. He didn't shave any time off the second time around, but Truth could see he was more sure in his movements. Truth nodded slightly. Harmony had a good head on him. No way he would screw up something this important. His System would be silently assisting him too.

At around the twenty-minute mark, Harmony was interrupted by a handsome-looking older gentleman.

"No, don't get up. Mr. Medici, I am Mr. Red. I, along with Ms. Black will be conducting this Grand Working. Now, I'm assuming that Ling didn't explain *why* we are doing any of this, yes?"

"She mentioned terminating a growing cost, sir?"

A meaningless smile flickered across the ritualist's face. He wasn't in costume yet. For now, Mr. Red wore a gray suit with a restrained tie. Not a speck of red on him.

"True, so far as it goes. I'm not accustomed to explaining my instructions, Mr. Medici, but this is one of the rare exceptions. It is actually important that you understand the significance of all this and why it must, specifically, be you that does it."

Truth's eyes widened.

"Mr. Medici, I trust you are aware that Starbrite has been under constant attack for almost a year now?"

"I hadn't realized it had been that long."

"It was somewhat covert before, but it has degenerated into outright terrorism and criminality. It was very quickly apparent that this wasn't mere industrial sabotage or espionage. These were deliberate atrocities aimed at our people."

Harmony nodded, his eyes going hard. Mr. Red continued slowly punctuating his words with little jabs of his hands.

"We haven't been idle ourselves. Both directly and through the appropriate agencies. Primarily, though, we have relied on our PMC. For every one of ours their butchers took, our brave soldiers killed ten or a hundred of theirs."

Harmony nodded even more firmly at that.

"But it was always a losing trade. We only have so many capable people. Our casualties quickly added up. Added up to disaster. We have lost members of the C-suite."

Harmony gasped.

"Oh, yes, and more than one at that. Our losses of personnel and irreplaceable magical equipment have exceeded our most abyssal fears. We haven't lost yet, Mr. Medici, but another year like this one, and we will."

"Sir?"

"Starbrite is eternal. We, the poor stewards of his will, are not. Corporations are people, Mr. Medici, and for all our power, we cannot defend everyone. As the saying goes, the defenders have to succeed every time. The assassins only need a single victory. Our enemies unmake us, one company funeral at a time. And it's quite intentional. By destroying certain key businesses, they paralyze our ability to move our armies. By pinning down our armies, our people become vulnerable."

Harmony looked sick.

"It's all of a single piece." Mr. Red gave another of his meaningless smiles. "The war with Onis is, at best, a distraction. A year ago, it never would have happened. I could have slapped their president in front of a full parliamentary meeting, and their vice-president would have been holding a basin for me to wash my hands in afterward. Then the worm would have thanked me for the privilege of serving. But now they think they can test us, because we are collapsing from within. Which leads me to you."

"How may I serve?"

"By doing your duty as instructed. As your brother did before you."

There was a sudden quiet in the room.

"We finally, *finally* got a piece of one of their top agents. 'They' being the enemy, likely Siphios, but possibly including elements here in Jeon as well. And you know what? Our best divination spells just . . . slid off it. In my one hundred and twenty years working here at Starbrite, I've never seen anything like it. They just slid right off. Like the person we were looking for didn't even exist."

"How is that possible, sir?"

"Oh, we figured it out. The little freak is some vat-grown *thing*, soaked in natural treasures and loaded up with a very specific set of spells. Useful for only one thing—murder. I wouldn't even trust this . . . creature . . . to boil water, let alone work out an amortization schedule. It's diabolical but effective. Still, our working wasn't useless. We were able to divine something with it."

"Me, sir?"

"*Who will lead us to our enemy? Who is their greatest weakness?* That's what we asked, and you were the answer."

Harmony blinked at that. Mr. Red smiled, a little more honestly this time. "Wondering how we could find their bane even if we couldn't find them?"

"Yes, sir."

"Very, very complicated spell design, and sacrifices made on a scale you hopefully cannot conceive. You might consider it the equivalent of sacrificing a good-sized town. Likewise, the spell wasn't aimed explicitly at our enemy. It took some finessing, and the results are naturally not guaranteed. But at this point, the cost is comparatively negligible. It's you. Which leads us to something rather interesting. Your brother."

"Truth."

"Yes, the remarkable Truth Medici. He was being groomed for high office. Very high. He might even have stepped into the C-suite one day."

"Sir?!"

"Oh, yes. Not in a managerial role, but his dedication and talents, properly nurtured, would have made him a world-class powerhouse. He would have been a second Frobisher. We subjected him, covertly, of course, to an incredible array of personality-assessment tests, and you know what they said?"

Harmony had learned to keep his face still, but Truth could see him biting back the words in his heart. "No, sir."

"They said he was, by all common usage of the words, a psychopath."

That made Harmony jolt.

"He had only the vaguest grasp of morality and was completely incapable of distinguishing right from wrong, good from evil, and evaluated the world entirely on the basis of benefits. With a single, massive exception."

"Starbrite."

Mr. Red sighed. "No, Mr. Medici, his siblings. You were the only things he was capable of loving. And he did love you. And since he did love you, he calculated what would provide you the most safety and opportunities within his limited means. And *that* was Starbrite. We delivered for him and you, so he was unquestionably loyal."

"He loved the company, sir."

"It looked like that, perhaps. But he didn't. He loved what the company did for him and for you. It's not a bad thing. Not a bad thing at all. It certainly never troubled his superiors. You see, he believed in the company like he believed in gravity. Without Starbrite, nothing made sense. Nothing worked. So, it was worth giving his all. By giving every scrap of himself to the company, the world kept working, and his siblings were safe. Even if it cost him his life, they would be cared for."

Harmony slowly shut his eyes. "Yes, sir, that does sound like him."

"Yes. And he did give it his everything. The details of his final mission are, as you know, so utterly classified that I cannot discuss them with you even now. But I can tell you this—there were recordings of it. He, almost single-handedly saved an entire team of elite natural philosophers as well as their research materials. The results of which . . . have been incalculable. Simply incalculable."

"Thank you for telling me, sir."

"He held the line against a literal army. He was shot, blown up, hit with flying stones, and still, *still* kept shooting. He managed the rare feat of killing not one but several people after he died, due to crashing spell birds and wounds that eventually turned fatal. Despite everything. Despite the pain. The fear. The chaos. Despite what it might cost him, he never quit. Not even for one second."

Silence settled in the ritual room again.

"I can see you understand my point."

"Yes, sir. This won't just hurt, will it?"

"No, Mr. Medici, it won't. I personally put your chances of leaving this room alive as less than one in twenty."

"As high as that, huh?"

There was another long pause.

"Why, sir? If I may ask?"

"You may. It's why I've explained all this. The spell will work infinitely better if you understand the risks, the consequences, and the intention of the spell. This spell will very likely kill you. You do have a slim chance for survival. You will need to fight like absolute hell and get some lucky breaks besides, but it is possible. The pain of the spell will surpass anything you have known before. Your very soul may be at risk of shattering. It's a nonzero chance, at least."

"But if it works, we kill the people who have been killing our people."

"It is more nuanced than that, but . . . yes. We draw them out. Force them to reveal themselves so we can focus our power on them and crush them. And yes, the weakest of them will simply be instantly exterminated. This move will slaughter their most effective agents. It won't save Starbrite all on its own, but it will go a very long way."

"So, what do you need me to do?"

"I? Nothing. Starbrite needs you. Your siblings need you. Everyone who counts on you needs you to step up. They need you to clench your teeth and say, *I can pay this price, and I will.* Because it's worth it. Because the company will keep your people safe. Because this world doesn't make sense without Starbrite lighting the way. They need you to push through, Mr. Medici. To reach the end of the ritual, performing every step as perfectly as possible."

"To be the willing sacrifice."

"Yes, Mr. Medici. To be the hero. To be the one who pays the price. To take the place of your late brother and be the man your family needs you to be. A Starbrite Man."

CHAPTER 36

A BIG JOKE

Nothing more needed to be said. Harmony was resolved. Truth could see it in his eyes. His body would break and his soul would shatter before he quit. The System had been working on Harmony for almost six years now. Truth had been brainwashed to near-suicidal fanaticism in one. Admittedly, in both cases, Starbrite had been pushing on an open door. With that little motivational speech, Mr. Red had ensured the perfect sacrifice.

Truth flexed his fingers. Mr. Red was a superb ritualist. Best he had ever seen. Really made Truth appreciate his deficiencies. As a thank you, he would make sure not a single bone in Mr. Red's body remained intact. Even the quite tiny ones inside the ears. Easily overlooked by the thoughtless. It might take some ripping and prying to get at, but that was fine. All in a good cause, and gratitude made souls grow strong.

"It's time. Ling will lead you to where you will be bathed and prepared for the ritual." Mr. Red gave Harmony a slight smile.

"Yes, sir. I will do my very best."

Mr. Red didn't say anything unnecessary, just nodded in appreciation. As soon as Harmony was out of the room, the smile drained from his face. He quickly checked over the ritual space. Truth kept moving, trying to stay in the ritualist's blind spot as much as possible. Truth could feel that his body was different now, his integration with the world subtly different, but he still wasn't prepared to test the observational abilities of a Level Nine. Seemed . . . unwise.

Some faint prickling of warning was on the edge of his skin. It wasn't Incisive, just the slumrat in him. Mr. Red looked like exactly the sort of person who liked to counter-ambush. If he was showing a gap, it was probably intentional. Hanging out by himself in the crucially important ritual room?

Well, they might not know he was in the base, but it was a cheap precaution to be ready for surprises, right? And Truth had proven that he could make his way in just about everywhere.

He half-expected the man to suddenly yell, *I know you're in here; show yourself!* But the ritualist didn't. Maybe he thought it was beneath him. There was a knock at the door.

"Everything set?" A woman, also still in her office gear. Her hair was cropped short, but it looked good on her. Truth was puzzled by it for a second until he looked over at Mr. Red. His hair was short too. Must be to prevent accidents during rituals.

Mr. Red nodded, keeping his gaze moving around. "Not so much as a dust mote out of place. The sacrifice is prepped."

"Mmm."

Ms. Black looked around the room as well, indifference smoothing her face. Eventually, Mr. Red broke the silence.

"Still have that premonition?"

"Yes. Going on two weeks now. Extreme danger. Could just be things getting worse outside."

"But you are certain it isn't."

She nodded. "It feels more personal."

The two shared a look, shrugged, and walked out. Truth carefully trailed behind them, trying to kill his existence as much as he practically could. It was a little frustrating, even with how tightly he was holding his emotions. It should be possible to ambush and kill the two of them, but he knew he would fail. They were waiting for it. Even if he had hidden himself like a rat in the walls of the world, they were waiting for him to pop out.

The two trudged off to a ritual bathing and changing room. Their vestments were already laid out. Silver ewers, inlaid with precious metals and gems, poured sanctified water over them. They dried using cloths woven of trees whose swaying leaves brushed away evil fortune. There was not a single thing in this room, towel racks included, that was not a precious treasure. So precious, most people wouldn't even recognize them if they saw them. Truth included. He could just smell the reek of money and power on everything.

"It's funny. Not ha-ha funny, but . . . funny." Ms. Black looked over at Mr. Red. They were both naked, and both utterly unbothered by that.

"What is?" he asked.

"We have worked together for . . . seventy years?"

"Seventy-one next month, yes."

"Had sex hundreds of times, if not a thousand."

"As part of rituals, not recreationally, but yes." Mr. Red nodded, clearly wondering where this was going.

"Lots of late-night meals together, on the job. A lifetime of shared experiences. Climbing the ladder of power all the way to the pinnacle together."

"Yep."

"And I just see you as a colleague. Not even a work 'friend.'" She did the little air quotes. "Just a reliable coworker."

"Same. Funny." Mr. Red shrugged. "I guess we just never clicked."

"I don't mean romance; I mean . . . That's really it? Seventy years. I have known you longer than any other person in my life, and we are on cordial nods. I don't think we ever had drinks after work or watched a fight together or . . . whatever friendly coworkers do. Scheme against our wives. Husbands. Whatever."

"Well, other than the company-organized socials. But so what? Did you want that?"

Ms. Red laughed silently as she started dressing. "No, not really. It just struck me how solitary my life has been, even with all the people around me. And then it struck me that I was content with that. It's been a good life. Fulfilling. I got to see, if not the absolute peak, then one step below it."

Mr. Red smiled one of his meaningless smiles as he put on his own costume. "Yes. I noticed it long ago. I was standing under a streetlight, waiting for a sacrifice to be hauled into the back of a wagon, and I looked up. I felt suddenly alone. Utterly, terrifyingly alone. Dozens of people around me, and yet I was alone and lost in the obliterating light."

He carefully eased his arms into the undershirt. There was some delicate magical embroidery on it. Truth imagined it was rather fragile.

"You got over it."

"No, I didn't." Mr. Red shrugged carefully and gave his torso a little shimmy, making sure everything fell into place. "I am still lost in that terrifying presence."

"Don't you mean void?" Ms. Black was, Truth noticed, practically mirroring Mr. Red's movements. Not intentionally, he suspected. Just the product of endless repetition.

"No, I do not. That's what's so terrifying. White light contains every color within it. Even more so than the sun, it fits my imagination of God. Infinite variation sublimated into a single, seamless, perfect whole. And the only fault in that infinite perfection, the only stain on that pure white, is me."

"Sounds kind of egotistical."

"Just my own perspective. I know perfectly well I'm not special in the grand scheme of things. But it did make something very plain. I am always alone, and never alone. The fact that I am capable of thinking both *I* and *alone* proves just how far I am from the infinite while immersed within that infinite.

"So . . . why get close to other little blots in the light? They are as limited and alone as I am. Nothing will be gained by clumping together, as twice nothing remains nothing. I should just remain in awe and terror at the infinitely surrounding light. It was that moment, I think, when I lost my final trace of empathy." Mr. Red's hands never stopped moving, fixing his vestments and trying to wear the surplice just so as he looked intently in the polished obsidian mirror.

"Huh. And here I was just thinking we are just shockingly antisocial." Ms. Black's smile was as meaningless as Mr. Red's.

"We are also shockingly anti-social. I suspect that's why we climbed so high. Lack of distractions."

"Yes, once I pushed past all those early years of trauma, it was remarkably easy to cut ties with the world. To drift past it, touching it only when and where I pleased or Starbrite required." Ms. Black finished buttoning the surplice.

"Oh, you had a messed-up childhood too?" Mr. Red sounded politely interested.

"I think it's more or less mandatory past Level Three. Cultivation of that quantity would be impossible if one was wasting time on family or friends or . . . whoever. Children, I suppose. Or pets." Ms. Black casually fixed her collar in the mirror, then made a few minute adjustments to her jewelry.

"Didn't you have . . . I'm going to say . . . potted plants? I thought you mentioned them once." Mr. Red wiggled his feet into the waiting slippers. He made it look easy.

"The various maids look after them. I don't even see them anymore. Not really. They became part of the background decades ago."

Mr. Red nodded understandingly. "I had an underling give me a potted plant. I stuck it on a side table and forgot about it. I was startled to find it had grown into a vigorous little tree when I noticed it again. Generations of housekeepers tended to it carefully, and I never noticed. Funny."

Truth nodded. It was funny. It was so damn funny. He controlled the urge to summon the Tongue and lay into the two of them. It wasn't time. Soon, though. He could feel it, feel Incisive coiling, the poison dripping along the fangs. Even Cup and Knife seemed eager to have a go at the two ritualists.

"Ready to end a bloodline?"

"If we did all that work and we *only* get his bloodline, I'm going to spend however much time remains exterminating all life in Siphios. I don't care what it costs. I'm going to do it." Ms. Black sniffed.

"Why Siphios? At this point, we know he's from Jeon. I would per-sonally put money on him being from the same slum as our sacrifice, if not the same building."

"Because fuck 'em." She exhaled through her nose and set out. Mr. Red blinked in faint surprise, smiled slightly, briefly, and followed behind her.

Amazing. Truth found himself smiling, too, and with no more feeling of humor than Mr. Red. It was really amazing. This was what the top of the pyramid looked like. This was the best of what Starbrite had to offer. He really wanted to laugh, and really couldn't. It was just too damn bleak. Then a real smile did escape somehow.

He only had sex once, and it was more special to him than the hundreds of times these two had fucked. Teenage Truth would never have believed it. Twenty-six Truth could barely believe it. He didn't want their stuff, either. Maybe just to use, but as something to work toward? He didn't want it. What would he do with it if he had it? Who, exactly, would be impressed if he waved it around? How . . . funny. It was just so damn funny. It was the biggest damn joke in the world.

Well, that wasn't fair. It was easy to not worry about starving or finding shelter when you just stole whatever you needed. He would take the more easily pawnable items, the ones with big chunky jewels in them. If he went off-world, he could probably sell them. And if he stayed local? Who wouldn't want a fancy water pitcher?

Into the ring they went. Truth quickly followed the two seniors down the hallway. He had an . . . unpleasant idea. All this spellwork, all these intersecting lines carved and painted and inlaid over every surface, all the scarification and potions and purifications and anointments, all the ritual prayers and blessings and invocations and banishments, all of it was just trying to operate machinery hidden behind a curtain. The magic wasn't there. All this *stuff* was to intercept the magic coming from higher levels of existence than this one. Starbrite got it. It was how his best tricks worked.

So, what if he were to just . . . bypass all the big-brain stuff and steal the ritual for himself?

CHAPTER 37

SHAKING THE TEMPLE

Thorough preparation means swift execution. The ritualists were met in the hallway by seven costumed acolytes, each carrying a beeswax taper emitting a terrifying white light and a musky, piney gray smoke.

"Now is the hour," Mr. Red and Ms. Black chanted.

"Now is the hour. Justice is at hand," the acolytes chanted back.

"The stars align."

"Darkness falls on the evildoers."

"The stars align."

"Enlightening the wise."

"Now is the hour."

"Now is the hour. Now is the hour. Now is the hour."

The acolytes arranged themselves in formation and marched in step toward the ritual chamber. Mr. Red and Ms. Black walked carefully behind them, each forming mystic seals with their hands and reciting certain names, calling upon particular Powers and Dominions, even Thrones, to bless their work this night. To block the eyes of their enemies and to grant good fortune.

Truth skulked behind them. This ritual was far, far beyond his limited experience. He could hear invisible bells tolling in counterpoint to the slow steps of the marchers. He could hear the whispers of terrible things slowly gathering, peering at them through the shadows and the cracks in the light. Emerging from the darkness under the candle's flame.

His shaky grasp on local reality was being steadily pressed. The island was already covered in one layer of reality manipulation, and to Truth's silent horror, the ritual was imposing a second layer. Or a third. He wasn't sure how many layers had been stacked up at this point. It seemed to be infinitely reflecting into fractal protrusions, each intruding unexpectedly into layers below and jutting painfully into layers above. He imagined a thousand sea urchins, all expanding and contracting from the size of a poppy seed to the size of a house. All of them violently flew through the air as Truth tried to cross a chasm on a slackline.

It seemed there was more to those ritual costumes and props than he thought. Starbrite had its faults, but its people were generally quite good at their jobs.

Truth wondered if the acolytes knew the walls were subtly bending inward, held back by the light of the burning tapers. He wondered if he knew the hymn they were singing reflected back on them from the hidden geometries of the black cathedral they inhabited. He was certain they didn't know about the uncountable beings waiting in the nave, watching their procession. Beings that defied easy categorization as angels or devils. Truth wondered what he looked like to those watchers.

What would he see if he looked for his reflection on a candlestick? Would his face smile up at him from the reflection in a baptismal font? In this strange place, what would the Tongue of One Who Speaks for God look like?

Truth let his hand drift over his first aperture, sensing the godly blade inside. He felt his eyes involuntarily widen. He had always wondered how the Tongue could just . . . materialize and dematerialize. How it could live in his aperture, appear in his hand, then return to its home, instantly and without pain.

Easy. In the finest tradition of jank craftsmanship, its forgers in Siphios had had no real idea what they did. The Tongue was built around a fragment of an angelic weapon. Literally a higher-dimensional construct. The steel was just something to hold on to. The actual *weapon* operated on a less-material level. It was quite smart enough to decide where and how to emerge in these shallow waters. Why did the sword get stronger along with him? Because he was better able to impose on local reality, and better able to endure the changes imposed by the sword?

He had the sudden eerie feeling that he was the bit of steel the weapon had wrapped around itself so that it could interact with this lower realm. He shook the idea loose and forced his awareness down to a more-secular level. The hallways had emptied ahead of the procession. It seemed to stretch endlessly between two points in a gray oblivion, punctuated by unmarked doors, the shifting harmonics of the hymn reverberating and disorienting listeners with the echo.

Truth didn't understand the magical technology operating the ritual, but he understood the intention behind the technology. *We come from the stars. We come from lands beyond your understanding. We are the hidden hand distorting the fabric of the world. In all our invisible glory and transcendent righteousness, we descend upon the world below. We part the infinite gossamer veil to slaughter the wicked.*

They reached the ritual chamber. One acolyte opened the door, while the rest formed a double line and preceded the ritualists into the room. In the center of the formation was Harmony. Knife in hand. The silvered steel nearly as hard as his eyes.

The chanting took on a new, more-urgent tone. The tapers were set in prepared holes in the floor. A thurible was lit and handed reverently to Ms. Black. She walked the boundaries of the ritual, the pale blue smoke mixing with the smoke from the candles. The smells mixed, layered over the shifting lights and vibrating sounds. The nature of the room shifted, changing from the peak of modern technology to something ancient. Something so ancient, it had become dislocated from time.

Truth could hear drums rumbling. Where were the drums coming from? No one had been carrying drums, but he could hear the basso thump in four-four time. It wasn't until the first splash of bright red blood from Harmony's chest that he realized. It was the thunder of heartbeats. The very first music any human hears.

Mr. Red was calling and abjuring, binding and forbidding, hands in constant motion, tongue never tripping. Harmony's hands never slipped. The knife cut steadily along the prescribed path. Harmony would pull his skin tight so he could make sure the cut was clean and straight. Truth felt an odd pang of pride. Harmony had only practiced twice, but he was still nailing it.

Harmony was always the steady one out of the sibs. Thoughtful. But not soft. Truth would never forget sitting at the table in the apartment they grew up in, seeing how calm Harmony looked when he said he would join the Meat Market, the cannibal gangsters that ruled twelve dense blocks in the slum. Literally cannibals—they had the cheapest ground pork in the slums, but you never found a body on their turf. Harmony figured they would be the best choice if Truth didn't get into Starbrite.

Harmony had been right. He would have done well. Someone with the guts to carve on themselves was at least lieutenant material. He wouldn't have ended up running the gang, though. Truth could see it in his eyes, even now. He was determined. Bravely doing his best for his people. Playing by the rules, patiently waiting his turn as he slowly built seniority. Truth silently sighed.

If you want to achieve greatness, you have to be ready to crash out. Harmony never was.

Truth, on the other hand, had beaten a Level One to death with a soup can before he opened his apertures. He didn't even hesitate.

The walls were shaking now. Truth suspected that the celebrants were seeing at least some of what he was seeing. Terrible faces pressing inward through the wall. Terrible reaching claws, stretching inward, recoiling from the light. They were hearing the baying of infernal hounds. They were hearing the creaking of the gibbets, smelling the hemp and the tar on the ropes. Tasting the rotten iron of the hanging hooks.

Truth forced himself to look at the truth behind the ritual. There was an enormous raising of power. The power wasn't just in the ritual implements or Harmony's sacrifice, though. There was a drawing maelstrom feeding into the room. A tornado running in reverse, sucking up energy from above and funneling it down into the room below. Truth struggled to imagine where it could have come from. Not from the atmosphere itself; there was too much of it, and it was too steady. Too pure.

The System. They are pulling magic from everyone with the System. It must be raising hell all over the world, even if they are only drawing a tiny amount from each person. Looks like Starbrite is ready to crash out too.

Layers of meaning were unfolding around Harmony. Truth couldn't understand what he was seeing—coarse thread stitching into him, flowers blossoming, rocks breaking, a fox trotting steadily. Truth forced himself to look away, to try to see the bigger picture.

A ritual was an extended spell. More complicated and more powerful, but still a spell. So, the ordinary rules must, at some level, apply. You have the mages' intention. You have the spellform. You have the sacrifice. And then the energy fills the form and catches the energy of the universe and acts as leverage, pushing around far more energy than was expended.

Reduced to that level, he could more or less understand what was going on. The first scream ripped out of Harmony. Harmony probably couldn't see what was gnawing on him. Hopefully, he couldn't see it.

"We summon you, Terrible Ones. Great Ones. From the Depths of the Infernal Realms, we call you." Truth watched the enchantments shiver and shimmer over Mr. Red and Ms. Black. Wards and protections against anything and everything that could be imagined. Certainly beyond anything Truth could comprehend. He had lost Obliteration, his sharpest weapon against mages. No sneaky one-hit kills available there.

The pressure was rising. Truth watched Harmony start to collapse. He wasn't done yet, but it was almost any second now. He could see Mr. Red and Ms. Black keeping a careful eye out, constantly moving, watching each other's backs. If someone was going to jump them, now was the moment.

Truth laughed. Yeah, they really never had little brothers, did they? Sometimes, big bro was just a prick for no reason.

Truth rushed into the middle of the ritual, breaking the lines and shattering runes as he went. He felt the instant reaction from the Ritualists, spells to bind, block, blind, and kill forming at the speed of thought. This was what they had been waiting for. The acolytes all collapsed, their lives forcibly ripped from their bodies and poured into some vile curse, lashing down on Truth. But Truth was *very* fast. Magic and curses had a hard time reaching him these days. And, he was willing to admit, he could be childish and petty as hell.

So, he rushed into the eye of the maelstrom. Grabbed Harmony by the ankles, spun him through the air once to build up speed, then smashed him right into Mr. Red, launching the ritualist directly at Ms. Black.

At which point things got messy.

CHAPTER 38

THE VIRTUES OF SIMPLICITY AND IMMEDIACY

Truth wasn't a simple man, but he liked to think he was.

Confront complexity with simplicity; defeat magic with beatings. All he had to do was sort out the order of beatings.

There were dozens of active spell effects in the room but only a few Truth actually cared about. There was the main ritual, which could be considered a strategic-level threat. The curse that Mr. Red and Ms. Black had just sacrificed their acolytes to power could be considered the tactical threat. Then there were the personal protections the ritualists had activated. Then there was whatever nastiness Starbrite was going to personally hit him with when he figured out who was wrecking his ritual.

Very complicated, and he had less than a second to start making things work. Smacking the ritualists together with their sacrifice might have scuffed up the sacrifice, but it didn't do more than disorient the two old monsters. It was enough. Part of the point of the ritual was to raise the focus of the ritualists to its peak. Likewise, all the protection of the ritual space was specifically to keep them from being disturbed. Because when you are channeling and controlling that much magic power, when you have summoned the attention of so many truly mighty beings, any slip in your attention might be fatal.

The curse writhed overhead. Truth could see it—a thing made of dripping venom and screaming ghosts covered in barbed hooks and promises of uniquely horrible ends. That death would not be the end of your suffering, merely the end of the beginning. It thrashed in the air like a snake pulled from its hole. It was supposed to have a target. Mr. Red and Ms. Black barely had hold of it after getting knocked around, but it was at the ragged edge of their grasp.

Give them just one second to think clearly, and they would drive it straight into Truth, shredding through his prided spell resistance. So, why give them that time?

That spell clearly has the wrong target. Cup and Knife.

Truth dropped Harmony and launched himself at Mr. Red. As he moved, he stabbed the curse with his spell. Manda didn't approve of this curse any more than he did. The ritualists didn't have a clear target yet, their intention not quite firm. Truth just had to tweak the spell a little. And keep them from thinking too much.

Truth brought his foot up to chest height and stomped straight forward. Mr. Red was shielded, but physics still applied. The boot to the chest smashed him right back into Ms. Black. Again. Just as she was getting up from the last time Mr. Red had knocked her over. He could hear the swears. Mr. Red let a chain whip drop out of his sleeve. Ms. Black was more straightforward, pulling a custom needler from inside her vestments.

Cup and Knife was struggling to crack the curse. Two Ninth-Level pros put a fair number of bodies on this spell. It wasn't shifting easily. He swore silently and called out the Tongue. Keep them distracted, keep them off balance. If he couldn't crack the shields, then keep them disoriented.

The fangs of Incisive lashed out, smashing into the shield around Ms. Black. Truth viciously stabbed down twice in an instant, making the ritualist reflexively bring her arms up to block. It wasn't rational—her wards were keeping him off for now. It was sheer instinct. And it bought him a fraction of a second. Time he used to smack Mr. Red around.

Truth hadn't scrapped with chain whips before, and he wasn't particularly eager to start now. Not with the hundreds of coppery glowing runes lining the links. He swept Mr. Red's feet out from under him. As the ritualist went down, he met Truth's boot rising up. This time, he was launched vertically, smashing into the spell-reinforced ceiling.

He hit hard enough to shatter cement. Truth grimaced in frustration. That would have killed almost anyone. He knew perfectly well that Mr. Red was fine and would be shaking off the confusion any moment now. Incisive screamed a warning. Truth slipped back and brought the Tongue up to deflect. Ms. Black was already getting herself together. Firing from her back, her aim was dead on.

Two-handed grip, hands not too far out in front, steady as a tripod, and that grouping is smaller than my pinky nail. Which, okay, at three meters, isn't insane.

Still a higher level of competence than he preferred in his enemies. Truth tried to deflect the needles towards the falling Mr. Red as he stepped over to Ms. Black, but he was pretty sure none of them actually connected. Incisive screamed and Truth dropped flat.

Ms. Black had remembered to layer spells on her needles. And now the room was on fire. He could feel the needles locking on to him, curving through the air. Becoming longer, moving faster, growing curses and banes like tumors.

From the ceiling descended a wyrm, lashing, hungry. Pale bone-rotting flames dripped from its maw as translucent wisps of coppery flame leaked from between its scales. Faster than blinking. Faster than the anticipation of pain. It came down like lightning and struck the floor like thunder. It was fast. But Truth was a bare fraction faster.

He smiled at them. Nicely. Cup and Knife had finished its work on the curse.

There are your targets. Get 'em!

Truth was looking up at Mr. Red when the realization hit the falling ritualist. It was eerie to watch. In the time it takes a spark to fly, the old man realized what had happened, figured out what to do, and executed the plan. Which was to kill Truth before the curse killed him.

The needles were still coming. Ms. Black had a full magazine and was apparently determined to empty it on Truth. He kept dodging, playing for time now. The curse roared down, smashing into the wards surrounding the ritualists. He could see it clawing at the spells, corroding them.

Ms. Black's aim fell off, but it didn't matter as much as Truth wished it would. She kept the tracking spells going, and the room wasn't that big. Truth frantically deflected the needles with the flat of the blade. This had the single advantage of keeping him from getting shot. It did not stop him from getting hurt. The needles hit like rushing wagons, the impact shock-wave ripping up his skin and scraping against his muscles.

Mr. Red wasn't waiting patiently for death either. The wyrm was unshakable, inexorable. Constantly closing on Truth, boxing him in. Pinning him up for the kill. Mr. Red and Ms. Black had worked together for most of a century. Their teamwork was flawless; no need for discussion.

Truth feinted toward Mr. Red, then lunged at Ms. Black. He dumped power into Earth-Folding Step. He couldn't move much, but then, he didn't need to. A half-meter step to the left, right, the side, anywhere but where it looked like he should land. He crossed the space between them in ten short steps. The needles flew wildly across the room, most not even coming close. The Tongue smashed down on her ward. Once, twice. Three times in a half a heartbeat. Always moving. Cutting from low to high, then high to low, then a hard thrust.

She snarled at him. Her wards flexed under the beating, but they held. Truth smiled back. He didn't need to break them himself.

There was no crack. No shattering or explosion of wild magic. Truth looked right in Ms. Black's eyes as the curse finally got through. There wasn't any despair. No fear. Just disappointment. He couldn't understand it. The spell ate into her. The curse ripped her apart, burning her magic as it rotted her flesh. He knew she was in pain. But she never looked scared.

"You dare to ignore me?!" The fire wyrm pressed in on him again, knocking him away from Ms. Black. Truth lined up for the rush. Without the threat of the needles, the fire wyrm was a hell of a lot less scary. He just needed to keep Mr. Red from thinking about what else he could be casting. With an explosive shove on his back foot, he launched. Mr. Red countered with a pencil-thin beam of heat so strong, it formed a standing explosion in the room where it passed. Hot enough to melt cement.

Truth kept leaning on his footwork, combining Incisive with Earth-Folding Step. It was so simple now—within his sphere of control, *he* decided where he was. The observations of others be damned; it was his opinion that mattered. He closed in a blur of shining steel and a thrum of cuts ripping through air. He got behind Mr. Red and hammered the Tongue into his shield, over and over and over. Smashing the pommel down on his head, forcing him onto the floor. Keeping him down and beating on him as the serpent tried to knock him away and protect its summoner.

He could feel when the curse got through. Everything went very still.

"Any last words? Any insights on what it means to be a human being?"

There was only some pained grunting, then the wyrm settled down directly on Mr. Red's flesh. He didn't wait for the curse to finish its job.

The ritualists were dead. The ritual was coming apart with ferocious speed, insane energies boiling and crackling through the air, through the walls, the floor, the ceiling. Harmony was on the floor. Torn up by explosions, burned, cut up, gnawed on by the sacrifice. His heart had stopped. Mercifully stopped. The brain trauma was surely enough to snuff out his consciousness.

Sorry, Har. Sometimes, I'm an asshole. And I'm doubly an asshole because I knew this would happen. It's okay, though. I'm not going to let you go out like this.

He sent Cup and Knife into the ritual. It was like trying to seize control of an active factory that was exploding and also flying through the air at twice the speed of sound. It lacked both a target and a proper sacrifice. Truth smiled bitterly. More of a sacrifice.

Now that he was in the storm, he could feel all the lives that had made it rise. He had underestimated what drawing on all that power would do to those being drawn upon. All the accidents when people collapsed where they stood. All the carriages smashed against each other or slamming into the side of a tunnel. Falling off the platform and onto the subway tracks.

This was it. Starbrite was eating the seed crop. If someone pushed on the spell even a little bit, it wouldn't just be Starbrite employees that were affected; it would be every single person with the System that the spell could reach. It wasn't the whole world, but it was already millions.

He . . . may have underestimated, somehow, just how badly Starbrite wanted him dead. Somehow, that thought didn't land right. There was something else going on there. Something he wasn't understanding about the situation. He didn't have time to figure it out. Harmony needed him.

Truth bent his will on Cup and Knife, forcing it to bridge the broken body of his brother and the ritual. *The ritual needs a target? What about the people who did this to him? What about the villains who tore up his soul before they tore up his flesh? What about all the other souls they mutilated and stole? It's not right. The spell should go after them. Look, there are two fresh bodies right here to complete the sacrifice. Their souls are already in agony, still trapped in this ritual space. Ignore this body and soul right here. He's what you use to aim with, not what you eat. Eat the others.*

It's everything you need. Now. Take all this power. All this pain. All this hateful energy. And kill every living member of Starbrite in this base. And as for their souls? Release them to Hell. Don't let a single soul outside this room get away.

CHAPTER 39

HELLO AGAIN

have no idea what I've just done. But I'm pretty sure it's going to fuck up ALL KINDS of things for Starbrite. So. You know. Going to take the win. Oh, and I just saved the sibs and myself. And my relatives, assuming any of them are still alive.

Harmony was lying very still on the concrete floor. He was short one relative. Short one sib. But it wasn't time to panic yet.

One more time. Cup and Knife.

Death, as Truth knew better than most, was not always a clean-cut thing. Alive and dead . . . weren't we always dying? And when we "died," didn't parts of us keep right on living? The soul was a tricky issue, certainly, but since Mr. Red and Ms. Black's souls had hung around, presumably Har's had as well.

The spell sank into the young man's body. He would be . . . twenty-four now? Maybe just twenty-three. Truth had completely lost track of time at this point. He carried himself like he was forty but hung on to that hard physique he had growing up. A fine body that had been torn into fine shreds.

Truth guided the spell through the body. *This isn't how it's supposed to be.* And it seemed Manda agreed with him. The ripped fibers of the muscles re-knit. The torn sacks of the lungs were sealed again, invisibly mended at the cellular level as the nerves that had once regulated them were reconnected. Around them, the snapped twigs of the rib cage were reformed into sturdy branches, guarding the healing organs. Marrow refilled the hollow spaces in the bones and flushed with blood. The eye that had boiled and burst from the heat was reconstructed, delicate layer by delicate layer.

The spell operated on a subtle level as well as an obvious one. From between the cracked plates of charred skin, nicotine-yellow pus and tar-black effluvia wept out, reeking. Stinking of ammonia and bile. He was puzzled about it. There wasn't much of it; it was just nasty. It took him a while to realize that it was all the crap Harmony had eaten and breathed that hadn't been cleared out by his kidneys. All the toxic metals, all the plastics, the pill residue from elixirs, it all added up. Cup and Knife scraped it out of him.

The little bones in the feet, shattered by a passing shockwave, slowly fused and smoothed back into their proper forms. The tendons relaxed, reconnected, tightened, became strong and elastic. Turning a bag of brutalized and disfigured flesh into well-formed feet.

Like a harp, Truth thought. *The bones are the frame and the tendons make the strings, but what music is played on it?*

Truth was a little lightheaded from it all. The ritual raged around him like a storm, its power lashing out ungoverned, ruled only by such laws as still remained in the ruined ritual chamber. There was chaos everywhere, but Harmony was in front of him, shattered and broken by cruel elders. He knew what to do in this situation. He had lived there most of his life.

I wonder if it's my past lives that got me through my childhood. I figure the memory of how to fight came from them. It's why I could use almost any weapon straight away—somehow, the memory of using them, of scrapping with my hands, stuck with me. But that's not what saved me when I was a kid. You can be the best boxer in the world and still get your head slapped off if you are six and they are twenty-five. It was the mindset. It was always the mindset.

The blood was full of poisons. Looking more closely, it was because the flesh was riddled with poison too. The toxic backwash of the curse, as well as the lingering damage of the scarification ritual. Things preventing blood from clotting, to wither flesh, to make bones brittle. Even in death, they didn't spare him. Necrotic venoms racing up the nervous system, destroying the channels of alchemical lightning as they went. No more of that. Cup and Knife washed it away, healing as it went.

The bone-rotting flame from Mr. Red's flame wyrm hadn't really landed on Har, but given the level difference, even being in the same room with the unholy stuff was fatal. It, too, was a sort of poison. One that took a great deal of care to root out. Fortunately, it was now a rootless flame—the summoner dead, the spell beast dissolved back into the void. The flame was, even for Truth, an eerie thing. It wasn't just a strange flame—it attacked on a higher level of reality.

The bone-rotting flame was like someone had lifted a spark from a fiery corner of Hell and forged it into a weapon. And in that corner of Hell were all the bones of everyone who died in a house fire set by an arsonist. All twisted and blackened and pieces lost in the fallen timbers and swept away with the rest of the trash when the ruins were cleared. He had seen similar fires when he fought the fire demons back in Xandre. The notion that a mage could take the flame and leave the demon, forge it into something wholly human in design, was astonishing. He really couldn't imagine how it was done. It was a wonder. A truly astonishing achievement at the apex of magical technology.

Bone-rotting flames. Behold—the very best we can do.

A lot of people had worked very hard to make that. And now he was lifting its remnants out of Harmony and burning through oceans of power, trying to heal what was left behind. His cultivation was churning, mindlessly hauling in the rioting energy around them and processing it. Dumping the power straight into his apertures and then straight out again into healing Har.

Truth was quick, and by now his body held far, far more power than his level would suggest. Harmony was Level Two and had never cultivated his body. There were a lot of serious problems to fix, but the final product was never anything really special. It was merely flesh and bone and water. Common stuff.

Truth understood the Ghūl a little bit just then. The body was beautiful but empty. You could put meaning on it. You could fill it with anything. But by itself, it was meaningless. The pitcher shaped the water inside of it, but didn't the water change the pitcher, too? There was all the difference in the world between an empty vessel and a full one.

Truth found Harmony's soul darting around, a little speck of light. Dim, flickering. Even to his inexpert eyes, it looked badly damaged. Truth had never learned exactly how souls left this world and descended to Hell. Even the demons didn't seem to know. Har's soul was still hovering over his body. It was more than good enough.

He cupped his hands gently around the dancing spark, then frowned. It wasn't dancing. It was frantic. Hurting. Scared. His mouth set in a grim line, and he gently set some ground rules with the Blessing of the Sea of Brass. Souls should be whole and not mutilated with bits stamped on them. Then he sent more energy into Cup and Knife. This was not what the soul should look like. The spell charged out, pouring its healing power into Harmony's soul. It seemed that Manda strongly agreed.

The soul . . . He groped for words to understand it. How do you describe the feeling of the intangible? What words can you use to understand the cracks and tears in something that couldn't possibly ever crack or tear? No wonder no one had ever figured out how the System worked. No wonder it had never been replicated or defeated. It was operating at a level most humans would never perceive.

Was this the big transformation into the Nascent Soul level? You were no longer pushing bits of matter around. You were dealing with things at a higher level. You could flatten mountains with a palm and turn seas to mulberry fields all because you could reach behind the world of seemings and manipulate the real. The whole Initiate level, those levels Zero through Nine, wasn't steps towards immortality. They were preparing you to *take that first step*. Preparing you to step away from the mundane.

No wonder angels despised humans. No wonder the Rough Patron thought people were clay dolls. They weren't real to them. They really were bits of dirt shuffling around and acting like fools. And the only bit of them that was really real, that really mattered, was this singular spark. All beat-up, worn-down, made grimy and dim from tumbling around in the red dust.

Well. That's how you polish things, right? Stick 'em in a tumbler with dirt and other crap, beat them up, then hose them down. Truth let the spell wash over Harmony's soul. He still couldn't see the System, but he could feel the flow of Cup and Knife. Feel the edges of it, the ground-in contours of it. Like someone had run a rotary grinder and traced the outlines of what would be kept. The rest? Not the maker's concern.

The grooves were terribly deep. Truth could feel the rest of the soul already fracturing away from it. He leaned in, pouring everything he could into it. Everything he had learned. Everything he had seen. How he had learned to love, to accept the love of others. How he had learned, slowly, to love himself. Feelings of gratitude echoed in Cup and Knife. Gratitude that he had the sibs. That he had Harmony. He knew what he would have been otherwise. He could see that future path. Another Frobisher?

No.

He would be no Starbrite Knight. He would be the Hell Prince, bringing infernal tidings of pain and reformation for all those who strayed from the path of duty and obedience to the Throne. A life spent in pain, his and others. A life he was saved from by a simple sentence. *A big bro looks out for his sibs*. It was a fragile thread to hang a life from. Like the slightest tug could break it. But it had held, and because it had, his life had become a thing of wonders.

His face twisted into an unwilling grin as he felt the soul heal. He wasn't getting paid for any of this. Sure, the tickets off-world, the house in Siphios, the various treasures and spells invested in him. But none of that was a paycheck, exactly. He was doing all this mad, painful, scary, frequently suicidal stuff because a big bro should look after his sibs. He was living his truth. And somehow, that was payment enough.

The soul was shining like a diamond in the sun. Truth pressed it gently back on the body, then gave the heart a little jolt. It quickly remembered what it had to do. Blood had to circulate. Nerve impulses had to race up and down the body. The lightning storm in every mind had to crackle and thunder. Eyes had to open.

Harmony coughed, dry, hacking coughs. His lungs had just been scorched. Even if the damage was healed, the body remembered the pain. Truth held up Har's head and slowly helped him drink.

"Thank you."

"No problem."

"What happened? I felt like I was flying, then everything went black."

"Oh, that's lucky."

"What's lucky?"

"Trauma amnesia. You really don't want to remember what happened in the next couple of seconds. You did not have a good time."

"I feel okay?"

"Yeah, after the first time you die, it's kind of a rush. In your case, it's all the healing I ran through your body."

"Heh. Died. Hah." Harmony went quiet, then frowned. Then started thrashing, trying to get up. "THE SYSTEM! I CAN'T REACH THE SYSTEM!"

"Easy, easy! Yes, I know you can't. Ease up! Relax!"

"Oh, God. Oh, God!"

"Easy now. Just breathe. You are going to be okay."

"I lost the System. I can't lose the System." It was brainwashing. He could fix Har's soul, but he couldn't fix five years of carefully guided thinking. Not yet, anyway. Not with his level of power and understanding. He actually missed his System. That bitter, acerbic bit of his soul. Was it also smoothed away, returned to the seamless whole? Or was it waiting in him, looking for that moment to be reborn?

"How can I be okay? I lost the System. Was I fired?"

"Manner of speaking, I guess. Set on fire, certainly."

"You are real funny for a PMC hitter."

"No, I'm not. I will have you know that I am famous for being bad with jokes. The world, however, is occasionally hilarious when looked at the right way."

Harmony settled down a moment. "I guess that's true enough."

"Yeah. Look, this base is utterly fucked and about to get so, so much worse. I'm pretty sure I know the answer to this, but do you happen to know if there are emergency life rafts anywhere? Or, like, one-off flying charms, or literally anything that would get you off this rock?"

"No idea. And probably not; it seems like an insane security risk."

Truth nodded sadly. It really did.

"Well. You hang out here, then. Don't come out until the water comes rushing in under the door, or I come and get you. Or use your best judgment; I don't know. Just . . . really. Stay on *this* side of the door if you value life number two. How long since you last ate?"

"Oh . . . hours ago, I think?"

"Here's a couple of bottles of water and some instant noodles."

"I don't have a way to boil water, though?"

"You ate them raw often enough."

There was a strange pause.

"Who . . . are you?"

"Me?" Truth laughed, and Harmony jolted. "Just another ghost. Stay safe now. I've got to go see HR about some back pay."

The door clanged shut before the words finished echoing in the room.

The hallways were chaos. Didn't matter. Truth's grin stretched into a skull's smile. Next stop—Starbrite.

CHAPTER 40

SEEING AND SEEING

Jank is a formidable power. It is also, regrettably, unreliable, inefficient, and prone to breaking. These are known problems and, Truth felt, entirely acceptable shortcomings provided you followed the cardinal rule of improvisation: "Whenever possible, experiment with *someone else's stuff.*"

The hallway was, most of the time. Sometimes, it was not. Truth struggled to hang on to some semblance of stability. It wasn't easy. Just to the left of the door, something was scraping a furrow in the hallway. Always the same width, always the same stroke along the same channel, always scraping in the same direction. The furrow in the cement was about three meters long and ten centimeters wide. He could hear the cement crumbling and moving, but he couldn't see what it was.

Letting his vision stretch beyond the mundane revealed a cube, slowly spinning and twisting in the air. The furrow was made by one corner dragging along the floor. Then he was suddenly struck by the feeling of looking at several cubes, then two-dimensional squares, all twisting and folding into and over each other in a way he couldn't comprehend. He could see but not understand, and his brain was desperately trying to make sense of it all. The image collapsed back into a cube that gently turned in space, and the cube dragged a corner along the ground and dug a furrow in the concrete. And then there was nothing but the hole in space.

Truth had to suppress a wave of nausea. The dark cathedral flickered in and out of perception. The shifts were so violent, Truth wondered if ordinary people could see it. People who weren't clinging with their fingertips to the cliffs of sanity. Wondering if he would fly up into the stormy sky or down in the crashing sea when his grip finally slipped.

The curse had blown out of the ritual chamber and into the base, consuming people as it went. Truth was pretty sure the rags and ruins of flesh that he passed had been people. Some of them were still recognizably wearing boots. Some human-looking teeth were scattered around. He wasn't sure what had happened, exactly. The curse moved like a consuming storm as much as it moved like a pack of infernal hounds.

Truth didn't mind the torn-apart bodies so much as the torn-apart clothes. Why? Why were they shredded along with the light talismans on the walls and the lock talismans on the door? They were notionally manufactured by Starbrite, sure, but so what? The concrete used throughout the base was manufactured by Starbrite too.

It can't be a good thing. Not caring about the bodies. I should care. This is pretty fucked-up. How damaged must I be to look at all these shredded people and wonder why their shoes were destroyed but not the ground under the shoes. For all I know, that was someone I worked with in the PMC. Or not. Maybe it was a complete stranger. Maybe they cheated on their husband with their boss but never quite got that promotion they were promised and wound up getting transferred here. It doesn't matter. They were human, lived as best they could, and died ugly. I should feel bad about that. I don't.

It took him a few minutes of cautious exploration, but he eventually figured out his emotions. The dead weren't a threat anymore, but there might be a hidden danger hinted at by the exploded light talismans and shredded clothing. Mourning could happen later, if ever. Pity, grief, disgust, all these empathetic emotions should be set aside for now. So, he set them aside.

The hallways had once been liminal tubes. Gray holes poked in space, with inexplicable, anonymous doors gently pressed into the walls at irregular intervals. The doors would flicker in and out of existence, replaced by sheets of fire, or grief. Sometimes, they wouldn't be there at all, and neither would the rooms behind them. What remained was a void, a hungry emptiness and a terrible stillness. He moved past those rooms with his back flush against the opposite wall. He didn't know what was in that darkness and had no interest in finding out.

Incisive was, for once, practically no help. Everything was dangerous. Everything was *fatally* dangerous. Sure, it was obvious when you saw tumor-spirits growing out of the ruined flesh of some working stiff, but having a literal earl of Hell tell you the entire situation was cursed . . . Well. It added a certain terrifying something.

His eyes stuck on one particular corpse. There was nothing special about it. Maybe they really were "somebody," but here and now? Meat. They were just meat. For some reason, he saw Dr. Sun's leering face, his eyes glowing with hate and his voice warm with contempt. Truth didn't remember exactly what he had said, but he remembered the gist. For someone who loudly despised Jeon's elites, Truth had barely laid hands on them. Hundreds of their employees, on the other hand, were left without intact corpses.

It was an immediacy thing. The bastard shooting you was right there, shooting you, right this moment. The system that put him there gave him a needler and convinced him that you needed to be shot? That was a lot harder to find. How do you exterminate a system? How do you behead a process that has made so many so rich? Should you even try? But if you don't do *something*, everyone dies. Just not right this second.

Someone with a needler might kill a few dozen people. Someone deciding which lowest-cost bid on construction materials to accept could kill hundreds or thousands. Someone setting trade policy or negotiating water-purity regulations might kill millions over time.

How much responsibility does Starbrite's tea lady bear for the plight of the slumrats? It can't be zero; she's participating and profiting from the system. But she's a victim too.

So many victims. And even the people notionally at the top were victims. Victims he might not waste any tears on, but they were as blind as all the rest. They had every opportunity to look up, and they still kept their eyes firmly fixed on any bastards after their cheese.

A spider with a human face stretched over its back crawled out of the shadows under a body. At first, it only had eight legs, but they quickly multiplied into the hundreds, then became uncountable. They flickered and merged and seemed to flow like bubbling tar as the face described precisely how it felt when it realized its marriage was over, and that they were the reason why it all fell apart.

A door shook and fell off its hinges. Like something inside wanted to escape, or an ingrown hair finally bursting free of its zit. Truth looked inside but couldn't see what was so special. The hallway was rapidly filling with more spiders, each reciting litanies of personal failings. Truth went in.

The room looked like a library in a wealthy home. The shelves were made of bones, and he somehow knew the books were bound in human skin, but it otherwise felt quite normal. There was nothing of immediate use or interest. He forced his perception back into the realm of the mundane and pulled a book off the shelf. It looked like a collection of business records. The dissonance between realms of perception was starting to do his head in. Truth knew he was holding reports about something or other, but all he saw were bloody ledgers and weeping runes.

The spell should have been over. The ritual wasn't designed to run indefinitely, right? Just force me out into the open and wipe out my family in the process. Nothing else. Right?

Regrettably, anyone who might have answered that question for him was now very dead. He tossed the book back on a table and turned to leave the room. He was after Starbrite, not his secrets. He heard the book land with a thud and a muffled yelp. Incisive *yelled* and Truth spun around, the Tongue ripping through the air. The books had exploded into clouds of gray-black dust. He could feel the poison in it. Feel the dust trying to seep through his sealed skin and rot him from the inside.

From within that cloud of corpse-poison he saw shapes appear. Like minnows or octopi fry sweeping through the murk. Bulbous heads with narrow trailing bodies. Black holes for eyes and where the mouth should be. Silently screaming. Swarming. Dozens of them, boiling out of the dark toward him.

The Tongue was an angelic blade, a jank product made by the finest holy blacksmiths in Siphios. Truth had to imagine they had labored joyfully, content in the knowledge that it wasn't *their* bit of divine junk, and happy that they had something new to experiment with. The Tongue lashed across a ghostly shape, and the blade suggested a bane. Truth agreed and cut back again. Holy fire incinerated the ghostly shape, and the dust around it.

One down. Seventy-plus to go. But that was fine. He found himself smiling. He had fought a swarm of demonic insects when he first got his hands on the Tongue.

"Just like old times. Old like . . . less than a year ago? This has been a short life."

The sword whipped across his body, the fire compressed to a bare shimmer above the blade. No need to waste energy. Who knew how long he would be fighting for? Still, he would use the old trick of using bodies to block bodies, limiting the number of enemies—

He watched dozens of ghosts swarm through each other as they closed in, forming a nearly solid wall as they rushed closer. He wouldn't be stacking them up. Biting back a curse, he went on the offensive instead. After one swift horizontal slash, he nudged the Tongue to change it up a bit. Might as well let the divine flames fly. He really needed to be clearing out a lot of enemies with every move.

The battle was furious but brief. The ghosts melted like frost under the divine flames, and while some did manage to claw at him, they couldn't penetrate his skin. They did, however, hurt like hell and leave a lingering feeling of burning and corrosion where they touched. He dithered a moment but opted to strip off his shirt and very carefully run the divine flames over himself. In the end, he was scorched but basically whole.

He looked around the ruined room. The human-skin-bound books had been destroyed, the tables smashed; everything was in chaos.

"So, what did we learn from all that?" Truth asked rhetorically. The howling of the curse through the base didn't give him a meaningful answer.

"Yes, that's what I thought. Nothing. I came in for no reason, picked up a thing for no reason, fought something that will probably give me nightmares years from now, and I burned myself. For not one goddamn thing."

"Well. Not nothing. You did exorcise us, which is a blessing." Truth jolted, barely getting a hand up before he slammed into the ceiling. It was a shimmer-outline of a face in a pile of dust.

"Books! Books and ledgers! I checked! Just what the hell—"

"Books and ledgers, yes. The master of this place is not a creative man. Reducing a soul to record-keeping appealed to him, I think. There never were many of us. Either he gave up on it or he found a better way."

The little face was fading away, the voice becoming thinner and thinner.

"Ah, who were you? How did this happen to you? Do you know where Starbrite is, or what he is, or how to kill him?" Truth tried to get all the questions out, desperate to learn something before the face vanished.

"No idea; my records were destroyed. Probably not important. As for what . . . Did you call him Starbrite? Weird name. As for what he is now, he's a losing gambler. Every time he loses, he bets bigger. He has to. He has debts to pay, and they keep compounding. If we emerged, then he's lost practically everything else."

"So, what do I have to do to kill him?"

"Not one penny." The voice was almost gone now.

"Don't let him win even one penny?"

"Don't take one." And the voice was gone.

CHAPTER 41

A PATH WITH NO TURNS

Truth nodded slowly. He stroked his chin and frowned thoughtfully at the wall. With deliberate emphasis, he tapped his index finger against his lip. A sage glint burst from his eyes, his shoulders screaming of insight!

I officially have no idea what that ghost was talking about. Just what the hell is a penny?

It certainly sounded like money, but he wasn't sure he had ever heard of one. Maybe a foreign currency? It tickled some misty part of his brain, but he couldn't quite put his finger on it.

Starbrite is a gambler? He owes money? To who? And why would taking money from him make him stronger? Surely, it's the reverse if he's got unpayable debts, right?

The room was completely trashed, and he wasn't seeing anything useful. If there was some dark truth hidden in the books, it was gone now. Time for him to move on. The spiders in the hallway had all vanished. The hallway now looked rather mundane, save that there was some twist to the light that seemed to pull all the life from it. Truth stood frozen in the doorway. The sensation that something about the hallway had managed to make the cement walls and steel doors more dead was nauseating.

He took deep breaths, trying to steady himself. Slow his racing heart. It was an illusion, or a shift in local reality. Some higher dimension trying to muscle its juniors. He could deal with that. He repeated the thought over and over until he half-believed it, shoved more power into the Blessing of the Sea of Brass, and stepped into the hallway.

Pennies and ledgers. Not creative. Truth started connecting things in his mind. The Shattervoid despised Starbrite, not just for kidnapping their kid but for his cheap magics and mutilated soul. The core of the System was more or less the same as any other high-quality business-management spell . . . as defined by the denizens of this particular rock. It combined HR, payroll, accounts payable and receivable, inventory management, sales, task management, messaging, and probably a bunch of other things that he was either not thinking about or were never introduced to him during his employment.

Not hard at all to draw a line from pennies and ledgers to the System.

Is a penny a lot of money or a little bit? I'm going to say . . . a little bit.

All right, so . . . why? Why all of this? If he was gambling, who the hell could take the other side of the bet with Starbrite? They would have to come there through the Shattervoid, and Truth had never caught a whisper of any foreign power trying to muscle in on Starbrite's turf. Ironic as that might be. And if there was some Nascent Soul hegemon aboard the Shattervoid, why not send them in to save Sally? Or to put Starbrite in a box?

Sally had been kidnapped for five years. The Shattervoid, with their monopoly on interstellar travel, *seriously* couldn't put together a team of mercenaries specializing in asset recovery? There was something else going on there. There was some fundamental rule at play that was strong enough to bind the Shattervoid and . . . everyone. Everyone who might come and take a bite of this rotten-apple world.

He kept moving down the hallway. His interest in opening new doors had dropped to nil. Staircases, on the other hand, were now very highly sought.

Even if we are a backwater planet, we still got by. We imported most of our food, which means people were buying our exports. All those talismans and minerals and other stuff weren't worthless. Someone was buying them, even if it was for short money. Except it couldn't have been that short, because otherwise, why go through all this nonsense?

It was the question he found himself swirling around again and again— he had more or less figured out *what* Starbrite had done, but the *why* was still shrouded in the shifting layers of reality.

Why does someone start a business? To make money. Why does someone want to make more money? Well, that's pretty philosophical, isn't it? Once you get past subsistence, it's ambition or desire for luxury or vanity—something like that. But Starbrite didn't have a mansion anyone had ever heard of. Never showed off in public, decked out in gems and spells. He made no public appearances at all. Nobody knew what he looked like or sounded like. So, why go through all the trouble? Just to collect the souls of his employees?

There simply had to be a better way. This way took centuries. Wouldn't arranging a giant war, where you promised one side victory by use of your top-secret System but were secretly also providing it to the other side, be a whole lot faster? Hell, he was a Nascent Soul powerhouse. Couldn't he just establish a ritual around a city of ten million and exterminate them? Or something? Why go so slow? Why be so secretive? Why just take *part* of the soul?

A better life for your children. That was the other reason to get into business—planting money trees to shade your kids. But Starbrite had never married, so far as anyone knew. Nor did he have any publicly acknowledged children. And again, even if it was about looking after the next generation, why all this? Why all this . . . everything?

The hallway was blooming now, fruiting and flowering with mushrooms and strange blossoms whose meaty petals hid hungry thorns. A warm air blew, promising comfort, carrying the smell of iron and salt. The wind seemed to rise from the shadows under the flowers and beneath the mushroom caps, twisting the air into braids of half-memories. And behind the wind, in the darkest parts of the shadow? Something vast. Something that eyes could not comprehend. Something already surrounding the hallway. All these phenomena were Truth's mind desperately trying to comprehend something that it should never have been confronted with.

He staggered down the hall. He wasn't hurt. It was just hard, pressing through the weight of these intrusive things. The base seemed to have stretched in length, or perhaps the floor was imperceptibly angled downward, descending deeper and deeper into the sea. In any case, he had been walking down a straight corridor for who knew how long. There was some trick there, and he didn't think it was as nice as a simple illusion.

The smell of iron and salt intensified. There was a familiarity to the smell. A calling to the memory. Nuances eased through the edges—meat, red clay, and the particular air you get just after a storm has passed over a salt marsh. He could see a great tree ahead of him, a willow that filled a space larger than the hall, its long, streaming branches tossed gently in the soft wind. In front of it was a patch of sweet grass and thyme, freshening the meaty air.

He reached the tree. The willow branches brushed their narrow leaves over him. The thyme was crushed under his feet, their sweet-spicy smell energizing him, sharpening his senses. The hallway ended on the other side of the tree. Just a flat wall that seemed to faintly bear the traces of a riverside view, painted in broad and bold brushstrokes. The tree and soft grass were surrounded by taller, spiky-looking rushes. The long, straight green leaves poked upward like clusters of misericords, with the central stalk forming an exaggerated estoc by coming to a conical point.

One such reed, far to the left of the tree, was particularly vibrant. He could see it was bullying the other plants around it, slashing at them with its sharp green leaves. A faint memory, almost an instinct, nudged him. He could stay there. Resting under the willow, enjoying the peace and beauty of it all. Or he could press on and face whatever came next.

He half-smiled. There were always places to stop, to turn back or find another path. He walked over and, minding the sharp edges, pulled up the bulrush. The reed left behind a small hole in the wet dirt, but it quickly spread and widened, getting deeper. Revealing what was hidden below. He had found the stairs.

They were concrete stairs. Some thoughtful soul had pressed a checkered pattern into them to improve traction. There was a metal railing installed at a sensible height, and when the light talismans were still working, they were more than enough to make the entire stairwell bright. Now they were just shattered wall decorations, adding a desolate flair to the crushingly liminal. But the intention had been good.

No strange scents, or scenes rich in subtle meaning. Just a better-than-average commercial staircase. Truth found it more restful and comforting than the willow tree. He had grown up in Harban and was a city kid to the middle part of his bones. Sitting on the riverbank under a willow tree wasn't his scene. Squatting malevolently in a dark stairwell was practically his birthright.

Down and down, deeper and deeper. One flight became ten, ten became twenty. Space was stretching there, or the meaning of the stairs was becoming more prominent. Truth was tempted to just jump down, but there was something in that void below. Something hungered for more than flesh. Wasn't like he was going to get tired, trotting down the stairs. He stayed patient.

He didn't know how long his patience held for. It ran out before the stairs did. He was missing something.

It isn't likely to be a deliberate trap. The curse has completely mutated at this point. It's running off the accumulated cultivation of who knows how many people with the System, and it's clearly smashed into the reality-shifting ward around the base. And it's doing so at a large enough scale that Starbrite can't just step in and immediately fix it. Which is . . . I kind of feel like I should pat myself on the back, but at the same time, that feels kind of tasteless. A lot of people are probably getting hurt or killed out there.

He thought about it, shrugged, and gave himself a little pat on the back. People were going to be dying regardless. He should take pride in striking a tangible blow against Starbrite. Moping sure wasn't going to achieve anything.

So, having determined that it isn't intentional and is almost certainly the result of several enormous systems going BOOM at the same time, I can . . . do what, exactly? Stab the stairs?

He scoffed. A moment later, he sneakily glanced around and prodded a step with the Tongue. It crunched, as concrete does, and crumbled. Nothing else happened. Truth coughed and acted like he hadn't just stabbed a staircase because he couldn't think of a better idea.

Hmm. Reality was being manipulated and space was being distorted. He didn't know if he was trapped in a loop or not, but the difference was academic. Was there a jank magic solution to this?

Of course there was.

He just didn't know what it might be. So, regrettably, that was out.

Violence was out, hacking together some nonsense was out, couldn't walk out . . . He was running out of options.

Heh. Walking. Running. If I knew where the bottom was, I could reach it in a step. Theoretically.

Truth nodded slowly. He stroked his chin and frowned thoughtfully at the wall. With deliberate emphasis, he tapped his index finger against his lip. Then gently banged his head against the wall.

I don't actually have to know what's at the place I step to. I can step through walls. The angel managed to send me tens of kilometers with a single step. That's kind of the point of the Earth-Folding Step.

He sighed. He still didn't know what was at the bottom of the stairwell, but Incisive was just giving him the sense that everywhere was dangerous. No special alert about what he was about to do.

Hell with it. He poured his magic into the spell, fortified the Blessing of the Sea of Brass, and stepped. When his foot hit the floor, he was standing at the bottom of the stairs, looking at an ancient bronze door.

CHAPTER 42

A VERY PRIVATE MAN

The bronze door was covered in neat inscriptions. That was the overwhelming sense of the door—three meters tall, and somehow, it was more orderly than majestic. Truth could imagine the architect and the thaumaturgist having an argument—

"It looks ugly, doesn't fit with the entire rest of the building, and is going to add a mint to the costs. You can't—"

"Take it up with the client. Inscriptions have got to go somewhere, and while it would do the apprentice good to spend a couple months carving them into the poured concrete, I have better things to do. And I can make the door in my shop, saving the call-out and onsite fees. So. You know. Savings."

"You work for Starbrite; your time-cost is irrelevant!"

"And yet, my boss still manages to bill me out to other departments. What a shame I got a double J-Thaum instead of something useful like an MBA or an architecture degree. Whatever you call that. Do you think the door will need special hinges? I bet it will. Lucky you spent a whole career learning that kind of thing, huh?"

It was like each subcontractor had to flex and prove they were the biggest pricks on the project. Meanwhile, security just got to stand around, being the universal defecation destination. Truth hadn't guarded construction sites, but he had heard things. He had certainly seen things guarding buildings. Security was like maintenance—everyone agreed that it was necessary and best accomplished by morons. Sounded dumb, but Truth didn't have an MBA. Presumably, it was explained in the course.

Credit where it was due, the inscription was excellent. Each line was exactly the same length and width, the letters formed perfectly and with absolute legibility. There was nothing, to his inexpert eyes, to nitpick. What it was all for was a little harder to evaluate.

He ran his eyes over the inscriptions. There were astrological records, mathematical statements, the names of numerous angels and demons, methods of divination and warding away evil. There were recipes for alchemical draughts and medicines, recipes for incense and perfume, recipes for adamantium and mithril. All things of value but none of it secret. Most of this could be found in any specialist manual for the relevant trade. And what possible use could it be on a door?

He didn't touch the door. Incisive wasn't warning him, but it was just too damn odd. Truth kept working through it, getting more and more puzzled as he went. Some sections seemed to be a sort of prescription for cultivation, like something usually taught with detailed manuals or in-class instruction was reduced to a few chilly directions and an expectation that the reader should figure out the details themselves. The spells were similarly brusque. Not incomplete, exactly, just not properly explained.

"*To ward away venomous insects, establish a spellform. Taking Mezzorsh as your starting point and working widdershins, draw a line forty-five degrees up to Czru . . .*" and so on, not mentioning little details like the recommended cultivation of the mage, the spell's range, duration, effectiveness against demonic insects, and other not-so-small matters.

Not exactly a high-grade ward protecting the deepest secrets of Starbrite. Truth had some vague thought that it might be a sort of . . . legacy relic or something. Something to restart cultivation civilization after the collapse. But it wasn't. Not really. The recipe for steel indicated how much carbon and how much iron but didn't explain how to make a furnace to smelt the metals. Same thing with the potions—the recipe was there, but nothing about how to cultivate the herbs or make the alembics and other tools needed to process them.

It finally clicked. It looked like a giant notepad. Like someone had written down a load of notes on a lot of things they thought were important but not *that* important, and kept reusing the same bit of paper until the whole thing filled up. Then someone else came along and tidily transcribed the whole thing onto a clean sheet of paper. Except the paper was three meters tall and made of bronze. For reasons. There weren't any spells active, and this seemed to be human weirdness as opposed to mystical or divine.

He gently pushed the door. It didn't budge. Truth had a look and discovered that the much-maligned architect had put the hinges on this side of the door. Truth's first thought was security. A simple locking bar would make the door a serious obstacle to smash through, magic or no. But a simpler idea replaced it. Policy.

It was a fire-safety policy. The doors in Starbrite facilities, absent a good reason, opened toward the exit. In the event of an emergency, nobody was getting stacked up on a closed door—the door would always open outward so people could escape. The architect had a policy manual to follow, so they did. The fact that they were in a secret underground base in the middle of a contested waterway was irrelevant.

But since it was a Starbrite door, built to Starbrite codes . . . Truth ran his hands down the bronze, exerting a slight pressure. A narrow rectangle of bronze was pushed in, revealing a spot to grab. Truth pulled the door open and walked inside, closing the door behind him.

On the other side of the bronze door was what Truth tentatively decided to call a temple. There was a stone basin with an iron brazier set above it, holding burning logs of some fragrant wood. The smoke didn't linger—it was pulled up into the high ceiling and merged with the carvings above. Angels and demons didn't watch over this place. They were geometric forms, infinitely repeating yet infinitely complex. Subtle use of colored tiles filled the arches with bewildering splendor, delighting the eyes endlessly.

The floor was simpler—blue stone tiles, arranged harmoniously. Here and there, the ground had been inlaid with spell formations and ritual sites. There was a bath large enough for two or three—Truth reckoned it was for baptisms and purification rituals. Same thing with the blackened iron hoop, the two burn pits, the smoke filling the air—all methods of purification and baptism. He had become something of an expert on the subject.

The altar was, likewise, plain and plainly meant for serious business. This altar was a stone slab two meters long and a meter high. There were a horn cup and a stone knife on top of it, and that was it. No inlaid spells or embroidered cloths, nothing to show to whom the altar was dedicated. Certainly nothing to lure in the curious or inspire the faithful. No Pragerite priest worth his per-diem would be caught dead in there.

Truth thought differently. It was unadorned because it was used to venerate multiple beings, and more importantly, anything summoned by Starbrite wasn't going to care even slightly about the magical furniture some hick scraped together. Like the way new money obsessed over tags and designer everything, while the old money didn't give a damn and wore what they liked. Anywhere those exalted beings went in the material realm was, definitionally, a slum. Should they be moved by the hovel-owner bringing out his best tablecloth?

Truth slowly walked into the temple. No astrological symbols, he noticed. Which was odd, given everything. No pictures of anything, either. The quality was superb, naturally, but unadorned. Out of curiosity, Truth sniffed the empty horn cup. It smelled like wine, with hints of something sweet and bitter herbs. If Starbrite was chopped up, who was using the cup? A servant? Did he manipulate it directly with magic?

He kept exploring. There was a little cabinet with ritual equipment—oils, incense, wine, candles, candlesticks, the usual sort of thing. He was also amused to find floor cleaner and stone sealer, as well as some large sponges, towels, and a surprisingly ergonomic bucket. Someone had to clean up the altar, after all, and it wasn't always wise to have the lingering energy of cleaning demons or talismans hanging around your ritual site.

Or so he had heard. Nothing he had ever worked on required that level of purification.

When you get right down to it, I'm a thug with a spell. I've learned a lot, grown a lot, but at the end of the day? I'm a fix-it-with-violence kind of guy. He saw an oil lamp burning on the wall. He hadn't seen one of those in this life. Truth let his eyes roam and saw more and more of them. In fact, there wasn't a single talisman light in this place. For some reason, that struck him as hilarious. It seemed like they were too unreliable for Starbrite's personal use.

Maybe it will turn up on the SAT? What is the expected service life of a brass oil lantern, and how often do you need to replace the wick?

No. No more SATs. No more Silent Nights where parents ensure the peaceful sleep of test-takers with garrotes. How had he not understood how sick the world was, that a single company's test could stop a city dead in its tracks for twenty-four hours? Silent Night wasn't a tradition reserved for the slum. He had to imagine it was, if anything, even more intense in the striving lower and middle classes.

Mom had painted her garrote with gold nail polish. He remembered that vividly. Dad just used whatever. Mom had to be fancy. Glam. A successful businesswoman, because in this world, if you weren't a successful business someone, what were you? A civil servant is still a servant. Only money and power could truly command. And Mom, in her limited way, understood that. Dad was too far gone. It had taken Truth a long time to realize that Dad wasn't beating them to make himself feel better; he was beating them because anything that pulled him out of his haze of scry and booze made him hurt.

The world was a scary, painful place. It had beaten Dad long before Dad beat Truth. Truth sighed and kept looking around the temple. He wanted kids one day. Let the violence end with him.

The temple continued, stretching out deeper into the water. Perhaps the reason for all the purification equipment and the simple altar was to prepare celebrants for the mysteries deeper within. The patterns on the ceiling mutated but remained geometric. Potted trees started to appear, with benches under them. Little alcoves were set with cushions on the floor, just missing a statue or painting to venerate.

He could see bits of broken technology here and there. Rows of spell bowls had been smashed and scattered in pieces like oysters on rocks. Whatever had been bound in them had escaped or been destroyed. There was a smudge of ash on a lectern—once a book, perhaps. Rolls of scrolls that had rotted into slime. Still intact was a bronze sheet with more haphazard notes—on the correct angle of arch to build into a road, on how to plant chestnut trees, the formula for a particular shade of blue dye. On how to make scented soaps and little pastries shaped like roses.

On how to make light talismans.

Truth stared at the tablet. He knew every centimeter of that design. He knew its variations, he knew what materials went into it, he knew it considerably better than he knew his own family. It was the basis for the standard Starbrite light talisman. A basic technology that could be tweaked dozens of ways, from wide floodlights to focused spotlights and in every visible color.

They really were his notes, Starbrite's notes. The Shattervoid charged a mint for books and things. Starbrite must have memorized all of this with a spell, then, once he got there, wrote them down in a hurry. Later on, after he built his empire, he had someone tidy them up and etch them in bronze. An enduring record of his brilliance.

Everyone kept saying that Starbrite wasn't creative. Starbrite didn't have that kind of mind. So, he had taken ideas from off-world, brought them there, and built a business empire off the back of them. He didn't have to worry about being outcompeted by locals, because he had the System and, by extension, slave labor. He only had to worry about getting materials and protecting both his investments and himself. He needed deathsworn. The PMC. Once he had that, it was just a question of time. Growing silently, invisibly, until he was in an unbeatable position. Until he, personally, was unbeatable. And yet, even now, even there, Starbrite was invisible.

CHAPTER 43

PULLING UP THE LADDER TO HEAVEN

*I*s this all the most powerful man in the world is? Jotted notes and a compulsive need to be spiritually clean?

Truth walked through the temple, trying to find some piece of Starbrite he could grab ahold of. Everything was just guesses. Based on evidence but still guessing. Would there be any real trace of Starbrite there? Some real, tangible thing connecting the monster and the man? Other than the man himself, of course. Assuming "he" was a man.

The temple was utilitarian. Beautifully decorated but built for a single person and a single purpose. Truth still wasn't sure he was clear what that purpose was. If he was going to hang a name on it, he would call it a workshop. The curse had rolled through there, but it had only damaged the more fragile things, from what he could see. Not that he would drink the wine or try the oil—it smelled fine, but who knew what it would do to you if you actually touched it.

It reminded him a little of the Army wagon-maintenance depot he had worked in at the end of his National Service. The garage had been mostly empty space with just a few fixtures and a few highly specialized tools. The more general-purpose tools like wrenches and drivers were stowed in one spot and one spot only. You used the tool, then you put it back in exactly the same spot. It had to be that way, because if it wasn't, nothing worked. It would quickly become a cluttered mess, nobody able to find anything and no room to work on the wagons.

Well, here, Starbrite had made a workshop to work on his connection with higher powers. Presumably God, but Truth had long since come to agree with Merkovah's description of the divine. There was only one God. And there were multiple versions of them, all equally real. All existing at the same time. And yet, only one of them was real, because there really was only one God. Like the shape in the hallway. There was only one hyper-dimensional object, but it sure looked like there were dozens of them, from what our limited minds could perceive.

It said something about Starbrite that he presumably knew that tidbit but still built a workshop around communion with the divine. Was he trying to get around the interference of the stellar eminence that was the world? Trying to communicate with that same being? Calling out to another power? Ultimately, there wasn't enough to go on. He simply couldn't tell from what he was seeing. It was like he was in the garage but didn't know it belonged to the Army. He could make a guess about the nature of the work based on the tools, but like hell could he have named the specific wagons or figured out they were war weapons.

Deeper and deeper into the temple. If he kept the workshop analogy in mind, it started to make more sense. The little nooks that looked like they should hold chapels probably did. The specific contents of them were just changed depending on the project being worked on. Same thing with the different baptismal methods, the closet with one hundred different types of candles, the racks on racks of carefully labeled oils. All available to properly venerate whichever singular truth was required.

Jeon Internal Security, and presumably their allies, believe Starbrite is sacrificing himself to himself for reasons unknown. Sally said that Starbrite's soul is all wrong, grossly bloated with all the soul fragments he has stolen, and he wanted to steal her body. Somehow. Interesting that they didn't try to bully her into taking an oath and accepting the System. After five years in captivity, with the aid of the System, she probably would have agreed to anything. The spirit in the library said he was a gambler with debts coming due, but . . . that just doesn't add up. One, who does he owe? And two, it doesn't match what I've seen of his personality.

Starbrite isn't just careful; he's paranoid. When he has to choose between maximizing his safety and maximizing his gains, he picks safety every time. As much as everyone sneers at the F, E, and D Tiers, basic Starbrite Security has been consistently competent. You can really see that they are well supervised and pushed hard to excel. That's got to come from the very top.

It occurs to me that if he can manipulate reality enough to hide what is clearly a massive military installation in the middle of a highly active sea lane, he can also manipulate it enough to obliterate his own traces.

When was Starbrite founded? Dunno. Where did his first shop open? Dunno. What does he sound like, look like, dress like? Dunno. It was all handled by a courtier, you see. And then he would make a gesture, and things would blow up. So, we believed him.

It became easier and easier to remove himself from the public consciousness. Becoming less and less himself and more and more the corporation. Unknowable, untouchable; not only could you not argue with him, you couldn't even beg. You couldn't speak to him at all. You spoke to the ministers, if you were lucky. He wasn't the CEO; he was the weather. An oncoming storm. And we all went along with it. Aided by some very unique magic, of course.

Was it paranoia? Was it *just* paranoia? Truth was above-average paranoid, and he was honest enough to admit he enjoyed walking through the masses unseen. This felt like more than that. Truth was hiding from the masses, yes, but really from one entity—Starbrite. And, yes, Jeon, Onis, and whoever, but only because he was fighting with Starbrite. He still did the things he loved. Still had people he cared about. He was still *him*, just growing and changing as time passed. Starbrite, though, wanted to obliterate all traces of himself as a real person and become, simply, a higher power.

No trace of a specific deity anywhere. No pictures of animals, or demons, or . . . anything recognizable, really. Just these endlessly repeating geometric shapes. And they don't feel like sacred art. It feels more like someone just wanted a nice ceiling and budget was no obstacle to having the best.

But why, though? Hiding out from his debts? Weird way to do it. Starbrite the person might be a ghost, but Starbrite the public persona was the most famous person on the planet and had been for centuries. Anyone even slightly looking around would discover this. And if you were chasing Starbrite-size wealth, you wouldn't be satisfied with a quick check on local notables.

Truth entered a small courtyard within the temple. It was essentially an empty square with a gravel floor and an artificial sky overhead. There was a double row of plants and dwarf trees leaning up against a wall, stuck in plastic pots. There were a number of pre-dug holes scattered around the courtyard. It was a sacred grove—assemble as needed. You could alter the sky above the courtyard. Did your ritual require it to be noon, or dawn, or the first full moon after the vernal equinox? No problem. Another room to try and fool God.

Leaning against the trees was a corpse. Truth didn't notice at first; the body blended very well. It was mummified, rigid, holding itself straight like a soldier standing at attention. Truth took a closer look. Female, no visible cause of death, intact corpse. It looked like they just . . . died. And then were washed, dried, treated with some sort of preservatives or enchantments, and left out in the sun to cure. He could see a few more stacked in with the trees, hidden in the foliage. The corpses were props too. Sometimes, you just need a body. Apparently. Not his department.

The door out of the courtyard was wood, weathered and sun-bleached. Truth opened it and nearly screamed. On the other side of the door were dozens of the eyeless homunculi. The Tongue was out and reaching for the first head when his brain caught up with his instincts. The homunculi weren't looking at him. Weren't moving at all. Incisive wasn't going off. The creatures had been deactivated or killed by the curse. If you could kill such a thing. Rendered inoperable.

Truth hesitated, then slowly reached out to grab one of the shiny freaks. Smooth latex under his fingers. Room temperature. Whatever they were, they only acted alive. He dragged one out into the courtyard, ignoring what was in the rest of the room. If it wasn't hostile, he would deal with it later.

All right, time to figure out just what kind of monster you are.

Truth used the fangs of Incisive along one finger, trying to slice open the rubbery exterior. There was a strange resistance to it. It couldn't stop him, but there was a vague tugging feeling on the spell, like he was trying to cut through a rubber mat with an unfathomably sharp pocketknife. He ran his fingertip from the clavicle to the bottom of the ribs, then made a Y-shaped incision over the belly. Finally, he pulled back all the flaps of latex. Time to see what had been troubling him all this time.

The skin was the first minor marvel—black and rubbery on the outside, the inside was inscribed with thousands of tiny lines of calligraphy. It appeared to be a recitation of mighty names, invoking some and forbidding others, forming a dense coating of spells over the exterior. When the little monsters were active, they would be essentially invisible and, like Truth, largely imperceptible to Level Zeros. He was sure there was more going on with the skin than that, but even figuring out that much made him smug.

The bones, by comparison, were basically trash. Quite literally unwanted leftovers. They were human bones plainly manipulated to reach a uniform size. He could see the sloppy way nubs of plastic or porcelain had been glued on, the way tendons were attached with haphazard screws or yet more glue . . . It wasn't jank; it was junk. Its creator just needed it to be able to stand up and move around slowly, not do anything fancy like "run" or "jump."

Or. Well. Not do those things well, at any rate. No real musculature there. Everything ran off enchantments. Some clearly witchcrafted organs filling the chest and guts, things that blurred the lines between biology, alchemy, and necromancy. He hadn't the faintest idea what they did. Sophia would know.

The skull was a lot more interesting. The brain case had been hollowed out and coated with spells, forming an enchanted space with room for a tiny . . . something . . . to be housed in the middle of it all. It didn't quite look like a demon summoning, but a lot of the elements were similar.

The holes where the eyes should be were the big prize. The sockets had been covered with more of the black latex, though there, it was left blank on the inside. The bone was etched at a near-microscopic level with spells. Truth had not the first idea what they all did. The way they interacted gave him a headache. Literally a headache. Truth jerked back with surprise. The spell wasn't active right now. So, why?

The spells twisted and writhed on him. He could swear he saw some of them vanish and reappear elsewhere in the socket.

There is no way. No way.

He stared a while longer, letting his focus on the secular reality slip a bit. He bit back a swear.

He was looking at a rather ordinary Jeon woman. Not a great beauty, nor terribly ugly, not old, nor very young. Average. Everything that made her her, that made her more than an abstraction, had been extracted, rebuilt, or removed entirely. As for her eyes, the whisper-thin sacks of saline had been etched with spells so profound, they pressed on the edges of the real.

The homunculi still had their eyes. You just had to be standing at a slightly higher level of reality to see them. That was their reliance against Incisive and similar spells. You want to hide by adjusting local reality? Starbrite can play that game too, and at an industrial scale. Truth had evaded them by literally turning himself into a corpse. They saw right through his magic, to the reality below. And the reality had been meat on a hook.

Meet increasing complexity with increasing simplicity. He swore he would never leave that righteous path ever again.

He dragged the mess over into a corner, half-hidden behind the trees. Not that he expected anyone else to be down there, but . . . just in case.

He walked into the room with all the watching corpses, gently shoving through their ranks. It was more of a storage room than a site of veneration. Like the closet with the candles or the shelves of oils. The homunculi might be needed for something, so there they were, tidily organized and to hand.

The next room was bare concrete. No decoration. No furniture. An empty room with a long sarcophagus in the middle of it, and against the back wall, an enormous stone stele. Etched on the stele were the words HEAVEN SEALING ORDER. There were no other doors.

CHAPTER 44

RUNNING FROM THE DEEP

Hear ye, O ye children of Seth, and give ear unto the words of Sariel, the servant of GOD, who standeth before the Most High and executeth His decrees. Thus saith the Lord of Hosts:

1. The children of Seth come upon this world by grace, not merit.
2. The children of Seth think as children, act as children, despoil what is good, venerate the bad, and worship false gods.
3. The Children of Seth do not treasure the True Path, do not strive to ascend, yet cry out to the Most High when their strength fails them.
4. Sahariel sees you, and Sariel hears you. Receive now our command.
5. Ye shall not depart from this world in body, neither shall ye ascend unto the heavens, for it is decreed that thy lot is cast upon the earth.
6. And it is further commanded that none among thee shall awaken from thy period of initiation in the celestial mysteries. Nor shall you awaken your embodied Soul, neither by strength nor by cunning, for the bounds of thy power are set and ye shall not pass beyond them.
7. Ye shall receive no teachings nor guests from the realms above the rank of Embodied Soul, for the knowledge of the higher realms is withheld from thee, and their presence is forbidden in thy midst.
8. Moreover, ye are forbidden the warmth and comfort of fellowship that is thy birthright, for ye shall dwell in solitude and know not the communion of the wise nor the gathering of the elect. For ye have sold your birthright for dross, yet lack the means to reclaim it.
9. Thus is commanded the will of the Most High, who hath appointed bounds for every creature under Heaven: heed these words and keep them, for they are established by the decree of Sariel, who executeth the will of the Almighty.
10. Let all the descendants of Seth tremble and fear, for the price of ignorance is death eternal. Let all the descendants of Seth weep, for wisdom is the path to eternity, and obedience to God is the walking of the path.

Truth had no idea what language the Order was written in. That turned out to be no barrier to understanding. Sariel wanted his meaning understood and wasn't afraid to stamp it directly onto the reader's brain. Truth knew a couple of words of Enochian, the artificial language used to converse with angels. Just picked them up here and there on the job. This wasn't Enochian. This was something more primal. Something shaped like words but transcending language and arriving at pure meaning. He could feel his mind creaking, scrambling to reduce the transcendent meaning into manageable words and concepts.

Eventually, he forced himself to look away, collapsing to his ass on the floor. Gasping. Hugging his knees. Trying to fit all the nuance that words couldn't capture into some kind of box, some kind of frame of understanding.

It's our fault? He's saying it's our fault? "Daddy doesn't want to hit you, but since you won't listen to him, maybe you will listen to the belt." There are probably layers to this. Lots to unpack. Truth quickly memorized it. At this point, he could handle a spell as complicated as Earth-Folding Step. This wasn't too much. Once he succeeded, he forced himself to his feet and called the Tongue to his hand.

He could feel something in the blade thrumming in harmony with the stele. The Tongue was his platonic life partner, but she wasn't going to forget her roots either. He shrugged that away too. The women in his life were a lot more religious than he was. But they were worth it, so it was whatever. Time to finish the job.

He walked up to the sarcophagus. Simple-looking thing, at least in the secular world. Essentially a stone box. Big, for something that was allegedly only holding parts of a person. Meh. Not his problem. He put two hands on the blade, lined up his thrust, and stabbed hard at the side of the box. The blade skittered off.

Figures. Time to say bye-bye to stealth and hello to excessive violence.

Truth let his awareness slip slightly into the higher levels of reality. He kept his eyes focused on the now extremely elaborate sarcophagus. He wasn't sure his brain would survive looking at the stele. The true appearance of the sarcophagus was a chest of porphyry inlaid with gems and spells whose intricacy was far beyond Truth's meager learning. It was beautiful. He didn't care, because sitting on the edge of the chest, kicking her little feet, was the System Fairy. Still in her office-lady outfit, smoking Golden Bats, and sneering at the pictures in a magazine.

Truth pulled back the Tongue again, lining up his shot. The System Fairy had always been a sort of hallucination, but who knew? He might yet get lucky. The sword ripped right through it . . . to no effect.

"Oh, shit, you can see me? How can you see me?"

"I was wondering the same thing. As far as I know, you are Starbrite's soul."

"Oh, no, no way. I'm like a tiny fragment of his soul. Like a single cell on the very tip of your finger is also, in the least way possible, you."

Truth nodded. That's what he had remembered the System saying all those years before.

"A sock puppet."

"It sounds bad when you put it that way. Also, yes." The office-lady Fairy put down her magazine, but the cigarette stayed.

"So . . . Starbrite is about to pop up out of that box, and then we get into the mix?"

"Unlikely." She shrugged.

"Why's that?"

"Starbrite is barely holding on at the moment. The cascade effects of what happened here are still rippling out across the world. I'm not going to spell it out for you, but an *unbelievable* number of things just went BOOM."

Truth nodded. "I believe it."

"No, no. It's way more than you would believe."

"I have an excellent imagination for destruction and devastation. I believe it."

The System Fairy raised a perfectly plucked and arched eyebrow in surprise and possible disbelief. "Bizarre thing to boast about, but okay. Hey, are you that Hell Prince guy? Weird question, but you really shouldn't be able to see me unless you were sworn to Starbrite, and you aren't, because I'd know if you were."

"On account of not having the System in me."

"Yeah, exactly!" She clapped her tiny hands.

"Yet you can still find the spot on my soul used to communicate *through* my soul, which should be mutilated and training me up like a dog."

"Nah, we use way more negative reinforcement on our employees than you should ever use with a dog. We're just old-fashioned that way—no carrots without sticks, and sometimes you need to rub puppy's nose in their mess. Not because it teaches them anything. Just to make yourself feel better."

"Well, out with the old, in with the new, and all that. Let's try prying up *this* seam." Truth found a micron thin gap in the purple-red stone of the sarcophagus and started trying to work the sword edge in. This was met with a great deal of nothing much.

"Yeah, no, this coffin is officially, and I do mean *officially*, the best-armored thing on this rock. Including the rock itself. You could drop it into the magma layer for twenty thousand years, and you wouldn't even fade the paint." The Fairy sniggered. It wasn't a pleasant sound.

Called it. I knew that was the backup-backup plan. He kept picking at the seam. Eventually, he would figure out something. Just took time.

The silence stretched for a few minutes. The Fairy went back to her miniature magazine, pretended to read it for a while, and eventually threw it aside again.

"Look, I said you aren't getting in there."

"No, you didn't. I was there. I would remember if you said that."

"It's what I meant, and you know it."

"Yeah, but I ignored that bit."

"What, you think something will eventually shake loose and you can pry your way in? Naive." She sniffed and flicked her hand. "He is a superior being."

"Can't be that superior." Truth jabbed his thumb at the stele. "He's got the same level cap we all do."

"Says who? Some basic-bitch angel?" She sneered.

"Not sure I would call a stellar eminence a 'basic bitch.'" Truth kept hunting. At some point, he would find something or make something.

"No, it is. It's not even a person. That stele? It's a joke. Just because the angel means it doesn't change that it's a joke. The road to Nascent Soul is forbidden? The hell it is. What's forbidden is doing it the way the angel expects you to. Human ingenuity is limitless. All it takes is a person of singular vision and will to turn the impossible into the inevitable."

"Someone like Starbrite?"

"Someone like you." The Fairy smiled. Truth nodded faintly. He had expected the change-up. Didn't slow down his efforts to find a way to crack the sarcophagus.

"Starbrite . . . What is his name, actually? Is he even really a 'he?'"

"His name is Starbrite, and yes, he is a 'he.'"

"No. No, it isn't. His mom didn't look down on him in the bassinet and say . . . Actually, what's his mom's name? What planet is he from? Where did his dad work? Does he put extra sauce on his egg sandwiches?"

"He's a very private man and doesn't speak on personal matters. Particularly with people trying to murder him."

"You really gonna tell me this isn't self-defense?"

"Yes?" The Fairy looked puzzled. "Starbrite isn't causing the apocalypse."

"The rollout of the System globally?"

"Not your problem, so why do you care?"

"Calling me Hell Prince and trying to turn the world against me?"

"You murdered . . . so many people. So, so many people. Just an astonishing, shocking number of people." The System Fairy spread her hands helplessly.

"So did Starbrite."

"Nah. The main function of a business is to bring the proprietor profit. As long as a corporation acts in line with that principle, whatever it does is both morally and ethically correct."

Truth jerked to a halt.

"You . . . want to run that past me again?"

"The purpose of a business is profit for the owners. Individual, partnership, shares, whatever. That's why companies are created—to make money. Doing things that *aren't* making money, no matter how 'good' they might be, is fundamentally betraying the owners and the purpose of the company. Want to do charity? Do it on your own time and with your own money."

"But Starbrite outright owns the corporation. Are there even shares in other people's hands? He could do immense good in the world."

"But he chooses not to spend his money and effort on the things you care about. And so what? That's his freedom of conscience right there." The Fairy sounded severe. "You are in no position to judge. And by the way, if you are going to judge, make sure you include all the good he's done. The world is a much more comfortable place to live, thanks to him. All those talismans, all that high-energy food from off-word. The hundreds of thousands of homes and apartments. Elixirs. Talismans. So, so many talismans. All those jobs. All that healthcare."

"The environmental and human costs—"

"Not the company's responsibility." The Fairy flicked it away. "The company's responsibility is to earn profits for the owner. Offloading costs onto the state is just good business practice. Which is why I'm talking to you."

"Eh? I figured you were stalling for time or something."

"No, I knew someone would be coming. Listen, the planet is screwed, but there is an immense opportunity here. Don't you see the stele? Even if the Nephilim do invade, they will be Level Nine or lower!"

"So?"

"So? SO? Starbrite is the only person in the world who knows how to get around the ban on Nascent Souls! He's going to be taking a little nap for a few thousand years. Totally out of it. He needs someone who can step in. Take charge of things. Guide the public and protect them from interlopers. Don't you see? All those things you hate? All the things that hurt you, all the injustice, all the unfairness, you can fix it all! You will be the only *true* powerhouse in the world. You alone will have the ability to summon the winds and the rain. And all it takes—"

"I know what it costs. I have wanted to try this for years." Truth channeled all his magic into the Meditations and focused them on his hands. The spell worked on a more than physical level. The System Fairy had been the first person to tell him that. She'd been right about it, too. He reached out his hand, and he grabbed her. Truth squeezed.

Something went crunch.

CHAPTER 45

NUMBER ONE IN THE WORLD

There was a brief moment of ecstasy. The sheer joy that came with crushing the little tormenting imp was convulsive, rising from the depths of his soul and the most resentful corners of his psyche. It was all the taunting. All the *A real mage would*—crap that it spewed. The fact that it trained him—like a *dog* it trained him!—to despise others as weaker and lesser. To ignore other humans, to avoid human companionship. To seek power for the sake of dominating others.

Enlightenment poured into Truth's mind like a waterfall. Why the System? Why just roll it out to employees? Because each Nascent Soul was made up of the interplay of spells and understanding about the spells that filled your apertures. A Starbrite employee, someone recruited immediately after they broke through to Level One but before they learned a spell, would have an empty soul. They would only be shaped by the System, raw soul stuff stamped with Starbrite's ideology.

The world really was Starbrite's pill farm. All those components refining themselves, with his thoughtful guidance. Then they just threw themselves into his mouth in a nice, steady stream. Perfect. The waterfall of revelation had a bit of a glitch, and the smile ran from his face. How did the global rollout of the System fit in, then?

Because he was running out of time. He needed more souls and couldn't worry too much about purity anymore. Which meant that his soul was in a very rough state. And Truth had just crushed a tiny part of it while the whole thing was dealing with a literal world's worth of stress.

Whoops.

If he wasn't there to kill Starbrite, this would be terribly embarrassing.

There was a high-pitched shriek, one that ran on and on and on without pausing for breath, and Truth realized he wasn't hearing it with his ears. He was hearing it with his soul.

On a certain mountain outside of Xandre, Merkovah stood and watched the stars. His fingers flicked at an inhuman speed. Calculations and magic spells, most forbidden since the settling of the world, rushed from him like a hot desert wind. Merkovah knew why these spells had received a divine ban—they worked. No boss liked being snooped on by their menials. That observation was supposed to be one-way only.

Merkovah could smell the change in the air. He could taste it shivering across his palate. Feel it wrapping around his fingers, scratching at his fingertips. His eyes were fixed firmly on the heavens. He had waited more than half a millennium. Watched every human he loved and cared about die over and over again. Watched his world slide into the most unbearably mundane ruin.

He had always been a romantic at heart. When he was offered a life of chivalry, of boldly charging against unholy forces anointed by the blessings of God and in the company of true companions, he hadn't hesitated to say yes. The shine had come off the dream a long, long time ago. But he'd do it again in a heartbeat.

The prisoner next to him started shrieking. Not with his throat; that had been torn out weeks ago. No, it was the soul itself screaming, hammering wildly against the jar it was sealed in.

God had forbidden a wide variety of necromancy, too. But since God had broken their contract with Siphios, Merkovah literally did not give a damn.

"NOW!" His voice roared, a lion in the thunder, an avalanche on a clear day. A meteor ripping across the sky.

Behind him, the massed teachers of the orthodoxy bent over and began to chant. Their students provided the power, filling ritual circles with white and gold filigree. The runes, holy symbols, infernal sigils, the names of beings both blessed and rebuked were inscribed, as vast wheels of green flame and black water turned. Slowly turned, feeding something intangible into the heavy millstones positioned according to numerical formulae and certain, once-forbidden observations of the stars.

The teachers were there in their thousands, their students in the tens of thousands, and the laity were present more than a million strong. They thought it was a prayer rally, and they were right, sort of. A great raising of power in the face of the end of the world. A million voices called out, reciting terrible names and invoking awful powers with the easy fluency of a lifetime of experience. This was Siphios, and they walked with angels and demons every moment of every day of their lives. If this was to be the final flower of the old world, they were determined to bloom bloody and bright.

In the Royal Palace, barely sixty kilometers from the ritual site, the King of Siphios sat with the High Priest in what was once a ballroom. By absolutely no coincidence, the King and the High Priest were cousins. They smiled wryly at each other. They could hear the screaming too. They had made a point of lining every surface of the ballroom with the trapped souls of C-Tier-and-above Starbrite employees.

"I went into seclusion to avoid exactly this kind of thing," the King groused, coming to his feet. His arches ached. It was a petty detail to notice at a time like this, but they did ache. It seemed unfair.

"I entered the clergy for the same reason. Well, that and the money, the power, the fancy house—" the High Priest agreed, pulling out his sword.

"You ever realize that you want something but it's in a different part of the house and it's so damn far away, you can't even be bothered to send a demon to fetch it?" The King stood and faced his cousin, his own sword loose in his hand.

"Yeah, daily. Still wouldn't swap the Manor for a two-bedroom economy, though. They don't come with a private grotto." They lined up their swords against each other's chests. "I liked that poem you wrote. The one about watching the dawn."

The King smiled. "Liar. Thank you. Goodbye, cuz."

"Goodbye."

There was a crack of lightning, and they stabbed forward. The swords flashed with golden script, snuffing the light from their wielder's eyes instantly. Extinguishing decades of resentment and hate. It was like a spark was lit, igniting all the trapped souls. The souls thrashed, smashing themselves against the walls of their glass tombs. They would have begged if there had been enough in them left to beg. The fire spread out from the ballroom and engulfed the palace in far less than a second.

Respected servants and ministers, honored for their decades of loyal service, collapsed, clutching their chests as blue-green flames shot from their mouths and eyes. Decades of loyal service, yes, but not to Siphios. The fires spread out into Xandre. Block after block, kilometer after kilometer, the fire raced out, burning out the souls of those loyal to Starbrite.

Some of those incinerated would have defended themselves strongly. They weren't Starbrite employees. They didn't have the System. But tonight was the product of Merkovah's patient malice. The grand ritual wasn't so limited. The victims had Starbrite in their hearts and minds. The old exorcist did them a favor and made sure the rot was cleaned out of their souls.

It wouldn't have been possible if Starbrite had been at his old strength. Wouldn't have been possible even yesterday. But that terrible soul was badly wounded, and Merkovah had been scheming for this very moment.

The more people the ritual burned, the faster it spread. It covered the whole city in less than a minute. It covered the whole country in less than ten. Then it crossed the national borders, and the chaos truly began. It wasn't just going after living souls at this point. The ritual had accumulated enough power to burn them out of the air. All those souls called back to Starbrite, all the fragments of divine self, all those mutilated chunks of System-ridden humanity, were ignited. Siphios was once again the torch that lit the world.

Siphios had, understandably, not adopted the System to manage its citizenry. Neither had the Free State, on account of there not being an actual government. Their other neighbors, though, had been eager to adopt the next big thing. Prompted, subtly and otherwise, by Starbrite's agents. A lot of people had gotten very rich making sure the new System reached as many people as possible as quickly as possible.

The money didn't seem to comfort them now.

There was barely enough time for long-range systems to notice a problem. For oracles to wake up screaming, for nation-guarding bells to start tolling frantically. A lot of questions were being asked, but no one had any answers to share.

The rollout had been far from total in any nation. Even in Jeon, the System was a long way from universal. Other countries were far behind. But Starbrite had been on this world for centuries, and his reach was very long. A scallop-fishing boat ran onto a shoal when their captain lit up like the starboard navigation light. A woman screamed for help, for the fire department, as her wife thrashed and burned. Not noticing that the pillows weren't even singed. Not noticing the way green light was pouring in through the window from a half dozen apartments across the street.

Over and over and over, each death harming Starbrite and fueling the spread of the ritual. And watching it spread was Merkovah, tracking its awful progression through his divination. Keeping a weather eye on his assembled teachers and celebrants, making sure the ritual stayed on track. Force of habit at this point. He had so many lifetimes' worth of watching plans collapse at the last moment.

All these deaths were necessary preludes to the death he really wanted to see. And it wasn't there yet. His fingers kept flicking out, making their calculations as his voice rolled on, every inflection on every syllable perfect. Every word of the spell had been memorized before Truth's parents were born and diligently rehearsed ever since. Just in case God really had abandoned them and it turned out to be needed. Some nights, it was the only way he could fall asleep.

He was a romantic at heart, but that heart had been torn again and again. It had never managed to go completely dead, and the fury had never stopped accumulating. There were days when he admitted to himself that he was probably no longer sane. That the stress and pain of the endless centuries of struggle had broken him.

It became a talismanic thought—once he killed Starbrite, he could rest. Once he finally, *finally* brought an end to their long war, he could put down his burdens and leave the tidying-up to someone else. Anyone else. He wouldn't, didn't care. He just wanted to rest. To lie down in the mountains and dream of his lost loves, old friends, favorite students, and the sweet smells of the magical forests of his childhood.

The spell swept across the world, burning up Starbrite's feed and gaining in fury and power as it went. Jeon wasn't on the exact opposite side of the world from Xandre, but the ritual was well controlled. The world was bathed in blue-green fire before the flaming tide came in at last.

Merkovah was smiling. He didn't know he was, but he was. His lips had pulled back in a mad rictus of ecstasy, showing all his teeth. Truth's magic was utterly profound and his blessings were more so, but Merkovah was the one who had provided them to him. The student couldn't completely evade his teacher's divination. He might not know exactly what was going on, but he knew Truth was exactly where he needed to be. Ready to kill a false god.

When they told the story of tonight, he would make sure Truth's name never appeared. There was no hidden assassin. Hell Prince was a lie invented by Starbrite. The real monster, the true Hell Prince, was him. Merkovah. King-killer, apostate, liar, thief, false teacher, terrorist, and the greatest murderer to ever live. That would be the story they told. He was big enough and ugly enough to hold up that title. His student couldn't even hang on to one name.

Truth didn't know why the screaming was getting louder and louder. Why the air suddenly had an itchy feeling to it, then started burning blue-green. *The color of toilet cleaner*, he thought. It was harmless but alarming. The painful screaming started ululating and shaking, the wandering harmonies vibrating the walls of the hidden temple. It started feeling a lot less harmless when the blue-green flames started melting their way through the purple-red coffin lid. It didn't feel harmless at all when the lid exploded off the sarcophagus and something terrible arose from within.

CHAPTER 46

THE HERO WHO TRIED TO SAVE THE WORLD

It was like being hit with a storm. Like a wind-lashed wildfire smashed into him. Starbrite didn't rise from the sarcophagus—he boiled up out of it. He rose like an arsonist's finest work. You could hear the screaming kids trapped on the sixth floor. Only faintly—it was hard to hear the screams over the roars. Starbrite had been run to ground. Forced out of hiding. His steady feed of souls had been shattered and his servants killed. Local reality was twisting and thrashing like a spider being lowered over a candle. He was not taking the loss gracefully.

Didn't . . . Merkovah say something about a bunch of old, near-death Level Eights and Nines who were on standby to jump Starbrite when he looked weak? Boy, they would be really useful right now.

The layers of reality were trying to stack, to superimpose into one observable "truth." There was a haggard man, and an unspeakable nightmare agglomeration of soul-stuff, and a god-king rebuking his disobedient subjects. There was a floating head, and a terrible void in space that consumed endlessly. They all burned. Truth didn't know what the particular significance of that was, but they all burned and screamed. Pain, but more than pain—outrage.

Truth quite understood. His mind had congealed into a slab of lucid terror. It was always like this with high-value protectees. Once your net worth reached a certain point, certainly by the third comma on the line, you were supposed to be untouchable. Things were supposed to go according to plan, because you had limitless servants eager to do whatever it took to *make* it go according to plan. And when things didn't go according to plan? They were furious, and they took it out on everyone around them.

Starbrite took it out on everyone. Truth felt Starbrite reach into the void and pluck a string Truth never knew existed, but the sudden thrum of it changed something, a song or chord he had been listening to his whole life without noticing. Truth didn't know what that meant. He just wanted to cry. Something so foundational, so important was now wrong. It couldn't be like this, but he didn't know what was wrong, let alone how to fix it.

The burning figure snarled and swiped his hand out again. Thousands upon thousands of symbols appeared, then spread and grew like frost on glass. Truth didn't recognize any of them, though they reminded him of the circuit paths of a talisman. But only the paths. The nodes seemed to be missing. Then the spell rotated through an angle Truth could only dimly perceive, and a rain of bitter steel arrows flew out and over the world. No indiscriminate slaughter; each of these arrows had an intended recipient. Mere walls or wards wouldn't be enough to slow them, let alone stop them.

The ancient monster waved another hand . . . and nothing happened. There was a sound like swearing but not in a language Truth knew. Then another wave, and ten thousand motes of light flew out of the chamber. Truth wondered if now would be a good time to stab the . . . thing. He was desperately worried about the chord, about that plucked string, but there really wasn't anything he could do about it. He could stab a bastard, though.

"Oh, don't think I've forgotten about you." The cloud of flames / god-king / wild-eyed man turned to stare at him. "I'd call you an insignificant worm, but worms are actually useful. Worms make something of value. You don't. You just kill. That's it. That's all you are good at."

"Well . . . not all I am good at." Truth's mouth was running while his brain was trying to chip off the ice. "I'm better than decent at talisman maintenance."

"No, you aren't." The cloud of fire rose over him, staring down at him. "I know you now, Truth Medici. I can see why we didn't figure it out before. You were comprehensively killed. Even reviewing the recordings now, seeing the System records now, there is no question that you died. But here you are. A special breed of hornet this hateful nest produced to torment me."

The rest of Truth froze alongside his brain. His anonymity had always been his greatest shield. To have it casually pierced was—

"No wonder the curse to kill you used your brother as the sacrifice. Did you know that? When you did whatever you did to sabotage the curse, you killed your brother, too. Oh yes. And when I put out this fire, his soul will be *mine*. Yours, however, will be refined into an artifact whose sole purpose is to know pain. Every sort of pain. I will create teams of researchers whose only function is to find nuances of suffering and determine how best to make you suffer from them."

Starbrite started laughing, the fury shaking the walls. "Do you have any idea what you have cost me? And for what?!"

"Well, be fair, you did kill me first."

Starbrite slapped him. The giant hand hit him hard enough to send him across the room and into the wall behind him. It had been a long time since he had gotten hit hard enough to see stars.

"No. I won't be 'fair.' One, because I don't have to. Two, because you, of ALL PEOPLE, don't get to talk to me about 'fair.' And three, because your whole pissant life exists only because I allowed it. I am the sole reason for your existence, in every sense of the word. So, killing you is fair enough! FAIR? Do you have any idea how much I have suffered? How much I have given you people?"

"No. Tell me about it." Truth was watching the fires on Starbrite. Didn't look like they were part of him. Looked like something that was happening *to* him. And rich people loved to talk about themselves, right?

Starbrite jumped him. Shrank down to a mere three meters and jumped on him. Truth's instincts had him dodging, but as he knew better than most, once the difference in physical capability reaches a certain point, any attempts to dodge become pointless. The uppercut lifted him up off his toes, smashing him into the ceiling. He was seeing stars again, and his ears were filled with tinny bells.

"Sure. I'll tell you all about it. FUCK YOU! FUCK YOU! You think I'm stupid? You think I'm dumb, you piece of shit? You like fighting? Here, I got something for you. Why are you dodging? I thought you loved throwing hands!"

Truth was trying to block, trying to slip the punches, but Starbrite was just too fast. He either went around his guard or effortlessly broke through it. Truth could feel his kidneys were shot after two hits. Another two broke ribs directly over his lungs. Starbrite wanted to make this hurt. Truth caught a glimpse of something when the ragged man appeared. Not the god-king but a man in filthy robes and worn-out sandals. He knew that thin face and those rabid eyes. He had seen them on the junkie he beat to death by the canal.

"This world was your big chance, huh?" Truth grinned through bloody teeth. "This is where you would make it. Where none of the gangsters could catch you and beat you. Again."

Starbrite smashed him up into the ceiling again. This time, a foot made of blue-green flames folded him in half on the way down. Funny—the fire didn't hurt him. Spell resistance again? The gut-kick sure hurt like hell.

"Gangster? You think I give a shit about *gangsters?* You blind, stupid son of a bitch! What do you think a Nascent Soul is?"

Starbrite paused, glaring up at something Truth couldn't see. "Yeah, I said it. Nascent. Soul. Oh, you angry? You going to do something about it? Maybe send some little juiced-up gutter rat to try and stop me? Maybe your pet humans in Siphios? *It didn't work any of the other times you tried, did it?!*"

Wait, what? Truth knew that Siphios had made other attempts on Starbrite's life, but—

Big hands grabbed him up off the floor, wrenched his head around. "You know what? I want you to know this. I do." I do. I want you to know *exactly* how meaningless this all has been. Nascent. What does the word *nascent* mean? I know your school was trash. I know the inseam and favorite pornography of every single person who ever attended, or taught, or mopped the vomit off the floors at every school you ever attended. I know every person who ever lived in that termite mound you grew up in. Did any of them ever tell you what *nascent* means?"

Truth wasn't sure any of them could even pronounce *nascent* and was about to say as much, but Starbrite slapped him instead.

"No. They didn't. Because none of you fucks ever bothered trying to elevate yourselves. You kept pissing the floor until the battery-acid urine etched a hole in the concrete, then you decided to live in the hole because who would turn down free real estate? Then you kept pissing, and screamed that I was drowning you. Fuck you." He slapped him again. "Fuck you." Another hit. "You know what *nascent* means? It means *coming into being*. It means being *born*, you shit-eating moron." Another hit. "And if you had enough brains to not drown *taking* a shit, you would be asking yourself, 'Born into what?'"

Truth called the Tongue into his hand, tried to jam it up under Starbrite's ribs. The old monster saw it coming a mile away, smacked his hand hard enough to send the sword flying and breaking Truth's wrist in the process.

"Fucking animal. Can't think your way through a problem, so you stab it. Over and over and over again with you animals. You insects. You eat shit, make messes, and when anyone disturbs your towers of filth, tries to make something good and decent and meaningful, you come *swarming* out."

Starbrite punched him in the nose. He could feel it break, almost lying flat against his face. He couldn't even gasp in pain with the broken ribs.

"Nascent. Soul. A soul that has just been born. Which means that what you have inside of you right now isn't even alive. Not even a real soul yet. You hear me? All that stuff inside you? It isn't even a real soul yet. I'M THE ONLY REAL PERSON ON THIS ENTIRE PLANET, AND YOU THINK YOU CAN KILL ME?!"

Truth gasped out a laugh. He couldn't help it. Everything hurt. He was going to die. Starbrite was going to kill the sibs if he managed to put out that fire. His mission was, in every sense, a failure. Failed at the final step. But it was still funny.

"A human is a person with a real, embodied soul, according to you. But look at your soul. It isn't even yours." The sound was wet. Choking. Hard to speak with all the damage. Starbrite signaled his disagreement with another punch in the mouth.

"According to me? No no no. According to the angel you grew up running around on. Look at that stele. LOOK AT IT!" Starbrite wrenched Truth's head around. "It's older than I am, by thousands of years. There was no chance anyone on this rock was ever going to reach Nascent Soul, and you know why? Because once you were a real person, *the angel would have to take you at least a little bit seriously.* You understand? You getting this? All these stellar eminences that treat you like shit, GOD HIMSELF turning his back on the planet, why?"

Starbrite started punctuating his sentences with slaps. "Because. None. Of. You. Are. Real. People." He flicked Truth into the corner. "You are little clay dolls carrying tiny fragments of something so much greater inside of you. Not a single one of you morons knew what to do with that spark . . . and then the choice was taken from you. You got to be clay dolls forever, until Sariel decided to tidy up his toys. And you know why he did that? Because I was winning. I was getting strong enough to call the shots here."

Starbrite crouched over Truth, flames licking out from his eyes and seeping from between his teeth. "Congratulations! You managed to stop the hero from saving the world. You must be very proud."

CHAPTER 47

PROSPERITY

You are the hero who is saving the world. Do heroes harvest souls? Genuinely asking; I don't know." Truth's mouth had run away from him. His brain could understand why—under the circumstances, none of his body parts wanted anything to do with the rest of him. They were too obsessed with their own pain to worry about the pain of others.

Starbrite nodded, a "cheerful" smile on his face as he reached down and snapped Truth's pinky finger. The bone shattered, and not cleanly. Truth screamed. Starbrite's smile got bigger. "Yes. Hero. The hero swoops in out of nowhere and makes everything better. Which is exactly what I did. This planet was a shithole before I got here. *Civil servant* was the peak of most families' ambitions, as it was a stable way to steal money."

Starbrite flicked his finger and hauled Truth into the air. "A planet full of people who could *bind demons*, and your number-one life path was subsistence farmer. That's not even pathetic. Your shit language can't even convey how deeply your ancestors failed. If you had any real concept of shame, your whole damn planet would sterilize itself to prevent its awful bloodline from continuing. And then I came and saved you ungrateful pricks."

Starbrite threw a sloppy hook and caught Truth's lowest rib on the right. It broke like kindling. Truth bit back another scream—this one in part frustration at just how sloppy the punch was. Starbrite wasn't good at fighting, Truth realized. He was just strong.

"I gave you good jobs. Better houses. Better *food*. I made you rich. Don't like your job? Just quit. You aren't tied to the land." Starbrite was working up his ribs. Some part of Truth was wondering if Starbrite was trying to break every bone in his body. The other part was just trying to not faint.

"A little loyalty isn't too much to ask for all that. A little bit of work ethic. And you know what? If you aren't putting your soul into the job, why the hell are you doing it in the first place? Especially since it's not like I'm blowing everything on hookers and booze like you freaks. I'm not the one shitting in trash cans or puking on strangers in the subway. No! I'm not!"

The last line was punctuated by two shots to the gut. Truth felt something rupture.

"I'm the guy who makes it so toilets can be in every house!"

He's dancing around the truth. Perks' whisper-dry voice sounded in Truth's mind. *Why does he need the souls? Why does the need for souls get bigger, not smaller, with time?*

Truth tried to fix Starbrite with a look, forcing his lungs to fill and his lips to work. "The souls. You keep needing more. You are bad at using them."

Starbrite paused. The look of utter shock and fury on his face twisted it into a demon mask, even more than the gouts of blue-green fire.

Starbrite slammed Truth into the floor. Then pinned him in place with barbed iron rods called forth by his magic.

"Bad. At using. The soul fragments. Bad at using them. Me. Bad. At using them. You . . . absolute insect. No, you aren't smart enough for an insect. You slime. You . . . goddamn bacterial raft. How do you not get this? How is this not immediately *intuitively* obvious after everything I've told you?! I BEAT THE ANGEL! I beat Sariel's whole game! You know *why* I need the souls? Because that GODDAMNED ANGEL keeps squeezing me! He keeps making me spend and spend to keep my Nascent Soul, and if I try to leave the planet, he goes fucking berserk with the lightning, and the WHOLE TIME, HE KEEPS SAYING THAT I'M NOT DOING IT THE RIGHT WAY!"

Truth nodded slightly at that. He wouldn't give a shit about someone else's rules either, under the circumstances.

"Well, guess what. Most people *don't* awaken their souls. It's pretty goddamn rare everywhere! And everyone keeps saying that you can't explain it, you have to figure it out yourself, that it's about understanding and, hah! Divine revelation."

"Convenient excuse." Truth mumbled through the blood. "Kind of thing people say to keep you down."

"Finally, a flicker of light in that dim skull of yours. Maybe I will refine you into an eternally screaming lamp. Seems fitting. Screaming on the inside, obviously; I don't want to be hearing that all the time."

Starbrite started gently twisting the iron bars back and forth, enjoying the muffled shrieks and the muscles that tore and shredded.

"Whoops—can't have you dying on me yet. Lemme hit you with a quick heal. On the house; I won't charge you a single credit. On the other hand, those iron bars are a really high-level spell! Can't let you enjoy them for free; it would throw off the whole economy of the System. I'm going to have to charge you, including my time, obviously, twenty billion credits a minute." Starbrite giggled slightly. "Unfortunately, your PMC discount no longer applies, or I could reduce it to fifteen billion, five hundred and thirty million."

Truth felt the spell go off, repairing his flesh and shattered bones, healing up around the barbs and hooks still embedded in him. Once he was fixed up, Starbrite gave him exactly one second to enjoy the feeling, then started twisting the rods again.

Truth could see it perfectly. Starbrite *had* to keep growing. It wasn't his power. It was all borrowed. The bet was against Sariel and on himself. Starbrite was betting he could reach some kind of point of stability where he wouldn't have to keep absorbing new souls and could just generate the power internally. But something from the outside always seemed to throw it off. Some pressure from the angel, or an attack from Siphios, or a new mineral deposit to exploit, or *something*. He could never get to "enough" because there would always be the instinct that he needed more.

Which wasn't crazy. After all, the bastards really were out to get him. Hard to feel safe when you know that, quite literally, the world is trying to kill you.

"Not content to just die peacefully and enjoy the next life?" He could talk more easily now—the internal organ damage had been healed up. It was just the agonizing pain as his muscles and tendons were shredded. He really wished he had a plan.

"Next life? Next? Are you . . . Oh. OOOOH! That's hilarious. That is actually completely fucking hilarious. Are you a reincarnator? I bet you are. You were a badass fighter since you could walk, according to your file. Well, no more cycle of reincarnation for you, fucko. It's eternity as a screaming lamp from now on. There won't be enough of you left to reincarnate as a dahlia. Nor time to live in."

"I meant Heaven or Hell."

The blue-green soul fire was dimming down. Starbrite didn't seem to mind. Truth really didn't want to find out why.

"Heh. Let me save you a little time. You know what's on the other side of all that celestial machinery? At the origin of the Pleroma? Once you get past the Archons and Aeons and Angels and Demiurge and heavenly demons and the Ogdoad and all that other bullshit? Nothing. Absolutely nothing. A void that obliterates meaning. I can't even call it a screaming void, because it obliterates that, too. I have seen it. I have *had* a divine revelation, oh, yes! I have had my own enlightenment. And you know what I learned? There is a God, and it destroys us.

"All that meaning we accumulated in life, everything we learned, everything we achieved, it all gets ground away, over and over again, until we finally return to the void and are obliterated. That's it. That's the end of the fucking celestial road. You keep climbing higher and higher, losing more and more, until you are completely unmade. So, *fuck* doing it the 'right way.' *Fuck* a quiet life and a peaceful death. *Fuck* God, the angels, the devils, and fuck you, too, if you think I'm going to feel bad about any of this. My only regret is that fucking space worm escaped before I could refine her into a new body. Now I have to spend who-knows-how-many years having a nap, waiting to build up the empire all over again."

Starbrite stood and smiled. "I'm pretty done with this rock. Well. Fuck it. Most of my souls have burned off, but the architecture is still there. Enough refined souls. Enough to keep me alive for a few tens of thousands of years, anyway. Just enough power left to kill off every single person who has ever irritated me, exterminate every single relative and friend you have, build that eternal-suffering engine, and settle in for my nap. I won't be starting from nothing next time."

Starbrite looked up at something only he could see. "Oh, yes. My very own road to immortality. TRUE immortality! This is a setback but only a setback. A blink in the span of eternity. Don't think I can't hurt your precious Nephilim too, Sariel. There are so many ways. So, so many ways. As long as your order is in place—"

"Why do you think that there won't be any Nephilim Nascent Souls coming?"

"Eh? Can't you read?! Any human—"

"Doesn't say *human* from what I'm reading. Says *Children of Seth*. And the Nephilim aren't. You already lost. You can't escape the planet, and once you are powerless, the Nephilim are going to stroll over and rip out your tendons. They were only hanging back because it wasn't worth fighting you before. Now? It's worth it. They love beating people who can't fight back."

Language was a *funny* thing, Truth reflected. Especially when the order was written in an angelic script that was using the angel's intent to communicate its meaning.

Starbrite looked upward. Eyes tightening at the corners. He was a cloud of burning soul-fire, a floating skull, a philosopher-king fighting on a higher level of reality than the merely secular. Truth saw the exact moment Starbrite panicked.

Now! Incisive told him this was the time to strike. He forced his body to tear off the hooks, leaving massive holes in him, leaving kilos of meat, organs, and blood on the floor. Willing himself to *move*. Cup and Knife to "correct" Starbrite's soul. It only lasted for a fraction of a second. For the barest fraction of a second. It was enough time to start falling forward. Taking a single step. Truth fell onto Starbrite, and his foot landed in the emptiness of space.

The floating head looked at him in horror and disgust. *"Insect!"* Hideous power came crashing back into the flaming cloud that was once the most powerful man in the world.

"We feel the same way about you."

The stars were blotted out. Massive forms emerged from the void, long black shapes. Long beyond reason. So vast, they shattered the mind's sense of scale. A mountain range moving with the speed and fluidity of a water snake. Bigger than mountains. There was nothing to stop them from growing as big as they wished.

"Oh, get fucked! You crooked thieves have been screwing over this planet since long before I got here!"

Truth tried to step away, but nothing happened. His legs barely twitched. *Oh, right. Blood loss. And . . . I think I am missing some important bits. Uh. Kidneys. Need those. My liver. I can get by on one lung, probably.* He watched the gushing blood forming an enormous bubble around him. *Gonna need to stop that bleeding.*

He called up Cup and Knife. The spell seemed to struggle—against what, Truth didn't know. He managed to stop the bleeding, at least. The rest would have to wait.

The Shattervoid weren't interested in talking any nonsense with Starbrite. Enormous screens of magic folded around the floating head, crushing inward. Truth watched the magic working across layers of reality— space twisting in the secular world, serpents crushing it in another layer, giant hands in another. Starbrite wasn't going quietly, either. He was fighting back with waves of fire, of twisting razor wire, the pronouncements of terrible laws. However badly damaged he was, he had been the god of this rock for a long, long while. And he had never minded using violence to solve problems.

Truth really wished he was farther away. The backblast had the advantage of pushing him farther from the fight but was also tearing him up. Tearing him up more. His heart hadn't stopped yet. He could survive awhile even if it did. Still, even a glancing blow would obliterate him. He was just Level Five.

It was at this point that Sariel decided to join the fight.

CHAPTER 48

A STARBRITE MAN

Truth respected a well-organized jumping. No sense in fighting one-on-one when you and five of your nearest and dearest gangmates could kill some lost soul from ambush. There was, however, a higher art. One that took you from a nobody to a certified menace. An art completely beyond the sorry and the weak. The legendary art of Reverse Jumping.

Starbrite had had most of his soul reserve burned away. He had been ambushed by dozens of the Shattervoid. He knew that Sariel was just *waiting* for an opportunity to jump in. Starbrite fought like a rabid animal. No more swagger. No more taunts. Just violence. And it was working. At the very least, he sure wasn't losing.

Truth did his best to imitate a dead rat off on one side. He was no use in this fight. These seniors were making moves on a scale he could hardly imagine.

The Shattervoid attacked by twisting space. Starbrite attacked with whips of fire the length of rivers. He attacked with swords made of billions of adamantine fragments, each a spinning saw blade that cut through those mountain-sized beings like he was slicing a mountain's reflection in water. He smashed a bolt of darkness into the flank of a Shattervoid clansman, and beetles the size of apartment buildings boiled out, eating the giant's black flesh as they grew and multiplied.

Truth had never imagined the Shattervoid screaming. Starbrite made them scream.

The void twisted and shook, mathematical cascades of sensations the mind desperately tried to sort and categorize and analogize into taste and touch and sound. To hear the color of the sky before dawn collapse and expand simultaneously into a fractal of suffering. To see the infinite curvature of the universe in a straight line that is constantly shifting between the color and the meaning of crimson. To know that a furious, vengeful family had gotten their daughter back, and she was mutilated in ways most things in the universe couldn't put words to beyond the anodyne *trauma*.

Starbrite was hurting them, but there were dozens of the vast beings. Being hurt wasn't going to stop them. They kept coming. Their magic raked over Starbrite, trying to shatter his material skull and his more-metaphysical body. It looked like it worked but, somehow, never worked *enough*. He kept re-forming and smashing back at them with comets, with droplets of true sunfire, with beams of green necrotizing light.

Odd. The spells he's using . . . they are doing damage. Enough to wipe me off the face of existence almost instantly. But they aren't doing the kind of fatal damage I would expect to the Shattervoid. They are terribly big, of course, and . . . Oh. Oh, that's interesting.

Since he had first heard of it, Truth had dreamed of getting the System. That magical, impossible thing that transformed a human into a demigod. That took a slumrat and, with a single hand, raised him to be a Starbrite Man. A Starbrite Man didn't cultivate spells in his apertures. He had no need for it—the System provided everything he needed. Whatever spell he needed, whenever he needed it.

But the System was Starbrite's soul. Perhaps supported by intelligent spirits and other servants, but primarily, it was Starbrite's soul feeding information into specially prepared bits of his slaves' souls. So, did that mean Starbrite had cultivated every spell?

Impossible. Regardless of whatever strange powers came with being a fake Nascent Soul, Truth flat-out refused to believe it included *Can cast every spell at will.*

So, how was he doing this? Simple. He wasn't really casting the spells. Not the *real* spells.

So-called "modern" magic. Magic with all the useless, nonfunctional bits stripped out. All those improved, optimized spells that spell researchers were so proud of. Truth had wondered for a long time what those extra bits did. He thought they contributed to the final Nascent Soul, and it looked like that was true, but there was more to it. Truth didn't realize he was smiling. It wasn't a very nice smile. A lot of blood smeared over those white teeth.

All that "useless" stuff? It was the parts of the spell that operated at higher levels of reality. Starbrite could, thanks to his actual, cultivated spells, memorize millions of "modern" spells. They had all the metaphysical significance of a blueprint for a garden shed. They only worked on the most basic, material, and secular level. Oh, he could put some heat on them. He had the magical muscle to turn dross into, if not gold, then gilt. But Starbrite was trying to slay dragons with a foam sword.

Now that he knew what to look for, he could see Starbrite maneuvering. It looked like he was attacking rabidly, but his "wild attacks" kept moving him closer and closer to the planet. Credit to the old monster, he was managing to at least hurt the Shattervoid. But it was all a front. At a certain point, he would turn and run for the surface.

FORBIDDEN. KILL.

Truth felt something seep into him, through a channel he didn't know existed. It felt like angelic possession, but this was deeper. Coming at him at a level beyond the physical. Sariel. He had received much from his angelic benefactor, even if he didn't know it. Time to fulfill his destiny.

With a thought, he restored his body to the peak of perfection with Cup and Knife. The Tongue of One Who Speaks for God was recalled to his hand. No wonder it had been so lethal. No wonder that Bane was considered unique and terrifying. It was barely concerned with damaging the things of the secular world. It was a weapon for killing at a higher level. The Meditations of Valentinian strengthened and armored his body. Incisive whispered, _Now!_ and with a single step, he was in the fray.

His sword whipped around and came slicing down on the floating head, looking to split the crown of the god-king. Starbrite made a noise between a yell and a yelp and desperately tried to dive out of the way while shielding. Truth only caught a piece of him, and that did make the old monster scream!

"Always thought it was funny the way you hid all the time. Weird behavior for the strongest man in the world." Truth's lips were pulled back into a death's-head grin as the iron blade spun through the vacuum. It was a strange feeling—he couldn't plant his feet when he struck. Each blow had to move in conjunction with the Earth-Folding Step to give the blows momentum and force. Didn't matter. He had always been quick at figuring out a fight. He would treat it like attacking from the back of his iron horse—cavalry slashes rather than dueling.

Starbrite didn't bother replying with words. He couldn't hear them, anyhow. He sent a barrage of iron arrows, each etched with runes spelling pain and defeat. Thousands of them, impossible to dodge or parry. Truth stepped on the void, his sword cutting out again. Once, Starbrite's gaze would have been enough to lock him in place. The all-seeing perception of the Shattervoid would have turned space into concrete. But Sariel was on him now.

Truth felt shields shattering beneath his blade. Felt the wards pop like soap bubbles. They couldn't hold up. Starbrite tried to cast something, swore, cast a different spell, and shot away at high speed, leaving exploding balls of gold-melting acid behind. Truth stepped just ahead of the leading wave of acid and brought his sword up in a thrust toward Starbrite's eye.

"Strongest man in the world is hiding all the time. Raises a pack of thugs he calls the PMC. Has people whose job it is to puppet governments and businesses to do his bidding. In fact, every time you have a chance to not do something, to farm out the work and the danger, you do it."

Starbrite continued to let his spells do the talking—balls of molten iron the size of houses, spellcrafted insects whose stingers dripped flesh-dissolving venom. Whips of raw ether whose lashes left eternal stripes of pain. Truth simply stepped past them, the Tongue lashing out and destroy-ing the more-inconvenient spells.

"I get it now. You are strong. You are. But you are hollow. All that's in you is fear of death, so all you care about is getting yours. Most pathetic of all, you still want to be loved. You want that reverence. You want people to say only nice things about you. You really don't like criticism at all." Truth didn't smile as he said it. His tone was casual and sincere. "If you did have to argue, you wouldn't do it yourself. You would hire someone to do the arguing for you. Then call it 'an efficient use of time' and pat yourself on the back for your smarts."

Starbrite read his lips. Somehow, in the midst of everything, he man-aged to be outraged.

"You take a shower recently? You're welcome! You eat fruit in winter? You're welcome! Trains? Tee shirts? Not having a church or temple run your life? Never have to bow for a king or queen? That's me! That's me! Medicine? I made it work! Mass production? I made it work! You want to know why there is so much good music, good shows, good books? Me!" Starbrite was throwing everything now, from snakes made of lava to cascades of needler rounds, each self-propelled and self-guiding. Nation-ending assaults. He was running away as he threw them, though.

And Truth just stepped right past them. Unstoppable, inexorable, inevitable. Whatever came at him, he ignored. Just evaded, and kept on attacking. When the homing spells doubled back, determined to kill him, he evaded again, putting Starbrite in the path of the danger.

Starbrite didn't like that one bit.

"Your pants—I made them! Your shoes? Me! That haircut? You saw an actor wearing it because I made it profitable!"

Truth could hear Starbrite just fine. He had to talk using his mouth. Starbrite wasn't so limited.

"You didn't do a damn thing. You set the ball rolling, got people moving, then sat back and enjoyed the profits. All that stuff you said you invented? Someone else did it first. All you did was figure out a way to take over the market and take the credit. Any time there was a price to pay, you shoved it off on someone else. Your employees, the customers, the government, anyone but you. Then you called yourself smart and got very sad when people said mean things about you. And you hid. Now you want me to be grateful for all the good you did me?"

Truth slashed out again, tracing a bloody line across Starbrite's scalp. "I'm grateful. But now you have to balance the books. How much are you holding?"

The Shattervoid hadn't let up on their bombardment. *Friendly fire* was only a relevant concept if anything downrange was your friend. Truth was evading it thanks to his spells and Sariel, but Starbrite was having to fight through it. He wasn't able to outrun the Shattervoid any more than he could outrun Truth.

"Oh, get fucked. I know that game. How about this one?" Starbrite slammed a fist down on the void, bringing a vast spell to life. "If you kill me."

Truth stepped and swung his sword, splitting the head in half. He could feel the angelic bane rippling through the ancient monster, first here, then down in the world below. Starbrite's body was in pieces. No sense in letting even a speck of him escape.

The spell tried to launch. Truth stabbed the spellform with his sword, breaking it. He could imagine Starbrite having multiple doomsday weapons set. Probably on a lot of redundant deadman's switches. It was going to be a hellish mess down there.

He looked up at the looming Shattervoid, their bulk blocking the stars. He looked down at the planet, seeing Sariel. Feeling the angel inside of him. It was, when you got down to it, a hellish mess up there, too.

He stretched out his hands, snagging the bits of Starbrite's skull. It had been, once, a thin face. Deep eyes, furious even in death. But there was something in that forever-young face. Something ground into the corners of his eyes and the creases of his scalp.

Fear. Something drove him to this particular sort of madness. Was it the divine revelation? Was it fear of mortality? Or did he just grow up poor, hungry, and sick, with an alkie dad and an abusive mom, in a poison hovel with evil neighbors? Was he terrified of going back to that place? So scared, he would sooner destroy the world than let it happen?

Didn't matter, really. Motives matter, but so does outcome. And speaking of—

He knotted the hair on each half of the head together and tossed it up to one of the Shattervoid. It slowly tumbled through the void, making a mockery of the inhuman distances involved. His fare was paid. If the offer was to be honored—

He could remember seeing the billboard, the handsome man in the cream trench coat lighting the beautiful woman's Golden Bat cigarette. *A Starbrite Man is always ready.* Promising himself that one day, he would be that man. Well. He wasn't a Starbrite Man. But whatever came next, he was ready.

CHAPTER 49

BEHOLD—A MAN!

Truth tried to cough politely, but it didn't seem to work in the void. Now that he wasn't constantly moving with magic, it seemed that not much *did* work in the void. There was a distinct lack of air, for one thing. Could he . . . tap on the storage ring or something? Maybe wave? He tried to wave. He could feel himself slowly spinning in place. It felt undignified. Worse, the Shattervoid didn't respond.

We were one hundred percent willing to honor the tickets. Unfortunately, the ticket holder never reached out to us, so after waiting the industry-standard three-tenths of a second, we left orbit. Regrettably, refunds and exchanges are not possible.

He spun in place for a little while longer. The angel was still possessing him. It was impossible not to notice. *Divine one, could you transport me back to the surface? I'm not sure I could step there safely.*

There was continued silence. He could hear the thunder of his heart beating. He could actually hear the blood moving around inside of him. It was that quiet.

Fantastic. I am very happy that this is my normal. Also, and not to be petty here, but there has been exactly zero loot off this corpse. I just killed the most powerful man in the world, and I have nothing to show for it. I'm not looking for money, but a spell library would be great. Maybe some decently enchanted weapons? Natural treasures? He must have a warehouse full of them somewhere. Yes, I am getting paid in tickets off-world, and there is the satisfaction of a job well done, but even a saint wants their palm crossed with silver, right? Pretty sure that's how the sermon went.

There was a slithering in his shirt as Perks worked his way out through the enormous holes left behind by Starbrite's torture.

Perks, while I am quite happy to see you, just how in the actual hell did you manage that? How are you alive?

Perks' tongue flicked out, tasting orbital space. *Sariel. He can do your unnoticeability trick even better than you can. Also, he kept prodding me to scoot around your body while you were getting smashed up. It got a little weird. I thought I should hold my tail in a strange pose, and then your elbow would come smashing down and barely miss it. Move my head down a little, and a fraction of a second later, there was a big iron stick where my head had been. Very odd.*

Truth nodded. Then frowned. He had been at the site of a remarkable number of coincidences and near-misses in his life. He had known he was getting puppeted around, of course, but . . .

Why did Sariel do all that?

Perks looked around. Truth wondered what his eyes were seeing. Did snakes have good eyes? Perks said he did, but how would he know?

He said it was the burden of serpents. Which I didn't understand, but I think I do now. He wants to talk to you, and I'm going to be passing your words back and forth.

Truth blinked. Which didn't do anything to change the slow spin he was in, but it was quite a powerful blink regardless.

Snakes are angel translators?!

I don't understand it either. Anyway, he asks what you would do if you did acquire all Starbrite's treasures.

Truth was trying to think of a diplomatic way to phrase *Laugh hysterically while rolling around in vast piles of silks and treasure-pills. Then power up enormously while I can, and bring the best of the rest back to the sibs, Etenesh, Jember, and whoever,* when Perks cut back in.

Got it. I think Sariel understands the "get stronger, look after my people" bit, but the rest doesn't translate. He says no.

No to what?

No, he won't give you those things.

Ah, hell. *Why?*

He didn't say. I think he looks down on them.

Truth nodded. That was fair, given who was talking. Then his eyebrows shot up. Also not slowing his tumble through space, but they really got up there.

Is he planning on rewarding me?

I . . . don't think so? Or maybe he doesn't really understand the concept of reward. You should do the things you should do because they are the things you should do.

Ah, yes, that sounded properly angelic.

Any chance my performance has persuaded him to lift his order banning human empathy and limiting our cultivation?

No. But he did say he is willing to lift the order now, as it has accomplished its purpose.

That's amazing! Incredible!

Yes, apparently, translating it as Children of Seth *is also not quite right, and there are things in there that would harm the Nephilim. Now that the planet has been so thoroughly depopulated even before the energy famine, there really is no need to keep it around any longer. Well, I think that's what he's saying, anyway.*

Truth was feeling a lot of feelings at the moment. It was quite hard to sort through them.

So . . . any humans left on this planet should look forward to a lifetime of slavery?

Yes. Ah, correction, generations of slavery. I think the concept he is trying to express is unending, *with the understanding that nothing below the Divine is truly eternal.*

Truth spun in place, rotating between the stars and the world below.

He is lifting the order?

It is already gone.

"Shattervoid Clan, can you hear me? Will you speak with me?"

He felt space firm up around him. There was suddenly a "down" and he was standing on it. There was an impolite cough from behind him. The same middle-aged-man illusion he had seen before was standing behind him.

"It's Ragnax, right?"

The illusion blinked momentarily, looked away, then looked back. A matronly voice replied, "Is that still a common name?"

"Sure."

"Then yes, I'm Ragnax."

Different person; the original person didn't want to talk to him. The Shattervoid had perfect memories. To say they held a grudge would be an understatement.

"How are the Nephilim going to get here?"

"Eventually, they will pay us to carry them."

"You have a monopoly on interstellar transport?"

"Below a certain level, yes. The economics of interstellar commerce don't work unless you can operate at a certain scale." Her smile was colder than winter on a comet. If there was one thing the Shattervoid had, it was scale.

"Could we . . . make a slight alteration to my ticket?"

"No."

"It would mean seeing less of me specifically, and people from my planet generally."

"Well, everything can be *discussed*."

"Nobody in or out."

There was a long pause. "Pardon?"

"Nobody in or out. You were already planning to blockade the planet, right?" Truth asked.

"Embargo. There is a technical difference."

"Well, I'm saying, rather than take anyone off-world, embargo it completely. For . . . I don't know, as long as the cosmic-energy famine is happening, plus a couple thousand years."

"That will be literally tens of thousands of years. Forty thousand at a minimum, and likely longer."

"Yeah, but you guys have a strong oral-history tradition, right? And . . . I have to assume you live a long time?"

Ragnax's mustache twitched, underlining a feminine snort of amusement. "Oh, it wasn't a problem for *us*. I just wanted to make sure *you* understood."

"I do. Nobody comes in. Not with grain, or books, or soldiers. Nobody. Especially not the Nephilim. And we don't go out. Or if we do, we do it under our own power."

There was another snort. "Good luck with that."

"I'm not optimistic on that front." Truth had a smile that looked like crying. "I'm a bit optimistic that humans will still be here at the end of it all, though."

Perks flicked his tongue. *Sariel will permit this. He will not aid you further, but given your body's repeated reconstruction, you will live longer than most. Cultivation will become more difficult for you but not impossible.*

And for others?

He expressed indifference while implying that he will do nothing to prevent the energy famine or to speed its resolution. If humanity figures out a way to cultivate, that's their fate. If not, that's their fate too. He won't aid the Nephilim in coming, but he won't stop them, either.

Demons were always his favorite. I think the Nephilim were Sariel's compromise for putting up with humanity.

Truth nodded and looked over at Ragnax. "Sally doing okay?"

"You can keep your bullshit nickname and any version of my granddaughter's name out of your mouth."

Well, the ring still worked, so she was probably doing okay. "Well. I wish her well regardless."

"Goodbye, earthworm. We will never meet again."

The universe twisted and Truth was falling. The air ripped at his clothes as he plunged downward. Over an ocean, thankfully, though he couldn't see an island anywhere. Which, given he was still high enough to see the horizon bending a little, was concerning.

Not doing that again.

Truth stepped on the empty air and crossed tens of kilometers. It felt effortless, so he did it again. Smiling, he began a casual stroll through the air until he found land. Sticking the landing was tricky, but he eventually shed the momentum with little upward steps and letting gravity and air resistance work their magic.

He looked at a street sign. Didn't recognize the language. Shame. It looked like the Free State. Not the language—the road. Empty, with a feeling of recent violence. He walked on. He found a city. Black plumes of smoke were rising; he could hear the explosions from the suburbs. Signs for an airport. He followed them.

The airport was a frenzy too, with spell birds fighting for runway position. He walked over to the biggest of them and stepped inside. There were four people inside, not including the pilots. Three looked quite wealthy; the other, some kind of spiritual grifter.

"Where's this bird headed?" He asked.

"Who the HELL are you, and how did you—" At least, that's what Truth thought Fatty #1 was saying. He didn't speak the language. Truth knocked him out with a slap. He repeated the question.

"Ganet-Sho. Apparently, they own a villa there." The grifter tapped their walking stick lightly against the floor, their face hidden under a long hood and loose robe.

"Is that anywhere near Siphios?"

"Not even the same continent."

"Okay, well, change of flight plan. We are going to Xandre."

"We are?"

"Yes." Truth nodded, with his best reasonable expression. He could feel Perks shifting around inside his shirt, then slithering out one of the holes and onto the floor. Sariel had thoughtfully returned him.

"They might object."

"Ask them if they would like to walk to Ganet-Sho from here or arrange further transportation from Xandre."

It seemed that, once he demonstrated the ability to snap a talisman clean in half with his left hand while having his right hand wrapped around a fat neck, they all desperately wanted to go to Xandre. A broad-minded flexibility he appreciated.

"So. My name is Truth. And . . . Oh, sorry, it looks like my snake wants to climb your stick for some reason?"

"No problem; quite nostalgic, actually. I've always liked snakes. Two would be even better."

"Wouldn't they bother each other?"

"Well, sometimes." He got the impression the grifter was grinning. "Your name is Truth?"

"Yes."

"Found any?"

"Lots."

That seemed to get the grifter's attention. He leaned in. "Really? Like what?"

"Haven't a clue. They didn't stay true, you see." Truth nodded seriously.

"Then were they even true?"

"Yes, it was reality that kept changing."

"How can reality change? It's reality!" The grifter sat back and scoffed.

"Can there be an objective reality beyond our ability to understand it? And if our reality is defined by our ability to understand it, doesn't reality always change with our understanding?"

That had the robed figure sputtering. "There are more holes in that than your shirt!"

"Isn't."

"There is!"

"There isn't. Would you like some crackers, by the way?"

"Oh, thank you, been a while since breakfast . . . Hey, you didn't bring any luggage; where did they come from?"

"Don't worry; they are imaginary crackers."

"They aren't; I'm eating them." The crumbs sprayed out from under the hood.

"But you couldn't perceive their origin, so it doesn't exist. They are therefore imaginary." Truth stuck out his hand. "I'm going to have to ask for them back."

"Oh, no, you don't; that was your position!"

It was a long flight. The bird really wasn't built for such a long haul, and they had to stop a few times along the way. Truth wasn't bored. He found bickering with the grifter effortless. For some reason, his very normal questions seemed to wind them up. Truth thought he was being quite reasonable when he asked them to define what a human was.

He was fairly sure a human wasn't a series of insulting hand gestures and a five-minute monologue on his persistent failure as any sort of sapient lifeform.

"But really, what is it? I keep asking everyone, and nobody can give me a good definition."

"That's because nobody knows! The point isn't the answer; the point is the question. To make you think, reflect, question your assumptions about . . . everything, really."

Truth digested that for a minute. "So, if someone told me they wouldn't discuss theology until I could answer, definitively, *What is a human—*"

"They were telling you to shut the hell up forever. But in a really classy way. I think I'm going to steal that one."

Truth bumped visiting Merkovah up his priority list. But there was someone else ahead of him.

The mountain was cool, lush, and green. Far from the smoke and bloodshed of the cities. There were people up there, but they seemed reasonably social, from what he could tell. The house was exactly as promised. Beautiful, with a wonderful attached food garden and fruiting trees. There were even coffee trees. No goats, though. Or at least not yet. And the view over the valley, with its thousands of shades of green and singing birds, was unmatched.

"All right, and I just . . . push the lever down? Then pull it up again? Then push it down again? Okay, I hear something— Water? Really? Water came out. Not a hint of magic. I would have put good money on that not working."

Truth saw a truly disreputable iron horse peeking out from under a tarp in the driveway. It looked glad to see him. Or maybe he was just projecting.

Etenesh was working the handle on a pump, filling a water cup with wonder. Her legs were long, peeking out from under a flowing dress that fluttered in the mountain breeze with her hair—wild and free. Her arms had gotten stronger. There was something in her eyes that said she had seen, and done, some things that she would never forget. But she was smiling. Marveling at this new wonder and laughing at the strangeness of the world.

Truth stumbled over, not minding his rags or the dust from the road. He collapsed down in the dirt in front of her, laying the Tongue at her feet. He looked up at her, smiling through the tears. "I'm home." And laughed as her kisses rained down on him.

CHAPTER 50

EPILOGUE

He was a man with no name. His identity had been carefully excised by means practical and magical. His face shifted and bent thanks to the carefully manufactured skin-masks the shadowy Mountain Hermits crafted. He had even cultivated a spell that allowed subtle adjustments to his physique. You could shake hands with him, walk around the corner, and sit down next to him again and happily chat over lunch together without the faintest idea you were talking to the same person.

The man with no name would be the first to tell you—changing the length of your vocal cords was the easy part. Changing your habits of speech, the tone, inflection, cadence, clichés—that was the hard part. But it was all worth it. The Hermits had shown him just who was responsible for all the pain in his life, and he had been slowly paying it back. Starbrite and their collaborators were losing. Losing people, losing power, losing their hold on Jeon. He was the arrow fired from the still night, the blackened blade plunging from a shadow into an unsuspecting back, the glass knife rising from clear water to slit Starbrite's throat.

He had pruned away everything in his life. Not that he had much, but those few connections to humanity had been severed as completely as he could stand. He owned . . . almost nothing. Actually nothing, if he cared about the "ownership" the Hermits claimed over his face mask, spells, and tools. He certainly had no friends, no lovers, his family was almost entirely dead, and the one who was *probably* still alive had been cut off for years now.

It was a hard life but a meaningful one. Which was why he had been sitting on the sofa in a newly emptied apartment, staring blankly at the wall for two days. What was he supposed to do when all his enemies were dead *and he didn't kill them?!*

The man with no name mechanically made himself a bowl of noodles. The noodles came out of their pack and were dumped in a bowl. Then the water went in, cool from the talisman. Then he sprinkled the seasoning packet. Three minutes in the hot box, and he had a piping-hot bowl of noodles in soup. Just like Dad used to make. But he shut down that thought hard.

There was a knock at the door. He ignored it—the prior owner had gone up in a cloud of blue-green flames, so this was probably just a neighbor checking in.

The knock repeated, this time with a subtle variation in the rhythm. The nameless man took a long sip of his broth and readied a cut-down Firebolt fetish. It tended to end fights very fast in close quarters, and in the unfortunate event of the magic vanishing . . . assuming he or anyone else could still move . . . it was one hundred and fifty centimeters of cold-iron-infused ox bone. Which also tended to end fights quickly in close quarters.

A third knock, a third subtle variation. The man with no name crouched by the side of the door and reached up to gently twist the knob. Twice to the left, once to the right. There were two coughs, loud enough to be heard clearly through the door.

"Come in. It's not locked." Which was true. For the first time in his life, he simply could not be bothered with locking the door. He was back on the sofa with his bowl of noodles in hand by the time the door opened. The Firebolt fetish was laid out on the sofa next to him. Trust in his circles was always conditional.

Two bland-looking women walked into the room with a practiced casual air. "Codename Adder?"

"No."

They smiled. It was not a warm or reassuring expression.

"Just checking," they chorused. Then one of them continued. "Mr. Hinds, we are here to deliver you onward. Your orders."

"I don't take orders." The man took a long sip of his broth. "But then, you know that too."

"You do on this." They looked grim. "I'm told you can decrypt the message in this crystal. It should explain everything."

The nameless man pressed the crystal to his forehead. A second later, it shattered into dust.

"Always gets in my eyes!"

"Ought to lean forward when you use memory crystals." One of the women shrugged.

"Never seems to help. It always catches on my eyelashes."

This got shrugs in stereo.

"I'm going to Siphios? To do what? Kill whoever killed everyone who worked for Starbrite?"

They shook their heads firmly. "We don't know, but we did pick up something at the Bamboo Hut."

"Oh?"

"Yes, Grandpa Stone said you were asked for by 'our friends in the Highlands.' By name."

"I don't have a name." The lips of the man with no name half-quirked upwards. It didn't really look like a smile.

"We know that too. But they don't." The bland women nodded. Then one couldn't repress herself. "Were you *really* named Vigor?"

"Oh. I . . . don't know why I'm surprised you are still alive, Professor. But I am happy nevertheless." Sophia didn't look happy. But then, she had been caught breaking into Professor Cuinoird's top-secret backup-to-his-backup, off-site, black-budget-funded biothaumaturgical laboratory. Strictly speaking, she was discovered *after* she had broken in.

"Miss Medici? Now this is surprising. I was quite certain you were dead. Either in the purge of everyone with the System or by vengeful Nephilim, depending on who got to you first." The professor's voice was rich. Which was fitting, as the professor was likewise. It also dripped confidence. Similar to the professor's laid-back swagger.

"I . . . declined to enroll in the System. And I suppose the odds of you being loyal to anything other than yourself were always zero."

"Indeed. Although I am somewhat alarmed to find you here. I was quite certain I had erased all traces of this location. What did I miss?"

"Nothing." She shrugged. She was wearing workout gear, without a talisman anywhere near her. This was probably adding to Cuinoird's confidence, as he conspicuously kept one hand in the pocket of his eight-thousand-wen overcoat. An overcoat he was wearing on a beautiful summer's afternoon with the temperature hovering around thirty.

"There must have been something. I don't believe you found your way into a bunker under the third subbasement garage of the new SupremeCRISP! Arena. Especially since there is, in fact, no door, and it takes a very particular set of spells and tools to pass through the layers of enchanted concrete." He slowly came closer. He had a good ten centimeters on her in terms of height. A good thirty years in age, too. At least one level on her. Lots of hidden weaponry.

Sophia didn't look intimidated. She seemed a little tired. "Yes, that was rather a bore to work through. Still. Managed in the end."

"How, *Miss* Medici?" Cuinoird wasn't smiling. But then, he rarely smiled. Once he sprang whatever nastiness he had in mind on her, then he would smile. Or if he was sucking up to a patron, but that was hardly relevant there.

"Oh, well, it wasn't an oversight on your part. Backup Plan 88-9, in case of incapacity, insanity, possession, or other malady of the mind. I found traces of Cheston Diplo in your lab's business records and ran him down with everyone else that seemed suspicious. From there, it was just getting the information out of him, learning about your various safe houses, and picking the one that would suit me best. Not an oversight, exactly. A known danger, I would say."

"Quite. Since Cheston was utterly entranced and geased to not say anything."

"No, I think it was the parasites you installed in his brain that were the real failsafe. Another double-edged sword, as it turned out."

"I find them to be generally quite effective." Cuinoird's lips were starting to tug up into a smile. "Which, I regret to inform you, you will be experiencing shortly. You won't be any more agreeable to look at, but your tone will improve. It's always been grating. This is really your chance to improve. Resign yourself, young lady. There is no door to run to. No help to call for. And you are not now, nor ever will be, my match."

Sophia cocked her head to one side. Her eyes carried almost as much baggage as she did. "Oh? But then why am I glad to see you?"

"Eh?" That pulled him up with a jerk.

"Could I get your evaluation on a project? I call them Aeons. No idea where the name came from, but I think it would look great on marketing materials."

Two flesh golems leapt into the room, moving faster than the eye could follow. Hands like hams came swinging down on the professor, who crushed a charm. Sophia had a wonderful view of everything unfolding. The hands swinging in, the golden bell forming around the professor, then that bell shattering instantly under the weight of her creation's mighty fists. The professor didn't quite have time to realize what had happened before they were on him. Then it was all over but the screaming.

There was a lot of screaming. Sophia had a healing talisman handy, along with some rather excellent blood-restoring medicine.

"YOU SICK FUCK! You wanted me raped by goddamn Nephilim to save on experiment material costs! Bastard! Bastard!" She knew she had repeated herself four or five times at this point, but there was a lot on her conscience.

"Do you know how much I had to *lie* to get that poor girl"—Sophia didn't realize she was avoiding saying her name—"to go along with the plan? You *made me murder someone who could have been a friend, you evil shit!*"

Cuinoird might have contested that, but every time he tried to speak, the Aeons crushed something painful, then Sophia regrew it. Which was equally agonizing.

Sophia wasn't keeping track of time. It probably took a few hours for her to vent all her feelings. Eventually, she joined the Aeons in stamping the professor out into a thin, meaty paste on the floor. She didn't mind the mess. Among her creations were things that would happily eat up everything and leave the floor hospital-clean. She had spent a month down there, and the Aeons had only taken up seventy-five percent of her time. Lots of time to make use of the more-ordinary materials stored down there. She had already put the best stuff in her Aeons.

She didn't take off the workout gear as she stood under an icy shower. Trying to not feel anything as she was bombarded by . . . everything. The universe seemed to crawl into her mind, unwanted and unbidden.

"Knock knock knock. Is this . . . whatsername? Loveseat? Sofa? Yeah, Sofa. The prick's sister. Sofa."

Amazingly, the sudden voice made her far more awake than the icy water. A small stone emerged from a wall, ignoring the banishments and anti-demon wards. Somehow. Should be impossible for an imp, but she was a big believer in the evidence of her own eyes.

"Who are you? And what do you want?"

"Who are any of us, really? And do I 'want' something, or have I been taught to believe I want it? I mean, I'm not Mr. Big Brainy Word Guy. It wouldn't be too hard for some little pisswizard or chatty birdfuck to convince me I want something, right?"

Sophia, for all her intelligence and experience on the pointy end of biothaumaturgy, had merely audited the mandatory courses on demonology. Since it was ungraded, she had spent her time in the lectures reading up on things she actually cared about. A bit of an oversight, she now felt.

"Why are you here, demon?"

"I gotta deliver a message and tickets." The rock-shaped imp went silent. The shower added a pleasant white noise to the room, which didn't soothe anyone.

"To me?"

"To you what?"

"Are you supposed to deliver those things to me?"

"I think so, but how should I know, you know?"

"Then how did you wind up here? Through the wards! And banishments!" Sophia thought she was hanging on to her temper well. Must be a great grip she had on it, what with her knuckles turning white.

"Those are some, just, shit wards. Like . . ." The imp's voice trailed off. "Like just super bad. I was following my summoner's orders and tracking the bloodline linkage, then *his* summoner, or . . . wife? Maybe? Could have been a dude? You know what? The whole idea of sex is sick. You are all sick. You are gross and weird."

This time, Sophia didn't jump in. She knew that if she opened her mouth, she would order the Aeons to smash this imp and then she wouldn't get any answers.

"Anway, this . . . thingamawhosit put a super spell-pokey bit on me and I went *zoom* and also *woosh* through most of the planet's core and mantle and junk and made my way here. To deliver your tickets and the message."

"What. Are. The. Tickets. For?"

"I dunno. You think I can read? That's real judgy of you. Goddamn shitheel wannabee fakeass punkass excuse for a mage. Fucking embarrassed to even be delivering things to you. Goddamn horrible to think that I now exist in your memories. Blow your brains out as soon as I deliver my message. It's the least you could do."

The rock spat out a short stack of tickets onto the floor. It looked like spell-bird tickets.

"Uuuuuhhhhhhhh . . . The message is from your brother. He said he's the one who you saw as a ghost that one time in your dorm. Message begins." The imp's voice suddenly changed, and she heard the warmest voice she knew.

Harmony sat in the empty ritual room. It was pretty smelly at this point, but the one time he stuck his head out into the hall, he deeply regretted it.

All things considered, he could be hungry a while longer, and the quantity of gore rapidly going bad in the room distracted him from the stench of the "toilet corner."

Needs must and all that. Felt like a return to childhood, in a way. He worried about what had happened to the System. It had just vanished, and for some reason, it wasn't coming back. Nor was . . . whoever it was that pulled him out of the ritual. He had more and more questions about that, but for some reason, the man's face never seemed to fix itself in his mind. He just had the eerie sense that he had never met the man before but had known him his entire life.

The door to the ritual chamber had been firmly shut. Nothing good out there. Proving the point, a crow flew through the door and landed in front of him. "Oh, how homey. I really don't often get sent to such *delightful* places. Mmm. Would you mind waiting while I tidied up?"

"Err . . . are you . . . Of course you are a demon; stupid question. Waiting for what?"

"No no, Sir is quite right to question his sanity. Trapped alone, in the dark, surrounded by the ruins of more-powerful beings and his own filth, knowing that he was put here and trapped here by forces *far* beyond his meager comprehension . . . insanity would be a blessed relief. Tell me, do you often think the world is off its kilter, that reality is nothing more than a painted scrim behind a blood-soaked pantomime? That the music of the spheres is a hurdy-gurdy dirge and you the dancing monkey?"

Harmony recoiled. "No!"

"Then you truly are mad." A storm of wind swept across the room, sweeping it clean. The filth was consumed with alarming cries of avian delight. Cries that sounded, too often, carnal.

"Delightful. *Such* a *nourishing* meal. My master does season his servant's food with exquisite care."

"You work for . . . him? The man who did this?"

"Oh, yes. Him."

The crow preened, then started cleaning its feathers.

"And . . . why are you here?"

"I'm to carry you to a boat, which will carry you to a small airfield, which will result, ultimately, in you reuniting with your family."

Harmony paused. "This isn't one of those word games where we will be 'reuniting' in Hell or something, is it?"

The bird seemed to hesitate. "Strictly speaking, you will all be in Hell at the same time. Your stay in Hell will last, approximately, for eternity. This is true for everyone. So will everyone who ever lived, lives, or will live all reunite in the boundless infernal lands."

"No, wait. I give to the Church of Prager very regularly. I had my sins eaten before I flew out here. I should be a straight shot to Purgatory at the very worst."

The crow looked puzzled. "Purgatory? I'm afraid I don't know that, Excellency."

"Purgatory! You know, instead of Hell—"

The crow chuckled. "Oh, I know that old lie; I was just . . . ah . . . teasing you in place of your brother?"

Harmony was very steady. He was now steadily considering snapping the head clean off a crow.

"Listen, imp—"

"I was promoted. It's why I can carry you out of here."

"I don't follow?"

"A pity. Then you will be trapped here forever. Well. Not forever. Once you starve to death, you will learn what *forever* truly means."

Harmony was steady. But he was also very ready to be out of this ritual room and out of this deeply creepy base. He stood and gestured for the crow to lead the way.

"How is Vig doing, anyway? Haven't heard anything from him in years."

The crow chuckled but didn't answer.

"You still haven't heard from Merkovah?" Truth asked. Etenesh just shook her head.

"Everyone and their dog-headed demons are looking for him, and not to shake his hand. He's vanished. Like as not he'll turn up again sometime. Possibly in our great-great-grandchildren's day."

"Shame. I have a lot of very interesting questions to ask him." Truth grinned. "So many."

Etenesh looked thoughtful and cupped her ear. "You know, I think I just heard him burrow more deeply into the bedrock. Amazing." Truth grinned and hugged her around her waist. The air was sweet, smelling of leaves warmed in the equatorial sun, passing rain, and distant flowers.

"You get the cosmic-energy-gathering array set up?"

"And a dozen more. Jember helped; his church is about thirty kilometers from here. My family owns this whole mountain." She flipped her hand casually. "With the exception of this property. Technically." She smiled back at his grin. "You never asked why they picked this mountain for our house, did you?"

"I did not. I'm just glad they did."

They looked out over the food gardens and the fruit trees, down the heavily forested mountains, and into the wider world.

"I dreamed of you, you know," she said. "Quite insane dreams."

"Oh? Was I naked in them?"

"You were not. But in the last one, you were happy." She looked up at him, eyes as deep as mountain valleys. "Will you be happy with me, Truth?"

"I will." He smiled again, then started laughing. "It's the craziest thing! I feel like I'm finally starting to live *my* life! Not rushing around, looking after everyone else's life, not waiting for my life to happen; it's here! It's right now! I'm living my life right now, and I'm exactly where I want to be, with the person I want to be with."

Etenesh smiled and reached out, her eyes asking for a kiss. He happily gave her the best one he could.

"Glad to hear it, Mr. Medici. Although that does raise a question."

"Oh?"

"Yes. What does it mean to live one's life in the face of eternity?"

"So, that's why I can't eat geraniums anymore. The sheer cynical immorality of it all got to be too much . . . Say, old-timer, why are you laughing so hard? You will choke on your peanuts!" The wandering mendicant pounded the beardy elder on the back so hard, his little hat almost flew off.

"Ah, I just felt one of my contingencies activate. It's not a bad old world, not a bad old world. Getting better every day." The old man's face looked surprisingly youthful for a moment. "It will hurt you badly. But you have to be ready. Always ready."

"To endure the bad?"

"To find the good. And to enjoy it. I think I will enjoy what comes next very much."

ABOUT THE AUTHOR

Warby Picus is a lifelong fan of science fiction and fantasy. One day, he figured he would see if writing books was as much fun as it appeared to be. He hasn't looked back since.

RESPAWN YOUR CURIOSITY

follow us on our socials

 podiumentertainment.com

 @podiumentertainment

 /podiumentertainment

 @podium_ent

 @podiumentertainment